★ THE FAR EMPTY ★

THE FAR EMPTY

J. TODD SCOTT

G. P. PUTNAM'S SONS | NEW YORK

G. P. PUTNAM'S SONS
Publishers Since 1838
An imprint of Penguin Random House LLC
375 Hudson Street
New York, New York 10014

Copyright © 2016 by Jeffrey Todd Scott
Excerpt from *High White Sun* copyright © 2018 by Jeffrey Todd Scott
Penguin supports copyright. Copyright fuels creativity, encourages diverse
voices, promotes free speech, and creates a vibrant culture. Thank you for buying an authorized edition of this book and for complying with copyright laws
by not reproducing, scanning, or distributing any part of it in any form without
permission. You are supporting writers and allowing Penguin to continue to
publish books for every reader.

Verses from "Tall Men Riding" by S. Omar Barker are quoted with permission
of the Barker Estate.

The Library of Congress has catalogued the G. P. Putnam's Sons hardcover
edition as follows:

Names: Scott, J. Todd, author.
Title: The far empty / J. Todd Scott.
Description: New York : G. P. Putnam's Sons, 2016.
Identifiers: LCCN 2016023481 (print) | LCCN 2016032229 (ebook) |
ISBN 9780399176340 (hardcover) | ISBN 9780698408272 (epub)
Subjects: LCSH: Cold cases (Criminal investigation)—Fiction. |
Family secrets—Fiction. | Police corruption—Fiction. |
Borderlands—Texas—Fiction. | GSAFD: Mystery fiction. | Suspense fiction.
Classification: LCC PS3619.C66536 F37 2016 (print) | LCC PS3619.C66536
(ebook) | DDC 813/.6—dc23
LC record available at https://lccn.loc.gov/2016023481

First G. P. Putnam's Sons hardcover edition / June 2016
First G. P. Putnam's Sons premium edition / February 2018
G. P. Putnam's Sons premium edition ISBN: 9780735218857

Printed in the United States of America
1 3 5 7 9 10 8 6 4 2

For Delcia, *mi estrella del norte*

Shine on, babe . . .

The Far Empty is a work of fiction, *more or less*. Murfee, Texas, doesn't exist. But I've been a federal agent for twenty years, a lot of those working on the southwest border. In 2010, more than three thousand people were murdered in mostly drug-related violence in Ciudad Juárez, right across the river from El Paso, Texas. In 2012, several police officers and deputies from a special drug task force in the Rio Grande Valley, including the son of a popular and powerful local sheriff, were arrested during a federal sting operation for hijacking drug loads and protecting drug couriers. A little more than a year later, the sheriff himself pled guilty to corruption charges. In 2014, at least ninety-seven bodies of deceased immigrants were discovered by the U.S. Border Patrol in Arizona's Sonoran Desert. And in 2015, a popular travel website named Big Bend National Park in West Texas—800,000 acres of mountains and Chihuahuan Desert along the Rio Grande—one of the fifteen most beautiful parks in America. *This is all true*.

This is the border I know.

We tried a desperate game and lost. But we are rough men used to rough ways, and we will abide by the consequences.

—COLE YOUNGER, 1867

This is the song that the night birds sing
As the phantom herds trail by,
Horn by horn where the long plains fling
Flat miles to the Texas sky. . . .

This is the song that the night birds wail
Where the Texas plains lie wide,
Watching the dust of a ghostly trail,
Where the phantom tall men ride!

—S. OMAR BARKER, "Tall Men Riding"

★ THE FAR EMPTY ★

TALL MEN RIDING

My *father has killed three men.*

The first was over in Graham, an undercover drug deal gone bad. He was a lot younger then, only a deputy, not yet the Judge, buying weed from a California nigger—his words, not mine. Put him in front of the right crowd, give him a few Lone Stars or a Balcones Texas Single Malt—he pretends it loosens his lips like everyone else, but it doesn't, not really, not at all—and he'll say *I shot that ole boy two times.*

Once for being a nigger in Texas, then again for being a shitty drug-dealing nigger in *his* stretch of Texas.

*   *   *

The second was right here in Murfee, late summer a few years back, when Dillon Holt held his granddad's Remington on his wife and baby daughter.

I go to school with Dillon's younger brother Dale, so I knew Dillon a little, not much. Enough to know that only part of him—angry, broken—came back from Iraq. He hadn't been able to keep his job at the Comanche, spooking the cows too much, and he got into more than his share of fights at Earlys. It got so bad they wouldn't serve him anymore, so he spent that last Friday night drinking a twelve-pack of Pearl alone beneath the pecan trees behind his house, before getting ahold of a little meth early Saturday morning. By the afternoon he was shirtless on his porch, screaming at everything and nothing, his body slick and swollen and glowing like it was on fire. His wife Brenda held baby Ellie and covered both their eyes so neither of them would have to look down the barrel of that Remington.

I know all this because I was there. My father brought me on the callout, left me sitting in the truck cab. Everyone knew I was watching, but no one was going to say a goddamn thing about it.

He wanted me to see how he *handled business*.

That's how he said it then, how he still says it today.

My father tried some to talk Dillon down, even let him rant a bit to see if he'd wear himself out, but when he swung that shotgun around one too many times toward Brenda's face, my father shot him clean through his naked, burning chest with his Ruger Mini-14.

There was hot blood everywhere, fantailed up on the porch screen, on the windows, all over Brenda and the baby. It fell fast, like falling stars . . . red streaks. There's a sound that blood makes when it hits wood or skin. Dillon's yelling was lost to his widowed wife's screaming. It was furnace-hot that morning, but my father didn't break a sweat. Afterward, when he bent down into the truck to put away the Ruger, still stinking of smoke and oil and warm to the touch where it hit my knee, his skin was dusty, cool. Dry, like a snake's. He winked at me like we were old friends.

And that's how he handled the business with Dillon Holt.

The third man was the husband of Nancy Coombs, the woman he was sleeping with right after my mom disappeared.

He didn't shoot Roger Coombs like Dillon Holt or that poor black kid in Graham, didn't even raise a hand to him as far as I know, but he might as well have, since it all turned out the same. The story I've heard (nobody will say it to my face) is that Roger came home after a Big Bend Central Raiders game and found my father with Nancy in their bedroom—all their wedding pictures and honeymoon pictures from the Excalibur in Vegas staring down at them as my father made Nancy moan. There were words, maybe even a punch thrown after my father got done laughing and wiping himself off on Roger's sheets, but not much more than that—not then, anyway. A lot of people in Murfee whispered about my dad and Nancy—suspected, anyway—but they weren't going to make much out of it.

Who was going to say a goddamn thing to the famous sheriff, Stanford "Judge" Ross?

That left Roger to deal with it: the whispers, the smiles, the laughs. Everyone knew about Nancy and my father, and Roger couldn't step outside his house without knowing about it as well. All day, every day . . . down at the Hi n Lo he managed, every time someone came in for Lone Stars or cigarettes or Skoal Long Cut Wintergreen. Every time my father came by and poured himself a free cup of coffee, black and sour, sometimes still smelling like Nancy, before walking out with a wink and that sharp smile on his face.

Because Sheriff Ross doesn't pay for anything in Murfee.

Not even another man's wife.

When he'd had enough, Roger pulled his old F-150 into the parking lot of the Big Bend County Sheriff's Department and took a brand-new Gillette to both wrists, bleeding out into the old McDonald's bags and other shit on his floorboards. Chief Deputy Duane Dupree found him first, his dying breaths fogging the truck's glass, but Duane took his sweet time making the call, even fired up a smoke while he rang my father first; then, a few minutes later, the county EMT. Roger was dead fifteen minutes before the ambulance arrived, and his last sight ever on this earth was Duane Dupree calmly smoking a Lucky Strike, picking at his teeth with his thumb, watching him die.

Roger left a note. I know because I overheard Duane and my father talking about it one night on our porch, but no one ever saw it or read it. Duane was carrying on, laughing about it, but my father didn't say anything at all, just gave him that look that only my father can, when his gray eyes go black and don't seem to reflect much of anything in front of or behind them.

That look, far more than anything he ever says, shuts lesser men up. We're all lesser men. Staring into my father's eyes, Duane said he'd take care of that damn letter, burn it all to hell on his Weber grill, and I bet my life that's exactly what he did.

*   *   *

My father's first wife was Vickie Schori. They met in high
school right here in Murfee and were married six months
after the senior prom. He was of course the king, she the
queen—but a couple of years later she ran out on him to
El Paso. Most people thought it was for the best anyway,
at least best for young Deputy Ross (he was still a long
way from being the sheriff). There had been ugly whispers about the Schori family as long as they'd been in
Murfee—as long as anyone, longer than most. They
started the West Texas Cattle Auction, managed it forever, but sold it off and left town themselves a few years
after Vickie, and it's the Comanche now. No one knows
where they went. No one ever spoke to Vickie again.

I've never seen her picture in our house, but there is
one at school, pressed behind glass near the front office.
It's part of a collage of a hundred other images, bits and
pieces of Big Bend Central's history. The picture is black
and white, faded. She's standing on a football field and
she looks like a ghost beneath the stadium lights. Her
dress has these huge sleeves and her hair is turning in the
wind and she's waving, even smiling . . . looking at something distant, and she's so beautiful.

All you can see of my father is his hand, heavy on her
arm, holding her. I know it's him. I'd know those hands
anywhere. He's there, present, but just out of sight. The
rest of him is covered up by a baseball picture from 1988.

My father's second wife was Nellie Banner, and they were
married less than a year after Vickie disappeared. She
came from a longtime Murfee family as well; she'd been
a freshman when my dad and Vickie were prom king and

queen. Where Vickie had been all Texas blond, Nellie was short, dark, with a drop of Mexican blood, although no one ever said that out loud. My father has never talked about her, but I think they fought a lot. Fought, made up, fought some more. Early on, they lived out on Peachtree, and I imagine the neighbors got used to a bit of yelling and banging around. Still, they showed up each Sunday at church, with my father in his uniform and Nellie in her Sunday white, even if she wore a bit more makeup than most of the women around here thought proper for church.

Maybe she liked the way it looked. Maybe she needed that extra color to cover up the blue of bruises.

Nellie died unexpectedly in about two inches of water in the big Kohler bathtub in the new house on Rustler they built after my father made chief deputy. It was a shock to everyone, a true tragedy. Nobody could explain it, even after they brought the ME from El Paso. My father hadn't been home at the time, out with Deputy Dupree near Nathan, coming in far too late that night to find her blue and unresponsive. Facedown in water long gone cold. Colder than her skin.

People say that my father was so upset and distraught at Nellie's death he tore that Kohler out and replaced it—people around here swear it. I've heard them talking about seeing it happen with their own eyes. But I know better.

That goddamn tub's still there.

My father's third wife, my mother, was Evelyn Monroe. They met in Dallas while he was there for a law enforcement conference. She'd just graduated from SMU but took to him right away, I guess, and soon they were calling all the time and he was heading up to Dallas on weekends to see her. She left her new position at IBM to relocate out to Murfee, sight unseen.

I've often wondered about her first thoughts when she got here, way out in the middle of nowhere. What did she think when she first saw her new home? Chihuahuan scrub and long rolls of grassland; the humps and hills of the Santiagos and the Chisos hammered by the sun. Dust on everything all the time, like the whole fucking world's covered in ash.

If it had been March or April, at least the Texas mountain laurel would have been blooming through the caliche, and the sides of the valleys would have been carpeted in purple. She would have liked that. Purple was her favorite color.

They married and she moved into the house on Rustler that Nellie and my father built and that Nellie died in. About a year later I was born. My father eventually won the sheriff's seat away from old Dugger Barnes, and my mom got involved in raising me, volunteering first at Barnhardt Middle and later at Big Bend Central.

My mother was beautiful, tall, thin, her blond hair always pulled back in a ponytail. There was always a hair tie or scrunchie somewhere around her, orbiting her like small stars: wrapped around her wrist, trapped on the shifter in her truck, tossed on a counter or hidden beneath cushions.

I still find them, even now. And when I do, I still cry. Not so much, a little less each time, and never where my father can see.

They smell like her . . . her shampoo. Mint and rain and green places far from here.

*   *   *

Thirteen months ago my mother left us, maybe to go to one of those faraway places.

That's what the note said—a note my father claims he found folded on our kitchen counter. A note written on a piece of Big Bend County Sheriff's Department stationery that somehow didn't end up on Duane Dupree's grill. It was three sentences long and all but got printed in the *Murfee Daily*, because everyone had to explain and understand and debate how Evelyn Ross—the beautiful, smart, and beloved wife of Sheriff Ross—could leave her husband and teenage son and disappear.

Gone without a trace.

People offered to go after her. When they weren't dropping off casseroles or checking in to see how we were, they wanted to help track her down and drag her back like an old-time posse, but my father wouldn't hear of it. He claimed she'd been unhappy for a long time, was quick then to reveal little bits and pieces of their lives—secrets he'd carried and never shared before to protect me and her reputation—all ready and at hand to explain her actions.

There were secrets, of course, real ones—not those he pretended to let slip at Earlys or at the Hamilton. Three weeks after she was gone he packed up all of her clothes and things she'd left behind and put them in boxes in the attic.

His hands were still dusty from the attic ladder when he sat me down and told me I was never to take those things out again. I had two or three days to grieve her, a generous handful of extra hours to be sullen, and then I was never to say her name again either, not in his presence. If I did, he'd have to beat the dog piss out of me, and he didn't want to do that. He would, though, because he'd said it, and once something was said, it became the law.

He hoped it wouldn't come to that, though. He really did.

After that he winked at me, patted me heavily on the shoulder, and got up to get a Lone Star and make a phone call. He left a dusty handprint on the shirt I was wearing, and later that night I tossed it in the trash.

I knew my mother. I *know* my mother. I know she would never have left so empty-handed, without any of the things she loved that he so easily boxed away.

Without her photo albums and books and the chalcedony ring and necklace her grandmother gave her when she was sixteen.

She would never have left all those things behind.

She would never have left me behind.

With him.

My father has killed three men.

My father . . . that fucking monster . . . also killed my mother.

BONE

1

CHRIS

The body lay exposed, barely visible.

Maybe there was the gentle knurl of bone, dirty and ivory, and something brittle and flaking that might once have been fabric.

Something else, spidery and matted and awful and moving thick in the breeze, something that might have been hair. Human hair. It rustled with the grass and the black brush and dry mountain laurel, as if alive.

Human hair . . . and a bone.

Deputy Chris Cherry stood over the body, thinking, as a couple of Bulger's tigerstripe Herefords silently looked on. Bulger eyed him as well, propped up on his dirty

Kawasaki four-wheeler, working a jaw full of Copenhagen and eating a peach.

That was fucking talent.

Chris bent down, slow and careful, looking closer, before standing up again and wiping his hands on his uniform pants, even though he hadn't touched anything.

"How's the knee?" Bulger asked over a mouthful of peach and long-cut dip.

How's the knee? That's what everyone always said to him . . . Murfee's version of hello or goodbye. Another way of saying *Welcome back* or *Damn shame*, depending on who said it.

How's the fucking knee?

Chris ignored it. "You found this earlier this morning?"

Bulger made a face, spit a dark stream that looked bloody. "Earlier, ayup. Didn't have time to call it in. Busy." He finished the peach, tossing it behind him in the direction of Chris's patrol truck, a Ford, painted Big Bend County blue and gray. It hit the ground a few feet short, and one of the Herefords slowly walked toward it, head down.

Chris knew that after he left, Bulger would call the sheriff and complain a shit storm about his driving the truck up onto the pasture. He wouldn't say anything now to Chris, just take it direct to the sheriff himself, who might or might not hear him out—and who might or might not turn around and say something to Chris. Tough to say. Either way, Chris didn't feel bad about not hiking the five miles up from the ranch road to here, avoiding ankle-breaks and snakes and jackrabbit holes and whatever the hell else.

Bulger on his four-wheeler sure in the hell hadn't.

How's the fucking knee?

*   *   *

Matty Bulger's place, Indian Bluffs, covered twenty thousand acres of crooked spine running along the Rio Grande river gorge. His family had owned it for decades after buying off a piece of the huge Sierra Escalera ranch. Matty had three sons and Chris had played football with the youngest, Nathaniel, at Big Bend Central. The two older boys still worked Indian Bluffs with their dad, but Nat was running hunting operations at Sierra Escalera, and Chris knew that pissed off Bulger to no end.

Nat had been a decent receiver, tall with good hands. He'd been difficult to outthrow, scissoring along the sidelines beneath the big lights. Chris remembered Matty sitting in the stands, hollering Nat's name, pumping his blue-veined fists and watching his boy run.

"What we got? 'Nother dead beaner?"

Chris shrugged. *Probably.* It was a fact of life in far West Texas, along the river: Mexicans crossing the border, looking for work, carrying drugs, carrying each other. The trip was hard and it wasn't unusual for a few not to make it whole, or at all. Some got sick drinking water out of dirty stock tanks; others were injured by the land itself. They'd been known to break into ranch houses to steal food or to hide out for days in abandoned homes. Dupree had told him about a group that even called 911 on themselves after jimmying their way into a house. Lost and worn out, beaten, they'd polished off all the beer in the fridge and sat outside smoking cigarettes, stinking of river mud, calmly waiting with four hundred pounds of weed sewn up in burlap, until Dupree and a couple of the other deputies showed up.

Dupree always laughed his ass off telling that story, drinking a Dr Pepper and drawing hard on a Lucky Strike.

*   *   *

The Big Bend of the Rio Grande was outlaw country. Always had been, always would be.

It was the sharp curve where the Rockies met the northern Chihuahuan Desert, tough and beautiful and unforgiving. It was so bad, so rugged, so broken that it had been used to train astronauts for lunar walks. Big Bend, along with El Paso, Jeff Davis, and a handful of smaller counties, made up the bulk of the Texas side—the Trans-Pecos—more than 31,000 square miles. Big Bend County alone, anchored by Murfee and swallowing up whole both a state and a national park, was ten thousand miles of pure emptiness, patrolled by only six deputies and Sheriff Ross; all of it bigger than Delaware, Connecticut, and Rhode Island together. Just a few of a thousand places Chris had never been, probably would never go. It was a patchwork of ranches and river frontages and gorges shadowed by the Santiago, Chinati, and Chisos mountains, like deep cuts in dirty skin. If you looked hard enough, there were still the black pockmarks of ancient burned-out middens dotting the land, naked Indian arrowheads on the ground, and fading cave paintings up in the rocks. There were hills and valleys of cat's-claw and blackbrush and desert willow and mountain laurel, so much of it that when it rained good and hard, the waters were soon followed by an explosion of ground color rolling away as far as the eye could see—all the way to Mexico, so bright it was hard to take in all at once.

The rest of the time it was only bone and rust, just as hard on the eye but for different reasons, save for the odd patch of Bahia grass some ranchers tried for forage—a green so pale it was merely a hint, so that if you looked one way or the other, it disappeared altogether.

Chris had once hoped to disappear from Murfee altogether as well.

Chris's dad used to say that the ranches squared the land into little kingdoms where men like Bulger crowned themselves kings. They didn't answer much to deputies like Chris, less even to the green-clad Border Patrol agents who worked the Rio Grande. The land got handed down from father to son, and they hired their own men— more than a few illegals from right across the water—and bunked them in cold barracks built with their own hands. They tended their sick and dying and buried them in family plots and paid out wages in wads of dollars. Some operations had gone modern and given up cutting dogs and horses for cutting gates, choppers, and four-wheelers. Loading chutes and trailer trucks had long replaced the dusty trail, and more than a few had taken to hiring hunting management consultants to set up big-game operations on back acreage. They streamed live video of elk and mule deer and made top dollar from weekend warriors wanting to pick their own antler racks with little or no fuss.

But the ranches, and the ranchers, were Murfee, and always would be. No different from the handful of other little towns held hostage by the patchwork of fences and pastures drawn in the dust beneath all the gathered mountains. They defined life here, the ebb and flow of it.

In his summers, Chris had worked his fair share of cattle operations all around Murfee. He'd long known men like Bulger who didn't give a damn about what happened outside their fences and couldn't see much beyond them. Not all, though—both Terry Macrae at Tres Rios and Dave Wilcher at the Monument set out food and clean water for the illegals crossing their lands looking for work, adopting a live-and-let-live view of it all. Wilcher went so far as to put up a small cottage near the gorge, a way station for those passing through, even though it drove the Border Patrol crazy. Chris had been out there and seen the wadded clothes, blown-out old shoes, even the maps the travelers had left behind. They'd bought the maps down in Ojinaga. Crude things, pencil lines showing bare trails and roads and checkpoints and ranches like the Monument where desperate men—desperate people— could hole up for a few hours.

Still, so many didn't make it: drowned in the river in heavy rains, caught up in a cold snap or a sudden snow squall, more than a few catching a bullet behind the ear. All left for dead where they'd fallen. Bodies were not uncommon out here in the emptiness.

Men like Bulger found them, unconcerned about the how or why, just waiting for men like Chris to clean up the mess.

Chris had grown up here and had been trying to leave it forever.

His dad had been the town dentist and they'd lived in Murfee proper, but after graduating from Big Bend Central, Chris had taken his football scholarship and gotten the hell out for what he thought was good, only to return for a hundred bad reasons that seemed far worse now— like this god-awful moment, standing over bones and hair in the cold wind, with rain up in the mountains, darkening the far sky. Coming his way. And Matty Bulger waiting impatiently for Chris to do some goddamn thing so he could get back to work.

His cell buzzed, dying before he even could reach for

it. Service was spotty out here, the towers few and far between, and the radio was sometimes even worse, with the repeater in Stockton blocked by mountains. Either way, he'd have to go back out to the main road to call this in. The lost call was probably Melissa.

The lost call meant he'd avoided another argument without even trying.

Chris was about to turn away, return to his truck, when something on the ground caught his eye. Not so much on the ground, but the ground itself: that little rim of earth holding the body in place.

Like hands holding something precious.

He bent down again, careful for the second time, for a closer look. Bulger shifted behind him, finally sliding his ass off the four-wheeler, angling for a view of what had caught Chris's attention.

His eyes followed the contours of the body, trying to make sense of it . . . where it began, where it ended, in the mess of earth. That disturbed dirt, loam broken up with rocks that might be bone—all of it turned up, stinking like cow shit.

Turned up.

Unearthed.

This body had been *buried* here. Not particularly well or deep, not at all, but it had been deliberately put into the ground until something, coyote or Mexican wolf, even a black bear, had scented it and dug it up.

Someone had hid it. The illegals crossing the area never buried one of their own, no matter how they'd died. They left them naked, exposed, knowing the sun, wind, and rain had more time than they did to make them disappear.

He saw it clearly then, perhaps the very thing that had made him take the second look to begin with—his intuition working overtime on a problem he'd been about to give up on.

Hands holding something precious.

The body's hands were all there, puzzle pieces suddenly visible, both of them, held together tight. Wrist to wrist and pulled up close behind what could only be the curve of the spine, knees up by the broken jawbone, the way you might rope up a calf . . . or tie someone up.

Skeletal hands held together tight by a thick zip tie, taut like a sunning snake in the upturned earth. It still looked new, untouched; barely stained by the earth it had been buried in.

Chris rose up, his knee popping. It was a hard, sharp sound, carrying all the way to where Bulger stood, waiting. The rancher had asked if the body was another dead beaner, dirtying up his property, spooking his cows. Deputy Chris Cherry, who had been a deputy for less than a year, didn't think so. He didn't think so at all.

2

ANNE

Anne stood in Tancy Garner's—the dead woman's—room, trying not to think about her. She had all the windows open, letting the October air wander through. A damp breeze shuffled the papers on the woman's desk. A ratty old solar system hung high in the corner, turning circles, orbiting itself and nothing at all. Saturn's cartoon rings bumped against water stains on the ceiling tiles.

Anne hoped the breeze, cold enough to pucker skin, might blow the dead woman's spirit away. Send it off to wherever it needed to go. She was ashamed that she was so grateful for the call that brought her here to Big Bend Central over a month into the school year; ashamed that it took another woman's death to get her back on her feet again. At least Tancy Garner hadn't died *in* the classroom.

She was found in her kitchen, facedown in blood and

milk, where she'd passed away the night before while putting away a glass bottle. A strange fall, an accident, clip-
ping her head on her counter on the way down. She'd
taught science, later English, at Big Bend Central
for nearly twenty years. She'd been a school fixture—
more like a monument—respected and feared in fair measure, with her stern face, carved and weathered like rock,
still staring out of old yearbooks and copies of school
newspapers. And she was local, having spent her entire
life in Murfee. Anne figured the old woman had been
able to rope and ride and milk and whatever the hell else
people who grew up on a ranch knew how to do. Things
Anne had read about and seen a few times on the Discov-
ery Channel. Of course, no one expected Anne to *replace*
Tancy Garner, just get her classes through the end of the
school year . . . finish things without too much disrup-
tion or chaos. Philip Tanner, BBC's principal, had made
all that clear. Very clear. They'd talk about a permanent
position at the end of the year, if at all.

We'll just see, Ms. Hart. We'll just see then. Anne shuffled things around on the desk—*her* desk, for at least a
while. It was a holiday, Columbus Day. The school was
pretty much empty, except for her.

She'd pulled into Murfee late on Thursday, got the
keys to the little house she was renting the next morning
right after she'd met with Tanner, and had spent the past
three days over the long weekend getting settled. Tomorrow there would be students sitting in these old chairs,
staring at her while they texted and whispered. A few had
gotten a glimpse of her on Friday, had maybe already
picked up on their new teacher's name, and if BBC was
like every other school—and it was—the rumor mills
would've been turning since. She figured she would know

by the second period on Tuesday, or Wednesday morning at the latest, just how much anyone knew about her.

Still, she'd reach out to Dial Montgomery tomorrow and thank him, and soon Sheriff Ross too, although he'd plead ignorance. She'd been searching for something permanent in Dallas or Fort Worth since Austin was still out of the question, even with Dial's help, and had been prepared to sub for the rest of the year in Arlington before heading back home to Virginia. Now Murfee was all she had. Her parents waited for her back east, unable to understand or accept why she hadn't already returned. They thought it was foolish that she had remained in Texas.

Destructive was the word her father used, over and over again. She wanted to believe it was rebuilding.

She went to one of the open windows. From the second floor, Murfee spread out around her, so small against mountains whose names she didn't know, painted charcoal and purple in the background. She could see the big lights of BBC's football stadium, the long edge of an end zone upright, and caught the echo of whistles, rising and falling along with the wind. The team was practicing hard, even on a holiday. She guessed there were rules against that, but who was going to say anything out here? Tanner had already mentioned the October game with Presidio, and Murfee's Fall Carnival, both of which sounded like big deals—*very* big deals. Murfee was a small town in every way. Sure, the mountains and the open sky gave the illusion of size—of infinite, unfillable space—but take that away, and it was no different from any of the small towns around Virginia. In that way, it was *too* small for Anne—her past couldn't help but overtake her.

For her, no place might ever truly be big enough.

She knew she wasn't going to have to worry about Tanner offering her a full-time position. She'd be here a bit, try to find her bearings again . . . find herself, really, and then move on when they asked.

Rebuild.

Dial, the only member of the Austin Independent School District's board of trustees who never completely turned his back on her, had mentioned the sad story of Sheriff Ross's wife when he'd called out of the blue about the job. Principal Tanner had touched on it too, just in passing—like giving away a secret he wasn't supposed to share, but enjoyed doing anyway. Maybe he thought it would make some sort of sense to Anne, explain everything to her; as if she and the sheriff shared a tragedy that really wasn't the same at all, not even close.

Evelyn Ross had disappeared about a year ago, running away with or without another man—no one was sure. It was a scandal—in a place this small, everything is—and the wife had been popular and well liked. She had volunteered at the school, worked in the front office, sold concessions for football and basketball games, and handled other odds and ends. Her son was still a student, one of Anne's.

A good student—or at least he had been. Over the weekend she'd glanced through Ms. Garner's grade-books, the older woman simply refusing to use any of the new computer-based grading modules, sticking to her old Whaley Gradebooks instead. She had stacks of them neatly filed away from the last decade or more, each filled with her small, blunt writing.

Tancy Garner had taught the missing woman's son English for the last two years. Even though there hadn't been a lot of grades thus far for the new semester, the pattern was pretty clear. The town might have recovered from the scandal, but Anne was pretty sure that Caleb Ross had not let his mother go.

What did it take for a mother to up and leave her son, disappear? She'd heard of this happening, of course, but it was still hard to wrap her head around. What could be so bad to make a mother flee, run off into the night, leaving everything behind?

Maybe there was something about this wild and distant place that made such an idea acceptable, even possible, at the outer edge of so much emptiness.

October wind brushed her hair, stung her eyes. She stared down mountains both faraway and close at the same time. She didn't know their names, didn't even know if they were in Texas or Mexico. Marc had called her *geographically challenged*, laughing at the broken compass she carried in her head—her inability to remember directions or state capitals and the trouble she had reading maps, even following MapQuest printouts. He bought her a GPS once, expensive and idiot proof, but— not surprisingly—she didn't know where it was anymore.

Like other bits and pieces of her life, it had been left behind somewhere.

Although she really couldn't comprehend abandoning a child, your own flesh and blood, the rest of *running* made so much sense that it hurt.

Like a sharp pain, cutting your finger on paper. Just like now, whenever she thought about Marc. She knew that desperate need to disappear; to leave broken, unfixable things behind; to run into the wild dark and get lost in it until the storm passed, if it ever did.

That she understood far too well. She'd make the best

of it here while she could. Even if she couldn't lose herself in Murfee, she'd lose herself in the work; try to, anyway. It was all she could do, and with all she'd left behind, it was all she had. She turned away from the window and back to the classroom, continuing to put the dead woman's things away.

3

DUANE

Hurting someone was easy, too easy.

But showing restraint? Not raising your hand? Now, that was goddamn hard . . . a cross made of razors and nails, too heavy and sharp to bear. She didn't understand that. Not yet. But she would, even though in this moment—right fucking now—he couldn't remember her name. It was somewhere out of reach, circling. Soon he was going to have to let his hands do all the talking, anyway.

It had started first with messages, little texts. His first words were sweet before turning ugly. Next were the pictures: the wind in the trees behind his daddy's house, the sun glowing red like hell over the Chisos; his gun in shadows on the kitchen counter. Even a dead jackrabbit rotting by the road, all tore up, dead eye marbled and staring right into the phone camera. He couldn't explain why he sent these things to her, what they were supposed to mean. Couldn't even remember sending most of 'em.

He'd watched the little Mex girl grow up, but really first *saw* her sipping a Dr Pepper outside Mancha's. Maybe it wasn't even a Dr Pepper, and it was possible she hadn't winked at him either, but there she was: dark hair, dark skin . . . dark mouth kissing a straw. He hadn't even realized how much she caught his eye until he started having all those dark dreams about her. He'd been having them for a long, long time since.

Now, finally, he was in her room—a first—one hand holding steady his duty trousers and the other his goddamn prick—embarrassed—limp and not working, although he'd wanted her to see it for so long. He might have already sent her a picture, but didn't remember whether he'd done that, either. He wouldn't touch her, not yet, not now, because once he started he knew he wouldn't stop, so better not to start at all; all that restraint he possessed that she didn't yet understand. Worse, there was no way she was going to touch him, not willingly, so he was left with his pants down around his legs, and none of it working out the way he'd wanted or dreamed about. He was too distracted, too busy cutting his eyes away from her to his portable on her nightstand, standing tall next to a pile of books and her cellphone. Taller than his prick, for damn sure.

That damn phone distracted him. Oh, how he wanted to have a little look-see beneath its bright pink case, to find out if she'd been saving his texts and his pictures and who else she was talking to—peek at her dirty secrets and make sure there was nothin' in there about him. She wasn't to talk about him to anyone. He didn't exist. He was smoke and dust and the wind in the picture he'd sent her—he was empty spaces. He'd told her what would happen if she ever snitched about the things he shared with her, and was pretty goddamn sure she'd gotten the message, 'cause he'd also put something sharp up near her eye or left a stray bullet in her book bag or sent her a picture of someone else's blood, although he couldn't quite recall which of those he'd done, maybe all of them.

No . . . taking a gander at her phone wasn't so much about her as it was about *him*—it might help him remember some things, that was all. It had been getting bad lately, all the little things he was forgetting. It was cigarette holes in a newspaper, black scorch marks where words should be. His daddy, Jamison Dupree, had known a thing or two about cigarettes and scorches. Duane still had the marks on his arms and back to show for it. The forgetting had gotten worse with the *foco* he'd been snorting, and if the Judge knew about *that*—well, he'd beat the dog piss out of Duane, so Duane had been keeping this dirty little secret to himself.

He did like that *foco*, oh yes sir, he did . . . *yes sir, yes sir, three bags full, sir*. Duane loved its strange magic—the way it sped everything up and slowed it down at the same time. The way it made him *sharp*, like he was all shiny knife edge and cut the goddamn air when he walked, drawing blood, and the way it let him see things that weren't there . . . see *right through* things.

He'd once spied a mangy Mexican gray wolf out on his property and swore the *foco* gave him wolf eyes, just the same—afraid now people might even see them glowing, reflecting in his own dashboard light or the high beams of passing cars on Route 67.

It wasn't even a matter of liking the *foco* anymore as

much as fucking needing it. It made him desperate, long-
ing for his sharp skin and wolf eyes to protect him when
he was awake, which was getting to be all the goddamn
time, since he wasn't sleeping so much anymore; or
maybe he was and just was forgetting that, too. His daddy
always said they had Comanche or Mescalero in them,
which by birthright gave the Duprees a weakness for
drink . . . burned as it was into their very blood, so they
couldn't help but lust for it. It had been for Duane's own
good that his daddy had touched those Lucky Strikes to
his skin, the sweet stink of Four Roses on his breath . . .
whisper-screaming never to pick up the bottle the way
he'd done, 'cause he might never put it down.

And Duane *had* listened to Jamison Dupree. Still did,
because even before the *foco* took hold of him with its
skeletal hands, before it had scorched him in its own way
like his daddy's cigarettes, he'd been dreaming of his daddy's long-gone voice at his ear. Sometimes, worse—not
just his voice, but *all of him*, rotted near away, standing
right next to Duane, smiling lightning and blackness. If
nothing else, he came by his needs honestly. They were in
his blood.

Then he was done, spent, barely realizing it . . . having
forgotten she was even there. She stared at him, waiting
for him to leave or whatever he was going to do next. He
struggled with his pants, tried to focus on her walls, the
posters and pictures there . . . magazine cutouts of places
she would never go because he'd never let her. School was
out for the day, a holiday, but her daddy was off to work
or out at Mancha's drinking a cold one. Maybe Duane
had threatened to kill her daddy or her mama, or both of
them. That's what he'd done, or something like it. Then
it came, slow, like a catfish surfacing in muddy water—

why it had been so hard to concentrate on the task at hand. *In his hand.* It wasn't about her phone, but his portable radio, black and sleek, and knowing in a way he couldn't explain that it was about to crackle to life and summon him.

He'd been forgetting things, true, no two ways about that, but that was because he now knew other things, too. Weird things, things he had zero reason to know. He tested himself all the time. Like guessing the color of the next car that would pass him or the next stupid words someone might say to him. Knowing when his dead daddy would be waiting for him in the porch shadows . . . staring with eyes like hard white stones, the air around the soapberry and the shin oaks ripe with Four Roses and dead skin.

So he knew all sorts of things, some useful, some not; secrets and mysteries and little peeks around the corner. *Gifts*—a fair trade, he figured, for all the things he was forgetting. Like he knew right now his radio was going to call him. Maybe it was his blood talking or the wolf eyes or just the *foco*. Maybe it was all his imagination. Or most likely, he was just going goddamn crazy.

She stayed across the room, wary, like a kicked dog. She was in a T-shirt and BBC sweatpants, and it was still kind of early, so she had no makeup, with her hair all a mess. But he loved her dark skin, like that bruised time of day when the desert sky was shot through by the setting sun and the ground was long with shadow, right before he was most likely to see his daddy standing beneath the leaves of the shin oaks.

He could make her come and sit next to him, make

her hold his hand and say things she didn't mean, but he wasn't in the mood for it. Not anymore. Messing with her was like messing with a kicked dog, and sometimes even a whupped dog might bite. Or at least bark. Duane smiled, chuckled. He finished with his pants.

"Vete a la mierda," she said through her teeth. Tough words, even if he didn't know the exact meaning. She might have learned to talk like that from her brother, but her brother had never been tough at all. She hugged her arms. No need to waste a breath telling her to keep that fucking pretty mouth shut. That threat was already deep down in her eyes . . . all the things he'd swore to do, the horrible world he'd shown her in *his* pictures, not her magazine cutouts.

They both jumped when the radio came alive, with Miss Maisie from dispatch calling his name. He couldn't hide a smile as he reached for it. Happened just like he knew it would. The girl inched around her room to give Chief Deputy Duane Dupree a wide berth. He skinned back his lips, flashed a bigger grin, let his wolf eyes *really* shine. Revealing them, wondering if his teeth looked sharp, too.

Before he got out the door they both heard Miss Maisie on the radio going on and on about something, a trouble or mess, out at Indian Bluffs. A body? That's what she'd said.

The Bluffs was Matty Bulger's place, farthest out near Chapel Mesa and damn near north Mexico, part of the Cut. The only property beyond that was the Far Six, and that hadn't been worked in years, at least not for cattle, although Duane knew it well. It seemed Bulger had found a body rusting out on the caliche. Chris Cherry had caught the call and was out there now, probably fuckin' it up.

A body.

Duane thought that should mean something to him, but like so much else, he'd forgotten what that could be.

4

MELISSA

She hated nearly everything about the place, but mostly the smell. That constant wet, heavy stink of cows—the high, ripe tang of cow shit. It was everywhere and it hung in the air and crept into her food; she even dreamed of it. It reminded her too much of the oil fields, of the stench of burning gas and rusted metal. Chris kept telling her it was all in her head, and maybe he was right. This place was all up in her head, holding her hostage.

Mel took another drag on her cigarette, tried to inhale all the smoke, but even that did little to make the cow shit go away. The cigarettes were her secret, stowed away like pirates' treasure around the house, even though Chris must have known about them and just wasn't saying anything. He must have smelled them on her too; ignoring it like he did the cow shit stink, figuring the fight wasn't worth it. Since they'd come here, back to his home in Murfee, a lot of things hadn't been worth a fight.

Except now . . . except for *the body*. Chris was all wound up about that in a way he hadn't been wound up about anything in a long time. He was excited to play detective, wanted to convince her that this wasn't just any dead body, not just one more wetback hauling ass across the caliche and scrub and dying on the way. Evidently, finding dead Mexicans was kind of a common occurrence around here. Is that what happened to people who tried to escape this place? And was that what she really smelled all the time—the dead who'd never made it? No, for Chris this wasn't just another death, but possibly a murder, and somehow that made all the difference in the world.

Mel fished out another cigarette, eyeing her chipped nails and rocking the back porch swing with her pale bare foot. Chris's dad had put up the swing with his own hands a year or so before Chris's mom died of cancer. It was held together by carpentry nails; the cushions were faded and thin, and the floral pattern on them now looked more like bloodstains. She could pick out the uneven scratch marks where over the years Chris had worked at the wood with a penknife. It was easy to imagine him out here sitting, thinking, whittling. And his mom before that, wasting away, wrapped in blankets they now kept on their own bed. By the time they'd come to Murfee, his dad was dead as well, and Chris had the house free and clear.

It was a small, sunburned affair, peeling paint, with a backyard much bigger than the house itself. It was filled with boxes of his dad's old books, dusty and dank and smelling only slightly less bad than the cow shit. The whole place needed so much work, and Chris had been at it for a few months now, tinkering here and there, with little purpose or progress. He'd promised her a pool, and there was zero to show for that. The backyard remained a stubborn flat expanse of grass boxed in by warped fencing and surprisingly tall, modern lights: stadium lights, rising high above the grass that Chris actually did tend, some. He cut it short, but it was still smooth and a deep emerald green. It looked cold, polished, unreal—reminding her even more of the actual pool she didn't have. At least this she understood. Chris had let it slip once, how he and his dad had thrown footballs out here all the time. They'd needed all the space because Chris had a hell of an arm, every toss a moonshot, and his dad had put the lights up so they could throw at night—back and forth, back and forth—over all that green grass.

His mom watching them both from the porch, this very swing. Melissa had come to accept the swing and spent more time on it than inside the house. The porch, the swing, was her place now, where she could sneak her cigarettes and watch the smoke disappear—watch it rise and twist in the wind, escape past the trees and over the mountains.

Anywhere away from here.

Chris arrived at Baylor big, heavy; got a scholarship on that cannon arm, but no one expected him to play, least of all him, and he hadn't really cared one way or the other.

She was a couple of years older, still taking a class here and there, since it gave her a reason to stay in Waco;

working also a few hours in the Athletic Department and fucking some of the assistant coaches, one of whom was married. That last had turned into a scandal, a real mess that finally ended after she got a late-night call from his wife. The woman hadn't yelled, hadn't called her names or threatened her. She'd just cried, asking through tears and gasps why Mel had to fight and hold on to something that wasn't hers, break something that didn't belong to her and never had.

And Mel had wanted to explain how school was supposed to have been *hers*, how being in Waco was damn near the only thing she had to hold on to—a way out of Spindletop and Goose Creek and the Spraberry Trend, all those stinking oil fields she and her daddy had moved through, even as she still hadn't been able to quite leave them or him behind. How her piece-of-shit daddy had a thousand reasons for his drinking: stress and back pain, slights and old wounds that no one could ever see and that never healed. And how she'd spent far too many nights tending all those hurts, real and imagined, watching over him long after he'd passed out or been beaten senseless, eyeing the ragged rise and fall of his chest, praying his breathing would never stop so she wouldn't be left on her own; but sometimes praying that it would.

She'd wanted to say all those things and more—explain every detail of her shitty life to the sad voice on the phone who'd dared question it. But instead, she just let that voice cry itself out, holding the phone tight to her ear for more than an hour, *making* herself listen, knowing that she had to hear it all, knowing that she owed the voice— that other woman—at least that much . . . until the woman finally hung up on her.

Mel had then sat for another hour in the dark, phone still in her hand. Before dawn, she deleted the assistant coach's number, and when that wasn't quite enough, she tossed the phone itself into the small fountain in front of her apartment.

Her daddy had always said: *It ain't stealin' if they won't miss it*. But no matter what, it always was . . . *always*.

After that came Chris Cherry. Even during his first year on campus—long past the time she should have graduated and left—she couldn't help but notice him walking as often with a stack of books in his hand as a football. For the longest time they said hi every now and then but little more than that, as she watched him go from big and heavy to tall and strong. The time on campus carved him, cut away the excess, but he never saw it himself. He towered on the sidelines, a clipboard in his hand that she later found out had class notes on it rather than play sheets. The plays were easy for him and the classes he truly enjoyed.

He was smart and came across as a gentleman through and through, moving slowly and carefully whenever they ran into each other, as if he was afraid his size would break her. He could also be shy for a guy so big, so much so that even as they started to speak to each other more and more, she felt like the one carrying both ends of the conversation. But he had an easy way of saying a lot without saying much at all, and a habit of listening serious and close, almost too intently. He could lose himself in a book that same way for hours on end, and even though they saw each other most often around the practice field and the Athletic Department, he never really talked about football or the team with her.

She wondered then if the game was just his way out of some other place, too.

And he never would have gotten off the sidelines had Tyler McGee not spun a shot glass off his girlfriend's head two days before their season opener against Wofford. Tyler wasn't even the starter, he backed up Billy Pressey. But when Billy suddenly got sidelined with appendicitis and Tyler got the call, he wanted to celebrate with a bar crawl, where he downed more than a few congratulatory Jäger shots and then got sideways with his girlfriend, Dominique.

He might have played anyway, the whole goddamn ugly episode buried, if not for the stitches. Not the fifteen it took to close up Dominique's head; no, it was the six tiny stitches on Tyler's hand, his throwing hand, cut by striking his knuckles on the bar.

That left Chris. Only Chris . . . suddenly walking into Floyd Casey Stadium in front of fifty thousand with "Old Fite" playing loud, over and over again, and his eyes hidden beneath his helmet.

Months later, when they were twined together in her bed, Chris admitted his hands had been shaking so badly he'd kept them clasped together in front of him like he was praying, and in a lot of ways, he was.

Still, it was only Wofford. The first game of the season, and the Bears would get back either Tyler or Billy before the real games. All Chris had to do was keep a cool head, not make any mistakes; let the defense and the running game hold the fort, and he'd have the win. But that game plan had only lasted through the first fumble, the first blocked punt, and a long run by a Wofford back who'd never gained more than eighty yards in any game. Chris once told her that when he walked onto the field for the second quarter, he didn't really think much about his BBC games—all the games he'd played and won in high school—choosing instead to remember only what it was like to be *here*, in his backyard with his dad telling him to let 'er rip, just so they both could see how hard and high he could throw it.

And for the last half of the Wofford game, that's all he did: let 'er rip. With fifty thousand fans watching to see how hard and high Chris Cherry could throw it.

He started the Louisiana-Monroe game the following week, and then again at Iowa State. Two days after that, Chris came up to her after practice and officially asked her out. He was so serious, so sweet and awkward about it, with his hair still wet from the showers and a bruise across his forehead from a hard hit turning blue to black, that she almost laughed.

Instead, she asked him why it took him so damn long.

They'd been together ever since.

Tyler McGee married Dominique and lost his scholarship, and Billy Pressey never took another snap as the starter. They talked about it a few times, how fast the pieces fell into place: Billy's bad appendix and Tyler's bad temper and a few stitches and some shitty team defense. All the little things adding up to Chris finally letting 'er rip all through the rest of his junior year, when packs of overweight, tired men with video cameras and cellphones and notepads sprouted in the stands like thick weeds, just to see him play.

And on through the long following summer, where they holed up in her apartment, sleeping but not really sleeping together in the bed that was too small for her, let alone Chris. Chris pushing himself harder and harder while she waited, supported. She didn't really understand the secret language of the game, but she didn't have to, because she understood the players . . . men . . . and all the things they needed. Although after they first heard his name together on *SportsCenter* she'd cried for an hour, while he sat there, quiet, twisting his callused hands.

Then his final year, and those first six wins and not one, but two, ESPN video profiles of Chris's high school career in Murfee: all grainy, washed-out footage of Chris towering over fields far too small. He was noticeably heavier, and that was the reason, according to everyone, he'd never been given a serious look . . . but there was still that goddamn arm, always that arm—lightning chained to that earthbound body.

And finally, that heartbeat moment of the Kansas State game beneath the lights, the ESPN2 Game of the Week, where K State's Lonnie Ray Holliday showed that he knew how to let 'er rip pretty damn well too, catching Chris clean from the blind side right at the knees and Mel knowing—knowing for goddamn certain—that it was all over even before it really began.

There was an agent, briefly, who popped in like a magic trick, wearing suits a bit too shiny at the cuffs, who talked big about Chris having the opportunity to show off all of his *intangibles*. But then his phone went dead and he was gone as if he had never even existed. Vanished like a rabbit in a hat. Mel had called the agent over and over again even after Chris wouldn't, standing over their sink, smoking cigarettes, trying not to cry.

When she was thinking straight she didn't blame Chris for the injury itself, no more than she'd blame someone for getting hit by a car he never saw coming. It was more about what happened after, all the things that *didn't* happen. Chris had started working on a master's degree in literature, but let that go. He rehabbed some more, worked out, but not that hard, not that serious, and the weight he'd cut started to hang on him again. He'd sit in her apartment in the dark, flipping through TV channels or reading books by whatever sunlight he let in through the windows.

Never sports, though, never that, and none since. Finally, when it was near unbearable, both of them washed out and colorless, he came in one afternoon and said he was going home, back to Murfee—a place to her that was only TV clips and high school game films. He'd made a call she knew nothing about to the sheriff's department and they'd agreed to take him on. It was decent, honest work he could be proud of, and the old family house was still there and it was all set, easy. She knew without his saying it that he needed to get out of Waco, away once and for all. And standing there in the jeans he always wore so no one, most of all her, could see that white and coiled snake of a scar from the surgery, he'd almost been happy. Almost himself again.

Even still, the words were right there on the tip of her tongue, ready to spit it out: *Go fuck yourself, Chris.* He wasn't going to make a decision like that on his own. He didn't get to play house with her and then walk away, leaving her with nothing. He was supposed to be—*was going to be, goddammit*—different from and better than every other man she'd known from her daddy onward. She almost said all those things too—staring into his eyes, which were most often blue but other times appeared bottle green—when he finally smiled at her, wide, embarrassed.

Misunderstood. That's when *she* understood he wasn't talking about leaving Waco alone.

While he twisted his hands, hoping she got his meaning without making him put the words together out loud, she tossed water on that match-strike anger she'd struggled with forever—the same anger that had gotten her daddy in so much trouble for so much of their lives. An anger that had lit him from within, so that he was nearly glowing with it, his fists throwing sparks, always trying to set the world on fire. Burning them both.

Instead, she'd hugged Chris, face tilted down and hard, so he wouldn't see her cry.

It took them a month to pack up what bits and pieces of a life they had in Waco, and then just like that they were here, in Murfee, unlocking the long-empty house he'd grown up in and where both of his parents had died. That first night there had been a rare West Texas rain, all noise and fury and white light against the dusty windows, and she'd given herself to him on a few blankets thrown down on the floor, with water dripping all round them.

She woke the next morning and stood on this still-wet porch and saw all the color that had sprung up overnight, the earth taking water like a dying man, with a pale mist falling skyward over hills that were the same sudden uncertain green of Chris's eyes.

That had been truly nice, her best moment since coming here. Now the rain only reminded her that there were still a few holes in the roof Chris hadn't gotten around to fixing yet.

Mel wasn't sure what Chris thought coming back to Murfee might actually fix: his life, his knee, her. Them. If anything, coming home had made him more withdrawn, more sullen. Beyond the job, Mel couldn't imagine what he was looking for here anymore. And that left *her* lost, alone, not knowing what she was fighting against or for.

But still they went on, rusting away minute by minute, until two days ago, when Chris had found the body out at a place called Indian Bluffs. It was all he thought about now—*his investigation*—and she hated herself for letting it get under her skin, letting it drive her fucking crazy. Chris was finally alive, awake, like those hills after the rain, and it had nothing to do with her at all.

Chris had snapped a few pictures on his phone and showed them to her that first night, sitting up in bed. She'd turned the phone this way and that, trying to make sense of the mess on the ground. That's all she saw of the body.

After he got up to get them both a glass of water, she continued to thumb back and forth through the handful of other pictures on his phone. She saw none of her, none of their time in Waco, none of anything that might even make sense to her. It was all gone, deleted. Instead, there were images of cliff walls out in the desert where you could barely make out faded Indian paintings; a few more of ghost towns whose names no one remembered anymore; some of cracked earth circled over by big black birds in ugly skies.

And that damn body. All of Chris's pictures were of dead places and things: memories and remains and ruins where people had once been and were no longer. By the time he came back with their glasses, she had put the phone on the bed and pretended to go to sleep.

She'd had a bad dream of her own last night, one where she was sitting on this very porch listening to a dying radio beneath a snapshot sky. She had tuned in to her favorite show, *Dark Stars*, hosted by a psychic who'd once been famous for solving murders and disappearances but now helped people connect with their dead relatives . . . with their ghosts. In her dream a voice had called in sounding just like her—in fact it was her—wanting to know what had become of Melissa Bristow. Rumor was, she'd gotten lost, disappeared in some oil field or ghost town that no one could find anymore. But Melissa had been right there, with a mouthful of dust, screaming at the radio, at herself.

I'm right here. But she wasn't, not really. *She* was the ghost, haunting herself and Chris and the empty spaces between them.

She'd woken up cold and afraid and gasping, wanting and needing Chris and putting a hand out for him to feel his warmth and maybe his heartbeat, only to find his side of the bed empty. Instead, he'd been across the room, hunched in front of their laptop, his face hard angles in the screen's glare . . . *investigating*.

Afterward, she'd struggled to find sleep, still angry. At him, at Murfee, at herself. The living she could compete with, fight against. She'd done it her whole life, so much like her daddy in more ways than she'd ever admit, who always fought for everything. But those things in his pictures? Ghosts and shadows and emptiness?

She didn't even know where to begin. It was like her horrible dream and this house with its bad roof and its old books and this backyard with its lights and green grass—she was trapped inside one of Chris's pictures, a picture of someone and something that didn't exist anymore. But before she'd closed her eyes again, dropping into a sleep free of dead things, she'd imagined or dreamed, or just hoped, that Chris had climbed back into bed with her and that she had reached out for him. Just to brush her fingers over him, to make sure he was real.

5

CALEB

There are so many stories about Phantly Roy Bean Jr., the infamous Hanging Judge Roy Bean—the self-proclaimed "Law West of the Pecos"—that it's hard to sort the truth from the fiction. It's hard to see the real man standing in the long shadow of one that may never have existed at all.

In eighth grade we had to write a paper about a famous Texan, and everyone thought I would write about Judge Bean. After all, my father is the new "Law West of the Pecos"—I read it all the time in the *Murfee Daily*, and that's how the *NBC Nightly News* once referred to him. He's a modern Roy Bean, always wearing either his custom Half-Breed hat or a Stetson; colorful and famous and outspoken, so much so that he's been nicknamed the

Judge. He's even originally from Pecos. His family was once famous there.

In Murfee, he's more than the sheriff. He's larger than life. He is judge, jury, and executioner.

I almost wrote my paper on Gene Roddenberry, but at the last minute, chose Clyde Barrow instead. I thought it was funny that the sheriff's son was writing about one of Texas's most famous criminals. It was my raised middle finger to him. I was younger and dumber, and it was my awkward way of letting him know that *I knew*. That I knew all about him. My mom tried to talk me out of it before finally letting it go. She neatly corrected my punctuation and bought me a nice blue folder to put it in, even typing up the label for the cover. Back then, when my father was still pretending to be fatherly, or when he just wanted to push me or mess with me, he'd go over my homework. My mom had to lay it out for him next to his breakfast plate, to the left of the juice but not touching the fork, so he could scan through it with those gray eyes of his, searching for mistakes, tapping his long finger against the papers like a clock-tick. We both knew he wasn't really reading. It was more about making me sit there watching him do it, waiting for him. But on that one morning, I saw that my Clyde Barrow report, that blue folder, wasn't in his stack. My mom had already slipped it into my backpack next to the door. She never said anything and I never asked, even though we both knew he'd probably hear about it anyway. My father hears about everything that happens in Murfee, and if punishment was ever going to be given out over my disrespectful report, my mom would have gotten her measure of it, too. She sat there next to him while he read the rest of my work, calm, sipping her juice, never taking her eyes off me.

Walking to school and remembering my mom's look—steady, warm, ready—I almost threw that fucking folder into the trash, willing to take the belt or the closet or whatever for the failing grade. But I didn't. I turned it in, my hands shaking, and that's when I learned that Amé Reynosa, who I'd never spoken to even though she sat next to me in homeroom because our last names both began with R, had written her paper on Bonnie Parker.

I knew I wanted to be her friend that day, and have been, ever since. I suffered for that paper later; my mom did, too.

But whenever I get to sit close and talk to Amé, I'm ashamed to admit I'm still glad I chose Barrow.

There are all these stories about Judge Bean, legends. Who knows what's true anymore? He left Kentucky when he was sixteen to work Louisiana flatboats, then opened a trading post for a time in Chihuahua, where he killed a Mexican, forcing him to move on to Sonora and later San Diego, where he shot a Scotsman in a duel over a lady. He was arrested, and while he was waiting in jail, women he'd courted brought all kinds of presents: flowers, wine, cigars, food, including an iron skillet full of tamales, hiding knives he then used to dig his way out of jail.

Allegedly a group of men tried to hang him in San Gabriel after another duel left their friend, a Mexican army officer, dead. The issue? A woman, of course. They put Bean up on a horse and strung a noose around his neck and slapped the horse's ass, but when it stood rock-still, just staring at them, they left Bean to twist and hang. The woman who'd been the source of all the trouble later cut him down, but Bean was forever branded with a rope scorch around his throat. He moved on to Pinos Altos in New Mexico and managed a merchandise store and saloon. Once he even used an old cannon to blast back an Apache war party. I read that you can still see that rusted piece of artillery.

Then he was running the Confederate blockades down to Matamoros, opening a firewood business by cutting down a neighbor's timber, operating a dairy farm and thinning down the milk with piss and river water. He even tried his hand as a butcher by cattle rustling. He married an eighteen-year-old girl, and after he was arrested for threatening her life, she still went on to have four children with him. He opened a saloon in his own tent city he named Vinegaroon, hard up on the banks of the Pecos River and deep in the Chihuahuan Desert, and got himself appointed justice of the peace. He heard cases in his saloon, drew the jurors from his best drinkers, and only ever used one lawbook—a dirty and water-stained 1879 edition of the *Revised Statutes of Texas*. Anything else he burned.

In a case where an Irishman shot a Chinese laborer, the Judge ruled that homicide was the killing of a human being, but he couldn't find any law against killing a Chinaman.

Later, he moved his saloon and his courtroom to a railroad right-of-way, where he homesteaded for twenty years, illegally. He always made sure the school had free firewood in the winter. He ended every marriage service with "God have mercy on your souls." They call Bean the Hanging Judge, but he really sentenced only two men to hang, and one of them escaped.

There are all these books and films, each one adding a little bit to the mystery and the legend, turning his violent exploits into jokes. He lied and cheated and stole at every turn; beat a teenage wife and killed men over other women. But he made sure a few cold kids got firewood, so all was forgiven or ignored.

He led a dark existence in a desperate time and place and became larger than life. He was life and death. But only in Texas, this godforsaken place where there's more blood in the ground than water.

I know the stories everyone tells about my father, those that get repeated over and over again so that it's hard to find the man—the real man—standing in the shadows behind the one people think they know or simply need to believe in.

How he saved Brenda Holt and baby Ellie.

How he arrested two Mexican drug runners up in Platas with an empty gun and a cold stare and two words of Spanish.

How he pulled out the tub that killed Nellie Banner-Ross with his bare hands. Everyone is positive they saw him do it—even though I know it's still there, clean and smelling of bleach and my mom's shampoo.

How he hands out Thanksgiving turkeys and Christmas hams and donates half his salary to charity.

How much he loves his one and only son.

Two days after my dad saved Brenda Holt from Dillon, she was kneeling in front of him in our garage while he leaned back against the hood of his truck, his hard hands wrapped around her head. She was crying, and even through his smile he kept telling her to take it easy as he listened to the Rangers on the truck's radio. The station popped in and out, static mixed with Brenda's sobs.

*   *   *

Once I saw him calmly washing blood off his hands in our mudroom sink, turning them this way and that, looking down at them as if they belonged to someone else, making sure there were no stains beneath his wedding ring.

There are times even now he stands in my doorway, watching me, unblinking, looking at *me* as if I belong to someone else, his gray eyes as unfathomable as the ocean, inescapable like the tide. Sometimes he lies fully dressed on his bed all night, those eyes unblinking, and I don't know if he's awake or what he sees or if he sees anything at all.

Every now and then, I feel again the hot touch of that old Ruger rifle. It's like the skin on my knee still burns, a phantom brand, from when the gun brushed against me, that moment right after my father used it to kill Dillon Holt.

What does it take to shoot another man?

How long do you think about it before you pull the trigger?

How long after? I looked it up. That Ruger has a rate of fire of 750 RPM and a muzzle velocity of 3,240 feet per second. My father was probably less than a hundred feet from Dillon when he shot him.

Not even the blink of an eye or a whole heartbeat. At that distance or closer, I guess you don't even think about it all.

*   *   *

I once had a dog, an Australian shepherd called, silly enough, Shep.

My mom got him for me in Braintree and named him while he was still in the cardboard box she used to bring him home. He was all paws and tail, high-strung and active, and I loved him so much it made my heart hurt. He slept at the end of my bed, and when my father came in to stare at me, Shep stared right back with his own bright blue eyes, growling, like he could see something none of the rest of us could. My father didn't like his bark, his look, or that growl, so while I was at school one day Shep mysteriously got off his chain and got lost in a thunderstorm, scared by all the crash and lightning, or so my father said.

I spent two days looking for him, calling his name until my throat hurt and I came home each night, muddy and cut. My mom sat on my bed and touched me up with Polysporin, drying my hair with one of her big towels. She never said anything, just held me tight without really seeming to do so.

I finally found Shep by Coates Creek way out behind our house. He'd been worked over with something small and heavy and left in the swollen water beneath the branches of an old, twisted desert willow. He was hidden, but not that well. I was meant to know, after all.

I buried Shep with my bare hands out by the creek and never said anything more about him. A month or so later my father offered to get me another dog, and I said thanks, but no.

I smiled when I said it, just like he expected me to.

6

CHRIS

Chris sat in a chair that was too small, hunched over Sheriff Ross's desk, even though the office itself was expansive—dark, hand-oiled wood and paneling except for one wall that was nothing but massive arched windows looking out over Main.

Now morning light came through those windows, muted by the old soda-lime glass in the panes. This building had existed nearly since Murfee's founding, serving at various times as a mercantile, a saloon, and a brothel. It had once functioned as a courthouse, and you could have stood in this room, looking through the thick glass of those windows, and watched more than a few rustlers and horse thieves turn at the end of a rope.

The building had been renovated numerous times, most recently around 1996, and served now as the Big

Bend County Sheriff's Department. Downstairs were a waiting room and office space and holding cells, all modern or nearly so, but this area up here was reserved for the sheriff alone. It was his office and a museum.

Chris had been up here a dozen times, seeing something new each and every time. The walls were covered with Murfee's history, framed photographs and tintypes of old lawmen and bandits, Indians and Mexicans. Each picture had a weird thunder-and-lightning cast, as if drawn in charcoal and quicksilver. Buildings and ranch houses looked barely able to stand under their own weight, the buckled timbers and sagging roofs—everything slightly off-kilter—captured for all time.

There were pelts on the floor, longhorn and elk and sheep; a mountain lion, even a Mexican wolf. Their heads adorned the high cavernous walls above the old pictures, staring down with dark, dead orbs. Chris knew the sheriff liked to hunt, had property somewhere, and went several times a year.

In one corner on a stand was a full saddle, Guadalajara style, with a big horn and a high pitch, stirrups touching the floor: hand-stitched Hermann Oak leather, a half-breed of tooled smooth areas with plenty of rough out for a better grip while riding. Parts of it were picked out in silver and gold and it gleamed in the light, winking, a distant skyline.

There were guns arranged all around the walls, several beneath glass and soft lights and not meant to be touched. Others the sheriff was fond of taking down and handing around, all loaded, and he always rechecked the load and wiped them with a special cloth before placing them back. There was a whole collection of guns John Wayne had used in his films. Steve McQueen's cutoff Mare's Leg .44-40 from *Wanted: Dead or Alive*. The Colt Monitor

30.06 rifle allegedly used by Texas Ranger Frank Hamer to gun down Clyde Barrow and Bonnie Parker, as well as his .44 Triple Lock Smith and a single-action Colt .45 he called "Old Lucky." Clyde Barrow's hat sat next to his Colt .45 and a warped and stained box of shells pulled from the car he was killed in.

A revolver belonging to outlaw Sam Bass, who robbed the Union Pacific gold train from San Francisco and was ambushed and shot by Texas Rangers and later found dying from his wounds in a pasture by a railroad worker.

Sheriff G. Cooper Wright's .44 caliber revolver.

Bat Masterson's .45.

Texas Ranger J. M. Brittain's Bulldog revolver, and Bill Doolin's derringer.

Last, and probably most expensive, a Model 1847 Colt Whitneyville-Walker revolver, once owned by Texas Ranger Sam Wilson. Only a thousand or so of these guns were produced, and for a while it was the most powerful handgun in the world. Its massive size and weight made Sam Colt himself say it'd take a Texan to shoot it.

The Whitneyville-Walker hung on a crimson backdrop in a special glass case right behind the sheriff's desk, over his right shoulder. Hidden light fell on it, and it was hard to sit where Chris was now and not have his eyes drawn to it, pulled as if it were a lodestone. Chris had once thought if you could get it out from under its glass, you might still smell the original oiled steel, the faint lingering odor of powder and smoke. Chris waited, staring at all the memorabilia, as the sheriff fingered the thin paperwork he'd written on the body he'd discovered at Indian Bluffs.

"You want to send it to Austin?" Sheriff Ross asked, still not looking up from the paper.

"Yes sir. Doc Hanson is afraid he can't work the ID. But we can send it out, let the DPS forensic lab have a try." Hanson was the county's sometime medical examiner, full-time pediatrician, and emergency veterinarian. What Chris didn't say was that the identification of skeletal remains was far beyond Hanson's capability. Chris knew from the call he'd already made to the Department of Public Safety lab that their techs might be able to pry secrets from the scarred and damaged remains he'd carefully wrapped in plastic and put in a cardboard box.

The sheriff continued to read Chris's report, or pretended to, out of courtesy, but there wasn't a helluva lot there.

The body had been stripped prior to being buried.

Dry desert conditions can slow the change in hair color after death, but the strands clinging to the skull were already red pheomelanin, a gaudy scarlet. Groundwater had seeped in from winter rains, worrying away the flesh and the hair, or at least whatever the coyote hadn't. Even Doc Hanson had been able to distinguish what looked like tooth marks against the dirty bone.

The skull concealed two silver amalgam fillings on the back molars, like coins in a treasure chest, although the rest of the skeleton's teeth were good. Chris knew forensic dental identification was possible, but he'd need comparisons—actual dental records—since no central dental database existed. Murfee's current dentist, John Snowden, was willing to search for a match against his patients, including most of the current population in the town and a few outliers in Presidio and Valentine, but wasn't thrilled about the prospect. He'd picked up almost all of Chris's dad's patients, and the elder Cherry had worked in Murfee for more than two decades.

That was his dad's legacy—dozens of boxes of hand-scrawled records and old file folders and X-rays, already turning brown at the edges from chemical burn, still housed in a U-Store-It off Highway 45. Chris had moved them there himself. Snowden used digital radiography and hadn't wanted any of Tom Cherry's rusting films.

It'd take time, a lot of time, but if the body found out at Bulger's place had lived in or near Murfee and had had dental work done here, Chris might be able to put a name to it. Eventually. Maybe.

Then there was the ten inches of industrial black plastic that had bound the hands of the body behind its back. It was quality stuff, not too unlike—but much better than—the plastic zip ties found all over ranches used to hold together fencing or for a thousand and one other purposes. That's what he had thought at first when he saw it at Indian Bluffs, still wrapped around the skeletal wrists. But after he got a closer look, even snapped a few photos to puzzle over later, he knew better now.

These ties were made specifically for human hands. Double-cuff disposable restraints—something like zip cuffs or FlexiCuffs. Professional; either military or police, state or federal. Doc Hanson hadn't been able to untie the plastic; fumbled at it with his surgical scissors. It had finally taken Chris a pair of tin snips to get it off the bone.

The sheriff lowered the papers, didn't quite release them. He smiled. "Sure, Chris, sure, if that's what we need to do, we'll do it." Then added, "What do you think happened out there?" He made a vague motion with the report, waving at an area past Chris's head.

Chris looked at his boots, shuffled them. He'd known Sheriff Ross his whole life, and it still felt weird to be here, working with him . . . for him. After he'd thrown four touchdowns against Pecos, the sheriff had come right down from the stands and walked straight and tall across the chewed-up, muddy field and shook his hand with that same high-wattage smile he had on now, bright beneath his silvered brush cut and unusual gray eyes. He'd grabbed Chris's hand and clapped him on the back and said, "Helluva game, son, goddamn helluva game," and then turned and smiled for the picture snapped for the *Murfee Daily*. Chris's dad had stood to the side, waiting to congratulate him, until the sheriff was done.

The man across from Chris now looked no different from the man on that field or in that newspaper picture Chris had found in his dead father's things—his dad nothing more than a blur in the background, out of frame and focus. Sheriff Stanford Ross seemed immune to time—impervious, impenetrable. Images of him would fade long before he would.

Like *The Picture of Dorian Gray*. As Chris and his dad had together watched Caroline Cherry wasting and dying in front of them, they'd retreated to their favorite books, and when Chris returned home he'd pulled them all out again, feeling the paper, bending back a creased corner here and there . . . remembering. It pissed Mel off to no end that those boxes of books were still stacked in the halls and the empty bedrooms, but he couldn't quite get rid of them, didn't have a place for them, not yet.

And Wilde's *Dorian Gray* was one of them, his dad's old Dell Classic, with Dorian's ruined face on the cover. Chris was afraid if he looked too close now at all the tintypes on the walls he'd find an aged, ugly semblance of Sheriff Ross—one corrupted, wasted—standing with a rifle by the furred hump of a dead buffalo, or milling with a crowd under a tree where a man swung in a slow arc over his own shadow and piss.

"To be honest, sir, I don't know. Seems like a river killing, but more than that? I can't say. Not yet, anyway. Too far from any main highway to be a transient thing or a dump-off, but . . . well, I'm pulling missing persons BOLOs from all over. It's possible something will come up." Or it won't.

A *river killing* was Murfee shorthand for the killing of a Mexican—an undocumented worker or a drug or alien smuggler who'd crossed the Rio Grande. Still, Chris couldn't bury that small, ugly hunch that it might be something else, something more complicated than that. It was far-fetched, but you were never going to find that empty bit of earth on Matty Bulger's land just by passing it on the freeway on the way to Beaumont or Houston. You had to know it was there. You *needed* it to be there.

The sheriff nodded. "Take the river out of it. Do you know how many murders we've had in Murfee in, say, the last fifteen years? Hell, include all of Big Bend." He tapped his finger on his desk on each of the last words for emphasis. Chris struggled, reaching back, came up empty.

The sheriff raised his fingers. "Two, Chris, two. And do you know how many of those remained unsolved? Exactly zero." He stretched back in his chair, somehow still sitting ramrod straight. "Let's see, the first was around 1992. Charlie Beamon got sideways with Morris Clayburg over a bit of fencing. A silly thing, the sort of thing two men ought to be able to talk out, but they didn't.

Charlie had a temper and liked to drink and they got into it at Earlys and Charlie pulled a little .38 he'd bought off a beaner in Nathan and put two in Morris, one in the face and the other in the foot. A helluva of a shot spread." The sheriff laughed. "It was the bullet in the face that killed Morris, by the way." Chris laughed too, joining him; it was expected. "Anyway, Charlie walked right over and turned himself in to me. Tears in his eyes, wiping his nose on his sleeve. He put that .38 right in my hand, and it was still hot, son, still so goddamn warm from the shooting that it felt alive." The sheriff stood, leaving Chris's report on the desk, walked toward the big windows, and looked down at the streets. *His streets*, Chris thought.

"The second was a few years after Charlie. Duane Dupree found her out near the Comanche, on one of the side roads. A pretty Mex girl someone had taken a knife to and dumped right out there along a cattle walk. She'd been rained on for two days straight when Duane found her. Two days . . . and it still didn't take long to figure out who she was. Her name was Adela. She worked over at the Pizza Hut, was married to Tony Gastellum, who bounced around all the ranches out here. We later found out she was only sixteen, although both she and Tony had claimed she was nineteen, twenty, depending on who you talked to, and she looked every bit of it. Tony found out Adela was keeping time with a ranch hand at the Monument and lost it. He killed her in their kitchen and tried to wash it all up with Comet and water and did nothing but make a bigger mess. There were bloody footprints all over their trailer where he'd paced back and forth smoking a cigarette while she died in front of him. He screamed at her while she lay there, spit on her, and had sex with her after her last heartbeat, although we kept that out of the *Daily*."

The sheriff said all this without skipping a beat.

"We knew he'd done it, he knew he'd done it, but he didn't want to man up and admit it. He sat in front of me and denied it for three hours, even as we were taking pictures of *his* bloody handprints and footprints in that kitchen. Hell, I put a picture of her in front of him, two of them—one before, one after—and he wouldn't look at either. You know what it took for him to finally confess? A cheeseburger and cigarettes. He said if I'd get him a burger and let him smoke a few, he'd tell me everything. And he did. More than I wanted to know."

Sheriff Ross turned around, backlit by the windows. He was a shadow, his face a blank. Two fingers still held up. "Two murders, two stories, Chris. Murfee is too small for much of anything else. Everything else *is* a river killing. They always are. Most of our dead were dying even before they crossed that damn river, and that's how it goes."

The sheriff moved back toward his desk, didn't sit down, switching gears from talking about the dead. "How's Melissa, Chris? We didn't see you at church this past Sunday. The last couple of Sundays, actually."

"She wasn't feeling well, sir. Not much more to it than that."

"Unwell? You and Melissa about to give BBC another quarterback?"

The room got small, hot. Chris felt sweat bead on his forehead and neck, kneading his hands together. They looked huge to him, unwieldy and dirty and wind-raw. He wasn't sure what to say. *Mel fucking hates it here and pretty soon is going to hate me too and I don't know what to do about it or if I can do anything about it all.*

"No, sir. Nothing like that. Nothing like that at all."

The sheriff shrugged. "Not meaning to pry, Chris, it's just we need new blood here in Murfee. Places like this don't last without new blood. I don't mean half of Mexico, either. I mean men like you, coming back home, raising families, settling down. It's a good thing. It's necessary."

Chris couldn't admit that he'd never planned on coming back. Would the sheriff's own son, Caleb, finally leave Murfee and never return? Chris had passed a handful of words with him here and there, nothing serious. He was a thin mystery in a black hooded sweatshirt, always standing at the margins, opposite in a thousand obvious ways from his father.

Chris could see—everyone could—how his mother's up and running off had hit him hard, but wondered if the boy struggled not because he couldn't understand why she'd left Murfee, but because he understood perfectly why she did.

"Yes, sir, that'll happen for us, just not now. I guess we aren't ready."

"You never are, Chris, not really." The sheriff sat down, shuffling Chris's report beneath other papers, dismissing him, but first there was a noise: Duane Dupree coming up the stairs, stopping in the doorway. The chief deputy had his hat off, turning it over and over again in his hands, like a pinwheel. He was tall and thin, but always stooped, feral, with his short-sleeve duty shirt revealing a rancher's sunburn, as if he'd been tattooed by the sun. He kept his thinning hair slicked back hard against his skull with a handful of pomade, and his smile, like now, was always dust-blown—there and gone again. He'd been with the sheriff for almost as long as anyone could remember, and nothing much happened he didn't have a hand in or a comment about. He'd been pushing Chris hard for a day now to close out that body from the ranch as a John Doe, or as he liked to call it, a *Juan Doe*.

"Judge . . . Cherry, sorry to bother . . ." He bobbed his head up and down, but didn't retreat. He remained there, listening. Chris stood, his knees tight. "About that call to Austin, sir? I was going to make it today, get those remains shipped out, if that's okay?" He pointed at the place where Chris's report had disappeared.

He needed the sheriff's signature, couldn't do it without it. Duane could sign off on some things, but the chief deputy had made it clear he wasn't inclined to, not on this, not over a dead beaner in a ditch. The release and DPS request form were stapled to Chris's write-up, now buried on the sheriff's desk. Something passed in front of Sheriff Ross's kilowatt smile, a brief flicker, a shadow, like a moth circling a porch light. There, and then gone again.

"Of course, Deputy. If you still think that's what we need. Let's get it done."

7

ANNE

There had been a note for her on her desk this morning, written on Big Bend County Sheriff's Department stationery—polite, professional. It was signed in Sheriff Stanford Ross's firm, almost antiquated cursive, welcoming her to Murfee.

All in all, it had been a good week. A decent one. A normal one, if she even knew what that was anymore. She still hadn't spent much time with the other teachers, only passing a few polite words here and there with Lori McKutcheon, who taught civics. *Polite*, just like the sheriff's note. She'd caught more than a few slowing steps by her door, the others pausing to listen to her teach . . . listening for what, exactly? Clues? Because there was so much to catch up on, she didn't take her lunch in the teachers' lounge or even in the cafeteria.

Rather, she sat at her desk, working away alone, stealing glances at the mountains holding up the sky outside her open windows. After the gray pall earlier in the week, that sky had turned hard blue, extending endlessly.

She guessed word had spread quickly among the teachers, probably leaked by Principal Tanner, that Hart wasn't always her name—that once she'd been another person, in another time and place. It didn't matter. Not the other teachers or whatever they might think about her. She just needed to get through the year, do her job well. *Teach.* Being in the classroom felt good, even with the two years she'd been away.

Away—like it had all been a sabbatical, a vacation. She'd probably never convince them anyway that the *other* woman they were hearing about was as dead as the former English teacher. So she watched her students take a quiz.

Even in Murfee, like teaching itself, school kids didn't change much. There were all the same types; the same cliques, forming and re-forming. Big guys in letter jackets; popular girls, and those who weren't. Kids who hung in the parking lot until right before the first bell, smoking or laughing by their trucks (in Austin, more than a few might have been leaning on BMWs), and those who were already in their seats fifteen minutes early. She'd taught at three different schools: in Virginia, Austin, and now Murfee, and although they were all very different places, the schools—with their peculiar rhythms and closed ecosystems—were not so different at all. They even smelled alike, whether it was the brand-new building in Austin where everything had been cream and silver and the floor had been polished tiles and the walls modular linen, or this one in Murfee, which was ancient as the mountains around it, carved out of wood and iron and old glass. All schools were haunted the same.

*   *   *

Caleb Ross was done with his exam, had been for several minutes, and she wondered if he'd dropped off the note on behalf of his father. Hands folded, he stared out her windows. He'd lived here his whole life and she wondered what he saw out there—if his view or perspective was somehow different from hers. He was a good-looking kid (*don't think that, don't ever think that*), although far too thin. She'd met his father once before in Austin, a tall, imposing man with high cliffs for cheekbones and iron-gray hair and eyes, and had seen him a few times here too, just in passing. Yesterday, driving away from school, she'd caught sight of him standing on a street corner in his uniform, every bit the cowboy, laughing with two men in a dirty truck. He smiled at her as she passed, gave her a slight wave as if they'd known each other their whole lives, and that had been weird, unsettling, because in that moment, he looked exactly as she always imagined Marc would at that age. She returned the wave without thinking as he retreated in her rearview.

There was very little resemblance between Caleb Ross and his father. The few times she'd seen Caleb outside of class, he'd been with America Reynosa—a pretty name, she thought, for an even prettier girl with a mass of dark hair, which reminded Anne of a flock of birds forever circling her. Anne couldn't decide whether they were a couple-couple or just friends. They were always smoking together on the benches in the breezeway—an avenue, really—stretching between the school and the giant football stadium; sitting close, but not too close, so it was impossible to read what passed between them. Amé was done with her quiz as well, or had decided not to do it at all. Her grades were a hit-or-miss affair, suggesting the girl was smart enough but didn't care all that much. Now she was staring down at her phone, her expression unreadable.

Anne could take the phone, probably should, but in another minute or so the bell would ring and this wasn't a battle worth having. Besides, she didn't want to spar over *Heart of Darkness*; she couldn't blame the girl if she wasn't into it. At her age, Anne wasn't, either. Still wasn't.

Then the bell rang and it was as if all the air in the room sucked upward. A dozen students stood at once, suddenly talking, picking up conversations they had left in mid-sentence at the earlier bell. The room became constant motion and sound, kids swarming past her desk, dropping off their quizzes.

She politely thanked the kids as the hastily thrown papers piled up, drifting higher. A few of them were talking about some reality-TV show they'd gotten hooked on. In the aftermath of Austin, Anne had treated the TV like a live snake, fanged, something to be avoided. For four straight months the nice flat-screen Marc had bought— the one he used to park in front of with a beer too dark and thick for her taste—had sat idle in their apartment, fleeced in thick gray dust, until she'd packed it away with many of their other things. Even turned off, unused, the TV had felt dangerous, poisonous. It held too many memories: shows they'd once liked and all those they'd never have the chance to see. It posed another threat too: of hearing her old name, that other name; or worse, of catching a glimpse of that other her on the news.

She'd looked different then, her dark hair now blond. She no longer had a tan, either. In fact, she felt completely colorless, a pale reflection of what she'd been— ready to disappear again at a moment's notice—and was even back to wearing her old glasses. Now if she caught a glimpse in the mirror, she didn't quite recognize herself, unsure of the eyes staring back at her.

That was good, had to be, because it also meant that other version of her was finally, mercifully, fading away. Her parents paid more attention to it than she did, and although they never said it exactly this way, *that* version had become old news. Last time they spoke, her mother reported there hadn't been anything written, nothing new—no mention or oblique reference—in more than six months. Anne's sixty-one-year-old mother, who thought the microwave was too much trouble, spent her days Googling her daughter's name.

The thought of her mom's face—anxious, lit by the glare of the laptop she and Marc had bought her parents—still hurt. It had been an investment, a down payment on their future, Marc once said. They'd wanted it for FaceTime, thinking they might soon get a chance to hold a baby up to the laptop's camera—the grandson or granddaughter that Anne's parents were more than ready for. Marc had joked they needed to have lots and lots of sex to justify the cost of that damn laptop.

Maybe today was the day to get over her fear of the TV. Tonight she could watch her rented set while she sat on her rented couch in her rented living room, grading quizzes on a book she didn't even like. Maybe she'd search for that reality show, gawk over someone else's life. There were worse ways to spend an evening. She'd learned that.

She looked up, expecting to be alone, ready to be alone, only to be startled that she wasn't. He wasn't in her classroom, not exactly, more like hovering at the door, hanging back a bit. It was as if they'd both hit pause at the same time, trapping them together for a moment. Caleb Ross stared at her from beneath the shadow of his hoodie, lost in thought, contemplating . . . *what*? Her? Or was he just debating whether it was okay to ask a perfectly normal question about the quiz or *Heart of Darkness*? Or to mention he'd dropped off his father's note for her. To fill her in on the fall carnival or that stupid TV show, welcome her to Murfee.

To mouth *You're so beautiful* where only she could hear it.

No, that was someone else, somewhere else. She held her breath or just couldn't breathe at all. *Please don't, please don't*. She willed him to disappear, closed her eyes and begged him to, and when she opened them, Caleb Ross and the boy she imagined him to be were gone. Anne waited, just to be sure; then without really thinking, she pulled all the papers together, shuffled and reordered them, bringing Caleb's to the top.

She hoped against hope that there was nothing there: no tiny note in the margin, no picture or image sketched in No. 2 pencil, no secret message to decode from the circled letters on the quiz questions.

Not again, oh god, not again.

She found his paper, stole a look, only to find *nothing*, just sentences in precise, feminine longhand, so different from his father's. There were three essay questions and he'd completed them all.

It didn't matter what his answers were, Anne wasn't going to read them. She dashed off an A on the top, near his name, pressing a little too hard so her hand wouldn't shake, and shuffled it back to the bottom.

Not here. *Not again*.

8

MELISSA

She'd made spaghetti. True, it was with store-bought sauce and frozen Pepperidge Farm Texas Toast from a box to soak it up with, but it was something.

Chris just moved it around on his plate, though, and she guessed he'd already grabbed a burger or two. He probably hid out in his truck down the street eating it all before coming home. Kind of how she'd hid her day's spent cigarettes in the empty spaghetti sauce jar. She felt her anger spark, ready to catch fire, but tried damn hard to stop it before it burned far and fast. He put his fork down, looked up, as if just noticing she was there.

"Did you talk to Will Donner over at Earlys?"

She shook her head, though she didn't have to. He *knew* she hadn't, just like she hadn't talked to Constance Merrill over at the Hamilton or Felipa at the Dollar General or whoever the hell it was who managed the Hi n Lo or the Napa Auto Parts. He'd been pushing her to find something, anything, to bring in a bit of money so they could keep fixing up the house, even suggesting she work weekends at the Comanche, the cattle auction. She didn't know what she was going to do with herself, but it didn't involve selling beers or burgers or windshield wipers or goddamn cows.

"I just know that he's going to be shorthanded over there. May Doyle needs to get to Abilene. Her sister's sick . . . or something." Chris saw her face, let it go. He picked up the fork again, and she knew he was going to make peace by changing the topic and eating her shitty spaghetti. "The body's going out to Austin. We'll know something soon, I expect."

"I'm sure you will," she said, taking his plate from beneath his raised fork, giving up on dinner for the both of them.

"I wasn't done with that," he tried. But she was.

Tonight there was a football game over at the stadium; next week, or the week after that, a carnival, too. She wouldn't have minded getting out a bit, sitting in the bleachers, sipping a spiked Coke . . . drinking and people-watching and letting the cold wind move her hair to hide her face. There was no way Chris would go or even suggest going. He'd barely glanced at the stadium since returning to Murfee.

She could go without Chris and he probably wouldn't say a damn thing one way or another, but she couldn't remember the last time she'd been anywhere, done anything, on her own. Since Chris, she couldn't remember the last time she'd wanted to.

*   *   *

He helped bring the last dishes into the kitchen, taking the ones out of her hands to scrub them in the sink.

"Look, babe, all that stuff about Earlys? It's no big deal. No pressure."

"I got it, Chris. I do, loud and clear. I'll check it out next week."

He looked at her, shrugged, worked on the dishes.

She thought of him sitting in his truck down the street, waiting to come into the house, then later tonight, wasting their hours by flipping through some old dental film all spread out on the floor—ugly, warped pictures he'd dug out of storage, his dad's things; something to do with the body he'd found. Holding them up to the light, then piling and repiling them because he'd already admitted to her he was afraid they wouldn't be much use, and he didn't really know what he was looking for anyway. Faded pictures spotted with rust—blood-colored, as if the film itself had bled. A thousand people she didn't know, would never know.

Slowly, deliberately, she picked her purse off the counter, rummaged around the bottom of it, and found a cigarette, lighting it in front of him. Letting the cat out of the bag, so to speak. He didn't say anything, didn't have to. He'd known all along. He turned back to the sink.

She blew smoke. "I thought you said no one else was big on going to too much trouble for that thing."

That thing. The body that had once been a living, breathing person.

His hands paused. "No, not so much . . . not really. The sheriff, everyone else, thinks it's just another drug runner or alien smuggler."

"It probably is."

He made a face, unreadable, careful while stacking the still-wet dishes, not drying them. "Yeah, I know. But do you know how many people go missing in this country a year?" She flicked ash, pretended to be uninterested, as he blinked through her smoke. He kept going. "Okay, about a million, give or take. Half of those are never found."

At least she knew what he'd been looking up on the Internet . . . all his investigating. "Sure, Chris, and probably half of those didn't *want* to be found. Maybe they got sick of their lives, got up and left and never came back. How many people go missing around here, Chris, in Murfee? Really?"

He shrugged. "I don't know, babe, but that body I found was *someone*. They once had a name, maybe a family that's still waiting to know what happened to them. I think that's worth a bit of trouble."

"You didn't find *anyone*, Chris. You and Matty Bulger, you found a *thing*, broken pieces. You're just scraping it up." It was too much and she knew it the minute she said it. All of her needling, pushing, about the body—because it was the only thing that mattered to him now, after months of nothing mattering at all. She raised her hands, surrendering. "I'm not telling you not to do this or that, but don't be disappointed if nothing comes of it. Maybe these people in Austin won't be able to tell you a goddamn thing. It'll stay a mystery. I don't want you moping around about it."

He turned to her, his hands red and wet. "Really? That's what this is all about? I'm doing my job, Mel, at least as I understand it. That's all."

That spark she'd blown out earlier flickered, alive. "Don't talk to me about *your fucking job*, Chris. You drag your ass around here for months, show no interest in this house, me, anything. Other than telling me what I need to do, all you do is come home and sit in front of the computer or bury yourself in those damn books. I don't understand what's going on, but it's got nothing to do with your job."

He stepped back. "Mel, I . . ."

She cut him off. "Think very fucking hard on what you're about to say right now, Deputy Cherry, because you've said very fucking little for weeks." She paused, breathed, searched his face. "Please make this count, Chris."

She hadn't planned on any of this—not here, not now—but here it was all the same. He'd seen her angry plenty of times before. They both knew it could get a lot worse before it got better.

He settled against the counter. "Okay, I know, I know. I haven't been easy. Coming back here, all of this"—he took in the house, her, with a tired glance—"it's just different than I thought it would be. Harder. You're not happy here."

She inhaled, buying a moment, before nodding. "I'm not *comfortable* here, Chris. All of this stuff is yours. This house, everything in it. This fucking town. It's all your old history. I don't belong."

"How do we fix that?"

"I don't know, but it's more than that. *You're* different, too. Nothing about this place has been good for you." She wanted to say *Nothing has been good since Lonnie Ray Holliday*, but stopped short. "Maybe you don't belong here either, anymore." Adding, "And if that's the case, maybe there's nothing either of us can do to fix it. Not here."

He looked around the kitchen, past her, down the hall where boxes still stood stacked.

"You're right, babe, I know you are."

In their other fights, he'd step forward now and put his arms around her, wrap her up for a heartbeat or two, and she'd be fine with that. Instead, he stood, arms crossed.

"Look, give me another couple of weeks. Let me hear back from the DPS lab and make a stab at closing this thing . . . do some good here."

She hesitated. "Okay, then what?"

"Then we'll leave, if that's what you want. We'll leave."

If that's what you want.

But that wasn't what she wanted, not exactly. She wanted *him* to say it, to admit that he was done here and needed to get the hell out of Murfee for both of their sakes. They didn't have to go back to Waco, just somewhere, anywhere, else. Instead, he was putting it off on her, as if his stake in it—his own unhappiness—carried no goddamn weight at all.

It was bullshit, unfair, but for now that was all he was willing to give, watching her through the smoke.

There were other things she could say, a hundred things she knew would hurt him bad—as bad as putting bullets in him. Killing, really, whatever they still had. But she'd given herself to him and wasn't ready to take it back.

"Okay, Chris. If that's what you want. If that's the way it has to be." She flipped her cigarette into the sink where he'd been washing dishes, not waiting to see where it landed.

9

CALEB

Nothing much interesting happens in Murfee.

Nothing much anyone knows about, anyway. Time here is like a bug trapped in amber, *fossilization*—we learned all about that in biology. Come back a year from now, ten years from now, and Murfee would seem exactly the same. You would be wrong. Our town does a pretty good job of holding her secrets close.

Two interesting things have happened in the past couple of weeks.

First, our new teacher, Anne Hart, has come here from Austin to replace to Ms. Garner, who died in her kitchen. I have her for English, and she's picking right up where Ms. Garner left off, with Conrad's *Heart of Darkness*.

I've already read the book several times and know most of the passages by heart.

Ms. Hart is a small woman, delicate, much younger than Ms. Garner—who'd long ago fossilized. She keeps her blond hair pulled back in a ponytail, kind of like Mom; a look I also like on Amé, although she doesn't wear it often—or simply won't—because she knows I like it. Ms. Hart doesn't use nail polish and her glasses seem a little too large for her face, unnecessary, when she could as easily wear contacts, but there's a point to them. Sitting at the edge of her desk, talking, trying not to smile or make much eye contact, she doesn't seem much older than us, but she could be prettier—much prettier, I think—than she's willing to show.

Her clothes and glasses and the carefully maintained distance from us are props—all part of a charade, a mask she wears. I recognize it because I wear a mask every morning I wake up here in Murfee. I guess Ms. Hart has her secrets, too.

Amé already doesn't like her, but I think it's a girl thing. Where Ms. Hart is light, Amé is dark—dark hair and eyes and skin—and she's a hundred percent Murfee. At least one end of Murfee, out past the stadium and beyond Mancha's, where all the little houses and trailers begin. She speaks Spanish there but never at school and won't practice it with me, even though I've been taking it since the fourth grade.

My mom tried hard to pick it up as well, always listening to her Rosetta Stone in her little Ford Ranger—the one I drive now, since my father kept it, just like that Kohler tub. We used to have days when we were allowed to talk to each other only in Spanish, at least outside my father's earshot. If I wanted something, I had to start each sentence with *quiero* and go from there, and I used to write down all sorts of phrases and questions that Amé would sometimes translate for me. I memorized the lines and stumped my mom all day with them, making her look up the words in the small Berlitz she carried for the occasion. She would laugh, flipping madly through her dictionary, trying to repeat and remember what I said.

Te quiero y te extraño y nunca te olvidaré.
I love you and I miss you and I'll never forget you.

I've known Amé for over three years now. We're more than friends but a lot less than something else. She's forever keeping me at arm's length, but never quite letting me go. She's got problems with her family and there's that mess with her brother. We both carry holes in our lives, and maybe that's all that draws us to each other, even if I want to believe it's more than that.

I think I love her, despite all the parts of her I never really see, but I'm no different. There's so much we don't show or tell each other, so much I guess we don't dare say out loud.

Amé, Ms. Hart, me—just like this goddamn town, we all do a pretty good job of holding our secrets close.

After Ms. Hart's first day, Amé and I were sharing one of her cigarettes and I mentioned our new teacher, thinking out loud. I suspect my father knows Ms. Hart a little, met her once, but I'm not sure. As I talked, Amé turned her head sideways, her big silver hoops defying gravity, and blew smoke in my face. That was the end of the conversation. But then there's the second thing that happened—

the most important thing. The body Deputy Cherry discovered at Indian Bluffs.

My father came home the night after Deputy Cherry found the body, and didn't say anything to me. I was in my room doing homework and he walked past my open door without a word. I am never allowed to close my door. He walked down the hall to his room but didn't turn on any lights or wash his face or brush his teeth. There was no movement at all. It was like he walked in there and disappeared. I waited an hour, let the house grow dark, and then I did what I've long practiced: I crept down the hallway to spy on him.

In my house it's important at all times to know exactly where my father is and what he's doing. As always, his door was cracked open as well. Not because he follows his own rules or cares less about his own privacy, but because he wants to hear clearly what I'm up to. Besides, he has nothing to hide. Not in his own home and not from his own flesh and blood.

There's a spot I stand in, as silent and still as him, where the hallway forms a T. From that point I can see right through the door to the headboard and the top third of his bed; clearly visible is the cherrywood nightstand my mom bought in El Paso, with a cream-colored lamp on it. The same King James Bible is always there and the same empty quartz glass, dry and dusty as the desert around Murfee. The books and glass are props—things a real, living, breathing person might have if they slept in that room.

I can also see the old Rowan Cheval antique bronze mirror in the corner. It's a full-size standing mirror, one of the few things my mom brought with her to Murfee, and I still remember her in front of it, brushing the desert dust out of her long hair or just pulling it up, all while seeing me over her shoulder, trapped in the glass.

Sometimes when I'm spying and the moon is right, when the entire room is pale and pearl, I see my father *twice*, one real and another, darker one, both reflected in the mirror my mother loved. It's like he's not alone, like there's another person in there with him, and when I've thought I've caught him whispering to himself in there, he must have been talking to that other man in the mirror. But when the moon isn't quite up or it's hidden by clouds, I can see nothing in the glass. It remains empty, black like pond water, as if he casts no reflection at all.

That's how it was the other night, after the body was found at Indian Bluffs. He was alone on the bed, the mirror empty, his arms rigid along his sides. He was staring straight up at the ceiling, and I looked close to see whether his chest was rising and falling, praying as always that it wasn't. Praying, hoping, that he'd been struck down by a mysterious illness or that his heart had just given out.

That he was *done*.

Instead, the index finger of his left hand was tapping against his creased pants leg. Tapping, tapping . . . just above the knee. Like a clock ticking, like when he used to read my homework. Slow and practiced and deliberate— the way the big garden orb weavers out by the creek pluck at the strands of their webs. Spiders eat their own webs at the end of the day. It helps them regather the energy they've lost by spinning them.

I always thought that finger tap just meant he was thinking or pretending to, but it might mean something else as well. Worry—*real* worry, that Murfee might have finally given up one of her secrets.

At dawn, when the sun's up over the mountains and it hits the far edges of town at the right angle, the pink caliche on the bluffs burns crimson and everything runs red. Murfee always wakes up bloody. *The dead are her secrets . . . The missing are her ghosts.*

I know who Deputy Cherry found out at Indian Bluffs, and so does my father.

My mother . . . his missing wife.

10

CHRIS

Later no one would be able to explain exactly how it started. For every person who would talk, and there weren't many, there was a different story. It involved a girl or a ranch job or a *fútbol* score; whatever, it didn't matter. One thing everyone agreed upon was how it started *to end*.

With Delgado and the knife.

Aguilar was already near dead by the time Chris got to Mancha's, with Delgado standing in a circle of people, his shirt torn off, revealing tattoos curling over his wasted stomach, like cursive writing, all the way to his throat. He was dark, darker than normal because of the blood all over him already going black; some of it was his own, but most of it was from Aguilar, who was on his back in the gravel. Aguilar kept kicking, struggling like he was trying to stand but had simply forgotten how, the memory of it lost, along with his blood, all over the ground.

Everyone around Delgado was yelling, spitting Spanish, waving at the man who kept them at bay with the knife. The lot was littered with crushed beer bottles, discarded balls of tinfoil, old condoms; jackets and cowboy hats and John Deere caps all forgotten on the hard wooden benches beneath the tin pavilions. Chris caught sight of Eddie Corazon standing in the concrete doorway of Mancha's, smoking a cigarette, calm, picking at his teeth with dirty fingers and eyeing the mess in his parking lot. Corazon knew that when it ended, however it ended, the men shadowing the bloody gravel would want more beers, more cigarettes. They'd sit around a few more hours until the naked bulbs strung up around the parking lot turned yellow, talking over and over again about what had happened, making up stories about it. Eddie probably hadn't made the 911 call. The fight wouldn't hurt business.

Mancha's was Murfee's only bodega—part store, part restaurant—a gathering place for Mexican families and the ranch hands and laborers. It had gotten bigger, seedier if that was possible, since Chris's teammates used to come to this side of town for cheap beer or condoms or weed. This tiny part of Murfee had a dozen unflattering names—Beantown, Beanville, Little Mexico—just like all the people who lived in it, their nearby homes wrapped by chain-link fences and patrolled by dogs.

Everyone talked about the place, everyone knew about it. Everyone always denied they came here. Fights and trouble had been common at Mancha's even when Chris was in high school, and like so much else about Murfee, that hadn't changed.

Chris parked hard, throwing gravel and painting the

crowd with his lights. He got out and approached with his Taser at high-ready. Not his Colt, not yet; he hoped there wasn't a need for the gun he had never pulled in the line of duty. He just wanted everyone calmed down, and a clear line of sight to Delgado. Now, though, half the circle was watching Delgado, and the other half was yelling at *him*, pointing back and forth between the man with the knife and the man they thought had a gun.

As Chris got closer, Delgado took up howling, jabbing the knife at the air, standing over the man he'd stabbed. *Stabbed* didn't quite do it justice—Delgado had all but scalped Aguilar, had worked the knife hard at the edges of the other man's face. In fact, Aguilar's hands were the only thing holding it in place, his entire visage lopsided, uneven, like a cheap Halloween mask.

Chris had never seen anything like it. Delgado didn't look much better. He was clearly on something—skin taut, eyes weird, sunken and blinking *up/down, up/down*, like a windup toy. There was blood in his mouth, in his teeth.

Chris tried to steady his hand, tightening his grip on the Taser, waving everyone back. If anything, the circle only tightened, protective; everyone now concerned about what Chris might do to their *compadre* Delgado. Sensing this, Delgado stood taller, shouted louder, curling his knife in graceful figure eights in Chris's direction. He hopped from one foot to the other as Aguilar's face slipped sideways in his hands. The crowd cheered and Chris had no idea who or what they were cheering for.

Chris was bigger than almost any other man there and still felt helpless, suddenly unsure of what to do next. Wishing his Colt was in his hand, even though he couldn't imagine how that would make the situation any better.

He couldn't shoot everyone; desperately didn't want to shoot anyone.

Fortunately, that was when Duane Dupree came to his rescue. Chris had been so intent on the crowd, on Delgado, he never heard Dupree pull up. Didn't even realize the chief deputy was there until he saw it on all the other men's faces. They fell silent, the circle widening a bit like it was alive—taking a deep, deep breath—as Chris turned just enough to see Dupree move up next to him.

Dupree leveled his Remington 11-87 shotgun roughly in Delgado's direction, gently sweeping the crowd with it as he did so, making his point. The Remington shined as if Dupree had been cleaning it with moleskin at his desk before appearing out of thin air here at Mancha's. The shotgun had a fourteen-inch barrel and rifle sights and Dupree's initials etched in pearl along the stock, a gift from the sheriff for his years of service, and it was weightless in Dupree's hands. He moved it as easily as Delgado had waved his knife; Delgado had now gone silent as well.

"Got a problem here, Chris?" Dupree spit a long cut into the gravel.

"Yeah, a bit of one."

"You want me to get on down the road, let you handle it?"

Chris shook his head. "No, don't think so. I think I could use the help."

Dupree grinned, ugly, looking no better than Delgado. He winked. "Well, okay then."

Chris waited as Dupree moved forward. He zeroed his sights on Delgado, taking one slow, steady step after another, calling over his shoulder.

"Eddie, you tell them beaner friends of yours to move back. You tell 'em *now*, or I'll blow a hole through 'em."

Duane said it casually, as if he knew Eddie well or was just ordering a beer. Eddie Corazon wobbled his head back and forth, considering, maybe loosening up a knot in his neck. His throat looked swollen, like a snake that had swallowed a dog. He eyed Dupree long and hard before finally saying something in Spanish.

It took a minute, but the circled crowd backed away slowly as Dupree got within ten or fifteen feet of Delgado. Dupree looked down at Aguilar. "Jesus Mother of Mary, you put a hurt on that ole boy." Dupree sidestepped Aguilar's slowly thrashing legs and cooling blood. "What a fuckin' mess."

Duane eyed Delgado. "Now, Eddie, you tell this piece of shit right here to drop that pigsticker. Tell him *rápido*. Tell him I'm about to get fucking bored, and that I'm fixin' to open up a fucking sunroof in that thick beaner skull of his."

Corazon made a face, said something to Delgado low and fast. Chris, still behind Dupree, couldn't hear what it was.

Dupree raised the Remington so it was pointed directly between Delgado's wild eyes. "Give me a reason, beaner. Any reason." Dupree chuckled, shrugged. "Come to think on it, I don't need a fuckin' reason. Not a goddamn one atall." He winked at Delgado, spoke just to him. "You wouldn't be missed, you hear me? Not missed atall. None of you ever are."

Eddie Corazon must have suddenly come to the same conclusion as Chris—that Duane Dupree really was going to blow Delgado's head off right there in the parking lot—because he started speaking faster, gesturing at Delgado, begging him to put down the knife.

Maybe it was the rock-steady muzzle of the shotgun or Dupree's eyes or the cool, detached way he had said it, but Chris had no doubt that Dupree would kill Delgado. *That he was looking forward to it.* But while Dupree had been giving Corazon orders, threatening him, he'd also kept moving forward, steady and stealthy as a man could with a hundred eyes on him, closing the distance between them before anyone realized it. Just as Delgado loosened his grip on the knife, started to let it fall from his fingers, Dupree lashed out with the Remington—swung it like a bat and caught the other man in the face, rocking his head back and driving him to his knees. While he was down, Dupree gave him another blow to the head, then another. Wound a leg up high to kick him.

He might have done more, a lot more—he might have *done it all*—if Chris hadn't rushed forward and put a hand on his shoulder. There was chaos and blood everywhere, but Delgado wasn't dead, although he probably wished he was. He was already in worse shape than Aguilar.

The crowd murmured, pulled all the way back to the far corners of the lot beneath a stand of sweet acacia trees.

"Whoo boy. Goddamn. Goddamn, that was good." Dupree laughed, slicked back his hair with his hands and clapped Chris on the back as if they had just scored the game-winning touchdown. Chris thought Dupree might have left Delgado's blood on his shoulder.

"Get in my backseat, Cherry, get out the big medical kit. We'll cuff 'em, bandage these two up a bit until the ambulance shows. Call it in too, will ya? I don't wanna transport 'cause I don't want either of 'em bleeding in my ride. Fuck, I sure don't want 'em dying in there." Dupree stared back at all the people watching. "You can't get that smell out. No sirree, it'll stay in the leather, never quite go away." He bent down to wipe something from his shoe, something that stained his fingers. "I'll have Eddie get us some cold pops while we wait, a candy bar too . . . hell, a beer if you want. What'll it be, Tex? Eddie's buyin'."

Chris shook his head. "Nothing, I'm good." Then he started toward Dupree's truck as Duane called out behind him. "Suit yourself. But next time, draw your damn gun. *Your real gun, Cherry.* Damn wetbacks don't respond to much else."

Much later, after they had wrapped everything up and headed back to Murfee, after he'd suffered through Dupree's telling the story around the old courthouse for what seemed like a dozen times—each one broader, more slapstick—he was finally able to escape, toward new twilight, toward air.

He left the department with the sun slanting down and Dupree's voice echoing behind him, stopping to steady himself with one hand by a lemon tree the town council had planted years ago. He needed a moment, had to pull himself together, but avoided putting his full weight against the tree, since it might snap in half. Main Street was lined with a dozen of them—stunted, barely surviving, barely hanging on, like the town itself.

He wanted to call Mel, tell her about Mancha's, but couldn't shake the sight of Aguilar holding his face together, all that blood so much blacker than the movies; or Dupree savagely attacking Delgado and grinning while he did it. And then, after that, casually wiping the man's blood in his hair and on Chris's uniform—smoking cigarettes and drinking a Dr Pepper until the ambulance came.

Most important of all, he couldn't shake what he'd seen in Dupree's truck . . . in the goddamn storage locker. If only that fucking medical kit had been in the extended cab like Dupree had said at first, then he'd never have gone in that flatbed locker at all. But Dupree had been wrong about that, had tossed him the keys to unlock it probably without a second thought, while he'd remained staring down at the two damaged men, casually firing up another Lucky Strike.

Dupree's back had still been to him, talking low to Eddie Corazon, when Chris saw them—looped together in a clear plastic pouch, shoved down between flares and a rain jacket and a spare pair of boots. Not damning alone, and maybe not even the exact same as what he'd cut from the skeleton at Doc Hanson's, but close enough—*oh fuck, so damn close*—even if you looked in squad cars all over the country and found ones that were all damn similar. Because really, sometimes your one pair of good American steel cuffs wasn't enough. Sometimes you needed more, a lot more, like if they had been forced to arrest that entire crowd at Mancha's. And that's when a whole mess of dual-restraint FlexiCuffs like those in Duane's truck locker came in handy. They were easy, expendable, portable, and cheap. One was just as good as another, and you could stick a handful of them in your pocket or keep them on your belt. You could lose one, forget it, and *not have a second thought about it*. A lot of big city departments swore by them, and issued them just like they issued Surefire lights or Sabre Red OC pepper spray.

But not the Big Bend. Not *his* department.

He returned a wave to Modelle Greer, who was closing up her knitting shop and had no idea Chris had just witnessed one man nearly stabbed to death and another almost beaten to the grave. Everyone in Murfee took up knitting for a while to keep Mrs. Greer's place running. Still, there were buildings up and down that were permanently closed, just soaped-over glass and boarded doors. From a distance it all looked beautiful—a movie set, the ideal small town, with the BBC Fall Carnival banner over Main curved into a smile by the wind. A perfect smile, until you got close and saw a hint of blood on the gums— a bad tooth or two, buried deep in the back.

He'd always hated so much about this town, but here he was all the same. Willingly chose to come back. Nearly ran—fucking limped—home. He'd tried at times to imagine what his life would have been like if his knee hadn't buckled, if he hadn't found himself on his back staring at the yellow wash of stadium lights as blood drained from his face and the crowd fell silent like a radio suddenly turned down. The only sound first his own heartbeat, then breathing . . . ragged but not panicked, followed by swelling, rising, hurtling pain. Pain with a voice all its own, screaming at him.

But hard as he'd tried, he'd never really been able to picture that other life, could never give it shape or color. It had remained unknowable, unsolvable—a cruel fucking riddle or joke, like Caroline Cherry's cancer going into remission before firing back twice as hard. Her eyes had turned black and her veins had disappeared beneath paper skin and there had been a smell around her, *coming off her*, while she desperately held on to hair that had fallen loose into her curled hands.

No, it'd been much easier instead to imagine a life where he had never started a college game at all. Where he'd remained on the sidelines, studying for the classes he enjoyed, reading his books, anonymous even with his size. But of course, in that life, the one that had been so much easier to see—*the clearer one*—he never met Mel at all.

That was the price of *that* life, but in that one, he never came back to Murfee, either. He never saw the body at Indian Bluffs and never got called out to Mancha's and never saw Duane Dupree nearly beat a man to death or saw another man piss on himself as he held the pieces of his face in his hand.

And in that life, he never looked in the locker in the back of Dupree's truck.

Chris needed to wander a bit more, kill some time and let the sun finish going down around him; watch the sky change a hundred colors and then become no color at all, just black. Then he'd call Mel and try to tell her something about this day, and when he felt sure the department had cleared out he'd send another e-mail to Austin, maybe even make a call himself to check on the forensic ID. In the meantime, he'd compare the pictures he'd taken of the FlexiCuffs with the memory of those he'd seen in those few seconds in Duane's truck locker . . . *oh fuck, so damn close*. He wanted, now more than ever in ways he couldn't easily explain, to put a name and face and story to that mystery in the desert.

Skeletal hands held together tight by a thick zip tie, stretched out like a sunning snake in the upturned earth.

He knew he couldn't escape what he'd seen in Dupree's truck; not damning alone, maybe, but damning enough. He was bound tight to it now, with cuffs of his own.

11
CALEB

A week had passed before Amé finally asked me about the body.

We were sitting high in the bleachers of BBC's stadium, a concrete monster like a starship hovering at the edge of town. The field was all activity, an anthill, with the team preparing for the upcoming game against Presidio. Balls flew back and forth in long arcs over the green turf and distant voices and shouts carried up to us, words lost to the wind. She sat close, stealing some warmth, wanting to know what I thought about what they'd found out at Indian Bluffs.

I know what she really wanted to ask, though. *¿Es tu madre?*

I've never said to her that I suspect my father had a hand in my mom's disappearance.

Hinted at it, like I hint at so many things in our talks, but we both do that—all these secrets and questions within questions, nothing real. If anyone understands loss, though—understands losing someone without closure, without answers—it's Amé.

His name was Rodolfo, Rudy. Everyone around here called him Rudy Ray. She last saw her older brother after my mom disappeared. He was a Border Patrol agent, a *green shirt*, driving his little white green-striped truck on the hunt for illegals crossing the Rio Grande, particularly in the Ojinaga Cut. The Cut was once part of a border dispute settled back in the seventies when the river changed course, Mexico taking one piece and Texas another, accomplishing nothing but swapping desolate Indian land back and forth. Unlike Amé, Rudy had spent a lot more time over the border, whole summers down south, and even felt easy about visiting family and friends in Ojinaga, Cuauhtémoc, and Delicias. He was fluent in both languages and knew the area and the people, so he was a natural fit for the Border Patrol. His parents had been proud of him, Amé twice as proud.

Amé's dad works at the Walmart over in Fort Stockton and her mom works at the Supreme Clean right on Main. I see Amé's mom, Margarita, all the time when I drop off my father's uniforms at the cleaners. She's a tired, round woman with gray shot through her hair like stray dust. I once heard Duane Dupree say in passing she used to be a stripper in Ojinaga, but that's hard to imagine, and I've never asked Amé about it.

Rudy Ray was short like his mom, good-looking, with thick hair and a wisp of a mustache and goatee that Amé said he thought made him look older, but that she was always trying to get him to shave. He was about Dillon Holt's age, so I knew *about* him more than I actually knew him; he moved out of Murfee and got an apartment in Nathan not long after high school. He spent some weekends in Midland and others across the border in the bars along Libre Comercio, wearing pointed fake-ostrich-skin boots, wide-open imitation Versace shirts, and big enamel belt buckles painted gold and silver and shaped like a bull's head or crossed revolvers. Amé showed me the pictures on her phone, including one of him standing by his black and chrome Dodge Charger with the custom paint job—a bright green snake coiled along the rear quarter panel. I thought both he and the car looked ridiculous, and it was that damn ugly Charger that started the trouble for him.

Rudy Ray had made good. He got a decent job that didn't involve serving food or cleaning shirts or working on another man's property. Still, it was a government job—he was never going to get rich doing it—but Rudy Ray *played* rich, acted rich, more so with each passing day. Whenever he drove that Charger through Murfee, people said he had to be involved with the narcos across the river—that he'd gotten tight with them through family or a girl in Ojinaga, a dancer whose job it was to find easy men like him. And maybe it had started small at first, just a few words about checkpoints or the names of agents and inspectors. Then later, looking the other way as loads came across the border, before the Ojinaga girl or the people who owned her (and by then, Rudy) convinced or forced him to carry the loads himself—tape-wrapped bundles hidden beneath a blanket in the backseat of his

BP truck. People whispered these things all the time, people who'd gone to school with Rudy Ray and remembered him from town and saw him driving that chromed-out Charger or flashing a thick roll while buying a round of Montejima Reposado shots. Amé knew her brother had also heard the whispers, ignored them, even as she was afraid that the Border Patrol might start hearing them, too.

He swore to her it was nothing, *nada*, even as he gave her a couple of thousand dollars to keep in a box under her bed for parties and school dances and dresses—things that Amé never does, clothes she's never going to buy. I think Rudy Ray had imagined a much different life for Amé from what she had ever imagined for herself.

He called her late one night, admitting there might be a bit of real trouble, but that he would handle it. He'd found a way out, so no need to worry.

No need to worry at all.

She could still be proud of him, and he promised to move her to Houston with him when it was all over. But until then he made her promise not to talk about the money under the bed or show it to anyone. He sold the Charger right after that, but couldn't shake his problems or the suspicions.

In his last call to Amé, he said he might be away for a while. He wasn't sure, might slip south for a bit and see the sights, spend time on the beach watching the blue ocean, but he wouldn't say what beach, what ocean. He made it sound like a vacation, even as she begged him not to go. He told her to be careful, do well in school, marry a nice gringo and have lots of gringo babies. He told her never to go to Ojinaga or Cuauhtémoc or Delicias; to stay on this side of the border, *always on this side of the border*.

Then he was gone.

That's what I know, what I suspect. It's everything I've pieced together from the things she's said and the silences in between. And she really believes he is coming back, talks about it more than anything else. She thinks he's going to come for her and drive her away to Houston, in a car far classier than that damn Charger, which was cursed anyway. Amé once said her mom was a witch—a *bruja*—who won't teach her any magic. I think she believes in that stuff, spells and spooks and curses, just like she believes Rudy Ray's coming home.

And because I wanted to believe right along with her—so badly wanted to help her—I once risked raising it to my father. I asked if he or Duane Dupree or anyone in the department knew anything about Rudy Reynosa.

We were eating dinner and I broke the silence with the question. My father had looked at the ceiling, claimed he didn't remember Rudy *specifically*, so couldn't really say one way or another anything about him, but thought Duane may have ticketed him once or twice in that Charger, ugly as sin and running way too fast out by the stadium. Then he wanted to know why I cared so much about a damn beaner, staring me down with a beer parked halfway to his lips. I let it drop.

I didn't believe him. Dupree knows Amé's family, and my father has always known everything and everyone in Murfee, but still, that was the extent of my bravery—one fucking question.

I wonder if Rudy Ray ever saw the ocean?

She believes he is coming back.

I never talk about my mom coming back, ever.

When Amé finally asked about the body at Indian Bluffs, she was really asking about *me*. Asking but not asking. Watching without watching—her eyes dark as spring wells, bottomless behind the smoke of another one of her ever-present cigarettes. I know from Miss Maisie that Deputy Chris Cherry sent the body to Austin, so I've been waiting along with him, just like everyone else.

Miss Maisie tells me stuff because she's old and likes me and doesn't know any better. She's worked radio dispatch as long as I've been alive, and is the only reason I know a damn thing at all about what goes on inside the sheriff's department, my own father's kingdom. Miss Maisie, and the local newspaper.

The *Murfee Daily*'s done one story and will do another. That first featured a black-and-white photo of Matty Bulger standing over a slash in the ground and a loose piece of yellow evidence tape trapped beneath his boot, his hands raised and captured right at that moment in a "Why me?" gesture. It was accompanied by a photo of Deputy Cherry next to his Big Bend County truck, awkward and uncomfortable in his uniform, looking away at something or someone in the distance. I don't think the picture was even taken out at Bulger's place, probably staged later, like a lot of things in Murfee—they feel staged, close to real, but not quite. Deputy Cherry comes off as decent, different from the other deputies and definitely no Duane Dupree, but he hasn't been back in Murfee for long and I don't know how close he is to my father. I've been nervous to talk to him, much less ask him anything about Indian Bluffs.

But when Chris Cherry gets his answer back from Austin, all of Murfee will finally know what I've believed from the beginning—it was my mom he found buried out there.

So that's what I told Amé when she asked me about the body as I took the cigarette from her and finished it off. My mom has lain there for the past year, lost, waiting; waiting for someone . . . *for me* . . . to finally find her.

And Amé didn't ask anything else, just went back to watching the wind pull and tug at streamers on the goalposts.

12

ANNE

Big Bend Central was losing badly. She came to the game because it was expected, and honestly, she didn't mind getting out of the little house for a bit. Win or lose, this game and the carnival afterward were a big deal.

She'd seen all the stuff set up in the field outside the stadium, the games and the vendors and the rides. Most of her students would be at the homecoming dance after the game tonight, but tomorrow they'd be out on the midway, trying to win those huge garish stuffed animals—purple bears and pink dogs and green monkeys—sneaking in flasks to spike the silly-shaped soda cups they were selling for five dollars a pop.

As for the game itself, Anne knew how serious Texas was about its football, and Murfee was no exception. The stadium seated over eight thousand—a huge concrete bowl open at both ends to knots of sweet acacia trees. It had a full press box and reserved seating and the latest artificial turf and a scoreboard with video replay. What it did not have, not at the moment, was a winning team. BBC was down early just as they'd been in nearly every game of the season. But the stands were full, and under the huge lights, with everything polished and painted and perfect, the entire stadium *glowed*. She could only imagine what this all looked like from high above, the surrounding darkness of the desert anchored by all this heavy light—a great bonfire, burning and bright, trying to escape skyward.

Marc would have loved this crazy stadium in the middle of nowhere, the circus atmosphere. Electricity— excitement—ran through the bleachers, through the entire town, even as Presidio scored another touchdown and BBC's coach screamed on the sidelines and tossed what Anne imagined must be a very expensive headset into the stands.

She was sitting with Lori McKutcheon and her small, silent husband, as well as two other teachers. They'd been nice to wave her over, passing small talk back and forth and including her in their chatter about the school, the carnival, the team. Lori's husband said one thing and one thing only—BBC sure missed Chris Cherry—drawing nods and agreement from everyone around them. Anne pieced together that this Chris had been a great quarterback in Murfee and had even played some in college, but was back home as a deputy sheriff. The same deputy she'd read about in the *Murfee Daily*, something about a body discovered on a ranch. No one cared about that now. Instead, the town just wished he could trade his deputy's uniform for a football one again.

*   *   *

She burrowed into her jacket, her cold breath adrift. Lori talked, and she nodded in all the right places and said more or less the right things, a well-honed ability since Austin. She was here but not here, a ghost, turning in a lifelike performance; maybe a mime, forever pulling at invisible strings and failing to escape from invisible boxes.

At one point she thought she saw Caleb Ross sitting with Amé Reynosa, but when she looked again, they were gone. She lost herself in the game, the rise and fall of small voices around her. There was another reason she was glad to get out of the house, not face the thought of being alone. She knew that on this night more than any other, she needed to drop into this ocean of unknown people, let the tide of their lives and conversations take her away. Tonight she needed to hide. There was another cheer, a roar like pounding waves. Lori said something to her and Anne smiled, not knowing or caring what she smiled to.

She'd already deleted the inevitable cellphone messages from her parents, unheard, because she knew what they would say, and she'd spent the whole day keeping busy, trying to ignore the calendar and the time. After the game she was going to walk the midway a bit, buy one of those stupid soda cups or an elephant ear, let herself get cold and numb until she couldn't feel her fingers . . . until she was so frozen by the night's cold, hard edges that the tears she'd been afraid of all day would be little more than stray frost on her cheeks—invisible, unable to flow. She'd stay away from the house until late, well past the witching hour, and then race her fears inside and take a couple of Ambien or something even stronger, pray she slept until tomorrow afternoon; so by the time she finally struggled awake, this particular day—this awful date—would already be behind her again for one more year, locked away in a box with all the others, and all the others to come.

But it was never that easy, no matter what games she played with herself, no matter what silly tricks she tried. The date *always* fucking won; impossible to outrun, to hide from. No amount of deleted messages or pretending ever made it truly go away. Because there was always that one moment, *like right now*, even as she tried so damn hard to pay attention to Lori's stories about her sister's lying, cheating husband, that she instead suffered an all-too-brutal flash of Marc, her once husband, all bloody and broken, with his hands reaching for her from their open front door.

Reaching to protect her, to shield her, as she tried to help him stand because he just couldn't do it anymore . . . knees buckling and his face pale as he lay dying against her. Feeling the last breath he ever took against her face, eyes blinking as his soul passed by her . . . through her and beyond. Blinking away tears.

So now here she was again, against her will blinking away the goddamn tears she'd held back all day. Now turning her face from Lori and the others, facing upward, to blind herself in the stadium lights.

At 8:45 p.m. a lifetime ago, Anne Hart, then Anne Devane, had felt her husband Marc Devane die in her arms trying to protect her, never understanding she'd never really been the one in danger at all.

13

CHRIS

He waited on the midway until the game let out, until the cheering and the noise died away. It was bad enough out here, but still better than standing in the shadow of the stadium or sitting in the bleachers. Days before, he'd tried to describe the scene at Mancha's to Mel, doing a bad job, failing to paint the right picture, failing harder to pierce the silence between them. She was unable or unwilling to see it as he had: the light and the dying and the noise, that horrible and calm look on Dupree's face.

You can't get that smell out. No sirree, it'll stay in the leather, never quite go away.

Maybe that was too much to ask of anyone. Later, though, he caught her looking close at a stain on his duty shirt, her fingers tracing Dupree's handprint in another man's blood. Tonight he'd thought about suggesting she come out to the carnival, and almost got the words out a couple of times. But in the end he'd let it go, not wanting to burden her with having to say no to his face, finally leaving her on the back porch listening to the radio, dropping spent cigarettes into a coffee cup. He did call once, standing next to a rusted merry-go-round, just to ask if he could bring her anything. She said no, she was fine, both of them knowing that wasn't close to being true.

If he heard it once, he heard it a thousand times, even before the game was done. All variations of the same thing:

> *Wish you were out there, son.*
> *Boys could've used you out there, Chris.*
> *Might want to give some throwing lessons to that*
>   *number twelve.*
> *How's the knee?*

He passed the sheriff a few times, holding court, moving through the crowd. One moment he was shooting out a red paper star with a rusty BB gun; the next he was having his picture taken next to the Ferris wheel for the newspaper.

Chris had seen Dupree early, before the game, wandering around in uniform even though he wasn't working, eyeing girls in their tight sweaters and jeans. They hadn't really talked about Mancha's or much after it; Chris was still relegated to the punch line of Dupree's stories, and word was that Aguilar and Delgado would likely live, although both would probably wish they hadn't. Delgado was breathing through a tube, might be for the rest of his life.

Whereas Chris felt bigger, slower, all the time, Dupree

only seemed to get smaller with each passing day, folding in on himself like a knife. Standing and smoking a cigarette at Mancha's while waiting for the ambulance, Duane had been all edges and angles, his bloody uniform a little too loose but still creased sharp, his duty belt too low on his waist, with his gun heavy against his knee. A *gunfighter*. He'd finger-popped to his own beat, drunk two or three Dr Peppers, and read the riot act to Eddie Corazon about everything and nothing at all.

Chris had found a small meth pipe and residue on Delgado, a glimpse of his demons, but there was no telling what demons possessed Duane Allen Dupree. Duane's father, Jamison, had been a little bit crazy and a lot of the time drunk; he was once found naked in his car with an empty wine bottle and a homemade tomahawk in his lap.

But crazy or not, Chris accepted that he'd needed the chief deputy at Mancha's, unwilling to imagine the ending if he'd been left out there all alone or one of the other deputies had shown up in Dupree's place. Even though Hawes and Miller and Busbee had all carried a badge and gun longer than Chris, they had even less of a clue about their job. Miller pulled some weekend shifts at Earlys, tending bar, and Busbee owned a goddamn tow truck. It wasn't unusual for Busbee to pull people out of ditches while still in uniform and then write them a ticket afterward. Chris didn't understand Dupree; didn't like him much and trusted him less, but other than the sheriff himself, he was probably the only real lawman in Murfee.

He moved along, tipping his hat, trying not to slow down enough so that someone might really be able to talk to him. The sheriff saw him, gave him a passing wave—a kind of cocked finger-gun effect—before disappearing again. He could make this walk blind anyway, the fall carnival remaining unchanged since he was kid—same games, same stalls, all sitting in their assigned places, like students in a classroom. Chris suspected even the carnies were the same too, just older, with a few more years of wear and rust—peeling paint and breaking down, just like the games and rides they brought with them. He'd be out here again later tonight, breaking up a couple of drunken fights. As a kid he'd always wondered where the carnival went when it wasn't here, and because he loved Bradbury's *Something Wicked This Way Comes*, he often imagined this place as Murfee's own Pandemonium Shadow Show, with its own versions of G. M. Dark and Skeleton and Dust Witch and Tom Fury. He was so busy trying to remember if his old copy of the book was still up at the house that he nearly ran over the new English teacher.

"Damn, ma'am, I'm sorry," he said, holding her up with one arm.

"No, no . . . I am, Deputy. I was trying to decide between the elephant ear and the cotton candy, a very important decision. Got caught standing here in your way, and to be honest, I don't need either."

Chris laughed, making sure she was going to stay upright. She was wrapped up in a brand-new BBC sweatshirt and a scarf, her hair tucked beneath a Houston Texans ball cap.

He pointed at the hat. "You might not want to wear that hat, ma'am, we're all Christians and Cowboy fans down this way."

She touched it, self-conscious. "Guess you can't be just one or the other? It was all I had. I'll be sure to do better next time." She squinted up at him, searching his chest for a nametag. "I'm Anne, Anne Hart."

"That's what I thought. New teacher, right?"

"Substitute teacher, for a while anyway, but that's the one. And you?"

"Someone who forgot to mind where he was going and his manners. Deputy Chris Cherry. Nice to meet you." He stuck out a hand and she shook it formally as a crowd parted around them.

"I just heard a lot about you, Deputy Cherry. You were quite the quarterback at one time. They could have used you in there." She nodded back at the stadium. "Did you watch the game?"

Chris considered lying, but thought better of it. "Not tonight, all official business."

"I see," she said. "Well, tonight, the team officially got its butt whipped."

Chris grinned. "So they're saying. Everyone's used to it by now this season, so it won't kill the fun. They'll still enjoy themselves at the homecoming dance, and out here." Anne Hart nodded in agreement, taking in the people and the rides, the colored lights reflected in her glasses.

She'd said she'd heard a lot about him, and of course he'd heard a few things about her as well, which is why he'd recognized her to begin with. She'd been teaching near Austin where there was an incident, some sort of trouble, but he never paid much attention to the story itself. It was just Miss Maisie talking to Duane; she was a known gossip and also known to be wrong more than half the time.

Still, Anne Hart was a reasonably attractive young woman who'd come all alone to Murfee, and that would have raised plenty of talk all by itself. Busbee with his tow truck kept saying he hoped her car broke down so he'd have the chance to "hitch 'er up, if you know what I mean," and everyone always laughed and said of course they did, even when they'd heard it a thousand times.

"So you grew up here in Murfee?" She started walking, so he fell in step next to her.

"Yes, ma'am, I did. A pure native. Went away for a bit and came back."

She looked up at his Stetson, down at his Justin boots. "Native? You really do take that cowboy stuff seriously here, don't you?"

"Well, it is kind of the uniform. Kind of expected."

She laughed. "Okay, but please, no more *ma'am* stuff. It makes me feel old, like I'm talking to one of my students. How about just Anne?"

"No problem, just Anne." She smiled, and he wanted to shove his hands deep down in his pockets, not quite sure what to do with them as they walked.

"How do you like Murfee so far?"

She considered. "I haven't seen much, to be honest. The school, that's about it."

"You mean you haven't seen Murfee's great attractions? The burgers at the Hamilton, the Comanche Cattle Auction? Our Ghost Lights? You've been missing out."

"The Lights I've read about. I haven't gotten over to the Hamilton, but the other teachers swear by it." She scrunched up her nose. "I think I'll skip the cattle auction, if you don't mind."

"Tell you what, I'll pick you up a Comanche ball cap. They sell them along with shirts, mugs, that sort of thing. You can ditch that Houston hat. It'll make everyone feel like you're going to stay a while, a native in your own way. Or better, I can get you a good ole Stetson, like mine."

"Well, Deputy Cherry, I'm not sure that I will be— staying, that is. I'm on a year contract. We'll see after that."

They came to a stop near the carnival's edge, where the lights gave way to the dark. To a roped-off area that served as the carnival's parking lot, the desert and the town lost beyond.

"Before your time here is up, I hope you see something you like."

She looked down. "Too early to tell, Deputy, but I hope so. Murfee is interesting, very much so. You came back here, so that's saying something, right?"

He shrugged. "It does, yes. Not sure what, to be exact. Not sure at all. But welcome . . . and enjoy your stay, however long it is. If you need anything, just look me up. And please, call me Chris. Deputy makes *me* feel old or too official, like I'm talking to a person in cuffs."

Something passed her eyes, a dark flicker hidden in her glasses, but not completely. Eyes a little too red, too weary, as if she might have been crying earlier. She smiled, a mask, even before it dawned on her he was just respinning her own joke from a few moments before.

She held up her hands, in mock arrest. "I'll do my best to stay out of trouble, Chris."

Even after they said their goodbyes, neither walked away—a certain gravity holding them in place, close. They talked for a few minutes more, mostly about books. He asked what they were reading in her class, all about her favorite books, and admitted he'd been thinking about *Something Wicked This Way Comes* when he almost knocked her down. She looked out over Murfee's carnival, at the lights and noise, saying she wouldn't be able to see it the same way now. She said she might even pick up a copy of the classic to read again, but he told her not to bother, he'd dig up his old one for her.

She glanced down once at her watch, so he offered to walk her out to her car, but she didn't want to be any trouble. It ended up not mattering, because the sheriff appeared to do the honors himself.

*   *   *

He walked right up, smiling, always smiling, tipping his hat to reveal his brush cut gleaming silver, a razor's edge. The sheriff asked Anne if his deputy was treating her okay and she said he was—a complete gentleman, extolling the virtues of Murfee. The sheriff put a hand on Chris's shoulder and said Chris was the best damn quarterback to ever play at BBC, maybe all of West Texas, and that he might turn out to be a pretty good deputy too if he shot a bit straighter and wasn't so nice all the time. He said Chris's idea of *deputying* was saving cats out of trees and escorting pretty ladies on the midway.

Chris took the cue. He excused himself, smiled at Anne, who smiled back, and turned into the heart of the carnival. He glanced back once, but Anne and the sheriff were already gone.

He saw the sheriff once more a little bit later. Sheriff Ross was near the entrance, saying bye to folks, shaking hands, telling them to come again tomorrow night. He reminded parents to check in on their kids as they left the homecoming dance, and pointed out that his deputies— *his boys*—would be out on the road tonight to make sure everyone got home safe.

Chris knew that before the night was done he'd pull over a couple of kid-filled trucks, beer cans and flasks rattling around their feet or being tossed out windows. But there would be no tickets, no punishment, just an escort home. It would be the same at Christmas break, when the kids had their winter bonfire. As a senior, he'd had too much to drink there, throwing up in the hay, and had been taken home by Duane Dupree, a long-ago moment the chief deputy probably didn't remember.

No trouble. That was the word handed down by Sheriff Ross.

The town loved him for it; they loved *him*—eating brisket and shaking hands and looking after their kids. In many ways Sheriff Ross was Murfee, and Chris wondered if either could exist without the other.

Before all the lights went down, Chris caught one glimpse of Caleb Ross, guessing he never went to the game or the dance, either. He was enveloped in the same sweatshirt he always seemed to be wearing, hood up, wandering the dark paths between the games and rides. He wasn't joining in any of them, just watching. By the time Chris thought to say hello, he was gone, too.

Cars left and the rides slowed to a stop, all the lights winking out one after another, at least those not already burned out or busted. Chris texted Mel, but there was no answer. He hoped she was asleep. He still had several more hours to go, anyway.

He'd enjoyed talking to the new teacher more than he cared to admit. She came across as smart and funny, sharing his love for words. Meeting her felt like holding a new book, the story within still a mystery, its ending unknown. He could catch up with Miss Maisie or Duane on Monday and find out what all they knew about her, but wouldn't. That felt like prying or spying, and he didn't want to do that.

Whatever drove her to Murfee was hers alone, her secret to keep.

14

MELISSA

Of course she saw his text. She was sitting in her car, smoking and thinking, just choosing to ignore it. Earlier she'd been in the lot, walking toward the carnival, when Chris and the other woman had come toward her. They'd been easy to spot—even without his hat, Chris towered over most everyone—and they weren't moving fast, just enough to sidestep the crowds. They paused to watch a young girl throw darts at tired balloons taped to a board, then walked on a bit more toward the carnival's edge, slowing with each step, stopping in the last circle of light.

And Mel had seen it all from the darkened lot, one hand steadying her on the warm and ticking hood of the car. She'd come out as a surprise. Even did up her hair, spent extra time on her makeup—made a real effort. She felt she owed it to him, to herself; felt she had to hold on to something good because there had been for a time something really good between them. Wanted to believe there still could be.

Only to find him walking, talking, laughing, with a stranger. Mel had no idea who the woman was, had never seen her around. There was a time not that long ago when Mel would have roared right up to both of them, glowing white hot, gotten some goddamn answers, but tonight she'd just stood in the dark and watched.

Watching Chris.

Saw him smile easy and natural, laugh, like whatever that woman was saying might be damn funny. Talk with his hands the way he did when he was nervous or excited. Then the sheriff had come up and Chris had left, but not before sneaking a look back at the woman in the ball cap. The glance had been quick, but it had been enough. More than enough. Mel had already retreated to the car when the sheriff walked the woman out to hers. They stood by it while the sheriff talked, where they were darker shadows. And when the woman finally got in her car to drive away, the sheriff had been left behind in the wash of her moving headlights, weird tattoos of light coiling up and down his arms, across his face like live snakes. Mel had imagined then he'd looked right at her, eyes holding the last of that light, but if he'd seen her, he gave no sign, making his way alone back to the midway— walking with both hands in his pockets, a man without a goddamn care in the world. Afterward, Mel had stayed in the car with the radio off, getting colder by the minute, until the rides died one by one and the carnival lights went dark.

And that's where she was when Chris's last text came in. Still sitting in the car, smoking and thinking.

15

DUANE

There was blood everywhere. He blinked, once, twice, before it was gone.

The little house smelled like cat piss, but Duane didn't own cats. Hated 'em. It was that fucking Mexican *foco*; smoking it left a burned matchstick stink in the air, like the devil himself had popped in for a quick visit. Tough to say . . . maybe he had.

Duane checked for ghosts whenever he got home now, looking in the corners where his daddy usually stood, but he wasn't there tonight—away on whatever ghost business he had. It was a bad joke, since Jamison Dupree for damn sure never had any real business to attend to while alive. Still, Duane couldn't shake the sense that something, someone, was watching him. He'd already been up to look more times than he could count, stark naked because his skin itched bad, leaving both the front door and the front windows wide open, inviting the night in, daring whatever else was out there to join it. Even the devil.

He'd been out to the carnival for a bit, but all the bright lights hurt his eyes, drove him away, all the bells and whistles too loud like gunfire and people screaming.

Not before catching sight of the new English teacher with Chris Cherry, and making sure the Judge knew it, too. The Judge had listened with eyes flat and hard like coins and then walked right off in mid-sentence to find them. Pussy was the Judge's weakness; always had been, always would be. He made too big a deal about it and let it get all into his head. Not like Duane, at least not until the little Mex girl had invaded his dreams. But before the Judge went off to hunt down Cherry, he'd made a point of his own—told Duane to be smart, keep his damn eyes open, *just in case*. He didn't say any more than that, but he didn't have to. That other thing troubling him was more than just pussy.

Chava . . . Rudy Ray . . . the Far Six. Of course Duane would keep a lookout, he always did. And with his new wolf eyes, the Judge had no idea all the things he could see. Duane was not a worrier. Before the *foco*, it had never been in his nature, not even while dealing with the Judge's crazy beaners at their makeshift airstrip past the Far Six— a long patch of flattened gravel lit only by the dirty light of pie pans filled with coal oil.

Rudy Ray had been responsible for the pans and never got it quite right, not fucking once. All he had to do was make a goddamn straight line, and that had escaped him. The other beaners never complained, though, only laughed a bit about it and cuffed Rudy Ray around, all in good fun. Rudy Ray had known 'em first, even got one of their special phones like the Judge; he'd been one of them in a way that Duane would never be. So much so, it sometimes seemed they'd all worked for Rudy Ray, rather than the other way around.

He hadn't liked any of them, but got to know one passing well: Chava, bowlegged and short, with a machete always in his rope-tie waistband and a bright gold tooth, too big for his mouth, right in front. He'd spoken a little English. Chava's head had been shaved, revealing scars on his skull, deep claw marks. He wore a dozen necklaces, little beads and bones, and when Duane had asked about them one night, Chava said they were gifts from their witch doctor. This witch doctor was half Mex but had spent time in Haiti, and they kept him around to cast curses and poison their enemies: other narcos, the *policía* and the *federales* and the *putos*. This witch doctor lived in a special ranch across the water, where they stored loads before the plane trips and where he fucked all the young girls they gave him on a big round water bed and where he also did his rituals and sacrifices, killing goats and zebras and snakes; once, even a fucking lion cub. He had a huge cauldron, an *nganga*, filled with bones that Chava claimed to have dug out of a graveyard. They'd had so much success and luck that the witch doctor's cauldron had gotten even hungrier and needed "fresh meat"—live human sacrifice. Chava had helped with that, too.

He'd touched a finger to his machete and rattled the little bones on his necklace, what Duane had thought all along were bird bones or rat teeth but suddenly wasn't so sure, before Chava had smiled and laughed and said something in Spanish and all the other beaners had joined in, even Rudy fucking Ray. Then a stupid grinning Mex had handed him another burlap bundle and told him in bad English to hurry the fuck up. They'd been fucking with him, probably.

Duane saw Chava two, three times after that, then never again. There'd been someone else, though, a beaner thinner and tall like a fucking skeleton, but wearing Chava's same necklaces and carrying the same machete like he'd had it his whole life. Even that hadn't worried Duane, not then anyway.

So the Judge didn't have to say it, but things hadn't been square in a long while. He hadn't sent Duane out to meet a plane at the Far Six in months, near a year—all over lost money and Rudy fucking Ray's mouth, which should've ended up in a fucking cauldron to begin with. After that, the line truly had gone silent on the Judge's special little phone; dead, like a dropped fucking call, and the longer the silence had stretched, the sharper it had become—a goddamn knife edge. Some days the Judge pretended things were fine, nothing to worry about; others, like tonight at the carnival, he acted spooked, telling Duane keep his eyes peeled, like maybe he was seeing ghosts of his own. Duane reckoned *his* ghosts, at least half of what he saw, weren't real—just the *foco* working overtime or his own brain casting shadows. The problem was, he couldn't tell which half was which anymore, and maybe the Judge couldn't, either.

A coyote made noise, a mama barking at her pups, forcing Duane to the window again, duty gun held low, scanning the cold dark. Starlight collected on his bare skin, made it glow, where he dreamed thick hair might soon grow to join his wolf eyes and his wolf teeth. When that happened he was going to show up at the door of his little Mex girl, huff and puff and really blow her house down. As a boy he'd once seen a wolf at the far edge of this very property, way past the pecan groves. It had laughed at him before slipping into the endless dark. His granddaddy had built this place far from Murfee's lights, passed it down father to son; but it wasn't a true ranch, just seventy-five mean acres of snakebit land worth even less than the house that sat on it.

After Old Dupree had passed, Duane's daddy bought, cheated, or straight-up stole a few head of Angus, deciding to try his hand at ranching. But they never thrived, because even a young Duane knew you had to do more than turn them all loose and hope for the best.

You had to *care* for them, get your hands dirty. Fill up stock tanks with good water and buy enough feed or plant hay for forage and repair fences, or at least build a few. You had to work the land and tend all the things on it, and those were two things Jamison Dupree was definitely never too keen on. Not his cows; not his family, either.

Duane had wanted to care for those damn cows, desperately, willing to do all the work himself—dreamed of taking a 4-H ribbon with the one he'd named Big Boss. But he was too young, too goddamn small, to do it all on his own. Most wandered off, lost, or got stole back by whomever his daddy had thieved them from. All of eight years old, and Duane had walked the fields alone before sunup, lugging buckets of feed and tap water almost as big as him, looking for those damn cows, calling out the names he'd given them.

The few that remained got bad sick, and with no money for a vet or medicine, they'd dropped where they stood. Breathing hard, laboring, blowing snot, their ribs raised like skinned knuckles on a fighter's hand. So Duane got his granddaddy's Smith & Wesson, the very same gun, ten years later, he would put against his daddy's teeth while he slept off a drunk, and walked around the back field, shooting them all. He had to hold that big fucking gun with both hands, kneeling next to their steaming heads and breathing in their last breaths; pulling that trigger steady, with their hot blood going cold in spray and streaks on his face. He kissed Big Boss once on the feathery star between his eyes and then blew his brains into the grass.

Maybe there *were* eyes watching him from beyond the very fields where he'd done that killing.

Or it was just a bit of shine off Chava's gold tooth, come back from the grave like his own daddy. He pointed his gun into the night, figured it was worth cranking off a few rounds and letting whoever or whatever was out there know that he'd seen them. His three sudden blasts echoed and rolled over the caliche and back, stirring up thunder and lightning in his head. Right after that his cellphone rang once, making him jump, so he almost put a bullet through that, too.

He chewed sulfur, tasted it at the back of his throat. He'd snorted up the last of his *foco* two hours ago, right after leaving the carnival, and he was gonna need more soon.

A lot fucking more.

16
CALEB

I followed Ms. Hart home after the carnival. I wasn't stalking her, just curious about where she was staying. She's renting a house over on Maple, a few minutes from school. She didn't check her mailbox when she got there, walked right in the front door and never looked back. She never even turned on any lights, but I thought I saw her move once past the window, a phantom, before she was gone. We both sat alone in the dark. If I ever told Amé, she'd give me hell. She'd be both jealous and not, all at the same time, and probably punch me in the shoulder and ask me what I'm thinking. Ask me if I am *loco*. I am scared I don't know the real answer anymore.

*   *   *

A few days before the carnival I was sitting in my room, doing my homework. My door was open and I looked up to find my father standing there, leaning against the jamb, arms crossed.

It was one of the few times since my mom disappeared he's been able to sneak up on me, because I do a pretty good job of keeping an eye out for him. This time, though, I had no idea how long he'd been standing there, just watching. I tried not to react when I looked up, so I gave an "Oh, hi" and turned back to my work.

I have to practice saying casual stuff like that, like we're a normal father and son. Not only when we're out together, but even when we're alone, just the two of us in the house. It still takes everything I have to turn my back on him, look away from him, like I did when I saw him at my door. My mom's been gone over a year now. Everyone says my father is still in his prime, eligible. Everyone talks about how hard it must be for a father to raise a boy alone, but they have no idea what that means. He stood there a minute longer, cleared his throat. "What do you think about your new teacher?"

I don't keep anything I write in the house. Not my stories, not my poems. Not these pages. Not the handful of 5.56x45mm rifle cartridges I stole from his truck. I never go anywhere important in my mom's old Ford Ranger, because I believe he always has his eye out for it, keeping track of me. I'm even careful with my cellphone. The account is still in my mom's name, and I pay it in cash, in person, every month.

My secret place—*my safe place*—is down by Coates Creek, near the desert willow where I found my dog hammered to death. Amé knows about it, and I've told her if anything ever happens to me, if I mysteriously run away, to go to my place and get my notebooks and all the other things I've hidden there. She laughs at me, though. Can't take me seriously, but I mean it. I once read in some fantasy book about a phylactery, a place or an object where a creature can hide its soul, protecting it from death. As long as the phylactery is safe, the creature can never truly die. It lives on, rising again and again. The plastic box buried at Coates Creek is my phylactery, my proof against death. Everything in it is my heart, my soul . . . I'm too scared to bring those things into the house, to keep them under the same roof with him.

But I worry he has one too—that his soul is locked away even farther from here. Far from Murfee, safe from all the things he's done. I've had nightmares about stalking him through our darkened house, trapping him in my mom's kitchen and putting him down with his own gun, that damn Ruger he used on Dillon Holt; pumping round after round into him until my arms ached from the gun's mule kick and my hands were hot from the barrel's heat, only to have him crawl upright and laugh, his body hammered into all kinds of impossible angles and his blood pooling and going cold on the floor between us.

The fear that I *can't* kill him might be the only thing that prevents me from trying.

Before I followed Ms. Hart home, I caught her talking with Deputy Cherry. If Deputy Cherry had been in regular clothes, not his uniform, you might have sworn they were college students on a date. They looked natural together, normal. They walked to the parking lot and stood there for a bit before my father showed up. He must have seen them together, kept an eye on them as well, circling back to catch up before Ms. Hart left.

My father makes these encounters seem so natural, normal. They aren't. Nothing with him is. My guess is he decided two or three days ago it was time to start paying some attention to Ms. Hart; at the very same moment he'd stood in my doorway and asked me about her. He probably knew a year ago he wanted to bring her here.

What do you think about your new teacher?

I was careful, able to keep them both in sight after Deputy Cherry left. Close enough I could hear a little bit of what my father was saying—his damn stories, the ones recorded so all he has to do is hit play. They always come out the same and he always smiles and laughs in the exact same places, even though he sounds like he's making them up on the spot.

They're fake, smoke and mirrors—like those in the shitty fall carnival fun house that break and bend you into weird shapes. Do those mirrors bend someone like my father back to normal? Once upon a time he told all those stories to my mom.

My father finally let Ms. Hart go, released her, letting her drive off. I had to stay crouched down next to an old dually truck while he took a good look around the lot before I got in my mom's Ranger and decided to follow her. I did notice one last thing as I made a wide circle through the parked cars. It was Melissa, Deputy Cherry's girlfriend, sitting in a car watching the place where my father and Ms. Hart had stood. She wasn't moving or talking on her cell or doing anything. I wondered what she was thinking.

Someone who reads this will come to all the wrong conclusions. I have no proof, no smoking gun, no evidence of all the things my father's done, the things I know he's capable of. All these words might be nothing more than *my* fun-house reflection—fractured, crazy, anything but normal.

But I saw the way he smiled and laughed with Ms. Hart . . . the way he can transform, like a snake shedding a skin. He has a horrible mirror of his own to bend himself back to normal, right in front of everyone's eyes.

Like he did for Nancy Coombs, Brenda Holt, Vickie Schori, Nellie Banner.

For so many others. For my mother.

But I've seen the man without the mirror. I know his real face. Everyone says Ms. Hart will be here only through the end of the school year, and if I got to know her, I'd probably like her. Right now, though, I want her to get the hell out of here as fast as she can.

Ms. Hart will never really be safe in Murfee. It might be that if I don't do something, no one will. As long as my father is alive, I don't think anyone is. He's fooled all of them except me.

Once upon a time he told all those stories to my mom.

17

CHRIS

I t was late when he wrapped up at the carnival, but he wasn't quite ready to go home. He figured Mel was already asleep, so there was no need to text her anymore, to lie that he needed to stay out and work the road. She wouldn't have believed it anyway. She knew as well as he did that the sheriff didn't care about his deputies patrolling U.S. Route 67, writing tickets. Route 67, along with 90 and Texas 118, were all part of one long black ribbon that curled tight around Murfee like a zip tie. Desolate, rarely used, going nowhere. There might have been a time when he would have caught joyriders or drug smugglers racing in the dark between the border and El Paso and Dallas, but that hadn't happened in forever, since long before Chris had joined the department.

The sheriff had made it all safe.

*   *   *

He was out near the Union Pacific rail line, up on Mitchell Flat, far west of town. He'd already watched a train move past him in the dark, counting cars, its three front lights like huge glowing eyes, leading the way. As a kid, he'd wondered about all the places a train like that might have come from, all the places it might go.

He was parked up on the grass at the Murfee Lights, the Ghost Lights, famous enough that the town had put up a small roadside viewing stand. They'd been seen and talked about since the fifties, tracing their origins back farther than that. The Lights were said to be glowing orbs about the size of basketballs, all ice-cream colors, floating and merging in pairs out across the flat. They appeared about a dozen times a year, explanations ranging from distant car lights off the state highway to small fires to temperature changes. None of these possibilities diminished their mystery, though, and Murfee kids had been coming out here forever, waiting for them, drinking and fooling around in their darkened cars. There was even a movie about the legend, a B horror picture with killer phantoms terrorizing a lost couple trapped in their car. He'd caught it a couple of times on late-night cable, more times than he'd ever seen the Lights themselves.

But it was black on the flat now—cold, dark. No ghosts floating there. He had his window down, listening to the night wind try to move the mountains. His good-time radio was turned down low to a repeat of that call-in show Mel liked, *Dark Stars* or *Dark Sun . . . Dark* something, and the host was talking about the power of letting go. Chris couldn't agree more, even if he had no fucking idea how to do it. His department radio was turned all the way up, but it stayed grave quiet, not even static. This time of night, unless she'd been asked to stay, Miss Maisie had long since gone home. After the train turned to echoes, he had the road—the whole world—to himself.

He'd known Mel was unhappy and had been for a while, never realizing how much, not until that moment in their kitchen. He wasn't willing to face how unhappy he was, either. Chris had always had a touch of claustrophobia, no surprise for someone as big as him—it used to come on in basements every now and then, or in a small car; the occasional football tunnel when he'd been crammed together with the team. But he'd always coped, never talked much about it, knowing it had little to do with the true size of the physical space and more with the threat of being closed in, trapped, unable to escape. Unsure of what to do, as he'd felt at Mancha's, as it had always been, growing up in Murfee, even beneath its endless skies, stretching forever. Empty, untouched, indifferent. Back then, books, as small as they were, particularly in his hands, had been his infinite worlds. They'd taken him to places far away from here; they were boundless. All of the books at the house had been escapes. He'd lost himself in them again and again to make Murfee bearable; this was why he still couldn't let them go. But Mel, who had spent most her life always *leaving* places, didn't quite understand that. Maybe she never would.

But still he'd come back. Had come limping home to Murfee on his broken knee because it *was* home, because he'd been too afraid to face anywhere else—the old devil that you know. Afraid also to face Murfee alone, so he'd brought Mel with him, only to turn right around and leave her in that gray, lifeless house full of the air of his dead parents and the decay and dust of all their old things, all of those old books. At least his job got him out, offered a hint of light and air, even as she stayed behind, buried. Her only escape—his best offer—was taking orders at the Hamilton or pouring drinks at Earlys.

Mel hates it and pretty soon is going to hate me, too. That was the heart of it. He couldn't hide how much he resented returning; he saw it reflected in her eyes every day. He was small here, folded, crushed, and diminished. *Claustrophobic.* Mancha's had reminded him of that. He couldn't blame Mel for not liking Murfee or him when he himself didn't like either very much. He'd been lost since the injury, getting Mel lost right along with him. They were like the couple in that horrible movie, trapped in their car, haunted by their ghosts. Had he been telling her the truth about leaving? Could he? He didn't know himself, not anymore.

Let go.

But Chris couldn't, didn't know how to. Not now. Not the body at Indian Bluffs, not what he'd seen in Dupree's truck. Not the sight of Aguilar's face in his hands or the ruin Delgado had become after Dupree was done with him. Not these last few cold, brittle weeks with Mel, and God knows, not all the warm times they'd shared before that. Because he still could remember Melissa *before* . . . before Murfee, before their kitchen. Before she'd tossed a cigarette into the sink that was really aimed at him, them. An act far louder than anything she'd actually said.

Before.

He'd heard things about her: how she fell in and out of the football program's orbit, how she was all kinds of trouble. How she had a thing for men and they all had a thing for her too, at least for a little while—but he never cared about those whispers and in-jokes. She was pure light, magnetic, drawing him to her. He was closed off and quiet and lived on empty movie sets in his head, and she was a star—a north star, and he followed her.

She took him into her bed before they had their first real date, tasting of cigarettes and Jack Daniel's, both she and her sheets smelling like her perfume, and when they were done, she got up and walked naked into the kitchen for beers, her body lit by passing headlights so that she glowed pearl and blue. She came back and opened his beer and ran the cold bottle over his chest, running her own hands up and down his arms in a way that had made his skin ache, fingers tracing veins and muscles as if she could touch, maybe steal, the tiniest bit of the current thrumming there.

She asked him then how he could throw the ball so goddamn far, and when he started to tell her he didn't really know—that his dad had always just told him to let 'er rip, so that's all he'd ever done and ever knew how to do—she'd put his warming beer on her nightstand next to a clock that was always off by an hour or so and rose up suddenly, arching in a way that made him hold his breath so she could straddle him first with her hands on her ass, then on his chest. Her hair falling forward in his face—mouth to open mouth—breathing all she was into him. Breathing, whispering.

Let 'er rip, Chris. And he did.

He might have slept, drifted, remembering or dreaming of Mel from that time *before*, when she'd been naked and electric and his—afraid to let it go, afraid he already had, even if she hadn't. Wondering where she'd gone, or if he was the one who'd left her behind.

But he was awake now, the radio playing music . . . opening his eyes to see, after all of the years, the Lights. Ghosts on the flat. He held his breath, mesmerized. They bounced along, a mated pair, locked together like dancers, shimmering the exact same cool pearl and blue of Mel's car-lit body from his dream, their first night together. They were eyes staring at him from the dark. Then he understood. *Headlights.*

Just headlights, turning off Old Ranch Road onto 67. His dash clock read 2:34 a.m., and he tried to guess who would be out that way at this time of the morning, where they might be going. He was still wondering when he caught the first sound of the car's revving engine coming toward him. They probably never saw him, not when he pulled out behind them, not until he hit his lights and sirens.

The car, a big dark SUV, went by him so fast—leaving a horse's tail of dust and rocks in its wake—that his response was pure instinct, without thought. He gunned his truck to life and flipped on the wigwags, the road beneath him blue and red drumbeats. He knuckled the wheel, coming up to speed, closing the distance until he was right on its tail. The SUV, a Tahoe or similar, bigger than his F-150, flicked its brake lights once, twice—like it was thinking, debating. Then the brake light finally held steady as the big car slowed, stopping. Decision made. The SUV pulled smoothly off to the shoulder, waiting for Chris to angle to a stop, where he had his truck's nose for cover. He rolled the wigwags over so they flashed behind him, not that he expected any other cars to come up Route 67, but he hadn't expected this one, either. He'd been asleep, for chrissake.

Nice work, Deputy.

He popped his spotlight, sweeping it twice over the

back of the vehicle. It was a late-model Tahoe with Texas plates, and in the harsh glare of his headlights and the mounted spot, he could read the digits. There was dirt and mud caked on the Tahoe's ass, though, sprayed as high as the back glass. Even through that mess, he saw two heads moving in the front seats, talking, but not turning back to look at him.

He fumbled on the Datalux, still off because when he parked out here, he'd never planned on seeing a car, much less stopping one. It took a long moment for the terminal to come to life so he could run the Tahoe's plates, check if it was stolen. It was not unusual for cars boosted out of El Paso or Midland or even San Angelo to make their way over the border to be sold or stripped in Juárez or Ojinaga. Sometimes those same cars showed up again months later, painted different colors, all the back-seats torn out to make room for burlap bundles of weed or coke or meth, but this car was going the wrong way for all that.

The Datalux told him the car was registered to some-thing called the Allegra Corporation in El Paso, and al-though a name like that could mean it was a rental, it could also mean anything or nothing at all. He wasn't sure who or what he'd stopped, but wished now he'd just let it go. It was past 2:30 a.m. and there was nothing out here anywhere, anyway—not for a hundred miles.

Let it go. But since returning to Murfee, letting go had become the hardest damn thing of all. In the tiny screen of his dashcam, the Tahoe sat ghostly and washed out, unreal. The camera had engaged the moment he hit his emergency lights. Sheriff Ross had been ambivalent about them, but they'd been purchased with a federal grant and installed in all of the department's trucks before Chris arrived. Duane and the other deputies routinely turned them off or cut the cable, but Chris always left his alone. The driver and passenger remained still, patient. There was no mad scrambling from inside, no one jumped out shooting; no muzzle flare lighting the dark as his windshield spiderwebbed from stray rounds. His window was still down and the wind tugged over the idling of both engines. It would have been peaceful if he hadn't been so damn nervous.

It wouldn't get better sitting here, though. Each passing moment gave the strangers in the Tahoe time to think a little more about what they might want to do . . . all their options. If they hadn't yet found the courage to fuck with him when he first lit them up, he was giving them plenty of time to find it now.

Fuck me.

Chris remembered Mancha's and flipped the thumb break on his gun holster before he opened his door. He stood for two heartbeats behind the nose of his truck, approaching along the passenger side of the Tahoe and staying off the road just beyond the sightline of the side mirror.

His right hand angled near his Colt, and his left swept the vehicle with his Surefire, checking the cargo area and the backseats. The windows were tinted, almost too dark, but not so bad that he couldn't confirm there was no one else crouched down in the Tahoe. It was only the driver and the passenger, but that was enough. The passenger window was already down when he walked toward it.

He saw her blond hair first, pulled back in a small, tight ponytail, but couldn't quite guess the woman's age. She wore dark clothes, a dark jacket with a high collar— high tech and expensive, rugged and outdoorsy. It looked new, hardly used. She had both hands on the dash, and he noted—weird—that she wasn't wearing any rings of any kind. She was pretty in a stern, athletic way; kept her eyes forward, not looking into his light. She was still, quiet, and being very, very careful. That made Chris twice as worried.

"Ma'am," he said, keeping the Surefire on her face, brushing it past to take in the driver—a man in a similar jacket with a thick goatee, peppered gray, hands on the wheel and fingers splayed and visible. These two knew the drill too well.

But the man spoke first. "Deputy, sorry if we woke you." He said it with a hint of a smile, a hint of East Coast accent, guessing correctly that they'd startled Chris. "We were zipping along back there. I know, I know, too damn fast . . . at this time of night I thought we had clear sailing through Van Horn."

"Well, 'zipping' is definitely one way to put it. I didn't expect to see anyone out here tonight, either. Guess by now we can both just call it 'morning.' How about a license and some registration? Where you coming from?"

The driver had his license between his fingers, quick, extending it. He used it to motion at his passenger—talking the whole time, keeping Chris's attention. "Is it okay if Sara grabs the registration? It's in the glove box."

Chris nodded and the young woman, younger than her companion, opened the glove box with one hand, leaving the other on the dash, pulling out a folded paper. Chris got a glimpse inside and saw *nothing*. No tissue boxes, no old receipts or folded takeout menus. Other than the Tahoe's driver's manual, still shrink-wrapped, the glove compartment was barren.

In the floorboard between the woman's sneakered feet, though, he caught a look at several empty water bottles and crumpled-up papers, an expensive black folio, and a package of half-eaten nuts. Chris took the registration and license. The man was Darin Braddock from El Paso.

"Sara and I were at Lajitas for a couple of days, heading home. You ever spend any time out there?"

"Not so much, no," Chris said. Lajitas was a popular golf resort tucked between the Big Bend Ranch State Park and the even larger national park, visited by presidents and actors.

"We were just looking for a little getaway."

"Sure, it's nice." Chris flipped open the registration, confirming the name Allegra Corporation. The rest of it appeared in order. Darin Braddock from El Paso was forty-seven, according to his license.

Chris knew he should walk back to his truck and run Braddock for wants and warrants, but hesitated. He hadn't been on the radar gun when the Tahoe blew past—in fact, it was still in its locked case—so writing a ticket was pure guesswork, an outright lie. And Darin Braddock, in a way he couldn't put a finger on, did not seem like the sort of man that was easy to lie to. Chris's curiosity was piqued by this pair and their vehicle—oddly empty and sterile and lived in at the same time—but was embarrassed for having been caught asleep at the wheel. Braddock seemed to know it, and that made Chris want even more to just get this over with and get home.

The woman remained silent. She hadn't really glanced at him or Braddock. All Chris had seen of her was the side of her face, unsmiling. She didn't look scared, only a little nervous. There was another thing too, a suspicion Chris couldn't shake: that running "Darin Braddock" in the Datalux would only give him answers as opaque as the vehicle's registration, as empty and clean as the Tahoe's glove compartment. More questions and suspicions, not less.

"Mr. Braddock, it's late, or early, depending on how you want to look at it, and I don't want to write you a ticket and I know you don't want one. If I walk back to my car and run your license, am I going to find any other outstanding tickets? Warrants? Anyone want you for any reason?"

Braddock laughed, now sharing a joke. "No, Deputy, you won't. My only trouble is a significant other in El Paso who isn't named Sara and who thinks I'm in Midland at a conference, if you know what I mean." Braddock reached out and grabbed Sara's hand, squeezed. She squeezed back, awkward, and turned to look up at Chris.

Smiling, embarrassed. She was pretty, prettier than his first take, and the story made sense. Older Darin and younger Sara—possibly his secretary or his student—sneaking away for a couple of days and racing back home before someone caught on. Chris handed back the license and registration, lit up the seat over Sara's shoulder with his Surefire to check for suitcases in the backseat and saw only small black cases, nothing big, and no golf clubs.

He smiled and made as if to step back, but stopped.

Let it go.

"I do know what you mean, Mr. Braddock, so no trouble here. I'll let you two get on home. One last thing, if you don't mind." Chris looked down at the young woman, giving her a chance to make eye contact if she needed it. "Ma'am, if I could just see your license too, you'll be on your way." Darin Braddock's smile flickered, reset.

Sara hesitated, as if waiting for Braddock to say something for both of them, but when he didn't—nodding a silent *Go ahead* instead—she said, "Sure. I'll get it." She reached toward the dark floorboard between her legs, between the empty water bottles, into the folio. Not a purse, not a makeup bag. Not even the back pocket of her jeans. She fumbled for a second at her feet, found the license, handed it over.

"It's a bad picture," she said.

Chris glanced down, read it, got ready to hand it back. He held it out a bit to make her reach for it, to give her one more chance to say something, anything, to him, but if she needed help, an escape, she wasn't going to take it. Her hands took back the license without shaking.

"No, no, it's fine, ma'am. My girl says the same thing all the time." Chris stood back, hand still hanging by his Colt. He and Braddock watched each other from their shadows.

"Be safe, Deputy, it's dark and empty out here. I don't envy you."

"Thanks, I will. And you drive safe. Let's keep your speed down a bit, at least until you're out of my sight. That way I don't feel too bad about not writing a ticket. If you come this way again, spend time looking for our Murfee Ghost Lights. They're kind of famous in their own way."

Chris walked away and got back in his truck. He was sweating and it had soaked his shirt all the way through, so bad he could smell himself inside the cold cab.

The Tahoe's lights flickered, faded, gone.

Until Mancha's, until *now*, Chris had never imagined himself prone to getting rattled. But he also still had no idea if he was a good cop, either, even though he could cite his criminal code and write a fair report, better than Dupree or any of the others. Because being the law in a place like Murfee was most often about breaking up fights and serving child support warrants, or pulling over knuckleheads like Carter Dale after he'd pounded down a few too many at Earlys and then drove around in his Dodge with his fucking pants down. It was *firefighting*, putting out the little flames that sparked around a small town all the time, which was one reason why he'd been so taken by the body at Indian Bluffs—it held the promise of being an actual crime, a real mystery.

And just like his mind had worked on *that* without even knowing it, standing there in Matty Bulger's field until the skeleton and the damage done to it had revealed itself, he'd been working over the mystery of the Tahoe from almost the moment he'd lit it up. It had been turning off Old Ranch Road, not the usual way to come from Lajitas—you couldn't even get there from here. There was nothing down that dirt strip at all—it angled south toward the old Far Six ranch, way past Indian Bluffs. It circled around Dupree's place, then along the Monument's fence lines. If you followed it long enough, you ran right into the Rio Grande. And there was the way Darin Braddock had very specifically addressed him as "deputy" right from the start, something that almost never happened when Chris pulled over a car. Nine times out of ten he was "officer," as in *Yes, Officer, I know I was going too fast*, or *Sir, yessir*. You had city police officers and sheriff's deputies and Texas Rangers all working West Texas, not to mention constables and Border Patrol and armed militia and God only knew what else, and few people could tell one from another and most didn't care anyway. But Braddock had, and he'd been very direct about it—almost like he knew Chris, not just the badge he wore.

There were the bags in the back of the Tahoe that weren't luggage. Instead, black hard-sided Pelican cases like those used to store expensive and breakable equipment—cameras and recorders. Guns, too. There were the matching high-tech jackets they wore, identical, like the kind that might be official issue or duty wear.

Then there was Darin Braddock himself, talking and smiling and spinning his off-the-cuff story of an affair to distract Chris so he wouldn't search the Tahoe or ask too many questions. Treating Chris like a rube, betting he was just a good-ole-boy county deputy. And Braddock had been good, very good, even after he had to have realized he'd been calling his companion by the wrong name the whole time; still betting or hoping this good-ole-boy county deputy wouldn't notice that, either.

But Chris *had* noticed just how startled and awkward Braddock's companion got after he grabbed her hand, not expecting it any more than Chris. And that was the moment he'd become afraid that the quiet passenger—Sara, *but not really*—with all her empty water bottles and no luggage and no purse, might be in serious trouble. So he'd played that little game with her license to give her a chance to say something, anything—to run or ask for help—only to end up with that stupid card in his hand, staring at a picture he couldn't even be sure was the same woman. They were similar, hints of each other, but the woman in the picture had much longer, darker hair. He would've had to get the blond girl out of the car, into what little light he had, to be sure.

Because whoever she'd been, she definitely wasn't Sara, and even if she wasn't a prisoner or a hostage or any of the other things Chris had feared, she absolutely wasn't on a romantic getaway with a man named Darin Braddock, either. Her license had been from Delaware, and said her name was Morgan Emerson.

18
ANNE

It was late when she came to, just as she'd planned. Dry-swallowing a couple of sleeping pills and three capfuls of vodka and falling down with her clothes on the night before had done the trick. Now sunlight washed her bedroom, bleached it. The room held so much light it hurt her eyes. She remembered . . . a game, her brain still foggy from the pills . . .

Sheriff Ross, smiling, going on about Marc and that one time they all met before; laughing at his own jokes and stories. Deputy Chris Cherry, dressed liked a cowboy, lacking only a lasso; talking about a thousand books . . . walking together for what had felt like forever, under a million stars wheeling and burning, before they all turned into cheap carnival lights.

She also thought she remembered, just before passing

out, glancing out her window to catch a figure standing there in the street, staring back.

No face, just shadows. Her dead husband, come to watch over her as she slept.

Later she found the Houston Texans hat Marc had bought her when he went to a game with other guys from the department. He'd gotten one for each of them, had worn his almost all the time. She found it in the trash while throwing out the cheap vodka bottle and the silly soda cup from the carnival, and couldn't for the life of her recall how it got there.

19
CALEB

MY MOTHER

These are things I remember about my mom. Watching TV in our living room in the dark. She liked crappy horror movies: *Halloween*, *Friday the 13th*, the original *Twilight Zone* series. When my father was out late or out of town, we'd set up camp and watch one. She popped popcorn or we ordered a pizza and hung out together. She talked to me about school, about Murfee, about whatever. She sat with her legs curled up underneath her, hair pulled back, wearing a BBC booster sweatshirt. I might ask about what high school was like for her or if she'd enjoyed college, but she didn't like answering all my questions, and just laughed many of them off or turned them back on me.

She came in from the rain, a few months before she disappeared. She ran into the house, soaking wet. I didn't know where she'd been, but her jeans were heavy with mud, her shirt streaked with long river clay that looked like she'd been holding an armload of snakes. She didn't know I was there, stripping off her outer clothes and putting them in a trash bag afterward, getting down on her hands to wipe up the floor where she'd been standing, trying to clean up any trace of her muddy footprints. She ran the shower in the bedroom for about thirty minutes. Maybe she was scrubbing away all that mud at first, then standing under the water after that, letting it run, letting it go hot then cold as the storm passed over our house with thunderous footsteps.

CHRISTMAS

My mom loved Christmas. Decorating the tree, buying presents, baking cookies. She loved it when it snowed, always wanted to stand outside, arms stretched wide and turning in circles, trying to catch the meager flakes that sometimes escaped the Chisos. When I still believed in Santa, or for as long as my mom begged me to pretend to believe, "Santa" left all of my presents unwrapped under the tree, assembled, ready to go. I'd come down the stairs to see my haul all laid out, gleaming, new, spotted by the colored lights of the tree. In the center was always the thing I wanted most—a computer or a PlayStation; one year a guitar, upright in a stand with its strings bright and silver like razors.

Later I learned that every Christmas Eve my mom hand-wrote a small paper sign with the year and placed it in front of "Santa's presents" to snap a picture, memorializing the moment and my presents hours before I got up to see them. I saw those pictures pasted in a book, all of them, year after year. There was an unchanging quality about them—the tree always in the same place, decorated nearly the same way. The light and chasing shadows even looked the same, forever trapped by the camera that had caught them. If you held all those pictures together, riffled through them with your thumb as with one of those silly flip books, the only thing that would have changed were the dates on the paper signs themselves, scrawled with a black Sharpie in my mom's handwriting.

SMOKING BY THE TREE

We have a large tree in the backyard, a pecan we've always watered like crazy just to keep it alive. When my father was out, my mom would stand underneath it and smoke a cigarette, make a cell call as well, or stare up through the high branches. I've stood out there myself, right in her spot, looking up through those same branches to see whatever mysterious place she peered into, and I've never seen much. Just the dark branches, skeletal arms, and brief breaks in the foliage where the sky might shine through, blue and white and harsh. I still go out there and sit underneath the tree, to read or think or to get out of the house, and I still smell her cigarette smoke, trapped in the leaves and the bark.

THE KITCHEN

My mom's sanctuary in the house was our kitchen, where she spent most of her time. The yellow paint, the black-and-white pictures on the wall, the dried desert flowers in the brightly colored glass bottles and jars and the way she never kept the blinds down or closed in there, always letting raw sunshine in—it was all her. Most days she even left the windows open so the wind could find its way in too, bringing with it a fine dust that coated everything. If she wasn't cooking, she was seated at the kitchen island, flipping through a magazine, writing a letter, drinking sun tea. Near the end, maybe four or five months before she was gone, she was there and my father walked in. He stood and looked down at her, arms crossed, and then picked up an oven mitt that she'd left on the counter. It was a silly thing, ugly, shaped like a rooster—bright green and red. I'd bought it for her one Christmas when I was nine or ten years old. My mom always used it, even though she had much nicer ones. My father slipped that oven mitt on his hand and walked over to where she was sitting. She saw him coming and didn't make a move. He smacked her out of her chair, hitting her flush across the face with his gloved hand, and she went to the floor without a sound. Her skin was red from her right eye down to her jawline, but it wouldn't bruise. The mitt had taken care of that. He pulled it off and put it back where he'd gotten it, straightening it out with the palm of his hand, and walked out of the kitchen past me, where I stood drinking a glass of milk, and didn't look back. My mom didn't use the kitchen much after that, but when she did cook, she still used that damn rooster mitt.

LOADING THE GUN

A couple of years ago my father was away, in Austin, and one rainy afternoon my mom caught me in our garage, loading and unloading his Ruger Mini-14 with a few of the rounds I'd stolen. I thought it was safe to touch because he didn't carry that gun anymore for work, kept it stored and empty in the gun locker at the house with several others he'd collected, including those he planned to display at his office but hadn't mounted or repaired yet. It sat there ignored, and I'd had the combination for some time, so whenever I thought I could get away with it, I'd sneak into that locker and stare at all those guns—dark and heavy, foreboding.

The Ruger most of all, the one that had killed Dillon Holt. I wondered how many of the others had a story, too. That afternoon I got up the nerve to get that rifle out, put my naked hands on it—spent an hour or more working the action, testing the sights, loading and reloading. I'd shot skeet once or twice, but until that moment I had never held a real gun as long as I held that Ruger, examining every inch of it, the metal and wood against my fingertips—feeling its weight, and how it settled soft against my shoulder as I aimed it through a wall, into the house beyond. When my mom saw me, I fully expected her to scream, to yell or come grab me. Something. Instead, she just stood for long minutes in the garage door from the kitchen, unreadable. Before reminding me that when I was done, I needed to put it back exactly as I'd found it.

Exactly. Then she turned away, shutting the door behind her.

WATCHING ME

My mom always used to watch me out of the corner of her eye, through her dark sunglasses—in the reflections of mirrors and door glass, thinking I never saw her. It was like OCD, a kind of mental handwashing: constantly checking up on me, to make sure that I was there or was okay. A little bit of it was wariness too, fear she didn't want to admit, couldn't admit—a need to know if that terrible dark thing inside my father had taken root inside me as well. What would she have done if she had decided I was like my father? If she knew for certain that awful and dangerous things hid behind my eyes and lurked in my hands? I don't know; maybe she didn't, either. Maybe there was even another fear, much worse. Not that I might be like my father, but what would happen to her if I wasn't.

She watched me all the time, like when I got pneumonia one September. I was sicker than hell, a sweating mess trapped in my bed, out of school for more than a week. My mom sat with me the entire time. I drifted in and out, waking up to see her at my bedside, reading a book, talking on her phone, but always watching me. She talked to me while I dozed just so I could hear her voice and know that she was there, finally revealing stories about herself. About college and someone named Jim she still dreamed about once in a while. About finding her mother dead on the bathroom floor from a heart attack, and the first time she kissed a boy, his hand fumbling underneath her shirt and how she'd been too afraid to tell him to stop, but not sure she wanted him to anyway.

All about how her favorite color was purple, but she was pretty partial to yellow as well; that she didn't like the taste of beer but could stomach it; was afraid she could find a taste for wine, so she didn't keep it in the house. How she hated Murfee but loved Texas, how she needed me always to be a gentleman and what that really meant, and how she liked to stand out in our yard in the dark and look straight up at the stars, count them until the blood drained from her head, leaving her dizzy, like she'd done when she was a little girl.

She knew I heard most of what she said, hanging on each of those tiny secrets, but she didn't care. She wanted me to know all of those things and more. She was gone a few months later and she might have seen that in the stars as well, a glimpse of things to come. Even now I can still feel the weight of her hand on my forehead, my burning cheek. The touch of her fingers pushing my damp hair back from my face. Her breath against my eyes, bending down to kiss me good night.

Goodbye.

20

DARIN

His name really was Darin; that part was true and
always had been. Just not Darin *Braddock*. He was
born Darin Braccio in Howard Beach, New York, where
his ex-wife Sara and their two girls now lived. She divorced him and returned there after she couldn't take
Texas or him or both anymore.

"I never knew Texas could be this cold," Morgan said,
shifting in the Tahoe's seat.

"Yep, my mother used to say 'cold as a witch's tit.'
Ever fucking heard that?"

"Um, no." She laughed, peering through her dark
window. Chief Deputy Duane Allen Dupree's house was
a couple of miles distant, the security lights visible, windows aglow, everything around it black and empty and
endless. Darin knew that's the way she wrote his name in

the notes she was keeping—the whole thing, every letter of it.

"He doesn't really, you know, do much, does he?" she asked.

Darin glanced up from the issued iPad in his lap. He was playing solitaire. If Dupree had lived, *you know*, like anywhere near civilization, they could have put a camera up on his house, piped the feed to the iPad or even back to the office. But the redneck deputy lived so far out, even for Murfee, that a video feed was tough, and the tech request would have tipped his hand anyway to Garrison about his real interest out here, forcing them instead to do it the old-fashioned way—actually following Dupree around, the other deputies too, even Sheriff Stanford Ross, whom Darin had heard speak at a Texas Narcotics Officers Association conference. *Lifestyle surveillance* was damn hard work anywhere, and damn near impossible in the middle of nowhere. He and Morgan had been in and out of Murfee for two weeks, staying at a hotel in Valentine, and hadn't seen a goddamn thing.

Not counting the night Dupree had cranked off a handful of rounds into the dark. Now, that had been exciting. Darin was almost to the point of conceding that he was barking up the wrong tree, even as his instincts, honed over all of the years, whispered otherwise. He might be a lousy husband and a marginal father, but Darin Braccio was a damn good agent.

For the life of him he couldn't figure out why he used that name, *her name*, when Deputy Cherry pulled them over. They were coming back from this exact spot, on the heels of a full night of watching Dupree's house after that silly carnival, when he'd been caught by complete surprise by the blue and red lights ablaze in his rearview. He even thought about making a run for it, but Morgan insisted they pull over and bullshit their way through the late-night traffic stop. Basically lie, because she didn't want some local deputy to flip his prowler, crashing trying to catch them. She had a weirdly honed sense of honesty.

His ex-wife's name had just slipped out, even though Morgan didn't have any kind of undercover backstop in that name or any other. She hadn't been in the division long enough. Hell, she hadn't been in Texas long enough for much of anything, including getting a state license. He should have just called her by her real name with a different set of lies, been done with it. The deputy had stared hard at her out-of-state ID even as he pretended not to, so he must have picked up on it—there was no way he missed it. But he never made an issue of it, and Darin couldn't figure out why. No matter what side of the fence he was on, what they'd dug up on Chris Cherry suggested he wasn't a dummy, not like this other country fuck-up they'd been watching.

Darin remembered seeing Cherry play at Baylor. Big guy, great arm.

If Morgan wondered why the hell he'd called her by his ex-wife's name, she was smart enough, even for a new agent, not to raise it. You learn a lot about each other when you're on surveillance, sitting in a car for hours together staring at someone, hoping something, any-thing, will happen. Right or wrong, Morgan had already learned plenty about him.

Though it was tough to call what they were doing real surveillance: just two weeks of sitting out in some fields behind this hick Duane Dupree's fucking shack, watching a whole lot of nothing. Darin wasn't sure what he hated more. His ex-wife or Texas. At least they'd agreed on the latter.

"You know, this sort of stuff, the job, always looked more interesting on TV." She chuckled, handing him the bag of almonds she'd been picking through. It was her joke, a favorite—she'd said it four or five times already. Before becoming an agent she had been an accountant—DEA was always on the lookout for accountants and stockbrokers, money people, because nowadays money was the blood, not the dope. You could seize dope all day and sometimes feel like it didn't matter, like it didn't move the needle. (Although it mattered to the bad guys, very much so; enough that some of them ended up in very small boxes or quartered into Hefty garbage bags along the freeway.) But take their money? That hurt the fuckers where it hurt the most. Darin wasn't a money guy, never had been. He couldn't balance his checkbook and hadn't tried to in years; his bad guys had stored their cash in ratholes and attics. The sly ones had used the spare tire in the trunks of their fucking cars.

Morgan was the new DEA. He'd read her academy profile, where she'd finished third in her class: shot well enough, aced the law and report-writing blocks, but exhibited indecision during practicals. He'd contacted an old buddy in training, and the real version squared pretty much with the write-up: polite and professional, very eager to learn. She hadn't broken up any marriages and was well liked, working hard to put in the extra time to get her gun qualifications up to par. El Paso, the border, hadn't been one of her top three assignments, but it never was, for anyone. Still, needs of the agency and all that found her shipped out here anyway. She was unmarried but had kind of a boyfriend back east. Her dad was ex-military and she'd joined DEA to push herself—make him proud and see the world and chase the excitement.

Murfee, Texas, wasn't what she had in mind.

She was attractive and had a weird sense of humor and an amazing way of stealing food off your plate without even asking, and sharing sips of your morning coffee, and a younger Darin might have fallen madly in love with her. It was probably for the best that this younger guy didn't exist anymore.

He followed up her observation. "Sure, everything always looks more interesting on TV. Ordering a fucking pizza, going to fucking Target. Drinking fucking orange juice. Nothing is that fucking exciting." He tossed a handful of her almonds down. Nuts, beef jerky, energy bars: the basic food groups for surveillance.

She threw an almond at him. "Please, really, don't try to protect my illusions."

"Fuck all that," he crunched.

"You know, you sure say *fuck* a lot."

He wasn't sure what they had, if anything at all. It had started and ended, and started again, with some radio and phone chatter, a handful of nonsense words bleeding between cell towers servicing both sides of the border: coded conversations bouncing between cheap radios and cellphones the narcos used to coordinate their dope moving over the river and across the desert.

DEA had long known that the Serrano brothers and Nemesio were both working this stretch of Texas, fighting each other for routes as they handed the border back and forth like a fucking baton in a bloody race. No one had been able to make much sense of the mess until a snitch surfaced. *The* snitch, wanting to come in bad, real bad, promising lots of good, very good intel. Not only about Nemesio, but even better—about cops on the take.

Darin hated crooked cops and agents most of all; all real cops did. Everyone had always been afraid the border was rotten on both sides, and here finally was a snitch claiming to know all about it. He should have. He was local, grew up in the area, and was crooked, too.

He was a BP agent named Rodolfo Reynosa. But just like that, he disappeared. Ran away, went south. That's what everyone figured at first—he'd played both ends and lost, or decided it was easier to spend Nemesio pesos than Uncle Sam dollars. That should have been the end of it—another snitch gone, another lost chance—and if he'd had a nickel for each of those, he could've retired a decade ago.

Except for that damn chatter, still bleeding all over the airwaves, and the fact that Darin was sometimes sleeping with Stephanie Ortega, an intel analyst, whose primary job was to analyze just that sort of noise. And she kept talking about it, wouldn't let it go, until he couldn't, either. Steph didn't cook worth a damn and was pretty average in bed, but worked absolute magic with her intercept data—like she had her own fucking crystal ball. She'd become convinced the narcos down here were looking for Reynosa as well, as if he'd up and vanished on them, too. She spun up some Nemesio call sheets of bad guys talking among themselves, a spiderweb in which each strand was a code word—*diablo* and *perrito* and *rana*—all tangled around Murfee. Steph believed one hundred percent Nemesio was out *hunting*, and these were very bad men to be hunted by. Half drug cartel and full-on lunatics, Nemesio wrapped themselves in witchcraft and worshipped narco saints like Jesús Malverde and dipped human skulls in gold to make fucking drinking mugs.

If Reynosa or another yokel out here in Murfee had crossed Nemesio—or if someone in a certain sheriff's department had gotten sideways with them—Darin might be here only to find the bodies and pick up the pieces. And if there really was a live public corruption angle, he was obligated to turn it over to the FBI anyway, or at least share it, sooner rather than later. However, since no one knew exactly what he was looking into down here, he hadn't felt pressed to do anything . . . yet.

He'd just wanted to come down here and poke around on his own, see what he could dig up, so had made up a bullshit excuse about another dead-end case so Garrison would sign off on the travel time and money. Of course Joe Garrison had *known* it was bullshit, complete bullshit right from the get-go, but let it pass anyway, because his boss also knew that Darin Braccio sometimes went a little stir-crazy if he didn't get out of the office—*out in the wild*—every now and then, but more often than not came through with something whenever he did. Garrison had been feeling extra generous because he'd also ordered Darin to drag Morgan along.

Darin wanted to say he agreed because she was new and needed the experience, but the truth was she was easy on the eyes and had a good sense of humor, and he loved the way she stole his food and drank his coffee. She also didn't know enough to question what the hell he was doing and how he was doing it. Not too much. Darin had been married for fifteen years and an agent for over eighteen, and that worked just fucking fine for him.

The lights went out at Dupree's house, but they were going to give it another final twenty minutes or so before heading out. He'd already replaced the iPad in his lap with two canned beers—tall boys, Budweisers. Another reason he'd been fine with Morgan coming on this little vacation—he knew she wouldn't rat on him. He didn't have a drinking problem, he drank just fine; just needed a few cold ones to round him out and help him sleep, and tonight he really wanted to sleep when he got back to their hotel in Valentine.

Already eyeballing his beers, he knew she was going to offer to drive, plead with him, really. But what were the odds they would run into Deputy Cherry or another one of Murfee's finest again? Pretty fucking slim. But she was looking out for him, and that wasn't a bad thing.

He was about to say as much, head off any argument before it had a chance to begin, when he stopped to look at her. Really look at her. She had her knees up, her chin in her hand, peering back out through the window as if something had caught her attention there. Her hair was free, hanging around her face, and although the car was dark, as dark as the night outside, he could see her clear. She was humming to herself, a silly song.

He didn't think much of his ex-wife, didn't see her as any sort of role model for his daughters, but Morgan Emerson? His girls could do a helluva lot worse than growing into the woman sitting next to him. Next time they came out to Texas for a visit, he might take them all out for a pizza, let them get to know each other. Let Morgan steal their food for once. He was smiling at that—about to mention it and hoping it wouldn't sound weird or awkward—when a sun flared behind him. Blinding him.

This time he wasn't going to fuck around lying. He was going to badge Deputy Dawg or the rancher out there checking on his cows and tell them it was government business and be fucking done with it. He slipped the beers into the floorboard and got his badge ready and told Morgan to do the same, reminding her to keep her hands visible. He was going to make it very clear that they were armed, so whoever the hell it was out there wouldn't freak out if they saw a gun. It was going to be real fucking awkward if it *was* Chris Cherry who'd slipped up on them again, but if it was anyone else, Darin figured they'd be okay. That's what he told Morgan when she asked.

"Are we all right?"

"Sure, we're okay, kiddo, no problem." He had only about twenty seconds to realize he was wrong. He saw it, but far too late. He'd told Morgan to have her badge ready, not her gun.

They really, really needed their guns. The man approaching with a flashlight aimed straight into their eyes wasn't wearing a uniform. He didn't appear to be wearing any clothes at all. And if Darin had lived, he'd have sworn that fucker's eyes glowed.

The first bullet came through the window. It punched glass and metal, sucking all the warm air and breath out of the Tahoe. Others followed, trailing glass and bits of seat stuffing and jacket fabric; the interior full of falling snow. Darin had enough time for one final decision: go for his own gun or throw his body over Morgan. She'd taken one already, blood hitting the windshield, rocking her head back and forth. Darin wanted to reach out, hold her head, pull her close to him, just to make that awful motion stop. He'd taken one or two as well; it might be his blood all over the windshield, too. It was pretty fucking tough to say.

Gun or Morgan? Morgan or gun? Darin Braccio never felt the final bullet take the top of his head off. He took it slightly under the left eye, traveling upward at an angle at 850 feet per second. That's because he'd covered Morgan Emerson, cradling her in his arms, his head where her heart would be. A shock wave rolled through his skull, turning the frontal and parietal bones into ash, leaving everything open and exposed. Revealing everything he had ever been to the night sky. He was long dead—gone—by the time the car burned, and the flames took all that had been left behind.

21

CHRIS

The morning after Darin Braccio burned, Chris was sitting at his desk when the early results on the body came in from Austin. Not a definite ID, not complete, not by a long shot.

Chris scanned through the e-mail as the DPS lab tech walked him through it on the phone. A lot of it was complicated, medical, hard-to-follow diagrams with arrows—ossification and sagittal sutures and sternum markers and pubic symphysis and pelvic shape. DNA typing from hair strands. It was still preliminary, the final report weeks away. He still didn't have a name, but he had something. Probably enough. A Caucasian. Most likely a Hispanic male, probably mid-twenties. A lack of bony ridges on the wrists indicated a person who never did a lot of manual work for a living, but then again, he hadn't lived all that long to begin with. Certain shattered bones and debris pointed to the most likely cause of death as a bullet through the skull.

After that, one or more large-fanged carnivores had worked over the extremities, the hands and the feet. One whole foot was gone, carried away. The other showed tooth marks. The dental ID Chris had hoped for? Next to impossible—all the dental work had been done south of the border. Shoddy, a couple of porcelain crowns, one of which had been blown through the lower palate by the passage of the phantom bullet. More than likely a high-velocity hand-gun round—a jacketed hollow-point—but they were still looking for fragments in the bones that remained. A serious bullet, but not a rare one. Not anymore. Not in Texas.

Long after Chris hung up, he continued to scan up and down the e-mail. He read and reread it, trying to fit the puzzle pieces together in a new way, hoping to come up with a different picture. The sky outside his window was cold and stale, the remnants of another, better day. It was the same color as all his worthless dental X-rays, scattered like fallen leaves around the house. With so little to go on—make that *nothing* to go on—identifying the body from Indian Bluffs was becoming an impossible mountain to climb; like the Chisos, all sheer cliffs and long drops below him. Chris had FlexiCuffs and a truck locker of suspicions, but those were damn small handholds. And no one was asking any questions, raising any concerns. Not one person was looking for the man he'd found; he was nameless, faceless, and destined maybe to stay that way. It was like he'd never existed at all. Everyone else had been right—a river killing. And to everyone else, that meant it didn't matter. It never did.

Just another dead Mexican in the desert, after all.

★ BLOOD ★

1
AMERICA

He hadn't put a hand on her yet.

Still, it took more than brushing her teeth hard, almost till her gums bled, or smoking a cigarette or some weed, or drinking three shots of tequila, to get the *thought* of the taste of him out of her. On more than one occasion, after getting one of his horrible pictures, she'd put her fingers down her throat and threw him up into her toilet. That was better, but not enough. Sometimes she worried she might never be rid of him. Sometimes she wanted to set herself on fire, just to burn herself clean. There was no one she could tell about Chief Deputy Dupree. How he wasn't afraid now to come right into her bedroom. How he called her *darlin'* and was always talking about taking her out to some abandoned lot or to the Comanche. How he sent her pictures of flowers and

dead dogs and once the picture of a knife held to a naked
throat and she didn't know who it was. How he strutted
around town with his badge and gun, *un gallo roto*, and
threatened to take care of her mama and papá and promised he knew all about Rodolfo: where he was and what
he was doing and how he'd take care of him, too. Dupree
had been stalking her for a year, but the things he'd already done would stay with her forever.

Dupree was one of those things she couldn't completely share with Caleb, like the money Rodolfo had left
her: double, even triple whatever number she'd told him,
wrapped in tight little bundles with electric tape. Like the
phone and, most of all, the gun. Rodolfo had given her
those too, in a plastic freezer bag, the night he left.

The last night she saw him.

The phone was cheap, an old flip unit, a brand she didn't
recognize. Rodolfo told her to keep it charged, to hold
on to it, but never to make any calls. If it rang, she was
only to check and see if it was him. If it wasn't, she was to
hang up. It rang—once—two weeks after he left. She'd
answered the call and heard a voice, scratchy, weak;
breathing from the other end of the phone.

¿Eres de Rana? ¿Dónde está Rana?

It wasn't Rodolfo, so she hung up, just as he'd told her
to do. The voice had asked about a frog, or someone
called Frog. She knew nothing about frogs, except they
were *verde*, green . . . green like Rodolfo's uniform, like
the stripes on his truck. She didn't understand and it had
scared her, but not so bad she hadn't carried that phone
every day since, charged and tucked into the bottom of
her bag, safe. Not so bad she didn't flip through the re-
cent call list looking for numbers she recognized, writing

them down on the back of one of her magazine cutouts taped to her wall. All Mexican numbers, but one. Just one number—*one call*—from a few hours before Rodolfo had given her the phone, his last night in Murfee, the night he disappeared. The only number she recognized, because for the last year she had seen it so many times on her own phone. *Darlin'.*

The gun was much nicer, but scared her in a whole different way. She'd never seen Rodolfo with a gun—he told her it was a gift. It was silver and pearl, had the image of the Virgen de Guadalupe and etchings of Pancho Villa and Jesús Malverde. It was stamped with several *calaveras*, grinning their toothy grins.

Rodolfo told her once about visiting the ranch across the river, that secret place where the gun had been given to him. All about the zoo they kept there, with real lions and tigers and peacocks; where he'd met a *brujo* who cast a spell on him to always protect him from harm. He brought her a peacock feather, or what he'd said was one, anyway, long and green and purple and shining like metal. There were other things he saw at that place he wouldn't tell her about, things that had made his lips quiver and his eyes go distant when he thought about them. He told her there was so much *potencia* at the ranch, so much power in those people, they glowed like the sun. They burned everything.

America loved her brother but had long ago accepted there was a weakness in him, a softness that drove her papa more than once to try and beat it out, to toughen him up and harden his skin. Her papa had wanted him callused, the way his own hands were cracked and bruised from hard work and the sun. But Rodolfo was pretty, like a girl, with a good singing voice. He liked his fancy food and cologne and both American and Tejano music and never roughhoused. To Rodolfo, it was better to make friends than fight. Better still to run away.

If their papa thought the Border Patrol would toughen him up, he'd been wrong about that, too. Rodolfo had looked good in his green uniform, shined shoes, and ironed shirt, but he worked just hard enough to stay cool in his truck, napping in the cab to music, with the dirty river rolling by, baking in the sun. For a few dollars here, a few more there, he let families slip across the border to look for work. Their stories, their troubles, moved him. America had loved her brother for that, but understood his flaws—flaws that had left her holding his money, a phone, and a gun. Left her worrying about where he'd gone and when he'd come home. *Better still to run away.*

Caleb had some of that same softness. He loved her, or thought he did, but she knew it was as much to hurt his own papa as anything else, even if Caleb didn't yet know it himself. They both lived in Murfee, but the river always lay between them. She was a Mex, a beaner, a wetback, and he was the son of El Juez. Caleb was too afraid to throw her straight into his father's face, but the time they spent together made its way back all the same. It was a foolish game, *juego peligroso*.

Foolish as allowing it to continue, but she was selfish in her own ways, because where there was softness, there was sweetness as well. Caleb had never tried to put his hands beneath her shirt or push against her, *pene* throbbing, asking her to *touch it a little, just look at it.*

He took her to Las Luces where they searched for *fantasmas* together, and he talked about the books he read and the journals he kept, and always, always, about leaving Murfee and taking her with him. Rodolfo used to say the same thing, so part of her knew those thoughts were all foolish too, but let him keep them anyway. Because she also had silly dreams of her own, things she'd never shared with Rodolfo, could never share with Caleb. Like how everything might have been different if *she*, rather than Rodolfo, had been wearing a green uniform and watching the river. Or how things might be after she finished school—moving away and changing her name, her hair; becoming someone and something else altogether. A doctor, a lawyer, maybe even *a deputy* herself in some other town. Carrying a badge and gun all her own.

So she liked hearing about all the places she guessed she'd never go while they lay on their backs in the bed of his truck at Las Luces, sharing cigarettes. As he talked and talked, she could see those places in the smoke above their heads: cities with tall glass buildings; beaches on a blue ocean with waves crashing and boats with colored sails. Caleb made those places more real than TV; he was a *brujo* and didn't know it. Casting spells she liked with his words.

According to Pilar, her mama's friend, her mama used to know *magia*—could weave small *hechizos* from hair and nails and drops of *sangre* and certain flowers. That is how she got America's papa to love her, and though America questioned the choice, she couldn't question the result. Her papa, old and battered and rough and quick to raise his hand to both her and Rodolfo, had never once done so to his *rosa*. He still sang songs to her, old ones that

America did not know, and every Sunday he brought her dusty flowers he'd picked from someone else's yard. Her mama always kept them in the same green jar until their petals dropped. America had asked her mama to teach her these things, but she'd waved America away, said Pilar was *loca*. It was all so much nonsense now. She'd lost her *magia* and all of her belief in it after crossing the river. Left it all behind in *el mundo viejo*, the small village in which she was raised. *Perdemos mucho*.

That's what had happened to Rodolfo. The spells cast on him in Ojinaga had lost their power here, leaving him no longer protected, no longer safe. Still, America longed for that kind of *magia*. For revenge, and Dupree's eyes bleeding and his *pene* turning black, exploding in his hands. For *lobos* sitting at his door to tear out his throat when he tried to run, *fantasmas* haunting him as he'd haunted her.

Dupree finally burning and that horrible smile catching fire.

Because even if there was no real *magia* in the world anymore, that didn't mean *those* things still couldn't come true; so much more real and possible than any of Caleb's stories or her own silly dreams of a different life. Her *magia* was Rodolfo's phone—the one he'd left behind and that she kept so close. He'd said they *glowed like the sun . . . they burned everything*. She didn't know who they were, had no idea what sorts of things might hold the other end of that phone or if they would even help her—*¿Dónde está Rana?*—but she knew where they were. At the ranch, with the peacocks and their metal feathers. Just across the river.

2

MÁXIMO

He drank horchata through a straw, standing by the gate. The machete in his waistband scratched him, rubbed sharp against his ribs, while he waited to kill the man. He wanted a gun but was told to use the machete. He was to make it messy. They wanted to send *un mensaje*.

He understood their messages. He'd been sending them since he was eleven years old, when he first killed for them, shot a man in the face with an old gun wrapped in tape while high on good weed. He'd laughed at the mess, the gun blasting sparks and powder, and hadn't looked back as the man fell, blood everywhere. He was chewing gum, American gum—Big League Chew—and almost choked on it because he'd been laughing so much. Happy or afraid? He did not know. There had been so many more since. He was seventeen years old.

He smiled at a pretty girl walking past his driver, Lugo, whose face was only a pair of dark sunglasses. Lugo didn't notice the girl, but he did. He finished the horchata but kept the empty cup, sucking on the dry straw, a kid waiting for a bus. It was one of a thousand little lessons Chava had taught him before Chava himself got taught a lesson, burning alive in a barrel full of diesel gas, a real *guiso*. He helped light his old friend on fire and had watched him boil, the stink of it gagging. He'd liked Chava.

They gave him two hundred American dollars a week and lots of weed and places to stay. He had a nice phone and girls whenever he wanted and *rojo* Lucchese boots with the shadows of naked *niñas* picked out in silver. He dressed nice and looked older than his age. He stayed out all night in bars wearing the jewelry of dead men and watched *fútbol* games and talked to real women, not just girls. If anyone ever said anything to him, even the *policía*, all he did was make his eyes flat and black like river stones and say Nemesio and they walked away, *rápido*. It was a good life. He'd run with a *pandilla* until Chava found him and called him his *hermano menor*. Chava taught him how to hold a gun and use a knife, took him to the *rancho* and showed him other secrets. Chava's *jefes* had liked him right off because he was young, smart, fast. They would not let him get tattoos of any kind and they talked about how he was an *americano* and how that was a good thing. *Una cosa muy buena*. Someday he would no longer have to make his way by killing. They told him he might become a *jefe* himself, at least a *jefe poco*, *un teniente*, like Chava. They smiled when they said it, a smile that died below their eyes, and then always put a gun in his hand anyway. He was in no hurry for *someday*. He liked killing, and he was very good at it.

Besides, he saw what had happened to Chava.

The man breaks from the door of the small street-level apartment; he's on a cellphone. He's been hiding in that spot a week, not showering because the water was off. He stinks, smells himself, his own fear. He's been collecting money but not fast enough. Not enough, because there is never enough time or money in the world.

He sees a thin kid in an Avengers T-shirt leaning against the light pole, pulling on a straw in a Styrofoam cup, a book bag resting against the tip of his red boots. Waiting for the bus. Tapping his foot to music only he can hear. His boot edge shimmers with silver, grinning like a skull. Once clear of the door, the man finally catches sight of the car parked sideways down the street, the driver thick and bug-faced behind huge black sunglasses. He hears the engine, the car running, waiting for him, and he knows what that means. He turns to bolt the other way, past the boy, who drops the empty cup on the ground and smiles.

The boy is the lookout. But he is wrong about that, too.

Máximo hit the man in the throat with the machete. Not the face. . . . They'd been very, very clear about that. They needed the man's face. The first strike drove the man to his knees, sent his cellphone flying and blood high against the door he'd come out of and all over both of their faces. The man pissed and shit himself, and Máximo hit him again and again, chopping him to the ground. The dead man fell beside the empty horchata cup, his blood filling it. It wasn't just about the face. They wanted the man's *cabeza*. The whole head. *Todo*.

Later he took a cold shower to get the blood from underneath his fingernails and out of his eyelashes and hair. Then he smoked the weed Lugo had brought for him and drank a cold beer, so cold that ice still hung on it, so cold it numbed the hand that had held the machete. He pulled on his Luccheses and his new green shirt and combed his hair back and sat on Matador's porch near the paper lanterns, trying to look for stars high above them and lonely girls beneath them at the bar. He was going to stay up way past dawn, until both the lanterns and the stars were pale and dead, anything not to sleep.

Anything not to dream of *todos los ojos*. He couldn't remember the faces of his brothers or his parents. His *abuela* was a haze of gray hair and curled hands and yellowed fingernails. He dreamed only of *los muertos*. They all stared at him the exact same way, with their dead *ojos*, asking the same thing; anything not to answer their question.

¿Qué eres tú?

3

THE JUDGE

Most people didn't know there had been an older brother, Hollis. They rode horses together on the family ranch in Pecos, land that had been his brother's birthright. Even after Hollis died—an accident—the Judge knew he would never have that land, the soil his father and grandfather had worked and owned and drilled and sweated and bled upon. He shot the horse that had thrown Hollis—drove up and dumped it on the close-cut grass for his father to see, while his mother cried. That's why he told everyone he was a self-made man.

The Judge listened to Phil Tanner, hearing nothing, even though his lips were moving. Mouth opening and closing like a big pale fish, standing in front of the computer running his PowerPoint presentation, aiming a laser pointer at the screen. Tanner continued talking to

Murfee's town council, but the Judge kept him turned down, like the volume on a TV.

It was a talent he had, to make people silent, mute, even when they were right in front of him. To smile and talk from behind a perfect mask so he could simply focus on other, more important things. Like now . . . and killing Duane Dupree.

The bodies had been discovered far past Valentine, in the badlands of the Ojinaga Cut. The man had been DOA, but the other, a young woman, had survived both the bullets and the burning—their car found on fire down at the water's edge by a handful of wetbacks making the crossing. Somehow, unimaginably, the woman had crawled free and put out her own flames in the river. Now she was in a coma in El Paso. The wetbacks had come forward because they were just smart enough not to want to take the fall for two federal agents. They probably saved her life, and their reward was a round of beatings and one-way tickets back to Mexico City. They'd each paid as much as $5,000 to get as far as they had, money it would take them years to earn again.

The story made the national press, a three-day splash. But other than the Dallas memorial for the dead agent, the story had started to fade. Muted, like Phil Tanner now. And that made no sense. The feds should still have been turning Valentine and the other nearby border towns upside down looking for blood, but they weren't, not publicly. He'd made a few calls, but no one was saying much, not even to him. There were whispers, suggestions: maybe the two had been off the reservation or were secret lovers. A Texas Ranger told him booze was involved. Whatever it was, everyone was treading lightly, and if that was a worry—and it was—the bigger one was that two federal agents were poking around to begin with, and he'd never caught wind of it.

Even after telling Duane to keep an eye out for just such a thing. The very *same* Duane Dupree already half-way to crazy like his dead daddy Jamison; leaving behind a trail of blood and fire. Of that he had no doubt, and that's what he should have seen coming. After all, he'd contemplated killing Duane Dupree before, but there was never a good time . . . a *necessary* reason. Now was pretty damn close, though.

Tanner finished his presentation, turned it over to Terry Macrae, the council chair, who brought the meeting to a close. Terry was a decent man, as good as there was in Murfee, not like Phil Tanner, who liked his kiddie porn, the younger the better. He kept it on his school computer, probably spent time with his pants down behind his office door, staring at his pictures and the kids out in the school hallways, even if they were a bit old for his taste. Murfee was full of long shadows, and the Judge knew all the secrets others tried to hide in them. He saved them, held on to them, knowing they all had value. More precious than gold, most became damn near priceless, eventually.

Tanner liked his kiddie porn and Matty Bulger got a nigger girl pregnant in Odessa. Johnny Mulgrew once beat a hooker to death in Hastings and thought every now and then about picking up another. He'd even dug a plot out at his place, a cellar but more like a cell, where he might keep her for a while.

His own deputy, Dawes, liked his kiddie porn too, and Carter Lawson's wife wanted you to punch her when you fucked her. Dana Lawson also liked to step out on her husband whenever he was on the road, which was a lot, and wasn't above snorting a little coke or meth she'd bought from Eddie Corazon, bought with her mouth around his cock, and inviting a couple of the high school football players over for a good time. Martin Thorn finally broke down and put a pillow on his daddy's head so he'd *just fucking die* because he needed that little bit of insurance money for his big gambling problem and a little beaner girl he kept on the side.

He drove around his town in the dark, watching it. Windows down, no matter how cold it might be outside. He was long past the point of questioning why. It could keep nothing from him, hide nothing. He cruised past Anne Hart's house.

She looked different now from when he'd first met her, and then later when he saw the news stories and pictures in the paper. He liked her hair color better before, the cut of it too, but there was plenty of time for all that. Tanner and his old friend Dial Montgomery had pulled her teaching and personnel records for him, and the Austin and Killeen police departments had generously shared their investigative files. He had a pretty good all-around picture of Anne Hart, had peeked a bit under her skin and knew what made her tick. It was another gift, like his ability to focus with the weight of the sun. But he still made a point of driving up to her place like this a couple of times a week to see what cars were parked outside. Just keeping an eye on what she was up to.

In the coming days he'd make a few phone calls, edge around the investigation of the burned agents, although he truthfully didn't expect anyone to say for certain they'd been spying on his town . . . on *him*. He'd find no proof or suggestion, no confirmation they'd been here at all, but knew better—and when someone else looked hard enough, they'd know it too, leading them inevitably to Duane, who'd been obedient, loyal, steady until recently. Duane—now gone rabid, a threat to everything and everyone that had to be put down. If he'd made any mistake, it was not dealing with Duane sooner. You always lived with the threat of a wellhead fire in a man like Duane, something finally blowing loose inside his skull once and for all. He'd watched many of those in his family's fields in Pecos, powerful coils of blood-black fire, visible for miles. Or Dupree was a sulfur flare: burning so damn bright, just to burn out twice as quick, with nothing left to show for it but a handful of bitter smoke and ash. Just like Duane had left that girl on the riverbank.

A very long time ago the Judge had spent days alone out in the Pecos hills, the badlands. Summer mornings he was gone before sunup, losing himself in the dark before the sun burned it all away. Once he stumbled on an abandoned mining camp, a few shacks choked with weeds and grass; so removed and out of place that he wasn't sure where or if there was even a shaft. He'd dreamed of all the things he could do with a deep hole like that all his own, a hole in the heart of the world. There had also been his grandfather's old wooden hunting blind, where he sat when the sun came over the mountains. Where he once took Celia Martin's cat and drove nails into it after it had bit him. There had been other animals, frogs and fish he took from the creek—so many that the stand itself went sour with the blood of things he had killed there. It stank, a smell so rank it kept the deer away and his father and Hollis were unable use it anymore, unsure of why the wood was always so dark and damp with fresh blood. He took no pleasure in the killing. It wasn't about *that*, it never was. He just wanted a peek under the skin, peel it back a bit to see what made other living things tick.

When he was a little older and had an old cast-off mare of his own, he rode along the dry creeks and out on the desert trails, searching for Spanish gold and bones and ghost towns. Riding as far as he could go. Until later, when he stole for the first time, but not the last—taking every thin nickel of Agnes Colfield's under-the-mattress money and adding it to what he'd already got from selling his old nag for dog food so he could buy a dented Pontiac from Buchman's and really wander afield. As far as he could go. Truth be told, he'd done more than just pinch Agnes Colfield's money; he hadn't left it at that. And her eyes, even thick with glaucoma, had been open and staring right at him the whole time, knowing who it was doing those things to her.

He wasn't worried she'd ever tell; knew she'd never breathe a word of it, or nothing anyone would believe. His father had once said she had softening of the brain, what they then called old-timer's disease, and how it made her tremble and forget things. Sometimes she saw things too, people who weren't there and never were. She also had a pretty daughter living in Monahans, not that far away really, not after he got that car of his own to drive up there and visit if he ever had a mind to. So he reminded Agnes of that as her brain slipped a gear and she started repeating the girl's name over and over again, crying out softly for the daughter who wasn't there, just as he got started.

Later, they saw each other at the Dairy Freeze, Sunday after church, and he bought her a cone with her own money. She took it from him without a word, her frail liver-spotted hand shaking hard, but only he could see, so everyone watching him that day—watching him buy old Agnes a cone, chatting her up—knew that he was a fine young gentleman, destined to go places. He had been ever since, as far as he could go. So far he could never come back. He drove back and forth across his town, as empty and distant as the heavens above it, with a gun in his lap—a habit he'd picked up so long ago he couldn't remember when it began.

4

CALEB

I didn't believe it at first. I didn't *want* to believe it.

I didn't learn it from my father, of course. I saw it in the *Daily* like everyone else, with Amé reading over my shoulder. I wanted to find Cherry and scream that he was wrong and somehow messed it all up. I wanted to believe my father or Duane changed the results or fixed the tests in Austin or paid someone to do it. The body at the ranch wasn't my mother, just another lost soul. It felt like I lost her all over again.

I've always lived with the fear that my dad might hurt me. It was only a few years ago that I finally understood why. Hunting is a big deal around here, and you might think with all the land and the desert that you could pretty much walk out anywhere and shoot just about anything, but that's far from the truth. Hunting has its own calendar, its own killing seasons, and since most of Texas is state park or private ranchland, you have to pay for the right to kill—like my father, who bought distant acreage from the Sierra Escalera for his deer and elk hunting. It's remote and untended and he could charge a fortune for other hunters to use it, but he won't, never has. It's all his. He built blinds overlooking the feeding areas and creek crossings so he can spot and stalk whatever is in season. That way he can kill without ever being seen or heard. He calls it El Dorado. He told my mom he was taking me with him to check the blinds and fencing and that we would be gone a few days. My mom stood in the driveway when we left at first light, chewing her lip raw, hovering too near the truck even as he backed out. She never said a word, just watched us all the way down the street. It was a long drive and my father made calls until he was out of cell coverage. Then he stared out the window while I read a book.

It's hard to say when the road gave way to canyons, when rural became wild. I dozed, already fighting some sort of cold or infection even before we left; woke up to gray skies, dozed again. When my father hunted alone he often used horses from the Sierra Escalera ranch, but we drove straight into the hills, following paths or roads or signs only he knew, high enough that the desert gave way to pine and ridge. We were at the blackened edge of the earth, at the end of everything with night rising fast, when he finally stopped. He sat with his hands on the wheel, watching the trees sway, before he turned to me.

"I thought I told you to handle that Carver boy," he said, and I shook my head, at first not even knowing what he was talking about. "I thought I told you to handle that *nigger*, the one that's been all over you. The. Basket-ball. Team. Caleb." He said it very slow, hitting each

"So what about you? And Caleb? You've never had a desire to leave?"

The sheriff shook his head. "I've been here so long even I tend to forget that I'm not a Murfee native. My roots aren't natural, but they run deep. Work takes me away quite a bit, but I always come back. I've had offers to do other things, someone always wants me to run for a state office, but nothing I've seriously entertained. Caleb, of course, will go off to school, and after that, I guess we'll see." The sheriff finished his beer, raised his hand for another. "How's Caleb doing, by the way? No problem, I hope?"

"No, none at all. He's a good student. Quiet." She paused, chose her words carefully. "I'm not sure he has a lot of friends."

"No, he never has. More of a loner that way, like his mother, actually. After his mother left, it got worse."

"I've heard that. I'm so sorry. It must have been hard for both of you."

The sheriff blinked, slow, as a new round of drinks arrived, unordered. "I think Murfee was too small for her, Anne. Nothing more than that."

During the rest of dinner he never mentioned Evelyn again or asked her anything else about Marc. His lost wife was a ghost the sheriff didn't believe in and refused to be haunted by, and if nothing else, she admired that will, that commitment. Instead, they talked about their respective lives, about the safe parts for her that didn't raise specters. Sheriff Ross proved to be charming, surprisingly eloquent; good-looking in a rugged, weather-stained way. But their ages surfaced nearly everywhere, their frame of references so different. She wasn't sure, but he word as if I was near deaf, but by then I understood. I was playing JV basketball at the time, not well or for many game minutes, but I was on the team. One of the other players who played my position, Antonio Carver, had been giving me a hard time, pushing me around, calling me names—*fag*, stuff like that. It was dumb, it was high school, but it had gotten back to my father, like everything.

He'd already told me a month earlier to take care of Carver, but I hadn't. My father came to the games because he had to, because it was expected, but he didn't like sitting there watching me sit at the end of the bench. A Ross in Murfee didn't sit at the end of the bench ever. My father brought me all the way out to the middle of nowhere to remind me of that, to have that one conversation. The trip was never about hunting; it was always about me.

The windows were down and the truck was cold, getting colder, and I was scared. The night was rusted, broken and dangerous, and I sat there with my own father, terrified of what he was going to say or do next.

"Did you know, Caleb, there was a time when I didn't think you were mine?" I didn't answer or dare move. "You may not believe me, but that's not an easy thing to say. I know it's not an easy thing to hear. That means I've had to live with the notion that another man crawled up between your mother's legs and put you there . . . put you on me. Can you know how that makes a man feel? The only saving grace is that I would feel no responsibility for you, either. I could abandon you, leave you in a place like this, and never look back. Who would blame me?" He sighed, looked beyond me to someplace else. "But I've had to accept that you are mine, blood and bone, and therefore every inch my goddamn responsibility. You're mine to raise and teach and by God, if nothing else, turn into a man." His eyes were the darkest thing in the truck. "And although before we're done you might wish it to be different, that's the way of it now. Do you understand me?"

I nodded.

"I told you to handle that business with that nigger and you didn't. Now you have that little nigger boy feeling comfortable pushing you around, and if you don't handle your business with him, he'll push you around forever and so will everyone else. I won't allow it, so you can't, either." He got out of the truck and walked around to my side, opened my door, a gentleman, holding it wide. I clung to the seat until he grabbed my shoulder and tumbled me onto the grass and dirt.

"It's okay to be scared, Caleb, I don't blame you. There are things you should be scared of. A smart man recognizes them, quick."

I understood it all, then: *One of those things is me.*

"I'm going to get back in my truck and drive away and you're going to stay here the night. This is your land, or it will be one day, and this is your first chance to get to know it. We've got a couple of big cats that prowl up here, old painters that have survived long past their time. I've seen their tracks. I could hunt them down, but I like knowing they're here. They keep the other animals vigilant. Hell, they keep me on my toes, too.

"You're going to find a place to tuck in and you're going to think about this talk. Indian tribes had ceremonies to make their boys into men. This is no different. If you come to understand me and you're ready to do as you're told, then in the morning when I come back for you, we'll make the run the rest of the way up to Sierra Escalera and have a damn fine breakfast, best in Texas. If you don't tell your mother, I'll even let you have a dark beer and a shot of whiskey with your biscuits and gravy, which is a pretty damn fine thing, too. But if you think you're already man enough, then you walk your ass out of here tonight and keep on walking."

He shut my door over me and returned to his side of the truck, leaning on the hood. He seemed larger than the trees behind him, and I couldn't find his face. "If you weren't my son, I wouldn't even come back for you. Never forget that." He slapped his hand on the hood, a sudden noise that carried forever, like he was summoning all of the night's terrors right to my spot, letting them know I was there. Then he drove away, whistling, with me still sitting on the grass.

I used to read about knights. About kings and castles and how a squire on the night before his knighting ceremony had to hold a vigil, staying awake and praying on his knees on a future life. Not so different from my father's Indian rituals. Some claimed they had visions or were visited by angels or glimpsed the future as they waited through the night. At the ceremony itself, the knight-to-be dressed in white cloth for purity and wore a red robe over that to prove his willingness to be wounded. Then they put a blade in his hands, to show his willingness to kill. Maybe all I had that night were visions, fueled by fever and sickness as the temperature dropped and the whole sky froze in place.

I know I curled against the rocks as the big cats screamed in the dark; got so close I saw their eyes on fire, felt their breath. I know I counted my own breaths and waited for shadows to move, and then they did, turning into snakes and other dangerous things that circled me in the night. I know at one point there was rain—quick, cold, like falling glass or broken stars—and I dreamed of a sword that became a gun in my hand. I know that the rain and cold worsened the ear infection I later learned I'd been suffering from, ravaging my left ear, so I've never been able to hear out of it quite the same way. I also know I saw *my* futures there, all of them, and understood then why my father hated me so much—not because I wasn't his son, but because I *was*.

And when dawn finally came, and with it a set of head-lights creeping over the hills, I was still right where he'd left me, frozen and pale and shaking so hard I could barely stay upright, kneeling in the muddy tire tracks from the day before.

Three days later I caught Antonio Carver behind school with a sock filled with quarters. He never saw me, never heard me, but I whispered "I'm sorry" with each swing. I broke that kid's jaw in two places, and after that there was some kind of trouble with his father, who also ended up bloody and battered by Duane Dupree and had to spend a day or two in my father's lockup because of it. Then they all moved away. I quit the team the next season. It was a week after I attacked Antonio Carver that I stole the first handful of my father's 5.56x45mm Ruger rifle cartridges.

I don't think Amé truly believed it was my mom anyway, but she put her arms around me and told me it was okay when she saw how upset I was. She held me tight. She held me for *real*, and her heart beat against me as she whispered, *Un día vamos a volar como los pájaros, muy lejos de aquí*. It was something about birds and flying away, and she didn't mean it. That's because we're both trapped here, held back by the hands of our ghosts. She can no more leave Murfee without knowing what happened to Rudy Ray than I can without proving what my father did to my mother.

I'd been holding my own vigil since she disappeared, one longer and darker than when my father left me on the mountain, right until that very moment I had Amé's face against my neck and neither of us was quite willing to let go—the moment I *had* another vision like those from that night, the very thing I'd missed all along. I'd been so focused on my mother, I had never even considered the *other* possibility, the only other one that made sense, right from the very beginning.

When I told Amé, she laughed without really laughing.

She called me dumb, *lerdo*, even as her eyes said something else. Her eyes *hated* me for even thinking it, let alone saying it out loud. *She believes he is coming back.* Just as much as I needed to believe it was my mom buried in the desert, she wouldn't accept the truth that Rudy Ray never left for Houston or Mexico or a beach somewhere. He's been here all along, still trapped, like the rest of us. And after I said it, gave it a voice, she pushed me away, hard, and then slapped me across the mouth before I could say it again.

5

CHRIS

After the carnival they saw each other all the time—running into each other at the Hamilton, walking past each other on Main. They always stopped and talked for a moment, about books and the master's degree he never finished. The places they both knew in Waco or whatever was going on at the school. She was polite and so was he—they both might've been sharing thoughts about the weather but knew they weren't, and each time they stood a little longer, a little closer, and talked for a few minutes more. The last time was in the Hi n Lo parking lot. Dusk—standing together in stray light—as cars maneuvered around them. He'd dug up his old copy of *Something Wicked This Way Comes* from the boxes still sitting in the hall and had been carrying it around in his truck, waiting for a good time, the right time. She'd

laughed when he handed the beat-up book to her, remembering their walk at the carnival. She promised to
read it again and give it back when she was done, but he
said not to worry about it, it was fine. They talked—she
holding the few groceries she'd come for, he juggling
the ones he'd bought but didn't need. Neither feeling
their weight.

He didn't know what he thought he was doing talking
to Anne Hart, thinking about her so much, but if nothing
else, she'd been keeping his mind off other things: his
problems with Melissa, the body from Indian Bluffs. And
that night out at the Lights.

He'd dumped the dashcam video on a thumb drive and
never said a word about it, and couldn't even think of a
good reason why. At the time, it just made sense. A week
later, when those two agents were discovered in Valentine, he still didn't say anything, but brought the video
home, hidden in his kit bag. He let a few more days tick
by. It wasn't that he didn't want to look at it; he just
didn't know what was going to happen, what he'd have to
do after he did.

He and Mel had another silent dinner and she was already in bed and asleep when he finally pulled out the
drive and downloaded the file to their laptop, pulling up
the video. He moused back and forth again and again.
Time, winding and rewinding. The two weren't visible,
less than shadows, and he was misshapen, monstrous,
leaning over the vehicle, which was also unnaturally
curved in the small-field view of the camera. None of that
mattered. The make and model and license plate were
clear.

In the picture in the *Daily*, the Tahoe was a burned-out hulk, the fire's horrible hands twisting it into even more impossible shapes than the dashboard camera. He couldn't imagine how "Sara"—Special Agent Morgan Emerson—had crawled out of that thing . . . how she'd survived. Word was she still might not. Agents Braccio and Emerson had lied to him from the get-go. Maybe because they were just sneaking around together, hiding a relationship. He thought about all of his run-ins with Anne Hart, and although it wasn't the same thing, not by a long shot—not yet, anyway—wasn't that how it always started?

"No, Deputy, you won't. My only trouble is a significant other in El Paso who isn't named Sara, and who thinks I'm in Midland at a conference, if you know what I mean."

But Braccio was divorced, his family in New York. His ex-wife and his two daughters had flown into Dallas for the memorial for his death. He'd seen a picture of them in their black dresses as someone in uniform out of frame, out of focus, handed the older daughter—but still so goddamn young—a folded flag. According to the paper, Braccio's ex-wife's name was Sara.

There was confusion about where they were staying. Some reports put them in a hotel in Valentine, about thirty miles from where they were found on the river— word was they had *separate* rooms—but the DEA wouldn't confirm it; not where they stayed or how long they'd been there. No one ever mentioned the pair visiting the Lajitas Resort, either, and Chris knew from a call he'd made out there—even before watching the video— that no one named Braccio or Braddock or Emerson had ever reserved a room.

He'd placed the call from his truck, on his own cell, away from the other deputies. And like saving and then hiding the video, he couldn't quite say why.

Valentine . . . Lajitas. You could draw a long crooked line from one to the other, and there was only one place between them. Only one place on the whole goddamn map that mattered . . .

Murfee.

He was still driving that stretch of road in his head when Mel suddenly spoke, sitting up in bed.

"What are you doing?"

He closed the video, hiding it. If she was watching him from across the darkened room, it looked secretive, and in a way, it was. "Not much. Couldn't sleep."

She ran her hands through her hair. "I know. Why do you think that is, Chris? Something on your conscience? Something I need to know about?"

"No, Mel, no . . . I . . ." She'd been at him like this for days, weeks, picking at his edges, suggesting and not suggesting all at the same time, in the same breath. He couldn't tell whether she was screwing with him or if it was something else, something specific. He thought of Anne Hart, the last time he saw her, both of them standing close, effortless, rising in dusky light. "Why don't you tell me?"

But she was too tired to spar with him. "It doesn't matter, Chris. Whatever you're doing, it doesn't matter." She paused. "By the way, I'm going to start taking a few shifts at Earlys. I finally spoke to Will Donner, just like you wanted." She held his stare and he didn't recognize the woman across from him. She was a stranger, a hint of someone he used to know, and then she collapsed back into bed, disappearing into the sheets.

He remained trapped on the computer screen, an afterimage slow to fade: still standing next to the Tahoe, haloed by light. He waited for his image to disappear, listening for more movement from the bed. When he caught Mel's steady, deep breathing, he knew she'd fallen back asleep.

He shut off the laptop and crawled into bed himself, slow and soft so as not to wake her, to lie flat on his back, staring at the ceiling lost above him. Mel shifted next to him, not closer, but farther away across the bed.

When he'd come home that morning after stopping the Tahoe, Mel's car hadn't been parked in quite the same way. Their bed was still cold, even with Mel in it. She'd been facing away from him, eyes closed, skin cool to the touch. It was so late, but he was sure she hadn't been sleeping long, if at all—there was the smell of smoke and the sheets still weren't warm from her body. She hadn't been in the house for long. Not long at all. And Chris had no idea where she'd been.

Braccio and Emerson had never been interested in Valentine or Lajitas. He knew that now. It was Murfee all along—something . . . *someone* . . . here.

They'd gotten only as far as the Old Ranch Road, by the Lights, more than an hour's drive from Valentine and even more from where they were found, burning, but an area that most would still think of as Murfee's backyard. *What was out there?* What had special agents Morgan Emerson and Darin Braccio been looking for? The only time he'd been out that far was when he found the body at Indian Bluffs.

6

ANNE

She saw him everywhere now: smiling from behind mirrored sunglasses, passing her on the sidewalk. At school, standing with Principal Tanner. She once thought he was parked outside her house in the dark, but couldn't be sure. Not Deputy Cherry, whom she was enjoying running into more than she wanted to admit, and would have been happy to see anyway.

Sheriff Ross.

Philip Tanner finally raised it, in a roundabout away. He fell in step with her in the hall as she was heading home, the sound of basketballs echoing from the nearby gym— the pop and pause of leather balls in flight. He was tall, edging closer as they walked through bands of late-afternoon light fading through the windows.

"Sheriff Ross mentioned seeing you back at the carnival, wanted to know how you were getting along here."

"Well, I hope okay," she said.

"Of course you've been fine, Anne. We're glad to have you. I've known Sheriff Ross since he first moved to town. He grew up in Pecos, came here not long after high school. Murfee's his true home, at least that's what he always says. We go back a ways."

"Neither of you look old enough to have known each other all that long."

The principal blushed, his thin hair barely concealing the red splotches on his skull. "Thank you. Unnecessary to say and definitely not true, but appreciated nonetheless." Tanner stopped, lightly touching her elbow and forcing her to stop with him. "Any man would age far too much after going through what he has, what with Evelyn leaving the way she did. He's held up well. Very well, considering."

She shrugged, wanting to sidestep talk of Sheriff Ross's vanished wife. "I'm sure he has. But how do you think Caleb has held up, considering?"

Tanner blinked once, in slow motion, as if the thought had never occurred to him. Maybe it hadn't. "Why, Caleb's done fine. It can't be easy raising a boy alone, but the sheriff's been there for him."

"I'd hope so. Caleb's quiet, but a very bright young man, absolutely no trouble in class."

"Oh, there'll be no problems with him. The sheriff wouldn't have it."

"I see." She waited while Tanner smoothed down his tie, over and over again. It was broad, striped brown and blue, and he'd tied it far too short, so it curved with his stomach. She wanted to tell him no amount of fussing was going to make it lie flat.

Tanner wasn't quite ready to let her go. "I believe you and the Judge have a lot in common. You've both experienced your share of tragedy and you're both moving on."

Moving on. That was a popular way to put it, but that wasn't how it worked. All the bad things that happened to you weren't just places that you packed up and drove away from, no matter how many times you tried. They weren't haunted houses you left behind. Wherever you went, you still brought all those memories—all those ghosts—with you.

Beads of sweat popped on Tanner's forehead, glistening, heavy; threatening to drip down his face. He'd called Sheriff Ross "the Judge" and though it wasn't the first time she'd heard it, she still found it off-putting. She couldn't resist tweaking the uncomfortable principal a little, standing in a school hallway trying to set her up with his good ole buddy the sheriff. She half expected him to pass her a paper note.

"Why do you think Evelyn Ross ran off?"

Tanner made a vague noise, as if the why of her disappearance had no more crossed his mind than her son's coping with it. "I'm not sure I could say." Then, vague: "She was troubled, I suspect."

Anne had talked to Lori McKutcheon. Sheriff Ross had experienced "trouble" with more than one wife. "Does he miss her? Sheriff Ross, I mean. Does he miss Evelyn? Now, still?"

Tanner looked lost, like he'd walked into a conversation he'd forgotten he started. "Well, I don't know that I . . . I'm really not the best one to say. He's got a son, has to think about Caleb, their future." Tanner kept messing with his ugly tie. "I imagine he's come to terms with Evelyn leaving. After all, she's gone. Not likely to come back, never to come back. When you lose someone like that, at some point you have to accept it, right?"

She couldn't stop herself. She reached out, pulled his tie straight. "No, Philip, you don't, really, not at all. You never have to accept it." She left him standing in the hallway, searching for something other than his suit sleeve to wipe his head. Later, it struck her that he didn't say he didn't know or didn't have any ideas about Evelyn Ross's disappearance. He just couldn't say.

In Austin it hadn't started with a paper note, but a text. She was never one of those people who did a lot of texting. Her parents were too old for it, and for her friends in Virginia it was just as easy to catch up with a phone call. She'd had one or two school colleagues who exchanged texts now and then on a place to meet for drinks or a sale or something about one of their classes, but that was about it.

Most of her texting was done with Marc, and because he'd refused to tap out anything but complete sentences— grammar perfect and punctuation proper—it was more of a nuisance for him than a shortcut. Once he discovered emojis, though, he wasn't beyond sending the occasional smiley face or tongue sticking out, those goofy symbols somehow more legal to him in a way that LOL and OMG were not, but it was never like they ever burned up thousands of texts between them. Still, it was only natural that when her phone buzzed that day, her first thought was *Marc*. She was at her desk, staying late after class, as she often did.

At over three thousand students, James Bowie High

School was the largest school in the Austin Independent School District. Anne almost always stayed until five p.m. or later, working with the debate team or the thespian troupe, preparing the latter for the state one-act competition. With Marc working in Killeen and her in Austin, they split the difference and lived in Georgetown, halfway in between. They both had to fight a commute, although hers was a bit worse. Staying at school allowed her to get work done, support her extracurricular activities, and avoid the worst of the traffic.

But she didn't really need to conjure a reason to stay late. She loved Bowie, loved the staff and the students. It was her home away from home, and she spent more hours on campus than anywhere else. She had a small fridge in her classroom where she kept bottled waters and snacks, since things had a habit of disappearing in the teachers' lounge, and Marc had bought her an XM radio that she put on when she had the room to herself. It wasn't unusual for a few members of the thespian troupe, seniors mostly, to finish up their homework with her after the last bell before going to rehearsal on the stage at the CPA, the Center for Performing Arts. She learned a lot about them during those sessions—as they joked back and forth, made cell calls, talked about colleges they hoped to get into. They shared their arguments and secrets with her and she felt part of them in a way the other teachers probably envied. They called her Ms. Devane, using her surname as they did with every other teacher, but she was more to them than that.

It was a Thursday and raining hard, water running in blurry sheets down her classroom windows, and about eight of the thespian troupe were in the room. When her phone buzzed, the little LED winking at her, she'd ignored it at first, finished grading an essay on *Darkness at*

Noon before finally picking it up, expecting one of Marc's funny digital faces or a needlessly long question about what they were having for dinner. It was neither, and it stopped her.

U r beautiful.

She had smiled. *She remembered doing that.* And if any of the students had been watching her right at that moment, they would have seen that silly smile on her face too, right until she realized the text hadn't come from Marc at all. Curious, she looked at the number, tried to decipher it. It was an Austin area code but otherwise meant nothing to her. The phone was still in her hand when the second message came through: *U r beautiful. I think about u all the time.*

She smiled again, held the phone facedown as if hiding it from unseen watchers. The kids in her room had become background noise, static. When she flipped the phone back over, the words were still there. She typed back: *Who is this?*

She waited for a response, watching the rain, her students. One of them was sitting away from the others, hunched forward, his dark hair hiding his face, typing slowly, deliberately, on his phone. His intensity held her attention. His name was Lucas, one of her seniors. He wasn't with the thespian group. As he finished typing his text, he looked up, caught her staring, and smiled.

Her phone buzzed.

First of all it was October, a rare month for boys . . . Anne flipped the book around, felt its weight, smelled dust. It was a Bantam first edition, second printing, 1963, with a cover of weird pink shapes and monstrous faces and the title marred by a streak of lightning. Trapped in front of it all was a young boy with the cuffs of his jeans rolled up, arms half raised—*Something Wicked This Way Comes.*

Chris said the book had been his father's, but Anne thought the highlighting and underlining between the covers were probably his, marking the deputy's favorite lines. She couldn't remember the last time she'd read the book. Chris had been thoughtful enough to remember their conversation at the carnival and dig it up for her. She'd give it a go; whether she got through it or not, she'd give it back in a few days, despite his protests, and thank him. She wanted to trade him a book, but all of hers—Marc's—were donated and gone. After her unpleasant conversation with Tanner and the memories it had conjured of her time at Bowie, she welcomed the distraction. She settled into the couch, thumbed a few pages, careful, since they were brittle.

The seller of lightning rods arrived just ahead of the storm . . .

Twenty pages later her cellphone rang and she thought about letting it go, figuring it was her parents, when she found herself hoping it might be Chris. They'd traded phone numbers, *just in case,* and although she couldn't imagine why he'd call, she did want him to know she'd started the book. But it wasn't Chris or her parents or even Lori. It was Sheriff Ross.

"Anne, so glad I caught you at home . . ." Then he was off and running before she could catch her breath, telling her how he enjoyed seeing her at the carnival and around town, reiterating that if she needed anything—anything at all—she just had to let him know. It made her wonder if Phil Tanner had called him right after their talk in the hallway. Had he told the sheriff how she'd asked about Caleb . . . about Evelyn?

He told her how much Caleb said he enjoyed her class,

but she couldn't imagine the two of them, father and son, ever having that talk. Then he slipped into a story from Murfee's past, about bandits and horses and Indians. From her debate and drama lessons she guessed he'd told this story a hundred times, a thousand. He had the easy, practiced speech of someone who seems not to have practiced at all; a powerful voice, deep, filling the phone and her room. She felt small listening to him, and wondered what it would be like to be this man's son—*his wife*—hearing that voice all the time.

At the end, he mentioned getting together for dinner, nothing fancy, just a little thank-you for coming to Murfee and helping out. She held a finger on the page of Chris's book as headlights passed her window before moving on. *She once thought he was even parked outside her house in the dark, but couldn't be sure.* He'd called her only phone, her cell. *How did he know I was home?* And then another thought, more insistent: she couldn't remember ever giving the sheriff her number.

7

DUANE

"'Nother, Miss Cherry, if you don't mind." He pointed at his now empty Dr Pepper, little more than slush. The heat in his hands had melted the ice, clear flames beneath the skin of his fingers making his nails glow. All because of the *foco*, leaving his heart and skin and skull full of copper nails and sparks. When Melissa, Chris's girl, took his glass to get another, he wondered if it felt hot to the touch.

She'd started at Earlys a week ago, picking up hours for May Doyle, who needed the time to go to Abilene to deal with someone sick. May had worked at Earlys for ten years and knew her way around a bar back. Melissa? Not so much. Still, she was a fine sight better than May. Her body was tight, looked real fine in jeans, with her hair half pulled up over bare shoulders. Whenever she bent down

to get something he tried to spy if she was wearing panties, but even with his wolf eyes—and they were sharp and
bright tonight—he didn't quite have the angle. He
pegged her as the no-panty type, wondering what the hell
she saw in Chris Cherry. She seemed twice the woman
that someone like Cherry could handle or satisfy. She
brought him a new Dr Pepper, too much damn ice just
like the last time, but he let it slide.

"Just Melissa or Mel, Duane. Chris and I aren't married, and I don't want to think I'm old enough for all that
Ms. stuff."

He raised his glass. "Why, no you ain't. Not atall." He
took a sip, slow-eyed her over the glass, imagined her
naked. Imagined a lot of other things, the sorts of things
he dreamed about his little Mex girl. His eyes and teeth
ached, one so loose he could work it with his tongue,
sucking acid, sugar, blood—all that damn *foco* unraveling
him and the too-sweet Dr Pepper making his gums sing.
"You like it here?"

"Here, as in Murfee? Or here, as in *here*?" She took in
Earlys—the old black-and-white pictures, the shot-up
stop signs; the antler racks on the walls and the dusty
permanent Christmas lights, hanging low.

He tipped his glass to her. "Both."

She rubbed a rag on the bar top, scrubbing at scratches
that would never go away. "How does that thing go? That
thing they always say on cop shows? I plead the fifth."

He yucked a little too loud, snorted in his ice. "It
grows on you, you just gotta give it a chance."

She tossed the rag aside, folded her arms. "Really? And
how's that?"

He tipped his pop, started searching his pocket for his
Lucky Strikes. "Darlin', you just have to see it with new
eyes."

*   *   *

He and Melissa had talked a couple of times in passing—
the weather, that sort of thing. But tonight they had the
bar almost to themselves, except for Paul Diamond and
Mitchel Gary at a corner table deep in their own talk, so
he got her going on a bit about her life before Murfee.
She talked just a little about her daddy, a wildcatter, who
reminded him of his own and in none of the good ways,
if there were any. He lit her up a couple of Lucky Strikes,
kept her going.

It was easy too, because she was killing a few drinks of
her own when she thought he wasn't looking. She had a
glass hidden beneath the bar, acted like it was pop, like
his Dr Pepper, but he could smell the whiskey in it, all
over her. No matter how many times she reached down
to take a sip, it was always near full. She just kept adding
more, talking, smoking his pack away. She didn't ask anything about him and he was more than fine with that.

He'd seen tire tracks. Heavy, big tread. Deep cuts in the
sand and rocks, a scattering of broken cacti—a secret trail
only his wolf eyes had been able to pick out, marking the
passage of his watchers. He'd followed it down to the
very spot on his daddy's land where they'd set up for a
good view of the house, near a small spread of anacahui-
tas. Sitting there, watching *him*, all those nights. Real, not
ghosts. After that, he figured it was time for some watching of his own, waiting for them to return. Ghosts didn't
drive big trucks.

So it had been easy enough, goddamn easy, when the
time came, with the *foco* boiling and burning inside him.
He saw the man first, thought it was Chava with his gold

tooth and machete, before something flickered on/off in his head, a faulty pilot light, remembering then that Chava was gone and had been for a while. And he never saw the girl, not until it was over and he looked into her open and staring eyes and didn't see his reflection; put his ear to her open mouth and didn't hear a thing, not a ragged breath or an echoing heartbeat. So he'd slipped a hand in her shirt just to double-check, not to feel her tits, although he did that too, and she never so much as twitched.

She was stone dead. Had to be, right until the car burned and the first oily flames had touched her cooling body. Until somehow, someway, the fire brought that girl back to life.

He'd thought about visiting the burned girl in the hospital, to stare at her and try to puzzle out how she'd died and come back. Not *back* like his daddy, who was little more than a shit-eating grin and whispers and shadows and old songs in his head—"Tall Men Riding" had been Jamison's favorite, so Duane heard that all the time now. But back for real, *alive*, or damn near so. He just didn't understand how it was possible. He for damn sure didn't see that coming. It was a long drive out to the Cut, way down by the water, and he would've sworn she was dead the whole time.

What he wanted to do—needed to do—was talk to the Judge: admit that he fucked up and share some of their secrets again, just like ole times. But the Judge was wary; not too close, not too far away, either. He was keeping his own eye on Duane but not wanting to be seen with him. Duane really thought they'd been through far too much together to behave like that now. Those things he could remember anyway, since so much was burned away like the fire itself from that night; embers through his fingers.

That girl hadn't been just another Chava or Rudy Ray or Delgado, another beaner no one gave two shits about. She wasn't some nameless wetback in Nikes running through the desert—she'd been a goddamn federal agent. Two of them, in fact, right here in Murfee. Where their blood still remained, staining everything. Blood *he'd* spilled, and dragging them to the river hadn't changed that.

He hadn't been in his right mind when he'd done it, but that wasn't going to make a difference to the Judge. Hell, after all, Duane hadn't been *right* in a long time, didn't even know what that was anymore, since he'd been going wrong for so long. And now he'd left behind a real bloody mess, one the Judge would need to clean up, since he couldn't risk the stink of it leading right to his goddamn door. That meant starting with Duane Dupree, and that's why the Judge was keeping his distance—he'd already looked into Duane's eyes and saw their newfound glow. The Judge was afraid if he stood close enough, Duane would see inside *his* head, all his goddamn killing thoughts.

Melissa asked a lot about Chris, about his job. Did he like it? Duane had no fucking idea.

"I reckon so . . . never heard him complain, not to me anyway. He keeps to himself mostly."

"Yeah, I know. Always has. It's his way. Too many books. He's always reading inside his head. Just more . . . lately." Her back was to him, straightening glassware, but he knew her attention was on him all the same. She was fishing, he just didn't know for what. Maybe she didn't, either.

"Sumthin' troublin' him?" He flicked ash on the floor.

"He's still not all twisted about that little dustup at Mancha's, is he?"

A shrug. "No, it's not that. I don't think so, anyway. He talked about it a little. He's just distracted. Coming back here, seeing all these people he used to know. Hell, I don't know. Thought it might have to do with work. He was going on for a bit about that body he found outside of town, but not so much anymore."

Duane raised his eyebrows, chuckled. "That thing? At Matty's place? Hell, darlin', ain't nobody distracted over that." He waved the thought away. "Not the first dead wetback we've found around here. Not the last." He was about to tell her about a picked-over mess he found last year near the Triple R, still wearing brand-new Nikes, but thought better of it. It was a helluva story, funny, but she wasn't looking for a laugh.

"Nothing else he's working on then?"

Duane pretended to think, looking for faces in their cigarette smoke; working his tooth, mouth full of blood. He could have spit it all out into his glass; probably fill it up, too. He was going to dig it out, probably leave a big damn hole in his head, but at least some of the pain would go with it. Maybe that hole would finally release other things too, all the horrible ghosts and shadows and his daddy's songs. "Not that I can say, not so much." He slid over another Lucky Strike, edged forward, like they were sharing secrets.

"You want that I keep an eye on him?"

Mel shook her head, dismissing his offer fast. "Thanks, no . . ." But he knew she wanted to say more, so he went back to waiting, swirling the last of the ice in his glass. Still too goddamn much of it.

"Anybody ever come around asking for him at work?" She finally looked at him, sideways. Her own eyes glowed, just too much to drink, but he wondered if she could see into his, which flamed for different reasons. He saw it all then, clear, as if written above her in the Christmas lights—her fears of Chris stepping out on her. That's what this whole talk was about, what the whole night had been about. Duane didn't really peg Cherry for the type, even with him talking up the new teacher, but he played along.

"Anybody particular?"

"No, just anyone. At all."

He pushed his glass forward, spread his fingers on the table. He let her misery drag, let her chew her lip. She was embarrassed for asking and worried, afraid, of what he might say.

"Well now, not so that I've seen, not down at work, anyway. But he does keep to himself. You said that yourself. Not sure what he's up to when he's not there, and he ain't there all the time. I can't imagine what might be keepin' him from home, though. If you was waitin' for me, darlin', I sure wouldn't be dilly-dallyin' around anywhere or with anyone." He winked, letting her know he was being funny, or not.

"That's sweet, Duane. It's not exactly like that . . ."

He shrugged his shoulders, like he'd said his piece and there was nothing more to add. "No, darlin', I'm sure it ain't."

She stared, silent, a long time, before going back to her glasses, back to her own thoughts. She'd wiped the glasses down so much they shined like diamonds, gleaming against the dark wood, but Duane knew she still hadn't wiped away everything that was bothering her.

"There is one other thing . . ." Melissa was still talking.

"And what might that be . . . darlin'?"

She stuck her hands in her jeans, steadying herself. Her

eyes were bright, new diamonds like the glasses had been, still lit by the booze.

"I'm sure it's nothing, just weird. Chris was watching a video the other night, at the house. It looked like something from work . . ."

8

MELISSA

It'd been a royal fucking mistake to talk to Duane
Dupree.

It had been the whiskey talking, the anger. Mel sat in
her car outside Earlys, smoking, sobering up. Her breath
turned the cold car hot with Jack Daniel's. Only her third
or fourth day of work and she'd drunk her whole way
through it, Duane watching it all. If Chris didn't figure it
out on his own the minute she walked through the door,
Duane might tell him . . . or not. It was hard to say with
the chief deputy, who'd spent most of the night grinning
at her with that awful smile—maybe the only one he
had—smoking Lucky Strikes and downing one Dr Pepper
after another. The thought of all that sugar, that cold,
dark sweetness wrapped in smoke, made her sick.

For the most part, she'd kept the bottle at bay. There had been moments, here and there, but not many, and not in a while. Not until tonight, in front of Duane. This place really brought out the fucking worst in her. Before tonight, she'd already gone through the inside of Chris's truck and his phone; had even driven around once or twice to put real eyes on him, when she finally thought to go back to their computer, the one on his dad's old desk in their bedroom. She started with his e-mails, then went through the browser history; next just started poking around, when she finally found a file she didn't recognize, hidden away. He must have forgotten it, abandoned it, that night she woke up late and caught him staring at the computer screen.

It hadn't made much sense, but after describing it to Duane, he'd explained it easy enough. It was a video file: footage from the dashboard camera in Chris's truck. A traffic stop where nothing much really happened, just Chris talking to one or two people in a big SUV, and that was all. It was at night and hadn't meant anything to her, and whatever interest it held for Chris also remained a mystery. But if that damn schoolteacher had been in the SUV, it hadn't been clear enough to pick her out.

At least *that* part wasn't a mystery anymore. Following Chris around, Mel had caught him running into that woman from the carnival again, Murfee's new English teacher, and finding out about her hadn't been that hard. She was from Austin, supposedly had *history*, which was the town's polite way of saying she'd gotten into some sort of trouble. But Mel didn't care about any of that; she had plenty of history of her own. What she did care about was how each time she saw Chris and the teacher to-gether she had to relive that goddamn look on his face,

the one he'd shared with the teacher at the carnival beneath the lights—the one that was no longer special or
reserved for her.

Duane had said it probably wasn't a big deal, couldn't
begin to guess why Chris had kept the video or brought
it home—it wasn't like he was breaking any rules—but
didn't ask a ton of questions about it, either. Instead he'd
gone out of his way *not* to ask much about it, telling her
all about how he turned that damn camera off in his own
truck because it felt like a big ole eye spying and prying
on him and he didn't like that, nicely salting the guilt she
already felt about shadowing Chris. In the end, the only
thing he did ask, like it was just an afterthought, was if
she remembered the time and date stamp on the video. A
string of white numbers in one corner—left or right,
Duane couldn't remember which—but all the video shot
by those cameras was tagged that way. Duane suggested
if he knew the date, he might be able to figure out what
Chris had been up to that day, where he'd been . . . who
he'd seen.

He didn't come out and say the teacher's name,
though; he didn't have to. And then pulling on his coat,
he'd smiled, and she'd had the craziest thought there was
blood spotting his teeth.

In all the best ways, Chris wasn't and never would be like
any of the other men she had been with. He had strength,
a *center*, unlike any man she'd ever known. But men
could still act like little boys sometimes, and she'd learned
long ago there was natural weakness in all unhappy boys
that made them fuck up perfectly good things. But Chris

had become *her* center; had been for long enough now that she wasn't willing to let Murfee or anyone else in it take him away from her. Not yet, not without a fight. And definitely not another woman, not Anne Hart.

And that's what had her·chasing him around Murfee, searching through his things—that's what'd brought her to their computer in the first place, watching and re-watching the strange video Chris had taken from work. Then revealing it, like a fool, to Duane Dupree.

Because she had known exactly what the chief deputy was talking about: that date and the time glowing bright on the video—the early-morning hours after the carnival. But with Dupree staring at her, waiting, grinning skull-like behind closed lips, she'd hesitated, before flat-out lying that she didn't remember anything like that at all. He'd winked, unconvinced, but had left it with "Of course ya don't, darlin'," only reminding her that if she ever happened to look at it again to let him know. Or better yet, maybe he'd just swing by anyway and take a look at it directly, to see what ole Chris was up to.

Then he'd written his personal cell on a napkin, folded it for her. After that he'd walked her out to the car, waited while she got in, and bent down to peer at her through the glass—leaving his breath against it and a palm print from a hard tap goodbye—before disappearing into the night. She could still see that print there now, smeared, a stain on the glass reminding her of a bloody paw. She didn't feel sober enough to drive, and couldn't shake the awful feeling she'd made a real mistake by talking up that damn video to Duane. It had all been in his eyes, the way he'd stared at her, unblinking—his eyes not quite match-ing the rest of his face, like they were too big and not part of the original design. She still couldn't quite see the en-tire shape of her mistake, only its outline, but it was enough. And there'd been no damn need to reveal it any-way: she'd already pretty much made up her mind the video had nothing to do with Chris and the new English teacher.

But . . . but . . . it might have something to do with those two agents murdered near Valentine that was all over the news. Not that Chris had ever said anything about it to her, even though she'd read the paper and heard it mentioned a few times around Earlys and the Hi n Lo. They'd been burned in a big SUV, not much differ-ent from the one in Chris's video. Not much different at all. The fact that Duane hadn't raised the coincidence gnawed at her; the fact that she couldn't talk to Chris about it without revealing her sneaking around only gave it sharper teeth. For once, she *wanted* to be mad, needed it—prayed for her old anger and any good reason to be flat-out furious, even though she knew there really wasn't one. Because anger was better, safer.

Because tonight, right now, she felt afraid, and that was a whole lot worse.

9

AMERICA

He wouldn't let it go, the thing she didn't want to hear, so he told her all about his papa, El Juez.

Everything. He told her about a dog named Shep and about a long night on a mountain. He told her they were all in danger. He told her all the things El Juez had done, all the things he could and would do. He told her it was her brother murdered and buried at Indian Bluffs, and if they could prove that, they might be able to put both their dead to rest and really fly away.

Pájaros para siempre. Birds forever.

He wanted to bring all their suspicions to Cherry, the deputy, but was too nervous to approach him. Instead, they'd go through Ms. Hart. He knew the two of them saw each other and talked. He wouldn't say how, but she guessed he'd been following the teacher around. He used to do that with her too, thinking she never saw him, but she always did. Murfee wasn't an easy place to sneak around, and he wasn't that good at it. They sat on a bench under red oaks bent sideways by the wind, planted in a line between the school and the football stadium. All the trees and the scattered benches beneath them had been donated by former students and local families and clubs, each with a small plate with the donor's name. On their bench, that name had been scratched off long ago, so it had become their "place," if they had a place, and if she let him believe they were a "they"—*una pareja*.

Caleb said they were hiding in plain sight—who would ever pay attention to two students sharing cigarettes on a bench outside the school? He never said what it was they were hiding from.

"Well?"

She sucked in smoke, counted tree branches above her head. He got in close, one leg curled beneath him and leaning forward like he did when he wanted to be serious, and he always wanted her to see him as serious. That was also when his eyes were best, when they were green and blue at the same time—bright, both young and old. Amé had never met Caleb's mama, not formally, just saw her around school, around town, before she was gone. But those were all her eyes, had to be.

"Try to remember, Amé, anything, anything at all."

He'd been at this for days, getting her to think back to growing up with Rodolfo, searching for something, anything, they could give to Deputy Cherry: a clue, a bit of Rodolfo's past that might prove once and for all that the bundle of *huesos* the deputy had found could be no one but her brother. But Rodolfo had been nine years older. There was so much she couldn't remember, so much about him she didn't know. Just like there was so much about her mama and papa and their lives over the river she didn't know, cousins and aunts and uncles who were nothing more than stories and names: Margarita and Luciana and Juan José and a mysterious Fox Uno, whom her mama did not speak of often and seemed truly scared of.

She'd seen enough TV—the same detective shows Caleb kept going on about now—to know that real life rarely worked that way. She didn't believe there were answers about her brother in any papers or reports Deputy Cherry might have.

"*No lo sé*. I don't remember anything. Not now. Not ever."

Caleb slumped, looked past her. "Dammit."

However, she did think more and more about Rodolfo's phone—picking it up, choosing one of its stored numbers. The person who answered it would not care about reports or papers; would not need them to help her do something about Rodolfo or Duane Dupree. But she always stopped herself. Using the phone was as dangerous as pulling the trigger on Rodolfo's gun; she'd have no more control over what happened next than catching a fired bullet. Still, she found it in her hand more and more often, not remembering how it got there. It had a life of its own, crawling into her fingers as she slept, beating, almost like a heart. She didn't want to be angry, but couldn't understand how Caleb made it all seem like a game, so easy.

"First, you *knew* it was your mama. You wanted me to believe it, too. Now you know it is Rodolfo. You don't make sense. You want all these horrible things and you don't even know why."

He threw his hands up, frustrated, almost angry. "And

you don't? You don't want to know? You don't want to do anything about it . . . to stop him?"

She pointed at the air. "*Him?* Your papa? Is that what all this is about? Or is it about you?" She laughed, bitter. "Do I want to know where my brother is? *Sí*. But do I want it to be that thing out in the desert? No, *no lo hago*. No more than I wanted it to be your mama. Don't you see, we get nothing by being right? It makes nothing better." There was no easy way to explain how she *needed* her brother to still be alive—to be free, to have escaped and gotten away from all of this for someplace safer, far from here, forever. In her *sueños*, her dreams, again— fewer now, but she still had them—she could almost see him there; clear, bright, waving to her, urging her to find such a place for herself. A place like the cities Caleb had promised her, or the paper beaches taped to her bedroom walls. That's what she had to believe, had to tell herself, even if it was all no more real or true than Caleb's TV shows. *Murfee was her real life*. Duane Dupree was real life. A gun and a cellphone and money under her bed were real. It was her *vida* and she hated it and there was nothing easy or good about any of it. Maybe it was worthless to hope or dream for better things, but as long as she believed Rodolfo was free, she could also hold tight to the idea, *the hope*, that on some other distant day she could be, too. It might be nothing, but what else did she have? It might have to be enough. She was stronger than her brother, always had been, but she was still too afraid to let that last dream of Rodolfo go. Too afraid it'd mean also letting go of her last small handful of hope . . . *her* last dreams.

She'd imagined once or twice showing Caleb one of Dupree's pictures, like the one she got this morning that she couldn't delete fast enough—a black knife held next to his *pene*, daring her to compare which was longer, sharper; begging her to dwell on which one was going to hurt more. What could Caleb do about that, about Dupree? How would someone like Caleb ever stop someone like him?

"I'm sorry, Amé. I just want to help us."

"No, you want to help *you*. You want this for you. You know *nada* about what I want." She hurt him, felt it. Those eyes she sometimes liked flickered, dimmed. He pulled back like she'd hit him, lost for something else to say.

She believed enough of the things he'd said about El Juez to know Caleb's own unhappiness, to feel it for him. But no matter how bad it was, he had a hundred more ways to walk away from his life than she'd ever have to run from hers. Caleb could never understand that; showing him Dupree's texts and pictures wouldn't change it. And no matter what he promised, when the time finally came, it wouldn't stop him from leaving, with or without her.

"It is nothing, Caleb. *Nada*, nothing. Let it go." She didn't have to say anything more, but she knew he heard it, felt it, understood it. Not today or tomorrow, but soon. *Let me go.*

But he wouldn't, not yet, so later Caleb came to her again. She thought about pretending she was out, but he knew better. He'd stopped first at Mancha's down the street and picked up gum and her favorite cigarettes. He peered in her window, tapping until she opened it, one of the few times she'd let him inside. She hated him being in her room now, knowing Dupree had been there as well. He took in all of her posters, her pictures. None were of him. Nothing in her room said they were friends or knew each other at all. If he was hurt by it, he didn't say anything.

She was embarrassed by all of her magazine cutouts, glossy and bright and taped to her wall—homes and beaches of the rich, the famous. There were several pictures of Rodolfo, one from when he was very young, wearing a cowboy hat, pointing his finger at the camera. She always thought he looked so small beneath the wide brim, his face lost in its shadow. Caleb stared at that for a long time. He also saw the ragged peacock feather stuck behind her mirror, colors faded by the sun. Finally he took one of the clippings from her wall, a city skyline along a beach—the one she'd written those mysterious phone numbers on—and put that in his pocket. Then he took the picture of Rodolfo in his cowboy hat and put that in her hand. He wrapped his hand over hers, over the picture. His hands were warm, gentle. "Try."

And that night she did dream of Rodolfo—*un sueño*—the first one in a long time, and different from the others. He'd been so good at *fútbol*, not what the gringos thought of as football but what they played in the dirt streets. Rodolfo had been thin like a reed along the river and could bend like one too, moving with the ball as if it were tied to him on a string. As he got older, there were fewer chances to play. Bigger clubs would not take a Mexican and the high school did not have a team, so Rodolfo gave it up for other things. But for a time there was always a ball at his foot—trailing dust around the house, leaving marks on the walls. There was still a black smudge in the kitchen, one her mama refused to wipe away.

She is sitting in the grass and they are calling his

name . . . Pasa la pelota, Rodolfo.¡Pasa! ¡Dispara! ¡Nadie puede atraparlo!

The sun is so hot and her mama and papa have promised her helado *if she behaves and she is clapping for her* hermano.

There is loud yelling and he is next to her on the grass and his eyes are so, so wide, and his arm is in her papa's hands and his hands are so big and gentle and dark from the sun and so is Rodolfo's arm but it doesn't look right and Rodolfo is holding her hand too tight and she is crying but she does not know why.

She is calling his name over and over again and her hand stings from where he is squeezing and she doesn't care whether she gets helado *even her favorite chocolate because Rodolfo is whispering just for her . . .* Estoy bien, pequeña estrella, estoy bien . . . *and then he is kissing her between the eyes and then he is gone.*

Rodolfo.

She sat up in bed with cold starlight on her sheets, Rodolfo's phone in her hand. She had fallen asleep with the phone or it had slithered from its place under the bed. It was warm, alive. She got up quietly and put it back in its place. The picture of Rodolfo, the one Caleb had handed her, was still on her nightstand where she'd left it, the last thing she had looked at before falling asleep. *Caleb had made her remember, made her dream.* Rodolfo had broken his arm bad, and her papa had taken him across the river to get it set because they could not afford the doctor in Murfee. He'd worn the cast proudly—it was so white— and he would not let anyone color it or sign it as they both had seen others do. She'd been five, maybe six; seven at the most.

He'd worn that cast for a long, long time.

She took Rodolfo's picture, held it tight, and went to her window. It wasn't dawn, not quite yet, the moon all but lost and the stars still the brightest things in the sky, as white and faceless as Rodolfo's cast. They were all she could see outside her window, the rest of the town, the whole entire world, having disappeared. She was alone. But maybe she could tell Caleb about that bad injury, and how whenever it was going to rain Rodolfo used to swear his throbbing arm, never quite the same, always let him know first it was on its way. Maybe she could tell him about Dupree's number in her brother's phone too, but not explain why she knew it so well, knew it by heart. Maybe she owed him that small thing, something, for wanting so bad to help her . . . for helping her remember. Maybe she owed it to herself.

It might be nothing . . .

But maybe for the first time in forever, something was better than nothing.

10

CHRIS

He was at home, thinking about pillowcases. The ones he and Mel were using on their bed. Floral print, old, they no longer held any color because they'd been washed so often. They'd been in his family since he was a kid. His parents probably got them when they were first married. His mother's head had once graced them, her hair turning as gray as the cotton itself before it had all fallen out. He was just thinking about going to the Dollar General and buying new ones, something he knew he should have already done, when his cell rang.

It was an unfamiliar voice, calling from far away. A man with a southern accent—not anywhere in Texas, but from back east somewhere—and he said his name was Garrison.

"I'm a friend of Darin Braccio and Morgan Emerson."
Chris first said he didn't know them.

The man laughed, said, "Sure you do, Deputy Cherry,
sure you do."

"Darin wasn't much of a report writer, worse about re-
porting in. He had what you might gently call *an author-
ity problem*. Morgan was better, really good. So new she
hadn't learned how to take shortcuts. She'd already
e-mailed me some of her notes for the reports she never
had a chance to write. You made an impression on both
of them that night you stopped them outside Murfee, a
week before they were attacked."

Chris wasn't sure what to say, his long silence almost
enough for both of them. Finally, "I think you should
talk to Sheriff Ross."

Garrison brushed it off. "No, I think he's really the last
person I want to talk to. Unfortunately, you're about the
only person in that ass-end of Texas I do feel comfortable
talking to right now."

"Why me? Why did you call me? Who are you?"

Now Garrison started with a long silence. "I'm *curious*, Deputy Cherry, like you. I'm curious why you
checked with Lajitas about Darin and Morgan staying
there. Curious why you're pushing the DPS lab over
those remains you found. Is it just good instincts, Deputy? Are you just a good investigator, like Darin Braccio,
one of the best I've ever seen? Or something else?"

Whoever this Garrison was, and he still hadn't made
that clear, Chris understood then he'd been monitoring
him, checking up on him. He had his cell number and
who knew what else. "I don't know anything about what
happened to those two out in Valentine."

"And that's what I'm most curious about. You're one of the few people who can probably guess my agents weren't really interested in Valentine, never were. Instead, they were up your way, being curious, for a reason. You've figured that out, but as near as I can tell, you haven't said anything to anyone about it. Why is that?"

His agents. "You think I had something to do with what happened to them? If so, this conversation is done."

"Deputy, if I already thought that, we wouldn't be having this conversation at all."

"Darin and Morgan weren't killed in Valentine or even down by the Rio Grande. I know that, courtesy of the same DPS evidence and forensic techs you're becoming so familiar with. Someone drove them there and then set their car on fire, probably after realizing they'd killed two federal agents. Their guns were found in the water, but their badges and creds were left to burn with them." Garrison paused, remembering. "So here's what I'd ask myself, Deputy, if I lived like you do all the way out there in the middle of fucking nowhere. First, where did they get ambushed, and why? Because it was a pure ambush, make no mistake about it. They never had a chance, not at all. Second, who drove their car all the way down to the river? And third, how'd that murderous fuck get back home? It's a helluva long walk from anywhere, so he probably had help . . . a few friends, maybe a whole bunch of them. I guess the only question that really matters is, who do you trust, Deputy Cherry? Can you trust everyone in your department? Can you trust anyone in Murfee at all?"

"And that's what I'm supposed to do now, trust you?"

"I'm betting we're supposed to trust each other."

Chris held the phone away, thinking. "That woman, your agent Emerson, will she live?"

Garrison breathed, hard. "I don't know. No one does. I want more than anything for her to open her eyes and tell me what happened. I want her to point out the person or persons who did this to her and Darin. Do you want that, Deputy Cherry?"

Chris ignored him. "But you already know, right? Or think you do. That's why you called me."

"I have some ideas, Deputy. I'm not clear on everything, but I'm clear enough. I'm getting there."

"So why aren't you down here taking care of it?"

Chris could hear Garrison struggle, imagined the other man carrying a great weight and praying for a chance to set it down, even for just a moment. It reminded him of his father caring for his mom, both of them carrying her through to the end. How Chris had washed the pillowcase he'd been staring at through this whole conversation, a day after she died.

"It's complicated. Messy and political and I wish it wasn't, but there it is, all the same. You have some popular, powerful people down there. The wheels might turn slowly, but I promise you they will turn, Deputy Cherry, even if I have to turn them by hand."

Chris knew nothing about this Garrison, but didn't doubt him. Despite how he'd said it, everyone knew there was only one powerful person in Murfee. That's all there'd ever been. *I think that's really the last person I want to talk to.*

"Okay, what happens next?"

"I want to meet you, Deputy, sooner rather later. Put our heads together . . . help each other out with this thing."

Chris turned it over, thought about what that might

mean, what it would have to mean. "Maybe . . . I'll think about it."

"That's a start, at least, but don't think too goddamn long." Garrison's anger, his frustration, was clear and real across the distance between them. It was *heavy*. "I don't know exactly what the fuck is going on down there, and maybe you don't either, but I do know this—one way or another, it doesn't end with what happened on that riverbank, not like that. *They were my friends.*"

"Is that a threat?"

"Absolutely."

Chris thought Garrison had hung up on him when he heard that voice again, faint, one more time. "Don't be a fucking hero, Deputy. Heroes end up dead. Just like Darin Braccio."

11

ANNE

He picked her up in his truck, held the door for her like a gentleman. They made small talk, his work and hers, on the drive to a little place he liked in Artesia—all smoke and dark wood and deer antlers on the walls; old pictures of places that didn't even look like Texas. It wasn't too romantic, more casual. The waiter knew him, everyone did, so she didn't even need to look at a menu. He ordered for them both. He was different in jeans and a button-down shirt, even with the gun and badge clearly visible on his hip, but not too different. Still recognizable. There was no mistaking Sheriff Ross. He'd followed through with his dinner invitation after all, caught her after school, and with no easy way to say no, she'd said the only other thing she could.

She'd seen him like this once before, in Austin at a

Texas Narcotics Officers Association convention. He'd been the keynote speaker, and she and Marc and several others had met him for dinner afterward at a steakhouse with sawdust on the floor. He'd been funny, engaging— entertaining the table with stories of his time as sheriff. She couldn't remember what, if anything, the two of them had talked about or if they had spoken together much at all, but she had caught him staring at her a few times, never inappropriately, just intense, focused. Right after Marc had died, he sent a condolence card to the house and may have attended the memorial, but there'd been so many people, she wasn't sure. Later, when things got really bad for her, he'd sent another hand-addressed note that she never opened.

She never figured out how he had their home address and didn't think much of it again—not at all, really—until Dial Johnson called about the job in Murfee. An old friend of his, Sheriff Stanford Ross, had asked about Anne personally—asked for her *by name*. The sheriff had re-membered her from the convention and knew about her situation in Austin, but didn't care about all that—the school needed the help, and with the sheriff's own son enrolled there, it'd mean a lot if she was available. The sheriff wouldn't have needed Dial to tell him no school in Texas would have her.

"Everyone says you've settled in well, Anne. I'm glad to hear it." Sheriff Ross smiled at her, a Shiner Bock in his hand.

"Thank you, I appreciate your help. I'm sure your word had more than a little to do with it."

He kept smiling, faking embarrassment behind a long sip from the bottle. "I've been around a long time, gotten to know more than my fair share of people. Texas often works on handshakes and favors, and I've done plenty of both."

"Well, thank you anyway. I wasn't sure I was going to teach again, not in Texas."

He nodded. "To be honest, I was surprised you were still here. Pleasantly, but surprised all the same."

She toyed with her fork. "Me too, I guess. So were my parents, my friends. It would have been easier to go back to Virginia, but I just couldn't, not yet. Marc wouldn't have wanted it. He liked Texas, it was our home."

"And you met in college?"

"Well, I was in college, Mary Washington. He was stationed at Fort Belvoir. By the time he was transferred to Fort Hood, we were married. After that horrible shooting there, he didn't reenlist. It changed him, affected him more than he wanted to admit, and he joined the police department in Killeen. He enjoyed police work more than anything he ever did in the army."

The sheriff smiled, serious. "Did you know he and I spoke a few times after we all met in Austin? I tried to sell him on Murfee's charms, but I think he figured it was too small for him, at least at that point."

She hesitated, finding it hard to imagine Marc talking with this man without mentioning it to her, harder to imagine his ever considering a job in Murfee.

"What do you think, Anne? Is Murfee too small?"

She laughed. "Too small? Too small for what? Murfee's very nice. I can see why people love it, how someone can live here their whole life and never miss a thing. It has an undeniable charm."

He raised his beer. "I like that. I've heard Murfee described many ways. 'Charming' is not often one of them."

She played with her napkin, folding and unfolding it.

was probably twenty-five years older than she was, maybe a little more. It wasn't that he tried to act younger—he was comfortable enough with his age not to be silly about it—and spending time with him didn't feel like being with her father, but it still felt *off*. Like that dinner in Austin long ago, or at least what felt like long ago, where she'd caught him looking at her—*studying* her, his eyes a few degrees cooler than the rest of his expression, which at any given moment might have been smiling or laughing.

By the end of it all she was tired, ready to be home, ready to curl up with Chris Cherry's old book, but just before ordering a dessert she didn't really want, she brought up the deputy in passing—how well the sheriff knew him when he was growing up in Murfee. The sheriff answered politely, went on about a couple of his football games and how more than half the town owed their teeth to Chris's father, but it was clear he hadn't driven to Artesia to talk about one of his deputies. Those eyes again gave it away. She didn't ask about Chris Cherry anymore.

Sheriff Ross had an undeniable presence—heavy, ambient. Under a bright sun, he might cast two long shadows instead of one. And he had that will, but so had Lucas Neill, until the very end.

Lucas Neill didn't grow up in Austin. The press liked to claim he hadn't really grown up anywhere at all, living with a man thought to be his father for a while, then his mother, finally an aunt in Austin, where he settled for the longest time and attended James Bowie. He was a good student when he chose to be. Like Caleb Ross, he didn't have a lot of friends. Much later they would call that troubled. But she knew that from the start.

It began with those texts, the first ones on that rainy

day in her classroom. She caught up with him after school that very day and told him his texts were flattering but inappropriate. Wildly inappropriate. She wouldn't bring it to the school's attention, but she wanted him to stop. He had to. He ran from her into the rain; pale, angry, his dark hair plastered onto his head, looking all of twelve rather than seventeen. It was the cover of a bad romance novel. The press was right, he never had grown up. She yelled after him to calm down, her words lost to thunder. But he did stop, for a little while. Before starting up again about three weeks later, the texts coming at various times both inside and outside school, her phone blinking at three a.m. while Marc slept or was on shift. She didn't respond, never responded, just deleted them as fast as they came in, but then there were other little things as well: a flower tucked under her car's wiper blade; a small, handwritten note slipped into a desk drawer; things appearing, disappearing, like smoke. Most of the later texts and notes weren't even about her, but his problems at school, at his aunt's home, vague suggestions of even vaguer abuse.

If his words had gotten intimate, too sexual, too fast, she might have shut it down just as fast—gone to the front office, asked for a transfer; just changed her goddamn number like she did after it was too late anyway, when it was only the media and worse calling her. Instead, she'd started *worrying* about him, pulled under by his rising tide of sadness and loneliness and frustration. Slow, inexorable, encroaching, so that she was up to her chin, then deeper, before she even knew it.

One night the phone had buzzed again and again, LED flickering, text after text. Marc was out and she'd tried to ignore it, curled up on their couch, but it kept on. It was Luke's way of yelling for attention. Something bad had happened. When she finally broke down and read his texts they hadn't made any sense, trailing off into random letters, numbers—half words or just her name, over and over again. He was hurt or being hurt. She tried to put the phone away, but came back to it again.

Where r u? Where r u? Pls don't fckn ignore me. Can u hear me?

She'd tried calling Marc, but he never picked up. Maybe if he had, if they could've talked for a few minutes about something, anything—about what they were doing for the weekend or his new pain-in-the-ass sergeant at work or even Christmas, which was still two months away—she'd have gotten up the courage to admit right then and there that there was a crazy boy from her school drowning her. How she was in way over her head and didn't know what to do about it anymore and couldn't make it stop. But he hadn't answered, and her phone had continued to act like a thing possessed, as if Luke knew she was alone. And it was possible he *did* know—that he'd been watching her all along—so it was no risk keeping it up until she finally broke down and texted back for the first time.

Three words, that was all. Three words to make him stop, though she should've known how wrong she was. Not even words, not really. *R u okay?*

"Are you okay?"

Anne pulled away from the window, where darkness ran past her and stars were faint and fading. "No, no, I'm sorry. I got lost in a thought."

Sheriff Ross nodded. "There's an area up here alongside the road. It's famous, known for its ghost lights. People say they've seen things out there, so the town built a little pavilion, like a picnic spot, for those with an interest to keep watch. Kids come out here, been doing it since . . . well, since I was still a kid."

"So have you ever seen any lights out here, any ghosts left behind?"

"Me? No, of course not. I don't believe in stuff like that, never have. Of course, can't say I ever took the time to look, either."

Like you didn't look for your wife? she wondered—a dark thought, probably uncalled for—as they passed the pavilion he'd just mentioned, a rickety wooden affair with a handful of small white signs and a little gravel turn-about. It was there, then gone.

"I enjoyed tonight, Anne. It's been a while since I've had a chance to get out. It was good of you to agree to come to Murfee. I hope at the end of the school year, you'll consider staying. I've talked to Phil Tanner, he let me know how much trouble we'll have filling Tancy Garner's spot. If you don't at least consider it, we'll be back to square one."

"That's very kind. I've enjoyed being here as well. I guess it's too early for me to say what will be best—for the school or for me—but I'll think about it."

"Please do. If I can put in a personal appeal, I wouldn't mind you staying on. New faces in our little old town aren't a bad thing. Not a bad thing at all."

"No, I guess not."

He tapped his fingers as if a thought had just occurred to him, but not really. "Thanksgiving is coming up in a couple of weeks. Unless you have other plans or were planning on getting out of town, well, Caleb and I would love to have you up to the house."

"That's nice, but I really couldn't impose."

"Not at all. I may head up to a piece of land I have and

see about grabbing an elk. Have you ever had it?" He caught her expression, laughed. "Now, don't make a face. Cooked up proper, it's not half as bad as you'd think, and I'm not a half-bad cook. There'll be all the traditional plates as well, and I'll get Modelle Greer to whip up a couple of pies, which are not my specialty. I'll invite a few others and it'll be fine, I promise."

R u okay?

The sheriff waited for her reply even as she fought another dark thought, a sudden suspicion that she'd be alone with him at Thanksgiving—all these "others" he'd mentioned suddenly having other plans, other commitments.

R u okay?

She wondered then about the real reason for her being in Murfee. Like that thing with her address in Austin and the notes he'd sent; all his calls to a cell number that she'd changed more than once in the last year. She could, with only a little effort, trace a faint but nearly straight line from their first meeting in that steakhouse in Austin to that call from Dial Johnson to this moment right here, right now, sitting in the truck with the sheriff. She struggled with the improbable idea that he'd somehow planned this all along, made it happen through sheer force of will—*his will.* Imagining too just how long he must have been thinking about it, thinking about her, while biding his time. And as crazy as it all sounded, now that she'd let those awful thoughts loose, she couldn't catch hold of them again, remembering each handwritten note and each call and each wave hello. His eyes kept hidden behind mirrored sunglasses but still watching her, and how she'd caught a glimpse of someone she thought was the sheriff sitting outside in the dark outside her house. Remembering, finally, the way he'd looked at her in Austin all those months ago, not long before his wife disappeared . . .

Murfee wouldn't be a new start for her even if she'd really hoped it could be. It was never going to be an honest chance to leave Austin and Lucas Neill behind, free and clear. She hadn't guessed it until now, but the sheriff had been the price of escape all along. As bad as she wanted right at that moment to get out of the moving truck, to run and put miles of desert emptiness between them, there was nowhere to go. Not now, not until the end of school. She had committed to being here, was committed to seeing it through. She had no good choices, just like she had no good excuse for Thanksgiving, either, which left her probably stopping in for dinner, at least for a little while. There was no polite or easy way to avoid it, but of course he knew that already, like he seemed to know so many other things about her. As long as she was here, she didn't want to anger him or upset him, even though she couldn't exactly say why. She didn't want him staring at her through his sunglasses, waiting outside in the night. But after the holiday, she'd do her best to pleasantly avoid him and finish up the last of the school year and then get the hell out of Murfee and Texas altogether. She was finally done, and she almost laughed out loud just to hide how badly she wanted to cry.

Is this how Evelyn Ross felt?

"Of course, I'd be happy to come up to the house for Thanksgiving."

12

CALEB

Amé once asked me about the last moment I remember with my mom. Was she worried, sad? Afraid? Was there any hint of what was going to happen next?

You can't live in my house, with my father, without sadness, without fear. It comes with the territory. She struggled with all of those things, and so do I now. Always. But that last morning I saw my mom, I saw none of that. She chatted with me, asked me about the upcoming week. She volunteered at school, but it wasn't her scheduled day. She said she had errands to run, might meet my father for lunch. She hummed in the kitchen, and early sunlight, not quite bright, fell on her face when she turned away from me.

I remember it so clear . . . how young she still looked with the sun on her. It lit her face, her eyes closed, lost in thought. It looked unreal. *She* looked unreal—beautiful, like a painting. Then I got up and grabbed my books and headed out and never saw her again.

But if I really concentrate on that last moment, and if I'm really honest, I can't say that she was afraid or sad, angry or hurt. If anything, in that moment—with light on her face and her eyes closed—she looked relieved.

Ms. Hart is avoiding me. I know she saw me after school yesterday, but she made a U-turn and headed out the other door to the parking lot. The day before, she saw me near her house and instead of parking, drove on down the street, disappearing, making sure not to look at me as she went by, and still hadn't come home an hour later. Today I tried to hang back after class to speak with her, but she stayed close to the other teachers and there was never a good opportunity. Later, she even spent a half hour talking to Principal Tanner, waiting me out.

Maybe she thinks it has to do with her having dinner with my father in Artesia, and in all the wrong ways, she's right. I need her to get Chris Cherry to meet with me. If I can make him see the truth about Rudy Reynosa, maybe he'll see all the truths about my father, too. Something has to happen soon. For Amé, for Ms. Hart, for all of us.

There was one moment after my mother was gone I thought about hurting myself. I got the Ruger out of the gun locker, put it deep in my mouth, making sure my arms were long enough to reach the trigger. The barrel tasted nothing like metal. I was still there with that gun in my mouth, my stolen shells chambered and tears on my face, when my father drove up to the house.

The garage door went up, loud, and the engine of his truck echoed like thunder below me. I had enough warning to take a position at the top of the second-floor stairs; crouched down, on one knee, the Ruger steadied against the wall. Back in the shadows, I was invisible. I had clear aim down the stairs, nearly into the kitchen. But for a man who's never been late to anything, he took too damn long in the garage, messing around, and I never found out what he was doing in there. That was my moment to *handle my business*, our horrible family business. But with so many minutes to think about it, I got scared and didn't do anything at all. I had more than enough time to slip the gun under my bed, leave it there for later, when I could get it back safe into the gun cabinet.

13

THE JUDGE

He didn't *dream*, so much. But he remembered things that only surfaced at night. Conversations he might have had, things that had happened to him as a boy. Things he'd done. More and more he remembered her hair. She'd kept it pulled up and he hated that, figuring she did it up so often *because* he hated it. He loved it when it was down, when it hung around her shoulders, falling like daybreak. It was blond and not blond, there and not there, the color of distant desert lightning. Lightning that came alone, without rain. He was always afraid to run his fingers through it, afraid of how sharp and electric it'd be and how it might hurt him. She wanted to color it once, darker, and he told her he'd kill her if she did. His moods regarding such things were unpredictable. But he remembered her hair, now more than ever, and he couldn't say why.

Dupree stank, sitting in the office chair across from his desk, a can of pop at hand. His eyes were deep in his head, lost, his skin paper-thin and greasy. If he hadn't known Dupree's history, he would have thought Dupree was coming off a three-day drunk, but his chief deputy had never taken a drop of alcohol. He was rank as a dead body, though—something someone had dug up and propped up in front of him.

He sat back in his chair, waited for whatever Dupree had to say. Dupree had caught him, trapped him. The other man rolled his eyes like marbles in his head, like he was trying to see backward through his own damn skull, casting around as if he'd never been in this office, in that chair. His fingers danced, did a little a jig, and he picked at invisible things on his shirt—dirt, maybe. Or blood.

"Been a while, you know? You and me, like this."

He sighed, tapped a penknife. "Like what, Duane? Like what exactly?"

Duane lost focus on whatever was on his shirt, rubbed at it, and sat up straight like he was now paying full attention. "I thought we was friends, always thought we was the best of friends."

"Have I done anything to make you feel different, Duane?"

Dupree laughed, little more than a giggle. "You don't call, you don't write. I was beginning to think you'd washed your hands of me, so to speak."

He stared at Dupree, trying to back him down with a look that had worked so often on so many. But whatever

Dupree saw behind his own bloodshot eyes was more sharp-edged and dangerous than he was. Then it fell together—the arterial cast to Dupree's eye, and his yellow skin. He wasn't drunk or being crazy, he was *wasted*, burned out. How, and for how long, he didn't know, but it looked bad, very bad. His chief deputy might have been getting it from Eddie Corazon, or anywhere, really. God only knew who he'd been talking to or who had seen him like this. Duane didn't have the sense anymore to be afraid, not of the things that mattered.

"I understand, Duane."

Dupree cocked his head, one eye shut like he was thinking hard. "Do you now, do you really?" He rolled his head the other way. "It seems to me you don't even know the damn question yet."

"Fair enough. You tell me, then."

Duane grinned with teeth too big for his head. "You get a piece of that little teacher yet?"

He hesitated, not sure where Dupree was going. "What's that got to do with—"

Dupree stopped him short, something he had never, ever done. "Seems to me you been spendin' time trying to get in her panties, not paying sufficient mind to other things . . . important things."

"Like what?" *Like you, Duane Dupree.*

Dupree seemed to read his mind. "Well, like *me*, Judge. Like me." Dupree cracked his knuckles, echoing like his entire body was breaking. "You know, Chris Cherry's girl thinks he might be stepping out on her, maybe even with that teacher of yours. Pretty Melissa ain't a happy camper, not at all. Lonely." Dupree hung on to the last word for far too long, in some weird way making it echo in his own damn mouth. "Maybe you should sniff around *that* for a bit, or I should."

He cut Dupree off. "Has Chris been spending time with Anne Hart?"

Duane grinned, happy, like he'd gotten blood from a scab. "Probably more than both of you might be comfortable with. You better slip in there before he does, if you get my meanin'. He's a young buck. But you and I? We're jus' old. Young pussy don't pay as much mind to us anymore, does it? Not willingly."

"Is there a meaning here, Duane? Is there a point to all this?"

Duane leaned forward, breathing hot and heavy, grinding like a diesel engine changing gears. "There's always a fucking point. You taught me that. *Always a goddamn point.*"

"Then get to it, Duane, or get the fuck out of my office. Don't come back until you don't look like dog shit. Or don't come back at all."

Duane rose up, nearly knocking over his pop can. "You don't talk to me like that now, not like that."

He didn't move, he didn't blink—just pointed a quick finger at Duane's chest. "Goddammit, you sit down, or I'll whup your ass the way your daddy once did." He wiped his hands on his pants, like he was wiping Duane off them. "You do remember how your daddy wasn't just plum crazy, but liked nigger dick, too? Hell, everyone knew it. When he was drinking bad, he'd give up his ass for a few dollars to buy his next bottle. He was popular in Van Horn, down in Stratton. That was *your* daddy, Duane, crazy and sucking nigger dick or a whiskey bottle, it didn't make any real difference because deep down inside he was equally partial to both. And when he wasn't doing that, he was whupping *your* ass because you weren't worth a nickel and change. He put your mother in an early grave with his antics, and nearly you as well. It all runs deep, Duane, and if I hadn't stepped in, kept an eye on you and damn near treated you like my brother, like my son, you'd be crazy or already dead or sucking nigger dick, too. So, you raise up out of that chair again? It better be because you're going to kill me. Otherwise, keep your ass planted and your goddamn mouth shut. *That's* the point, Duane, the only point."

Duane hung in the air, propped up by hands turning white on the desk. He looked as if he'd been struck, whatever fury and anger having built up in him suddenly spent, gone, drained all out on the floor. Slowly Duane sat back down, still shaking.

It was a risk pushing Dupree in his state, a monstrous risk—the exact size of it difficult to judge, like looking up at a mountain from its shadows, but it had to be done. He couldn't let Duane blow sky-high right here in the office, within earshot of the world. "Now, I assume there's a real reason you're here. Whatever it is you really came to say. So say it respectfully, and then get the fuck out of my office."

Duane nodded, ran a sleeved hand across his mouth, left a wet trail on his cuff. "Yeah, yeah, there's a reason, a damn problem."

He raised his eyebrows, waited.

"You need to open your damn eyes, Judge. Stop messin' with that teacher. I think we have a problem right here, right now, with Cherry."

"*We* don't have problems. Indian Bluffs? He's nearly off that. Not paying any more attention to it. No one is. There's nothing to find."

"Not that, the other thing. Those two who were here . . . who got burned."

Tense. "Who says that, Duane? Who says they were here in Murfee?"

Duane stared ahead, *right through him*, eyes dark and bloody at the same time. Shark eyes, dangerous. Yes, it had been risky to push Dupree, and the Judge wouldn't do it again.

"*That's* the problem, Judge . . . what I found out, when I was talking to Melissa . . ."

Duane was long gone, the office empty, except for his stink, hanging over the chair he'd occupied.

He got up and went over to one of his favorite pictures, black and white and very old, of a man in a small white hat, playing faro in a saloon in Pecos, one hand poised near where he wore a gun. In that old stained photograph the saloon looked hot, noisy, full of commotion, but the man in the center sat calm. It was one of the only photographs taken of James Brown Miller, known as "Killin' Jim" or "Killer Miller"; later "Deacon Miller" for his habit of attending the Methodist church and wearing a long black overcoat even in the worst of a Texas summer. Miller had been polite—a God-fearing man, a family man. He didn't drink or smoke, but was a wizard with a scatter-gun. He killed his first man, his brother-in-law, in 1884, with a shotgun blast to the head. He took to wearing metal under that long frock coat for protection, and was responsible for the deaths of at least twelve people, although Miller himself claimed he'd killed more than fifty. He'd killed for sport or for money, charging about one hundred fifty dollars a head. An angry crowd finally lynched Miller in Ada, Oklahoma, and his last words were, curiously, *Let 'er rip*, as he stepped off the scaffolding.

*   *   *

He lifted up Miller's picture, careful. Hidden behind it was a small safe. He spun it open, reached deep into its snake mouth, where there were two small cellphones. One was older, given to him by Chava's people, the one and only time he ever met them in person. After that, they talked to him only if he called from that phone, refusing to answer if he called on anything else. They were shadows. But they'd stopped calling since things had gone south—all thanks to Rudy Ray.

There hadn't been a card game back in Jim Miller's day that hadn't involved a little sleight of hand, accusations of it. That's why in his one known photograph, Miller was playing with one hand on his gun. It was the nature of the game and everyone knew it: gain an edge, take an edge, or be cut by one.

The second phone was newer, but the same as the other, more or less—just different voices, different shadows, on the other end; just someone else dealing out the cards in the same crooked game. He turned it over in his hands. Deacon Miller had killed for sport and money. He'd killed for those reasons too, and a few others. The reasons never made it easier. Just doing it enough did.

14

CHRIS

Chris was about to call Anne just to say hi, when his radio popped. It was Miss Maisie, letting him know an alarm had been tripped over at BBC. It happened every now and then, kids trying to get into the school, or more likely, onto the field at Archer-Ross Stadium. Usually it was enough to roll slowly through the lot with the emergency lights flashing, just in time to catch a glimpse of a shirtless kid hightailing it over a fence, tripping, laughing. Next morning someone might find a few crushed Lone Stars, a used condom. It was cold out tonight, though, hardscrabble winds, sharp enough to cut your breath away. Any kid screwing around out there was really desperate for a good time.

The sun had gone down a couple of hours earlier, but

the edges of the surrounding mountains and mesas remained, sharp and tilted, cutting against the sky. They
stayed there, stubborn, like the afterimage off a flash-
bulb. They trapped the setting sun's rays in the higher
reaches, reflecting that dying light against the dark. He
might never love Murfee, but at times he did love *this*
place: the old ghost towns, the high desert; the mountains and valleys and cliff walls. The daylit sky when it
was only the color of salt or sand or chalk. All the empty
beauty of it—an incredible hardness made up of so much
nothing.

When he rolled up, he hit his lights, circling the big
lot. There was nothing to aim his spotlight at, so he
didn't. He went around in loops like the fall carnival
merry-go-round. Up close, in the dark, Archer-Ross was
as high as the Chisos, so circling it was like driving the
length of a great sunken ship, resting at the bottom of
the ocean. He was about to radio Miss Maisie, let her
know it was probably nothing, when there was a flash to
his left. It caught his eye so quick he hit the brakes too
hard. He revved the truck, brought it around with the
tires protesting, scanning the length of the stadium. After his conversation with Garrison, Archer-Ross, already
huge, was now ominous and twice as large: *Who do you
trust?* Everything extended into the dark around him,
surrounded him—the whole place a black concrete
maze.

He punched his spotlight, used it to paint the parking lot
and the stadium walls. There, *right there*, he caught a
figure walking toward his truck, trapped by the sudden
white light. Hands raised, smart enough to stop even

without knowing how Chris had spooked himself—how he'd already drawn his gun and was aiming it through the windshield. The hands were up, no gun, no gas can. Nothing. Just one man in a hooded sweatshirt, waiting for Chris. Not even a man—younger than that, a kid. Chris knew who it was; knew that sweatshirt, had seen it or one just like it a hundred times. Caleb Ross. He put his gun away before Caleb got into the car. The boy still might have seen it pointed at him, though. If he did, he didn't say anything.

"What the hell are you doing out here?" Then, peering into the black behind Caleb, "Is there anyone else out here with you?"

Caleb shook his head. "No, just me. I'm alone."

"You weren't messing with anything? I'm not going to find graffiti painted somewhere?" Chris looked down at Caleb's hands for paint on his fingers or on the edges of his sweatshirt. Caleb wasn't that sort of kid, but nothing else came to mind. If there was a girl hiding out there in the dark, it was easy enough to admit it. If there was a boy, Caleb might have a lot of reason not to.

"No, sir, nothing like that."

Chris searched the dark again. "Don't worry about that *sir* shit. I need to know what you were doing. Then I'm going to call your father—*my boss*, the sheriff . . . remember him? Does he know you're here?"

Caleb gave him a look that was answer enough.

"Where's your Ranger?"

Caleb said something weird. "It was my mom's, right? So I don't trust it. It's over at the Pizza Hut, where I'm supposed to be, where my father thinks I am."

Chris let that go. "Look, you're too smart for whatever the hell it is you're doing right now. You're the sheriff's *son*. You know better than to screw around near the stadium. It has your family name on it, for chrissake. It's about the only thing worth anything in this town."

"I know."

Chris dwelled on that, reading the heaviness in Caleb's voice. He didn't like what was there. "Damn, son, that's why you're here, isn't it? You wanted someone to come out and find you."

Caleb wouldn't catch Chris's eye. "No, not just anyone . . . *you*. I knew you were on shift, I found out from Miss Maisie. If someone else had showed up, I was going to bolt."

Even more, Chris didn't like where this was going, not at all. "Look, I'm taking you back to your truck, and then you're going home."

Caleb settled into the seat, pulled back his hood, revealing dark, tousled hair. He was pale, thin; looked older and tired, too. "Please, I need to talk to you. There's no one else. I made a promise. I need your help."

Chris started to say something, but Caleb's face stopped him. "And no matter what, I don't want my father to find out."

"You know, you could have just called. Miss Maisie could have given you my number."

Caleb nodded, his shoulders too thin for the thick sweatshirt. "I know, but it seemed too risky, too easy for you to ignore me."

Chris still felt the weight of his gun that had just been in his hand, pointed through the windshield. "And standing out here in the dark, pulling alarms or whatever, isn't? Accidents happen, Caleb."

The boy's eyes were deep, knowing. "Yes, they do."

They stared at each other across the truck, desert wind working the windows and door handles—ghosts wanting to get in and join them. Chris ignored them. "Okay, you have my attention."

"I wanted Ms. Hart to talk to you, but she wouldn't see me." Caleb rubbed his chin, at stubble that wasn't there.

Chris was taken aback. "What's Anne got to do with this?"

"My father's interested in her. They had dinner the other night, his favorite place in Artesia. Did you know that? I think he met her once before. I'm sure he had a hand in bringing her here."

Chris didn't answer, didn't even know what to say.

"Look, I know you've been talking to her, and since this involves her too, I thought she might help us all meet. Not just me, but a friend as well. I spooked her, though. She's been avoiding me. After she went to Artesia, I got afraid she might mention it to my father, so I did all this tonight."

Chris felt heat at his temples, sparks. "How do you know I've been talking to Anne Hart? How much have you been sneaking around? You've been following me, her?"

"This town isn't that big, not nearly big enough. If I know, someone else does, too."

"What the hell does that mean?"

Caleb shrugged. "I'm saying you grew up here, you have to remember what it's like."

Chris nodded. "Consider me reminded. Now I'm getting you home."

Caleb put a hand on his arm. "No, this isn't just about you and Ms. Hart. Not now, anyway. I want you to help a friend of mine. Amé Reynosa. America Reynosa."

The name didn't mean anything to him.

Caleb took a deep breath, released it like he'd held it for a long time, maybe forever. "I think you found her brother's remains out at Indian Bluffs. Rodolfo Reynosa— everyone called him Rudy Ray. I wanted to believe it was my mom, but it's him. It has to be. He worked for the Border Patrol and everyone thinks he got in trouble with the cops or drug dealers and ran off. No one really searched for him, no one gave a shit. Everyone thinks they know what happened to him, just like they think they know about my mom."

"And you're not like everyone else, Caleb? You don't think he ran off?"

"No, *no*. He was murdered. You found him buried at that ranch, and I think I have a way you can prove it."

A Caucasian. Probably a Hispanic male, probably mid-twenties. Rudy Reynosa was a name Chris remembered, mostly from high school; a little bit older than Chris, but not by a whole lot. He might have heard it since then too, something to do with the things, the troubles, Caleb had mentioned. He never knew Rudy had a sister. "Okay, say you're right, why was Rudy Ray murdered? Who killed him?"

Caleb looked out the window, searching the same dark that had eluded Chris moments before. "I don't know why, exactly, but Amé knows *who* . . . and I believe her." Caleb pointed at Chris, let his arm hang there. A heartbeat later Chris realized Caleb wasn't pointing at him, but at his chest. At the Big Bend County Sheriff's Department star on his jacket.

Chris heard him out, everything he had to say, while they drove back toward town. About an injury that Rudy had suffered as a kid, bad enough that it might still show up in a forensic exam, if someone knew to look for it.

Also about a phone Rudy's sister had kept full of mysterious phone numbers and one not so mysterious at all, possibly Duane Dupree's. Chris thought there was even more the boy wasn't telling him, didn't feel yet he could tell him, but he'd heard enough.

"What do you think? Will you help?" Caleb asked, and Chris said he didn't know, needed time to think. Not much different from what he'd told Garrison. He planned to drop Caleb about a mile short of his truck. Caleb knew a place and guided him there, behind the Dollar General store. After they stopped, Caleb held on to the door handle like he was holding on for dear life, and maybe he was. "Thanks for listening and not shooting me back there at school." Caleb had seen the gun after all. "After this thing with Rudy Ray is over, I hope you'll help me."

"With what?" Chris asked.

"Finding my mom. She didn't leave Murfee any more than Amé's brother did. She's still here somewhere."

Chris raised his hands. "Caleb, I . . ."

Caleb stopped him. "Look, I know you don't believe me, not yet, but when you prove it was Rudy Ray at Indian Bluffs, you will." Caleb got out and stood beside the truck, alone in the dark, lost in it. "You know that place in Artesia where my father took Ms. Hart? He took my mom there too, all the time, and his second wife, Nellie, because I've heard him say it. Hell, probably Vickie as well. It's been there forever, just like him. They've all gone there, and now they're all gone."

"Jesus, Caleb, you don't really believe your father killed your mother, do you?

Caleb worked hard at the words, as if he had never practiced them, never really imagined saying them out loud to another person. "I *know* he killed her."

Before Chris could say anything else, his phone rang. He checked it, glanced at Caleb, who didn't miss his look.

Caleb's eyes were wide, nervous. "What? Who is it?"

Chris held on to the phone, ready to answer. "Get on out of here, get going now. It's the sheriff . . . your father."

15

MELISSA

She was surprised when he came into Earlys. Whiskey Myers was playing on the radio, a band they both once liked, a long time ago. Chris was slow getting to the bar, stopping to say hello to a few of the regulars. Seeing him like this, she noticed he'd dropped a few pounds, not much, but his uniform didn't seem as strained, as uncomfortable. He hadn't shaved in a couple of days, so maybe he was trying to grow out a beard or a goatee. He had a goatee in *ESPN The Magazine*. That had been a great picture, a photo that made him look even taller and stronger than in real life. It'd been snapped mid-throw, his arm braided, taut. The football was still resting on his fingers, aiming upward, surrounded by the glow of stadium lights. If she hadn't seen it in person, she never would have believed it was real.

"Hey," he said, sitting on the same stool Duane Dupree had occupied a week before.

"Hey, yourself. What brings you in here?"

"Was out by the school . . . a false alarm. Thought I would drop in and see how it's going."

"Paradise, absolute paradise." It came out harder, had an edge she didn't really mean. She didn't want to fight with him, not here. "You want something?"

"Coffee if it's made up. It's damn cold, and not even Thanksgiving."

She searched for a mug—always a pot brewing behind the bar to help the regulars sober up. Some came in just for the coffee and talk. She put the mug in front of him. He got lost in it, staring into the rising steam. She left him there and checked on the real drinkers.

He sat for a while, talking to her whenever she had a free moment. Small stuff, nothing important. She had a mug of her own tucked beneath the counter, but with him right there, she let it be. If he had something particular on his mind, he didn't share it; just sipped his cup of coffee, and then another. He told stories about his parents, his time in high school and other things; thoughts, disconnected, all random. He asked her about her work before drifting sideways into silence. His handheld radio rested on the scarred wood next to his cellphone, in case Miss Maisie called him out, but it stayed quiet. He never once looked at the cell or checked it. If his eyes weren't in his coffee, they were on her. She had no idea what he was seeing.

If he'd ever just opened the door a bit, said, "Hey, it's funny but I think I stopped those two agents," she would have said, "I know," finally admitting to searching his things and willing to suffer whatever anger or disappointment came with it; how she'd watched the video and told

Dupree about it. But he never did. He finally got up to leave, fumbling in his pockets for a few bills, even though Earlys always gave out coffee for free. She could tell he was going to wave goodbye, slip out the door, but she came over, pushed the money back across to him.

"I don't want you to get in trouble," he said.

She laughed. "It's a bar, Chris, there's nothing but trouble in here."

He smiled, joining her for a moment. "I'll be home when you get there. Call me, let me know when you're closed up."

"Okay, I will," she said. He'd never asked her to do that before. It was strange.

He shuffled from one foot to another. "There's another thing. I talked to the sheriff tonight. He wants me to head out with him day after tomorrow, take me elk hunting on the land he owns up toward Sierra Escalera. I'll be gone a day or two."

She turned his empty mug in her hands. It was still warm from where he'd held it tight. "Chris, you've never been hunting." It was half a question.

"Once or twice when I was kid. Mule deer, that sort of thing."

She wondered if he'd ever told her that. "Do you want to go?"

"He's my boss, Mel, the sheriff. The almighty Judge. Can't say no."

"Elk are like big deer, aren't they?"

Chris cracked a smile. "Yeah, very, very big deer. Big enough that I might even hit one if I see it. Guess we're having elk for Thanksgiving, babe. That's what the sheriff wants, to bag one for Thanksgiving."

She didn't like his look, the whole tone. She surprised herself, maybe him too—reached out, put a hand on his arm, holding him back. It was the first time she could remember touching him in weeks. It had been good having him here tonight.

"Hey, you okay?" she asked as he turned for the door. What she almost said, what she wanted to say so badly and what was on the tip of her tongue: *Are we okay? Are we ever going to be okay again?*

Chris smiled right at her, right *into* her. "Right as rain, babe."

"It doesn't rain much here, Chris. It's a fucking desert."

He smiled again. "Yeah, I know."

16
ANNE

Her phone rang late. She was afraid it was Sheriff Ross, but was relieved when she saw the number, more than relieved. Happy.

Chris Cherry said, "Hi, hope it's not too late," and she told him it wasn't. He asked if she liked the book, and she said she did, might even try and slip it into the curriculum before the end of year. Kids nowadays might think it was quaint, but she was enjoying it. He hemmed around. She could tell he was in his car, window partly down—caught the sound of night air, moving. She guessed he was closing down the shift for the night, heading home. He mentioned going hunting with the sheriff and that got her attention.

I may head up to a piece of land I have and see about grabbing an elk. Have you ever had it? Then Chris was asking about the sheriff's son, Caleb—how he was doing in class, that sort of thing. She couldn't figure out where this call was going.

"He's fine, a bright kid. It's been a tough year."

"What about a girl, Amé Reynosa? She's a friend of Caleb's, right?"

"America? Sure, I've seen them together . . . I guess that means they're friends."

Chris was silent on the other end. Then, "Amé lost her brother, too. Supposedly ran off, like Evelyn Ross. He worked for the Border Patrol and got into trouble."

"That's so sad."

"It is. I guess it makes sense for the two of them to hang out together . . . kind of going through the same thing."

That's what Phil Tanner had suggested about her and the sheriff. "Yes, I can see that," she agreed, waiting for him to say more. When he didn't, she took a risk, pushed a little bit. "I get the feeling this is an official call, not so much a social one."

Chris laughed. "Am I that transparent? I'm sorry, Anne. I did call to talk to you, really. I just had a couple of questions about Caleb, too. Nothing official, he's not in any trouble." He paused for far too long. "Actually, it's the damnedest thing. He's been trying to talk with *you*, meet with you. As crazy as it sounds, he wanted to get the three of us together. It's no big deal, and I don't want you to be alarmed. I've spoken to him about it, so I'd appreciate if you didn't say anything to anyone, most of all Sheriff Ross."

She almost asked *Why would you think I'd say anything to the sheriff*? Understood then that Chris must know about the dinner in Artesia by now. Hell, all of Murfee probably knew about it. The whole town holding its collective breath, watching and waiting to see what might happen next.

"Caleb wanted to meet with me, *us*?" She waited, but Chris didn't fill in the blank for her. Talking to him was like reading a book; she had to turn the page herself to find out what happened next. "Well, okay, of course, I won't say anything, but if this is about the dinner I had with Sheriff Ross, well . . ." She stumbled. "I'll be honest, I was avoiding Caleb, but it's a lot more complicated than—"

"Anne, please, you don't have to explain yourself to me, or anyone. I know what Murfee is like."

"But I want to. I want you to understand."

Heartbeats passed. Saying it out loud . . . *I want you . . .* even if that hadn't exactly been what she'd meant, still felt like walking them both out on a very high ledge.

Finally, he said, "Okay, we can catch up after I get back from this trip. As long as you know you don't owe me anything. I'm just a guy you met at the carnival, a lightning-rod salesman, like the book. But if you have free time, we could get together."

"Sure, I'd like that, very much."

She thought, hoped, he might say, *Me too, I'd like that as well.* He didn't.

It was part memory, part dream, part something else altogether. First, it was her sitting in her car with Lucas Neill, *the car too goddamn hot and Lucas going on and on and his hands shaking and then those hands grabbing hers, too warm to the touch, her pulling away realizing this has gone too far.* That was the memory.

Then it was Marc in her arms . . . *and both of them covered in blood but this time he doesn't die right away, most of his heart blown out against the wall and all over her, even in her mouth so that she has to wash it out before the police come and never mention to anyone, but he has the time to look at her and whisper, although no sound comes out,* I love you—*not* oh my god oh my god oh my god, *which were his real last words—still reaching for the gun not at his belt but left behind on the nightstand, before he was shot again, and again.* That was the dream.

Then looking up and realizing it's not Lucas with the gun in his hand, but Caleb Ross . . . *in his hooded sweatshirt, not smiling or laughing or making any face or sound at all. Caleb Ross, who for the first time looks exactly like his father. He's a wanderer in her nightmare, an intruder—a bunch of folded shadows in the shape of a boy, standing where Lucas Neill should be.* Where Lucas Neill really had stood over a year ago, so that when she finally woke up— gasping, crying, heart hammering through her chest and hands balled in the sheets—that was the part that was something else altogether.

17

AMERICA

He drove her out to the Comanche. Everything smelled like *vaca*, although the big building and the pens were empty. You couldn't live in Murfee and not go out to the Comanche at least once. Inside there was a ring with a stage surrounded by raised bleachers, almost like sitting in a circus or a movie theater. The ring had fake grass, too bright, too green, where they walked the bulls and the calves; men bidding on the flesh, while other men sat behind a desk talking into big silver microphones, writing notes down on colored paper and typing on laptops. There was a method to it, but she never understood it any more than *las vacas* themselves, staring dumbly through the slats of the ring, pissing or shitting on the fake green grass. Tonight the Comanche was locked up tight, the main building silent, gravel lot stretching on endlessly. The cold mud of the pens, still scarred deep by the hooves of *las vacas* long since gone, was ugly gray—cigarette ashes—in the big overhead lights.

He parked between the lights, settled them down in his own private patch of darkness, and unzipped his pants. Leaned back, waiting for her to begin. And there was a moment when she thought he'd actually fallen asleep with his eyes open, he was so still. He looked bad, *malo*, his face a *calavera*. The Comanche smelled like shit, but he smelled worse, much worse. Smelled like he was dying.

You could roll sand off his eyes, they wouldn't blink, wouldn't move in his skull, but he wasn't sleeping or dead. He tried to get himself hard using his hand, but it wouldn't work. Nothing was working. He kept muttering *goddamn* under his breath, frustrated. He said other words, names. She heard El Juez. His eyes glowed in the big mercury security lights.

"Do it . . . do it anyway."

She leaned back against the door, waited, daring him. If she waited long enough, he might die right in front of her.

Minutes later: "Goddammit, girl, I ain't playin', do what I said." He struggled, got his gun out and pointed it at her across the truck. It trembled in his hand.

She wondered then if he might really shoot her, right here in his truck, and how he'd explain it; or worse, if he would ever have to explain it at all. As she stared at the gun, her phone buzzed deep in her purse. They both heard it, breaking the moment, and although her purse was on the floorboard, he could grab it if he wanted to. She got to it first.

He barked at her, "Fuck, who's that? Who izzat?"

She knew who it was, didn't need to look down at the phone, but didn't want Dupree in her purse, where other secrets hid. *Caleb*. He'd texted a couple of times already, wanted to talk to her. He'd met with Cherry.

"*No es nadie,*" she said, but the phone was better than him finding the other thing.

"Fuck that, let me see." He said it all in one word, slurring, *fuckthatlemmesee,* and the gun still hung between them. She flipped the screen around, the phone still vibrating, caller ID visible. It flashed only two letters, CR, but he either guessed right or recognized the number.

"Darlin', darlin' . . . playin' around with the young Ross is playin' with fire. You give him a taste too, the way you're gonna give me?"

She wasn't going to *give* Dupree anything, ever. He'd have to take it. Take it all, everything, or kill her trying.

"You think the Judge's ever gonna let the two of you be?" Dupree's eyes were shot through with blood, lightning. "It don't matter. 'Bout the only thing he likes less than a Mex like you is that son of his. You know that? He lets you two alone 'cause it *amuses* him, gives that pissant boy something to do . . . something the Judge can take away from him when it suits him." Dupree drifted, the gun drifting with him, away from her face, toward the floorboard.

Her phone stopped, went still, but still she held the purse tight. It was heavy, hiding Rodolfo's gun—silver plate and pearl. What sound would it make going off in the truck? Would it blind her? Deafen her? She'd started carrying it for just this moment—alone with Dupree. But now there were all of Caleb's texts from earlier, saved in her phone. Excited, relieved: *going 2 b ok now . . . promise . . .* over and over again. Chris Cherry had promised to help them . . . help her, just like Caleb had said he would. *Luv u . . . won't let anything happen 2 u . . .*

Caleb believed he'd risked everything for both of them; needed to believe he could save her, even when she wasn't sure he could save himself. Dupree reminding her that *the only thing he likes less than a Mex like you is his own son . . . something the Judge can take away from him when it suits him.*

She had her hand on Rodolfo's gun when Dupree came back around, focused on her again. "I can't get it hard, darlin', not tonight. Guess you're gonna be okay for 'nother day." He shoved the gun in his unzipped pants, not bothering with the holster. "So goddamn tired. You ever get like that, darlin'?" Almost a real question. "Can't even remember when I last slept, closed my eyes. Maybe I only dreamed about sleeping."

Dupree reached toward her, but stopped short of touching her face. "You were there in my dreams." He coughed, spit blood into his open hand. "Is this a dream now, darlin'? Did I never wake up?" Then he forgot about her, fumbled around with the keys to start the truck, talked with someone who wasn't there—someone only he could see or hear in the backseat.

Going 2 b ok now . . . promise . . . She put her purse back down in the floorboard and let Dupree drive.

18
DUANE

So he didn't get hard, she never did get him off. But he had gotten angry. Smacked her once or twice if he remembered right, left her three miles from Mancha's in the dark so she could walk her sorry ass home. Unless he had that all wrong; instead threw her out in the mud all the way back at the Comanche. Left her there facedown. But before that, had she talked to him about his dreams . . . her dreams *of him*? He just couldn't goddamn remember. His head was so full of ashes and embers.

He wasn't sure how he was getting his *foco* anymore, either, since there was almost none to begin with. He'd already picked through the threadbare carpet of this floor, nearly pulling over the stove to look behind it. Used a steak knife, too, on his own mattress, which he didn't need for sleeping, searching for any that might have slipped inside. It had been so long since he'd met the beaners at the Far Six that their little packages were long gone; memories, if he still had those.

It was possible he was changing into street clothes, taking his daddy's old truck and driving to Fort Stockton, buying it there. Or breaking his own rules and getting it from Eddie Corazon. But he was finding *some* from somewhere—never enough, never ever enough—always a little pinch to smoke up fast in one of his old lightbulbs. He'd taken all the bulbs from his kitchen, where he didn't eat anymore anyway.

It should bother him more that he couldn't pin down when and where he was getting it, but maybe it was just the ghosts, after all—because there were more now, always waiting for him, hanging out with his daddy on the porch. So many he couldn't name them all, even if he could remember them. A goddamn reunion.

The Judge told him he was taking Chris Cherry up to his hunting property, El Dorado. There was a lot of nothing out there. Just badlands, bad things: a place where Cherry could very easily fall into trouble, like falling down a well. But that had never been the Judge's style, not really. That's what he'd always had Duane Dupree for.

Still, the Judge swore he was going to handle Cherry. *Handle it all.* He'd been talking to some new friends and promised Duane there might be a little work coming their way again. It wasn't a sure thing, not yet, but he just needed Dupree to sit tight, hold it together, and for fuck's sake, not fall apart.

The Judge had no idea how hard that could be, when you couldn't even find all your pieces anymore.

19

CHRIS

In the car on the long drive, started just after dawn, they talked elk. All about bulls and solos and harems, about how big they could get—well over seven hundred pounds—and how late September and early October was the real rutting time, although a late-season hunt could be just as successful. Chris also messed around with the cow call; checked out the rifle that the sheriff had lent him (along with all the other hunting gear)—a Weatherby Vanguard Back Country. It was a beautiful weapon, and even with the heavy scope, barely weighed in at seven pounds. Still, it didn't hold a candle to the sheriff's Sauer 303, built to take boar in Europe. Both rifles were more than Chris felt comfortable with. Both were made for a better hunter than he. The sheriff told him not to worry, Chris wouldn't be taking the shot anyway.

Once on foot, they lost themselves in the oak brush and red oak and mountain scrub, in a maze of canyons. Snow dotted the highest peaks, but the sheriff said the elk were down below, where there was still forage. He knew these lands like the back of his hand, had built tree stands along good water and wallows. They'd first see if they could draw in and stalk a bull before resorting to tracking one. They'd lay up overnight and try with the dawn.

When Chris asked if Caleb enjoyed coming out here to hunt, the sheriff looked at him for a long moment before saying that Caleb never had the stomach for it.

They kept moving as a light rain fell. Chris hadn't used these muscles in a while, and it played hell on his knee. He lagged behind, the sheriff a shadow constantly appearing and disappearing ahead. That's what happened out here, in this place; everything disappeared eventually. Chris imagined it all as nothing but one huge ghost town, just memories of people and places and things that were long gone. Scarred middens and pictures painted on rocks. An abandoned mine and a lone wooden lean-to, battered by the wind. Arrowheads and old shotgun shells and musket balls left on the ground. Fool's gold and the bones of fools.

The going was even harder as they worked their way down the roughs, cutting through a mosaic of spruce, fir, and aspen. They finally found a break in the basin and a scattering of monstrous boulders thrown up hard against a water run, trees circling like a crown. The sky turned dark at the edges with dusk. Sitting on a rock, taking water from his borrowed canteen beneath cracked limestone looming close and tight, felt like being gripped by a huge fist.

Chris was breathing hard, trying to hide it, but the

sheriff laughed. "Haven't been out like this in a while, have you?"

"Hell, I've never been out like this. I did a little bit of hunting with my dad, but not way out here. I'm not sure I'm going to be much use to you."

"Your dad was a helluva dentist, best this town ever had."

"Yeah, but not much of a hunter."

The sheriff said, "Well, let's see what you're made of."

By the time they camped they still hadn't seen another living soul—an eagle, maybe, before nightfall. Something small and dark and distant, high on invisible drafts, held aloft by unseen hands. Later they drank coffee spiked with Black Maple Hill, stared together into the fire. There would have been a million stars if the clouds from the earlier rain hadn't held over, smattering drops that were now flakes—like white ashes—blowing down and catching in Chris's hair. Something howled high on a ridge behind them; became a series of barks before fading to nothing.

"Do you like what we do, Chris?" The sheriff nudged the fire with a boot, poured out his cold coffee and bourbon and set up another.

"I'm sorry?" Chris said, unsure.

"Being a deputy, working in Murfee?"

"Sure, sure I do."

The sheriff watched him through the fire. "Maybe it's not what you thought you'd be doing, but we're glad to have you back home. The people like you, they trust you." The sheriff sipped from his mug. "I'm not always going to be sheriff. May not seem that way, but my day is coming, sooner or later."

"I think you've got a lot of years left. Remember, I just hiked around these woods with you today."

The sheriff grinned, pleased. "Well, it's still best to plan, to look ahead. And that's part of the reason I wanted to spend this time with you. Looking ahead. Someone will sit in my chair one day and they'll have to run for my office. That'll be easier if that man has my support."

"Sir, I appreciate that, but there's Hayes and Busbee. There's Duane . . ."

The sheriff kicked at the fire again, releasing smoke, embers. "All good men in their own way, necessary men. Duane is a fine example. You always need a Duane Dupree because he serves a purpose; makes the hard decisions, the ugly ones. The people of Murfee need him and don't even know it and will never appreciate it the way I do. They can't, so they won't follow Duane, and that's the difference. I think they'll follow you."

"I don't know what to say."

"Of course you don't. You're not the sort of man who thinks that way. You don't covet another man's possessions." He held on to the last a little too long. "That's another reason why people trust you. They believe you're decent, and so do I."

"I'm trying to do a good job, that's all."

"Everyone starts that way, Chris. You'd be amazed at how hard that can be." The sheriff looked up to the dark trees, the faintly falling snow. "Anyway, I want you to give it some thought. There's still time. I'm not quite ready to hang up the spurs."

"No, I don't think you are, and Murfee isn't ready for it, either."

"Ah, the town gets on, it always will." He took another long sip. "How about you? How are you and Mel getting on? Duane's been chatting her up at Earlys. She seems to like the work there. Is she finally taking to Murfee?"

Chris held his own mug tight. Mel hadn't said anything about Duane Dupree, and as far as he knew, she sure as hell didn't like Earlys. "She needed to get out of the house a bit. Earlys is a way to do that. She's fine."

"Well now, you know Dupree. He can't stay away from a pretty lady. If he's bothering her over there, tell me and I'll handle it. He doesn't need to be lingering, drinking his damn pops."

"No, I'm sure it's fine." But Chris didn't know whether it really was or not. The fire popped, throwing a handful of sparks. They hung in the air, burning in the dark, leaving orange trails in their wake.

"He's been eyeballing that new teacher, too. Anne Hart. I've heard around that you two are friends." The sheriff's eyes reflected new fire.

Chris's hands were as cold as the mug in them. He shook his head. "Not so much. I've introduced myself, talked with her in passing, like at the carnival. But just about books. There's still a bunch of them up at the house. My dad and I saved almost every book we ever had. Mel wants me to get rid of them." He trailed off.

"Mind that woman of yours, Chris. Otherwise, she'll bring you sorrow . . . I should know." He shifted, backing up a bit, disappearing into deeper darkness. "I actually met our new teacher even before she came here, before she'd gone back to her maiden name. She was married to a police officer in Killeen. She was Anne Devane then."

The sheriff said it as if the name should mean something to him, but it didn't. "The pair of them got into a mess of their own up there. Tragic. You didn't know that? Maybe it never came up when you two were talking about all those books."

"No, no, it didn't."

The sheriff was so completely hidden by the dark and fire he might as well not have been there at all. "I'm surprised at that, Chris, really surprised. It was quite a big deal in the news for a while . . ."

20

AMERICA

The house was beautiful, like a picture in one of her magazines. Better than her magazines. It was wide, open, real. Rambling on and on, one room spilling into another, like the whole place was taking wing. There was nothing scary about it at all. Caleb always talked about this place in hushed tones. In the years she had known him, this was her first time inside it—*la casa del Juez*. Caleb said he was out hunting with Deputy Cherry and wouldn't be back until tomorrow or the day after, but he didn't look happy about it.

When she asked about that, something passed in front of his eyes before he said, "I think he'll be fine. It's all still okay."

She didn't ask anymore.

*   *   *

He got beers from somewhere, warm bottles, too afraid
to drink the ones already in the house. She held one but
didn't sip it as they walked from one darkened room to
another, everything wrapped in shadow, all light and
color gone. He showed her the things his mama had
bought, put up on the walls. She'd cleaned out everything from the other wives and tried to make the place
her own. Amé knew it didn't matter—those past women
still haunted the place, and Caleb's mama had known it
as well, every time El Juez touched her. Men didn't dis-
card things, places, people. They forever held on to the
touch and scent and sound of every woman they'd ever
had, like holding on to whatever years had passed them
by. El Juez saw those other women—remembered
them—in every corner, in every shadow, of the house
he'd shared with them. Even when Caleb's mama was
here by herself, hanging her own pictures or repainting a
wall, she was never truly alone. Her own mama used to
say, *"Las paredes todavía tienen ojos."* The walls still have
eyes.

   If Amé had been Caleb's mama, she would have
burned this place to the ground before ever setting foot
in it.

The room for El Juez was different. Simple. If it had ever
had a woman's touch, it was hard to tell. Caleb stood at
the door, afraid to enter, leaving the hallway light on for
her to see. They were reflected in a big mirror, smoke
trapped in the glass, and the bed was smooth as a stone.
There was a dresser of pale wood, no pictures, and little

else. Caleb stayed silent, like this room explained so much
on its own . . . that it revealed secrets. Amé felt her life
was nothing but empty rooms just like this, going on and
on, revealing nothing. Then they were in Caleb's room,
door shut. The lights were off, only the glow of the iPad
on the desk as it shuffled through songs. Songs he liked.
They were lying next to each other on his bed.

Earlier they'd stood outside on his back porch and
smoked the weed she'd gotten from Eddie Corazon until
they were both too cold, her bare arms left shaking. But
it was warm here, now, lying next to him. They'd never
been this close for this long. He whispered that Deputy
Cherry would finally prove that her brother had been
murdered, that Duane Dupree had done it. He whispered that everything would soon be different. She didn't
know if he was trying to make her believe it, or himself.

She rolled over, propped herself on her arm. What if
no one cared about Rodolfo Reynosa, like no one had
cared when he first disappeared? What if no one believed
the deputy? Or he told El Juez? He was out there with
him now, somewhere in the mountains. What if he was
left there, like Caleb had been left, but now forever? If
something happened to the deputy, what would happen
to her, her family?

"It won't be like that," Caleb said. "It won't. I promise." But his eyes weren't convinced, and neither was she.
But she let his arm creep over her stomach to hold her
and then she let him kiss her—what he'd wanted for so
long. And it was okay. For a few minutes, she wanted it
to be. She accepted he was incapable of seeing, no matter
what she showed him. His beautiful eyes were blind and
always would be.

His music stopped, started again, at the first song. The
room was so warm—like the paper beaches taped to her

walls—and so was he. She remembered then something Rodolfo once said when they were coming back to the United States over the Puente Ojinaga, the bridge above the Rio Grande. Hidden behind his big narco glasses, shiny like mirrors, Rodolfo had watched all the people crossing both ways over the bridge, Mexican and American. He'd said in his perfect English: *More than a river will always separate us.* He hugged her then, laughed at his own silliness, dropped back to Spanish and called her his star, *mi estrella.* He reminded her that as long as she glowed, he'd always find his way home.

He disappeared two weeks later.

Caleb's mouth and hands and body found her and she didn't stop him. Let the walls watch all they want. No matter what happened, she wanted him to remember this, hold on to it forever. It was all she had to give.

21

CHRIS

He was covered in blood.

They got up before dawn, not that Chris had slept much anyway, to the sounds of bugling and other animal noises, and made their way toward them. They broke cover at a wallow—cold water and colder mud spotted with hooved tracks the sheriff said were fresh—finally settling into a killing spot the sheriff favored.

The sheriff put him downwind with the cow call, told him to work the plastic horn. The sheriff set himself up high in a ridge of Hinckley oak. The elk, if there was one, would come direct to Chris's calls, sounding him out of his hiding place, but it would be leery, looking hard. Elk were big, but not necessarily dumb. Even if it spied Chris, it might never see the real danger lurking a dozen yards away. He had a hard time focusing and fumbled with the cow call, but kept at it. An hour became two or more. He couldn't see the sheriff, only wind moving pale branches and flakes in the air. The sky was the color of a bullet.

He couldn't concentrate, not only because of what the sheriff had revealed about Anne the night before, but because of the call he'd made to Garrison before leaving Murfee. He had a day before they came to El Dorado and pushed the DEA agent on getting the full forensic report on the body from Indian Bluffs; told him it was important, to use whatever pull he had, if any. After that, Chris would meet with him and help him any way he could. Garrison had wanted to know what he was supposed to be looking for. Chris had said he'd know it when he found it.

Chris was finally about to give up on the horn, stand and stretch and tell the sheriff he needed a break, when he heard shuffling, breathing. The elk came into view. It was bigger than he thought possible, the musty stink of it carrying to him. It was losing summer weight but gaining a shaggy winter coat, its heavy antlers crooked, dipped low. It was a bull, the points of the rack wide and sharp like an iron crown; lord of a harem, and curious about that solitary cow that it thought was lost or injured, calling from the underbrush.

It came, slow, nose down and huge dark eyes up, scanning. It spotted Chris, saw right through him, and stopped.

Chris glimpsed the sheriff, picking him out of the undergrowth. His gun was up and aiming and Chris could see right down the barrel even though there was no sunlight to gleam off of it. It was as wide as a canyon, a void big enough to lose the sky in, darker even than the elk's eye—the big animal a sudden blur and burst of motion

at the sheriff's presence. Kicking and turning and running. It looked back once, accusing, as if to let Chris
know it was onto the trick all along. But the trick was on
Chris. He knew where the gun was aimed, and he yelled
when it went off, surprised it sounded so goddamn
loud.

He was covered in blood. The sheriff's shot took the elk
through the rib cage, right in the lungs. The beast
dropped in mid-leap, stumbling and pissing everywhere;
went down headfirst, huge lungs filling with blood.

It never even made a sound.

The sheriff slid out of his hiding place, leaving leaves
and dirt in his wake. Chris imagined the gun was so hot
it glowed like a lit match.

"Damn, that's a big one," the sheriff called out, mostly
to himself, approaching the creature carefully. Chris
joined him, breathing twice as hard, as if he'd run a mar-
athon. The sheriff, smiling, knew the answer even before
he asked the question. "Damn, son, what was all that
yelling about?" Then he poked at the elk's open eye with
the muzzle of the gun, to make sure it was dead.

He was covered in blood, the natural consequence of
field-dressing the kill. The sheriff showed him how to
cape and gut it, how to cut its head off. They removed
the innards, split the brisket open, and pulled the wind-
pipe free. They tied it up by its legs over the little
stream and let the blood run out, which the sheriff fa-
cilitated by taking handfuls of muddy water and tossing
it into the ruined body, watching it all drain out at their
feet.

They did more cutting and quartering and the sheriff

got out his collapsible dead sled so they could drag their kill back to the truck. It was going to be a long trip. Chris's hands were red going to black. All that strange blood was trapped beneath his skin and he felt stained, marked, like he would never get it off of him.

The sheriff clapped him on the back, offered his canteen. "It's a helluva feeling, isn't it, Chris? A helluva feeling."

Later they were crawling hand over fist through the undergrowth, dragging that damn dead elk, when the sheriff finally asked him about the agents. They were just stopping for a break, the sled between them stinking of cold copper, pennies, when he brought it up.

"The feds are still poking around, asking questions. It's a tragedy, a horrible tragedy. I never want to see any of our own hurt. If there's one thing that keeps me awake, Chris, it's that." The sheriff squinted against a sun that wasn't there. "A damn shame. That memorial was tough . . . emotional. And that young girl, all burned up, still hanging on like that? A lot more questions than answers."

"A lot of bad luck. Wrong place, wrong time," Chris said.

"Possibly." The sheriff rubbed his jaw with a bloody glove. "Neither were born or raised in Texas, so they probably thought they were in the wrong place every goddamn day. This place isn't for everyone." He tried a smile. "And that's what bothers me. What were they doing all the way out in Valentine? Working? Seems like we should have known about that . . . spotted them around. A big ole black Tahoe like that? You know, passing on the road, if nothing else."

Passing on the road, if nothing else. A cold knot turned

in Chris's stomach. Chris wasn't sure how, exactly, but the sheriff knew about his stop on 67, maybe even the video.

Who do you trust, Deputy Cherry?

"Maybe we didn't know because they didn't want us to." The sheriff eyed him. "Common courtesy says if you're working in another man's backyard, you tell him. Feds, locals, it makes no difference. Trust is necessary. It's a courtesy that keeps blue-on-blue accidents from happening. Secrets only lead to trouble, Chris. Good people get hurt that way, happens all the time."

The dead elk was still leaking blood all over the sled. The severed head stared back at Chris with glassy eyes. If he bent closer, he'd almost see himself reflected there. "I don't know. I really don't." But pushing a bit, "I wonder if it had anything to do with that dead Mexican I found at Indian Bluffs?"

The sheriff spit, wiped his mouth with that bloody glove again, and picked up the sled's nylon rope. "Now why on earth would you think that?"

The full report was done, being signed off on. Garrison would have it officially in a few days, but he'd been better than his word and got what Chris had wanted—needed, anyway—just before he'd set out with the sheriff. He'd taken the call with the sheriff's truck still idling in his driveway, Garrison reading fast in that brutal early-morning hour from all the pages that had been e-mailed to him the night before.

The ulna is one of the two bones of the forearm. The injury on the remains from Indian Bluffs was an ulnar shaft, or nightstick, fracture—so called because it's the sort of break common when someone gets hit with a nightstick, raising an arm up to defend himself, although Chris guessed that wasn't the case. When it's bad enough, displaced, it's repaired through open reduction and internal fixation, basically the insertion of a strong metal rod—plates and screws. That was something Chris *did* know about: when his knee shattered, the bone below it had cracked, too. He'd gone through the same procedure. After all, ulnar fractures are a pretty common injury for athletes, especially football and basketball players. Soccer players, too—if they're struck by the ball in just a certain way, kicked in just the right place.

According to what Garrison had read to him over the phone, this particular fracture had happened when the deceased was young and had been left to heal with only a cast. Not the best treatment, because the fracture was very serious, serious enough it was still evident in the adult bones—like a crack in a pane of glass—all these years later. Evident . . . *evidence*. Just the sort of thing that might identify the bones Chris had found at Indian Bluffs if you knew to look for it. And that treatment, shitty as it was, might have been all that someone without a lot of money or no medical insurance could ever get— someone who might have found it easier to cross the river to have it done in Mexico.

Someone like Rudy Reynosa.

They didn't talk much more as they made their way back to the truck, getting there as night started to fall. Really, they didn't talk at all. There was nothing more to say. They had a long drive back to Murfee in the dark, both of them covered in dried blood the whole way.

Who do you trust, Deputy Cherry? Can you trust every-

one in your department? Can you trust anyone in Murfee at all? Chris couldn't shake the memory of the sheriff's big Sauer 303 pointed at him. For just a heartbeat, it had been pointed at *him*, not at the elk.

Just a heartbeat, but long enough.

22
CALEB

When I woke up, she was gone. I knew she would be. I rolled over, searching for the fading warmth of her body, the only thing to even hint she'd been with me at all.

Later I went into my father's room and contemplated searching his dresser drawers, his nightstand, looking for clues. Secrets. But standing near his bed, I had images of traps, land mines: a feather or piece of fishing line falling to the floor; my breath hanging in the air, still visible, long after I'm gone—a thousand clues that might reveal my presence to him when he returned. It's so goddamn funny that we both spend so much time hiding from each other, pretending.

Him, that he's a loving father. Me, that I'm a loving son.

We'd traded numbers that night outside the school, so I texted Chris, asking him to tell me when they were on their way back. I had to check in and make sure he was okay. It was a risk, and I knew he wouldn't even get it until they were well on the road from El Dorado. There are no cell towers out there, and phone service is nonexistent. It's like a piece of the world that's fallen off, a jigsaw puzzle piece lost on the floor. I wasn't even sure he would answer me. I just wanted to know . . . something. No matter what I'd said the night before, I was worried.

I was afraid of my father's room, but not of the attic. That's where he'd put my mom's stuff, and with him gone and still hours from home, I pulled down the ladder and crawled up there to look through those things one last time. Mostly I just wanted pictures—to see us together again. I wanted to see her face one more time, afraid I might not be remembering it right. That her hair was brown and not blond; that I had been dreaming her eyes were green when they were really blue. All these things I thought I knew and remembered, that I'd had wrong all along. That she never existed, was nothing but a dream.

But the boxes were there under the roof just where my father had put them that day he slapped me on the back, leaving a dusty handprint. They were neatly stacked, along with other things from other wives. I sat for a long time in the still and gloom before I opened up the first and looked through it. It didn't hold my mom's clothes or her old Christmas decorations or even the photos I'd been looking for. It took me a few moments to even figure out what I was looking at.

Then I dumped the box all over the attic floor.

*   *   *

I heard from Chris a little while later, two texts, both simple and to the point.

A warning: *On our way.* And the second as good as a promise: *You were right.*

23

MELISSA

She was outside smoking, listening to *Dark Stars*, when she realized Chris was home.

The shower was running hard.

She came in, still wrapped up in blankets, to find bloodstains on the edge of the sink, on the tub. Through the old shower-door glass, fogged and green and thick, all she could see was red. Her heart hurt and she pulled back the door fast to find him standing there, head down, water running over him, scrubbing at his bloody hands. She made a noise, half reached for him.

He told her: "It's not mine, I'm okay." They'd just shot an elk, a big one.

She asked if he'd done it, pulled the trigger himself, and he shook his head no. He was just the decoy, the dummy.

He turned away, leaned his head against the wall; held his huge bloody hands at his side. He said, "I think I'm in trouble, babe." The water was so hot Mel could feel it from where she was standing, like Chris was trying to set himself on fire. Trying to burn all the blood away.

She slipped out of her blanket, out of her clothes, and got in the shower with him. She gasped at the scalding water, but it hurt less than her heart. She filled up her hands with soap; put it in his hair, all over his chest. She held his hands in hers and scrubbed them with her own. She washed all of him until the blood was all gone.

24
ANNE

He called and asked if they could meet outside Murfee, away from town. When she asked where, she heard him thinking on the line before he mentioned a place called the Lights. Wondering if she knew where that was. She said she did.

She came late after school and he was there before her, sitting in his truck, heater running. The little gravel lot was empty except for a few crushed beer cans, loose paper blowing across the ground. Also, two beer bottles standing upright like lonely sentries on the table under the pavilion, catching and then throwing a last bit of winter sunlight. If they talked for any length of time, night would find them, and maybe she'd see these mysterious lights after all.

As she got out of her car there was a train coming

toward them, slow and lumbering, but it was too far away for any sound.

"Hey," Chris said, surprised when she got in and handed him back his book. He turned it over in his hands, back and forth, like he'd never seen it before, and then placed it up on the dashboard.

"How did your hunting trip go?" she asked.

"Bloody."

"Oh." She glanced around the tight interior of the truck, at all the police gear, as if there might really be blood there.

"Thanks for coming all the way out here. I know it's weird. I didn't feel comfortable in town."

She smiled. "Yeah, I know that feeling."

He shifted, facing her, and sitting this close to him in the car, she got a sense of how big he really was. He hadn't shaved, not recently, and a fine line of hair ran along his jawline, pale, almost blond.

"I'm going to tell you some things and ask you a couple as well," he said. "I hope you'll hear me out first. And look, you don't have to tell me anything you don't want to. I'm just trying to understand exactly what I've gotten myself into."

"That sounds serious. Are you in trouble?" she asked.

He shook his head, but she didn't quite believe him. "It's not so much that I'm *in* trouble as that I've stumbled on some, if you get my distinction . . . if there really is one." He paused, the train lumbering toward them. "And I think it involves you too, Anne."

Anne held her breath. "God, I don't need trouble, Chris. I came here to get away from it."

"I know," he said. "Or I guess I know now. Sheriff Ross told me all about it, his version anyway. How he met you before. And well, that other thing, with your husband and that student. I'm so sorry."

Breath escaped her; she felt herself get small. There was no avoiding it. "I wish *he* hadn't told you, not like that."

"It's okay. You can tell me here now, any way you want."

Now she heard the train, felt it, as it went by. After the last car had passed—the last of the sun gleaming on its metal skin—she finally turned to him again. "His name was Lucas Neill."

She told him about that day in her classroom, with the rain pounding outside and his very first texts. She didn't leave anything out, right up to the day she'd gotten so worried and finally broke down and returned his messages. How they met outside a Big Lots and he'd tried to kiss her, and how she said no. How she hit him across the face and left him angry, frustrated. That was what she really wanted Chris to understand—that no matter what people thought, no matter what the news hoped to report (and went on ahead and suggested anyway, because it made a better story), she never had any sexual relationship with Lucas Neill.

She'd made mistakes—God knows that, a hundred of them—let Lucas get too close, listened too damn much, but she had never crossed that line. She told Chris how much she'd loved her husband, and how she sometimes wondered if she'd just gone ahead and slept with Lucas Neill, if he might still be alive. It was a silly thing to believe—to beat herself up over—but it haunted her anyway.

"A couple of days later the doorbell rang," she said.

"He rang the damn doorbell, like he'd been invited over."
She could still hear the cheap sound of that doorbell. She
heard it all the time.

"It was this time of year, right around Murfee's Fall
Carnival, when you and I first met." But that felt like
forever ago. "Marc and I were talking about dinner, of all
things, a simple conversation, like everyone does every
day. It was late, but I wanted to go out and get something and he wanted to heat up hot dogs, scrounge
around the kitchen for leftovers. There was a game on TV
he wanted to watch. I can't even remember what it was,
who was playing." She wondered for a moment if it was
possible that Chris had been on TV that night.

"Anyway, I was irritated, because he knew I didn't like
fucking hot dogs and I just wanted to go out, someplace
stupid like Olive Garden or Red Lobster, and we were
bickering. And then I got even more irritated when the
doorbell rang and he stopped in mid-sentence to go answer it and . . ."

*It's Lucas, she knows that, even though his face is dark
inside the hood of his sweatshirt. He says something, but it
doesn't really matter because the gun is louder, oh so much
louder, and she is screaming both* Why? *and* No! *at the
same time and Lucas is both laughing and crying and all
Marc is doing is reaching for her to protect her, to shield her,
and then she's trying to help him stand up because he just
can't do it anymore, as Lucas fires again into the back of
Marc's head and his knees buckle and his face turns pale
while he dies in front of her. She feels the last breath he is
going ever to take against her face and it makes her eyes
blink as he passes through her and Lucas is still standing
there aiming the gun at her and then finally thank God he
puts it in his own mouth . . .*

"He said later the plan was to shoot Marc and then

himself. He had a moment's thought about shooting me, but it didn't matter anyway, because he didn't shoot either of us. Only Marc, only my husband."

She told him the rest, all about the trial and how it broke the remaining pieces of her life. Lucas Neill was convicted and sent to Austin State Hospital, a psychiatric facility. She admitted she read an article recently about a spike in patient-on-patient violence at Austin State, and how she hoped someone there was hurting Lucas Neill. She had dreams about that, hated herself for them. She tried a joke, how it often felt like Lucas wasn't the only one sentenced to that place, but she was crying when she said it.

"I guess Sheriff Ross remembered me from that stupid awards ceremony and the dinner after, then all the news following Marc's death. When there was an opening at Big Bend he helped make it happen. I don't know how many strings he pulled, but enough. And I needed it, because I needed to get out of Austin. I needed to get away." She wiped at her face. "You know, once I got here, a part of me suspected that he was waiting for me, just waiting for the right time to . . ."

Chris stopped her. "Anne, I understand. I do. Look, this thing with you and the sheriff? That's all . . ." He was struggling, searching for the right words, if there were any. "Well, it's fake, like the carnival . . . the Pandemonium Shadow Show from the book. With the sheriff, with everything he says and does, there's always this smoke, right? It hides everything, and you have to feel your way through it slowly, to see the real thing at its heart."

Chris shook his head, still not sure he'd said it right.

"But my dad used to say, where there's smoke, there's fire."

It was his turn. He told her about the body at Indian Bluffs. He told her that Caleb Ross and his friend, America Reynosa, believed that body was America's brother, Rodolfo—a former Border Patrol agent—and how he believed that now, too. He thought he might even be able to prove it, all because of an old sports injury. Not his, Rudy's, and if nothing else, it was a start. Pointing him in the right direction, so he could keep feeling his way ahead, searching for the real thing.

He told her it was also very possible that Chief Deputy Dupree was Rudy's killer, and that it was done with the sheriff's knowledge or on his orders.

"Caleb wouldn't go quite that far, but he said America believed it, the part about Duane, anyway. And he's convinced his dad is at the center of it all."

"God, Chris, why?"

"Not sure, but it might also have something to do with those two federal agents that were attacked, their car set on fire."

Anne remembered that.

Chris said, "You know, more smoke, this time for real." Then he pointed out to her where he was parked the night he pulled over Darin Braccio and Morgan Emerson.

"Caleb is worried about you . . . for you. He didn't quite come out and say it that way . . . but, you know the sheriff was married before, right?"

"Of course, his wife, Evelyn. Caleb's mother."

"Well, before Evelyn, there were others. Nellie died in the bathtub in their home, the house he and Caleb still live in. There was another one, early on, ran off to El Paso, I think."

"I heard those things." Her expression must have been clear even in the truck's dark, as Chris smiled, cold.

"Yeah, the sheriff hasn't been too lucky with love. All just coincidences, right? But between his wives and now Rudy Reynosa, we have a lot of people running away from Murfee. . . . You know, disappearing."

"More smoke," she said.

"Yeah, a lot more."

They both sat for a long time, silent. She understood now why Caleb had been trying to talk with her, following her around. He was keeping an eye out for her, trying to protect her. Her boy knight in shining armor.

She wasn't sure whether she grabbed Chris's hand or he grabbed hers.

"Okay, so what does it all mean? What now?" she asked.

Chris touched the badge on his shirt, a gold star. "I'm not sure. Not yet. It could be a whole lot of nothing."

But she knew he didn't believe that, not even close. "Are you upset I didn't tell you about Sheriff Ross before . . . that I knew him? How I ended up here . . . about my husband?"

"No more than you're upset that I haven't told you about my girlfriend. Her name is Melissa." He released her hand, pointed at the book on the dash. "But it's about the books, right? We both just love talking about books."

She laughed, and in that moment, he could have fallen

forward to kiss her, his big hands finding hers again and pulling her to him, where he'd feel twice as warm as the car, his own gravity holding her close. Safe. She would have let him, wanted him to. But Deputy Cherry, with his girlfriend Melissa at home waiting for him, didn't do that, and it meant twice as much to her.

He finally said, "Be careful, okay? Just do that. And I'll let you know how things go."

"I will. But you're the one who needs to watch out."

"Fair enough. Oh, and he invited you over for Thanksgiving, right?"

"Yes, he did." She was hopeful. "Are you going, too? I wasn't sure how to get out of it. The sheriff isn't an easy man to turn down."

He pulled the book down from the dash, thumbed the pages, and then carefully slid it between the seats for the drive home, or wherever he was going. "No, I'm not. But you'll be having elk for supper."

25

THE JUDGE

There was a clock ticking all the time in his head.

If he questioned it, which he really didn't, he might think it was just the memories of that old West Country Longcase clock his grandfather had been so proud of, dominating the foyer of the big ranch house outside Pecos. It had been mahogany, shined so bright each and every day by the nigger house help he could see his face trapped in the thick wood. He'd been switched in front of it, knelt down by both his father and his grandfather at one time or another—Hollis sometimes looking on—with their rough hands on his neck, leaning hard into the birch rod and bloodying his shoulders, his back, his ass.

If he thought much about that, which again, he didn't, he might wonder why he remembered the beatings in front of that damn clock, but never the reasons that had him kneeling there to begin with.

He sipped coffee while Caleb finished breakfast and got ready for school. He timed the boy's movement to the ticking in his head, found him always moving too goddamn slow. He knew Caleb had let someone in while he hunted at El Dorado, guessing it was that wetback girl he'd been sneaking around with. She'd changed the very air trapped in the house; if he stood close enough to the boy, he'd probably smell her on him. He both cared and didn't. Not so much the boy would try such things, but that he imagined himself safe enough to get away with them.

Like his truck, or his phone. The phone had been in his mother's name, her account and Caleb's held jointly down at Murfee's only cellular store. The boy paid the bill in cash from his allowance and always in person, no records ever showing up at the house. He *thought* he could keep a handful of secrets that way, but the boy was wrong. Caleb's life was like one of Evelyn's snow globes, the ones she used to collect and set out at Christmas. All that occurred under the boy's clear heavens were the movements of his hand, tilting it one way or another. They were his acts of God, granting an illusion of freedom. Caleb might look up and see sky, but he'd never touch it—never know it wasn't real.

He dealt with his son no different from how he might a horse, giving just enough rein to keep the animal content . . .

Once Caleb was out the door, still silent, he checked his watch. In an hour he'd visit his old friend Mimi Farmer down at the Verizon store. She'd been the manager for more than a decade, and worried about Caleb, and knew how much *he* worried about and loved his only son. She'd been kind enough several times in the past to pull up Caleb's phone records so he could keep an eye on what his boy might be up to. She knew it was a father's duty. No reason she wouldn't do it again.

Later, he sat in the truck. It was cold, Thanksgiving the next day. The sun was distant, retreating, a hint of itself. The desert was always cold at night this time of year and the days warmer, but not now. He couldn't remember a spell of weather like this—this soon for this long. Cold all the time. Where the sun was farther away, the Chisos and the Santiagos felt closer, clearer. They were all bright and dark, capped with white snow.

Men who wore guns, like his grandfather and his grandfather before him, once rode at the feet of those mountains, carving a place for themselves out of the very rock. They fought and died and killed in the shadows of the peaks, down along the Rio Grande's muddy banks— lives worth no more than whatever they had in their pockets. The strong rode on, the weak did not. It made sense. It was the natural, violent order of things. They'd had plenty of blood on their hands, but the blood washed off eventually.

He'd always longed for that clarity of action and purpose, that awful, brutal simplicity. He'd practiced it when possible, but it was not always easy.

He neatly folded the papers Mimi had given him, a crease as sharp as an axe blade, sharp enough to draw blood if he held it wrong. He put them in the glove compartment. There were things he needed to do, calls he needed to make—a final dealing with Duane and more; clarity of action and purpose, brutal simplicity. Blood washes off.

He sat in the car with that ticking still in his head, even though the clock and the house that held it were long gone. They'd both burned, along with his grandfather in his bed—blind in one eye and too weak to rise as the flames found him. Flames so hot he'd melted to the bed's frame, so you couldn't tell bone from iron, blood from ash. No one had ever figured out how the fire started.

26

MELISSA

Chris was already out of bed when she woke, moving around in the house, and there was the smell of coffee; a hint, the potential, of other cooking. It was Thanksgiving, and although he could have had some of the elk meat he and the sheriff had killed up at El Dorado, he'd passed on it. Yesterday he bought instead a boneless Butterball turkey breast at the Hi n Lo. It was in the fridge when she got home last night, next to a six-pack of Mexican beer, with one bottle missing.

She wandered through the house, noticing that most of the boxes in the hall, in the living room, had disappeared. There were just a few left, only a stray book or two to be tucked away. She picked up one and slipped it into the box waiting for it.

She found him in the kitchen, sipping coffee, with the

makings of a Thanksgiving dinner spread out around him on the counter. She hadn't thought about cooking, but here he was, picking through cans of green beans and corn, a box of Stove Top they might have brought with them from Waco. He had a random assortment of spice shakers arrayed like soldiers on the kitchen table and was holding one now, squinting at it; too small in his hand.

He caught her staring, laughed. "Hey, babe, hope I didn't wake you. I thought we ought to have a meal. It's silly, I know."

"No, no, it isn't." Mel wasn't much of a cook; blamed the mother she'd never known for that, and had never in her life thought of making a Thanksgiving meal. If she remembered right, last year she and Chris had eaten at a Luby's. Still, she could try. They could figure it out together. About mid-morning, as they fumbled around in the kitchen, talking, he switched to the beer he'd bought, and then, a little later, while she was taking a shower, he turned on the TV. She came out with her hair wrapped in a towel to find him watching football for the first time in forever, a warming beer bottle in his hand.

They ate their scraped-together meal, and afterward he went out to his truck, limping a bit from the hunt with the sheriff, and came in with a bag. It was turning dark outside, so he cranked up the big stadium lights and the backyard glowed beneath them, taking on a whole new dimension. Light poured through the back windows, pooling on the floor, and dust floated through the halls of the house, glimmering.

Chris shrugged on a jacket and took a fresh bottle of beer and his mysterious bag and went outside, standing for a while just looking up at the lights, before dumping the bag, spilling eight or ten brand-new footballs on the ground. Mel watched from the kitchen window as he picked one up, bounced it in one hand while holding the beer in the other. She could tell it felt uncomfortable—he almost dropped it before he found a good grip, swung back, and let it go into the night. It wasn't the tightest spiral, but it sailed high, got lost in the lights, falling silent on the ground at the back of the yard.

Warming up a bit, putting the bottle down, he got another ball. He gingerly bounced on the balls of his feet, scanning downfield like there might be receivers there, patting the ball with his free hand, timing a pattern that didn't exist. He put some muscle into this one, and it vanished into the night.

Even craning around the window, she couldn't see where it landed, if it ever did.

He blew out, really starting to crank up. The next one he fired straight upward through his own cold, hanging breath. It trailed smoke, like a rocket ship, pulling free from the earth. He kept throwing deep balls into the night, to people who weren't there to catch them. Maybe just to ghosts. He had one ball left to throw when he stopped to reach down to answer his phone, although she couldn't hear it ring through the window glass. He looked at it for a long minute before taking the call, but once he did, he forgot about the ball in his hand. When he came inside, he left the football behind, resting on that old chair on the porch.

The night following his bloody shower, after he'd mysteriously gone out for a while and then came back in, he sat her down and told her what had happened. Out on Route 67, and with the sheriff at El Dorado. He told her a little about a man named Garrison. So she told him some of the things she'd let slip to Duane Dupree, things that might have made everything worse. He held her and told her it was okay. It started and ended with him.

"I gotta go," he said. She stood with her arms still crossed, waiting for a better explanation.

"It was Dupree and the sheriff. There are lights, engine noises out south of Indian Bluffs, way out at the Far Six. Something's out there, maybe a plane landing." He'd talked about that before, stories he'd heard of small planes out in the badlands, dropping off drugs.

"Chris, it's Thanksgiving. You've had a beer, or five. Isn't there anyone else who can go?"

"No, guess not. The others are with their kids, the rest . . ." He let it go—there weren't that many to begin with. "It's me and Duane. I'm going to meet him near there." Chris was doing a few things at once, none of them well: looking for his duty gear, trying to talk to her, taking off and putting on his jacket at the same time.

She put her hands on him. "No, no, you're not. You're staying here with me. You're not going with fucking Duane Dupree anywhere." She searched around for his phone. It was sitting unattended on the kitchen counter while he fumbled around. All she could think about were all those boxes and books finally disappearing, those moments of watching him throw balls into the dark, so hard and so high no one might ever find them again. They might still be circling up there now, a handful of new stars. That's how she wanted to remember today. That's how she was going to remember it.

"This isn't right, Chris. You know it isn't. You stop and look at me."

But he didn't. "Mel, I have to go. That's the right thing. If I don't go, it all comes back here, to you . . . the town. I gotta see this through, all the way. Besides, nothing's going to happen. You . . . the sheriff . . . hell, everyone knows I'm going out there. It'll be fine."

She kept her hands on him, trying to hold him down.

"You better not be lying to me, Chris Cherry. Goddamn you, you better not be lying to me."

He got to his phone before she did, didn't know quite where to put it; he had the phone in one hand and his holstered gun in the other. To keep from crying, to hold it all in since she couldn't hold him back, she hit him in the chest, hard. "All right, slow down, cowboy. If you gotta go, you gotta. But let's get your shit together first."

She kissed him before he went out the door, tasting that shitty Mexican beer on his mouth. She didn't know why he'd bought it. But he wrapped her in his arms, strong as always, strong as forever. He kissed the top of her head, told her to watch TV. She wanted to say more, something that would keep him with her forever. But she'd said everything she knew how, and he was already gone.

27
ANNE

She told him she was sick.

She'd called the sheriff first thing Thanksgiving morning, embarrassed, begged off that she couldn't make supper later that day. He held his end of the phone silent for a long time before telling her it *was fine*. He completely understood, hoped she felt better. If he was angry or hurt, he hid it well. After that, she'd curled up on her couch watching old movies.

She was still there, asleep without dreams, when Chris went out to meet Duane Dupree.

28
CHRIS

When Chris was far away from the house, before he hooked up with Duane, he pulled over to the side of the road and checked his gun, then checked it again. He hadn't wanted to do that with Melissa watching him.

His hands were shaking.

He also called Garrison, left him a message when he didn't answer. They were due to meet in a week, but he wanted the man to know what he was doing out here now, in case he wanted to talk Chris out of it. A part of Chris really hoped he could talk him out of it.

When his mother had been diagnosed, she came back from El Paso with his dad and they'd gone directly to their room, sat behind the closed door for two or three hours. Although Chris couldn't hear them so well through the door, he thought she was crying. They both were. But when they came out, Chris saw no tears. They didn't want him to know, as if he couldn't understand why they all might *need* to cry at the news she had to tell. She'd put herself back together—what little makeup she wore was movie-star perfect—and held his hand as she told him she was going to die.

Yes, there were treatments, things she could do. But all of them would take her away from home, away from her husband and son. They'd make her feel worse than the sickness itself. It was no way for a person to live or die and no way to leave this world, so she would have none of it. She was going to stay there with them, with her little flower and herb garden at the side of the house. Life would go on without change, without panic. He wanted to argue, to fight with her, but there would be no more discussion, because there was nothing more to be said. Then she'd reached up, held his face with her fingers to steady them, so he wouldn't see them tremble, and told him: "Chris, I love you, but I have to do this my way." Then she went to the kitchen to finish the pot roast she'd planned for dinner. She walked away, smoothing her dress with her hands, and started to die.

By the end, when the porch was where she most often sat, wrapped in blankets against a chill that may not have existed, he'd watch her from the back door, wondering if she was already dead. She sat statue-still for so long, too weak to make the porch swing sway, with only the thinning wisps of her hair shifting in the breeze, and her eyes sunk into hollows so deep that her face seemed unfinished, incomplete. And in those moments, wrapped in anger and sadness as much as she was in her blanket, he absolutely wished her dead, so that the *always waiting* might finally fucking stop; hating himself for thinking such a thing, for believing his mother's dry-eyed acceptance of her end was somehow selfish. But just when he couldn't take it anymore, she would move, a slight uplift of the head; a subtle shift beneath the blanket, trying to follow a bird's mysterious flight across the sky. A hawk rising higher and higher, turning in great circles, leaving everything below it until it was lost in the blue and haze.

He went to her then, always, adjusting the pillow behind her head—covered with the same pillowcase he'd been thinking about replacing when Garrison first called him but still hadn't—and held her hand and felt its papery weight and tried, as she'd done for him, to not let her see how he'd been crying.

Yesterday, after getting the turkey at the Hi n Lo, he'd driven all the way out to Mancha's, looking for Eddie Corazon. He wasn't in uniform, and it was the first time he'd been out there since the incident with Delgado and Aguilar. Before he found Eddie, though, he found Amé Reynosa.

She was coming out of Mancha's, lost in thought. She didn't see him at first, maybe didn't recognize him without his uniform. She was a pretty girl, prettier than even Caleb or Anne had described. A girl used to being looked at who had mastered the art of ignoring all the stares; staring right back, staring down everything and everyone. She reminded him of Mel, destined—he desperately hoped—to escape this fucking place if that's what she wanted, to grow into one tough woman.

She wore a hooded sweatshirt and jeans, big sunglasses, although there wasn't enough sun for them. She was smoking a cigarette, blowing smoke sideways, and nearly ran into him.

"Hey, you're Amé, right? America? It's Chris."

She stopped, took a step back to open some space between them. "*Lo siento.* I wasn't paying attention." She hesitated, brushed her hair back with a hand and looked around the parking lot, probably for more deputies, more gringos. "Why are you here?"

"Sightseeing," he joked. When she didn't smile, he pushed on. "Anyway, I wanted to talk to Eddie. Is he in there?"

She nodded, shoved more hair back. "He's there. A piece of shit."

"I've heard that," he agreed. "Actually, I know it firsthand." She was sizing him up from behind her glasses, waiting. He wasn't sure if Caleb had told her anything yet, was less sure that Mancha's parking lot was the place to talk about it. There was still so much he didn't know, but he wanted her to know he was trying. That she wasn't alone. "I'm working on this thing with your brother, Amé, I hope Caleb has told you that. I believe both of you." He hit the last words slow and hard, but soft; hoped she understood.

She abandoned her cigarette, let it fall to the ground, and stepped on it. Her hidden eyes were drawn to the badge clipped to his belt, his department gold star. Even out of uniform, the sheriff felt his deputies were never really off duty, and he wanted them to wear the badge and their guns. "Do you think it matters, really?"

He looked past her, past Mancha's, through the parking lot and the chain link to the little houses beyond. "It has to, right? We have to try. This is our goddamn town." He was surprised by his own anger, his quick defense of a place he'd spent a good portion of his life trying to get out of.

She laughed, mocking. "*Our* town? *No lo creo.* This isn't *my* town."

He wanted to reach out a hand to her. "But it should be, Amé. It's supposed to be. And it will. I'm going to do everything I can, but I just need a little more time. And I'm going to need your help . . . both yours and Caleb's. I don't think I can do it alone. I wish I could."

She stayed silent, her face turned away from the cold or from him. He wondered what she was thinking, what lay ahead for her—for all of them—despite all of his promises.

"Ya veremos." She started to walk past, but whispered to him as she went by—urgent, honest. "Be careful. Our town is a very dangerous place . . . even for you."

Inside Mancha's he'd wandered the shelves, finally picking up a six-pack of Mexican beer he'd never had, while Eddie eyed both him and a busted-up TV turned down low. The store was tight, brightly lit, filled floor to ceiling with packages and things he couldn't read, didn't understand. In the back there was an old air hockey table, scuffed, unplugged, where some ranch hands played dominoes.

The cooler where he got the beers wheezed and chugged, pissing water on the linoleum floor. The beer bottles were warm in his hand when he placed them on the counter. Eddie looked at them, eyes bloodshot, waved him off.

"Take it, you don't pay here."

"I do." Chris fumbled for some bills, far too many, slipping them between the long necks of the bottles. Eddie shrugged, picked at the money with a finger and a tipless thumb before deciding to ignore it all and going back to whatever he was watching on his TV.

Chris tapped the counter. "Okay, I'm not paying for the beer. I'm paying for you to talk. I want to know about Rudy Ray . . . Rudy Reynosa. Did you know him? Ever see him around? Who did you see him with?"

Eddie looked over Chris's shoulder at the men playing dominoes, who ignored them.

Again: "I'm asking if you ever saw him with Duane Dupree. Did they know each other?"

Eddie bit his lip, showed teeth as dirty as his hands, smiling. "You say you care about Rudy Ray? Now? *Ha estado fuera mucho tiempo.* Anyway, go talk to his little *hermana.* She was just in here. Pretty, yes? Sexy?"

"I'm asking *you*, Eddie. Just fucking you."

Eddie winked in slow motion, a clown. "No, I think you are really here to ask about Dupree, *verdad*? Nothing to do with Rudy, not anymore." Eddie made a disappearing motion with his hand, turning a closed fist into waving fingers, waving goodbye. "He's gone forever. *Por los siglos de los siglos.*"

"Just tell me what you know."

Eddie took a sip of his own beer, hidden behind the counter. "Nothing changes, *mi amigo.*"

"You're right, nothing changes if you don't talk, right now."

Eddie pulled the money out of the beer bottles. "Are you sure you want to know these things, gringo? I can get you *drogas, mujeres . . . niñas.*" He arched his eyebrows as if he knew all about Chris's talk with Amé in the lot. He counted the bills, pretended to. "All cheaper than what you ask."

Chris waved at the money. "That's all I have now. I can get more."

Eddie neatly arranged and folded the bills, tore them in half, shoving the ripped money back into the six-pack.

"*No todos somos a la venta.* But okay, gringo, the price is you answer my questions. ¿*Claro?*"

"Like what?"

"Like why Señor Dupree made me pick him up one

night smelling of gas. So bad I had to wash my truck out with a hose. Like a fucking barbecue. *La parrillada*."

"What the fuck? What are you talking about?"

Eddie took one of the beers out of Chris's six-pack, popped it open, and slid the rest over to Chris as torn pieces of money drifted to the ground. He gulped most of it, turned back to his TV that was little more than static, the sound of whispers, but not before raising the beer bottle, a mock salute; another wave goodbye.

"*Gasolina, mi amigo. Gasolina.*"

This is our goddamn town.

He waited as long as he could, giving Garrison every chance to call him back, but when he didn't, and when Dupree started reaching out for him on the truck radio, wondering where he was, he knew his time was up. He thought about Mel and Caleb and Anne and dark-haired Amé Reynosa.

Be careful. Our town is a very dangerous place . . . even for you . . .

And he thought about his mother—*I have to do this my way*—searching the sky with clear eyes. Without tears . . . without fear.

He pulled the truck back onto 67 and drove on, with one hand on his Colt.

29

DUANE

He picked up Cherry by the Lights, made him leave his truck since they didn't need both.

He'd gotten the call from Inez Mason, then Matty Bulger—the sound of a low-flying plane, maybe ground lights too, or a fire. It made sense; you could draw a straight line right from the Rio Grande past the Mason property and then up toward Indian Bluffs, over the Far Six. It was a hop, skip, and a jump for even an unskilled pilot. Of course he'd gotten the call first from the Judge, a day before.

He drove with his lights off, picking his way across the fields. Even with his wolf eyes, it wasn't easy. So it was a good thing he'd been out this way before—not the first time he'd made this drive, although it had been a while. It also wasn't the first time he'd brought someone with him, either. There had always been Rudy Ray, no one else. But the Judge had been very clear. *Bring Cherry*. Nothing more to be said.

Cherry, however, wasn't a complete rube. Maybe he thought that Duane hadn't seen it, but when he got into the truck, he already had his Colt unholstered, ready. It was still there now, in his lap, covered by his hands, aimed across the cab at Duane.

"I think I see something," Chris said, almost surprised, pointing through the dark. There was a flicker out there, a distant glow. A little fire, another. Pie tins filled with oil, spaced out to create a makeshift landing strip. Duane had been amazed too, the first time he'd seen it like this. At how beautiful it all was, like fallen stars, burning on the ground.

Duane brought the truck up short, killed the engine. They both could see the small plane looming, barely visible by the light of the oil fires. There were men too, standing around, flickering back and forth, in and out of existence.

"Holy shit," Chris said, and Duane could hear him breathing hard. Duane could smell him too, the beer he'd been drinking and the toothpaste he'd used to cover it up. His nervous blood hot and rising close to the skin. Chris shined almost as bright as the oil-pan fires, he was so afraid. He had good reason to be.

Duane told him what to do. "You move a little left, I'm gonna move right. Creep closer, stay down, wait for me to yell out *policía*. They'll probably scatter your way, and then you pop up, let 'em know goddamn good and clear that you're there. Send a round skyward if you need to."

"What if they keep running?"

"Don't chase. Shit, it's dark and cold and they don't know where the hell they are, even less than you, although they got a good sense of where the river is. Like a goddamn radar. We'll scoop up the ones who get lost in the morning." Duane pulled his own gun and Chris flinched, just a hair. "Keep your eyes open for other trucks showing up, they're out here to meet someone."

"You mean someone other than us?" Cherry asked, giving Duane a look so knowing, something so much more than instinct—like Cherry had already caught a glimpse of his *own* future—that Duane almost put a bullet in him right there.

"Yeah, other than us. Another reason not to run around after 'em is they might crank a shot over their shoulder while running, and damn near certain they'll hit you. That's the luck of it. Most times these beaners don't want to fight anyway."

Chris nodded. "And if they do want to fight?"

Duane barked, laughed. "Well, by God, shoot every last damn one of them. That's what you got that big ole gun for."

They were out of the car, moving their separate ways, and Duane's eyes *glowed*. It wasn't just that he could see, it was all the *things* he could see. Like the plane still vibrating, its propellers still turning, moving the flames on the pie plates. Like the men not even pretending to take anything on or off the plane, no shitty off-load truck anywhere to be seen. And of course, no Rudy Ray either, to put out the lights. These men—definitely not Chava's people—deathly quiet, silent and near still. Not talking and not laughing; smoking, but careful to flick their dead butts into the open hatch on the plane and not on the ground. Every one of them with a small ugly rifle slung over his shoulder, hands near the trigger. Professional. And *there*, right over there in the ocotillo, two of them settled into the deeper darkness; scanning, looking, waiting; using scopes . . . hunting.

Duane could see their hearts beating right through their damn skin and shirts; could read his future written there, *saw it*. Exactly who and what these men were waiting for.

Of course he'd known it when Cherry had come back from El Dorado with the Judge, all safe and sound. Duane knew he was mightily fucked then, *expendable*; that's what his daddy had whispered—one of his *ten-cent words*, throughout a lifetime where Jamison Dupree had less than a dollar's worth to spend. Still, Duane had seen his daddy's truth in it and was set to kill both the Judge and Cherry when the Judge met with him first and told him not to worry—it was all just being handled a different way, promising things were going to be good again. Duane just had to get Cherry out here tonight when the call came and then they were back in business, like old times. *He was handling business.* And if things were going to be good again, that meant Duane was going to be good too—the free *foco* was gonna flow, and maybe he wasn't so fucked after all.

He'd hung on to the Judge's words with both hands, hung them like a noose around his neck. Because now he needed that *foco* so fucking bad that he would have crawled on his hands and knees out here for it—sucked nigger dick too, right on Main Street, right at the fifty-yard line of Archer-Ross Stadium. Even as it became clear and bright to him now—bright as the oil burning on the ground—just how the Judge had decided to handle their business together once and for all, just how expendable both Cherry and Dupree really were.

They'd already spotted Cherry, pretty much no way they couldn't. Duane, though, had barely left the cover of the truck, hanging back and expecting the shots; leaving Cherry out there exposed, alone. The original plan—and it probably saved his life, at least at the start.

The rifles sounded like whipcracks, then the bang of the hangman's trapdoor. Glass shattered over Duane's head, a window gone, pieces of it falling into his hair, into his open hand like he was trying to catch them. Muzzle flashes nearly blinded him, and he had to turn away as a second round, then another, all searching for him too, skimmed off the truck, throwing sparks into his face. He kept turning and ran off into the night. There was so much shooting he couldn't tell if Cherry ever had the chance to shoot back.

30
AMERICA

It was late, really late, when she got the texts, so she knew it was bad, really bad. They flew in one right after another, Caleb panicking. Deputy Cherry had been shot out past Indian Bluffs. Out past where he'd found Rodolfo. He was dying, probably already dead.

im sorry. im sorry. wat do we do?

Caleb kept texting until she turned off her phone.

But she lay awake for a long time, remembering Deputy Cherry. Tall, strong, the gold star at his belt shining even in that thin, cold sun. He'd seemed nice, determined, in the handful of moments they had spoken outside Mancha's. A good man. She understood then why Caleb had wanted to trust him. He'd promised to do everything he could for them . . . *for her*. And she had trusted him, like she'd finally let herself trust Caleb and this whole idea. Let herself believe in all of their promises. Tonight Deputy Cherry had died alone.

She got Rodolfo's phone from under her bed, where it was in a box tucked underneath the last of the money. She'd stopped carrying it after Caleb had convinced her it was *evidence*, that she needed to keep it safe. When she showed it to him, he didn't want to touch it.

Safe—that word meant nothing to her now. Deputy Cherry was dead and Caleb still had to deal with El Juez, who must know all the things he'd told the deputy, all the things *she* had shared. Caleb would run, sooner or later, and that left her with Dupree, far worse than before. That left her with almost nothing again . . . except for the ranch across the river.

She'd tell them about Dupree, about El Juez, about everything. Maybe they'd come here for them or take her away once and for all to the place with the peacocks—a place where Dupree would never reach her, a place where even he'd be afraid to go.

She was crying when she turned it on. She held it tight, warming it with her hands, bringing it to life. There wasn't much of a battery charge, but there was enough. She scrolled to the only number she had ever called, where that secret voice had asked her for Rana over and over again, and hit send.

ASHES

1
MÁXIMO

He went to the border wearing his Avengers T-shirt. He'd seen the movie, badly dubbed, although his English was good enough. He liked Viuda Negro the best—he didn't know any girls or women in Ojinaga who looked that way, had strength and spirit, and when he was done he would go to Los Angeles and find her, meet her. How hard could it be?

He crossed at Boquillas del Carmen, the water nothing but spit in the sand that he could have waded through. But instead he waited his turn for the ferry, practicing his English by reading the little cardboard signs by the side of the road, where children not much younger than him sat in the dust.

PLEASE PURCHASE TO HELP
THE PEOPLE OF BOQUILLAS MEXICO.

WALKING STICKS	6.
ROADRUNNERS	6.
SCORPIONS	6.
OCOTILLOS	6.
BRACELETS	6.
ROCKS	6.

He wanted none of those things, but gave a dirty boy an American five-dollar bill all the same, peeling it from the small, tight roll that had been given to him. Americans came the other way, a couple of old people with copper skin beneath big floppy hats even though there was very little sun, struggling to get up on burros to ride to Boquillas, one mile away. He'd been dropped by a truck in town, bought a street taco and a Coke, and walked to the river on his own, refusing to pay for a burro or horse ride. He waited his turn, listening to Victor the boatman sing "Cielito Lindo," and although it took another five dollars to use the ferry, he gave it and went across. Returning home in style.

They chose Boquillas rather than Puente Ojinaga, because the port here was unmanned—just the park rangers every now and then and a little kiosk where he could walk up and scan his papers, and then talk through a camera to a border agent a hundred miles away.

They wrote out for him what to say and he'd practiced hard and could repeat it without mistakes or looking at his little piece of paper, both in English and in Spanish. He knew how he looked in the big fish-eye of the camera—a skinny *niño* in torn jeans and an Avengers T-shirt, visiting family. Smiling, happy to be here, still drinking his American Coke. He was no *problemo*, no threat, and he was a hundred miles from anywhere.

He waited another hour for the truck on this side to get him, an old man and woman together, who said nothing to him as he climbed into the back. He had no idea what threat had been made for them to drive all the way here to pick up a boy that they did not know. In the old straw scattered in the truck's bed he found a small brown sack, still warm with handmade tortillas wrapped in paper, and a small plastic container of frijoles and cheese and a bottle of water. The old woman watched him through the back window and nodded when he smiled at her, chewing one of her tortillas. She was old, beyond old, more weathered than even the rocks and hills they drove past.

He wondered if they had been threatened, but couldn't be sure. Promises or threats, silver or lead. *Plata o plomo.* The colors of his life.

He lay in the straw in the back, with the sky streaming above him. Except for the clouds, he might not be moving at all. And he saw things in them—faces, a burning tree, a rearing horse. There were times when he thought about writing down all these things, like in a story or song. He could sing such a song to girls he knew, one better than silly "Cielito Lindo." His songs would be dark and beautiful and they would be all his secrets and dreams for everyone to hear.

A song about crossing the ferry and children sitting in the dust, selling little toy scorpions to a boy just like him.

Then he remembered this place he was going and the things he was supposed to do, and knew that no one would ever want to hear songs about him. No one could bear his secrets or his dreams. He put his arms over his head, shutting out the weak light and all the pictures in the sky and clouds. He wanted to sleep, if he could, before he arrived in this place they called Murfee.

2

CHRIS

H e was covered in blood.

The dream goes like this. He walks in darkness, toward flame. Small fires burn the ground, casting monstrous shadows of men. A constellation he uses to navigate, tacking toward them—left, right, left. He breathes hard and he's as scared as he's ever been and his knee starts to throb and then all the stars flare, so bright they nearly blind him—do blind him—and the night turns metallic and something parts the air by his face, fingertips drawn across his skin, startling him so much he leaps back, like he's been touched by a ghost. Another puts a fist through his chest and his heart nearly stops. Then his father is there, at his ear, telling him to just let 'er rip, Chris, just let 'er rip . . . and he does.

*   *   *

He was covered in blood.

But he had returned fire . . . *let 'er rip* . . . remembering that now, not just dreaming it; blasting holes through
the gathered darkness and running, calling for Dupree
but leaving Duane to take care of himself. When he
started shooting back at the plane, his Colt had come
alive in his hand, glowing like a fiery star of its own.

He took rounds, more than one—his own blood hitting his face. He'd felt it on his hands, leaking out of his
heart with every breath. Still he kept firing, trying to run
backward toward the cover of Dupree's truck right up
until he hit a snake hole, his already damaged knee
protesting—buckling—and then tossing him over the
ground.

He rolled over, searching for his gun, trying to reload,
scrabbling at the caliche. His hands hurt from nettles and
thorns and rocks but still he crawled, not even sure where
he was crawling to anymore. He was covered in blood
and going to die. So he stopped—the truck too damn far
away—accepting that between his knee and his wounds
he was never going to make it. He waited for someone to
come put a bullet behind his ear and blow all he'd ever
been and might be right into the desert, leaving his pieces
for a different, distant deputy to find, the way he'd found
Rudy Reynosa.

He'd refused to die facedown, though.

Rolling over, stretching out his hands, one last chance
to protect himself; reaching out. There had been stars all
above him. *God, so many stars*, right at his fingertips.

There had been other things, after that. But it was a
movie forever missing a few frames, from all those moments he'd been unconscious or dead . . .

Duane Dupree staring into his open eyes, putting a gun muzzle against one, the way the sheriff had done with that elk, checking to see if he was dead. Lights, maybe a million of them, from a city, or just more stars. His face reflected and distorted in chrome—a fun-house mirror, and the sheriff watching him with those same mirrors for eyes. Mel crying and her hair brushing his face . . .

All of those moments and so many others, lost, leading up to this one—*now*—and a man he didn't know, sitting at the end of an unfamiliar bed. No more dreams: a stranger pulling photographs from a manila envelope, shuffling them like cards, waiting for Chris to wake up. He held them up and asked Chris names he didn't know, so Chris was left only with *Who are you? Who are those people?*

The man smiled and said they were all dead men.

3

MELISSA

The hotel was nice, a lot nicer than most, but still reminded her of all the shitty roadside motels she'd spent so much of her life falling into and out of. She and her daddy had moved a lot, bounced around by work, his mistakes, the ever-present anger. She got to know peeling paint and swimming pools of rusty water and dead crickets—that weird color of neon particular to those places: harsh and hot, yellow and red. Colors promising carnivals.

Outside Odessa they lined the freeway like a string of fake pearls, downwind from the oil platforms and the fires, flickering in the distance. In Galveston they sweated in their own heat, near the sound and smells of the ocean—the hard rock of waves against concrete, salt and rust. She remembered once her daddy sleeping off a one-night drunk that stretched into three days, so she'd walked out on her own with two fingers' worth of his whiskey in a paper cup to watch the huge cruise and container ships turn out to sea by Pelican Island. They'd been as big as cities, lit from within, drifting in their own yellow haze, always heading somewhere better. All those different motels in different places, and they were always the end of the same line.

They'd airlifted Chris to the medical center in El Paso. The sheriff himself put her up in the hotel, so she could see Chris most every day, but each day was also a reminder of exactly what she was *not*. She wasn't *family*. She and Chris weren't married. She couldn't make decisions or sign things or agree to things or speak for him— all she could do was wait her turn. She had to ask the sheriff for the information the doctors were unwilling to share, even though he'd told them more than once that it was okay. The only thing that was okay was that moment she had each day to hold Chris's hand, marveling that he could hold hers back. It felt weak, faint, like holding the hand of a ghost. At least he was there.

He'd been shot three times, lost nearly three pints of blood. It had poured out of him nearly as fast as they could put it in, but when the doctors who didn't want to talk to her had learned she shared his blood type, she'd offered them as much as they needed before they could even ask, and they took it.

She still didn't understand all the damage, all the medical jargon, just enough to grasp that it was bad, real bad, though everyone promised it would heal with time and effort. She knew from the experience with Chris's knee that even after skin and bone were whole again, some things might never quite heal. They'd worry about that later, though. Now Chris was a hero. He'd killed three of the fucking men who'd tried to kill him—one for each pint of blood he'd lost. Everyone agreed it was a miracle that he was alive, and a credit to the other hero from that night. Chief Deputy Duane Dupree.

She had driven to El Paso escorted by the other Murfee deputies, and they had come up I-10 right along the border, on the razor line between Ciudad Juárez and El Paso. In Murfee, she knew Mexico was *right down the way*, across the river, but she never saw it, except in the faces of people working in the mini-marts or driving in some shitty pickup after a long day tending another man's lands. They didn't even come into Earlys, staying instead out at that other place, Mancha's, where on any given Saturday the gravel lot would be filled with cars with Chihuahua plates. But here Mexico sweated and breathed right beside her, piled in little buildings the color of wet cardboard all along the interstate. It stretched into a muddy haze, a huge city but mostly flat, as if it had been crushed by a hand, ringed by small ugly hills where someone had picked out Mexican phrases with colored rocks.

At night, heading back to the hotel, the lights of Ciudad Juárez stretched on forever and forever, almost beautiful, reminding her of Galveston's huge cruise ships heading out to sea. These lights didn't go anywhere better, however, just more of the crushing same. Endless and unchanging, everyone over there trying to get over here, and all it took was one look at those shantytowns lurking on the freeway, wasting under the weight of the sun, to understand why.

The men who'd tried to kill Chris—and Dupree too, although it was easy to forget that—had come from such a place. To her, it was a city made out of nothing but the motels she and her daddy had lived in. Burning it all to the ground was too good for it.

Days passed. Every morning one of Murfee's deputies—not Dupree, who was back in town—picked her up from the hotel and drove her to the hospital to see Chris for a couple of hours. Afterward, they brought her back or ran her by the store first, even though she had her own car; she'd insisted on bringing it from Murfee, just in case. She knew without knowing that Chris wouldn't have wanted her completely at the mercy of Sheriff Ross and the Big Bend County Sheriff's Department.

In between those rides she sat in the hotel, smoking cigarettes and drinking whiskey and Coke—but not too much—watching game shows and old movies but never the news, and waited to take Chris away.

4

CALEB

I know he knows, and still we pretend.

We've both gotten so good at it. Maybe it's the only thing we share, the only thing that ties us together as father and son—our ability and our need to lie to each other. We don't know how to do anything else.

I didn't pull the trigger on Chris Cherry, but I might as well have. All the times I've held a gun in my hand, *dreaming*. The things I said to him were no different from loading one and aiming it at his heart. Part of me knew the risk, but I did it anyway. I did it for me, for Amé—promising her it would all work out—but it was never my promise to keep. Chris did his best for both of us and nearly died because of it.

So I guess I did shoot my first man, just the wrong goddamn one.

*   *   *

I read in the paper that another millimeter or so and a bullet would have gone right through the left ventricle of his heart. He would have bled out long before Duane Dupree ever got him back to Murfee, and still, he nearly died anyway. In the *Daily* there was a picture of Duane's truck, full of bullet holes and empty windows. Chris's blood was dried all down the side of the open door, and there was a bloody handprint too, against the window-pane. It could have been Duane's or Chris's, I don't know. I saw that same picture on ABC News, CNN. I saw that picture behind my father in an interview he gave to Fox, and it'll probably win an award.

They're calling it the *Shootout at the Far Six*—Murfee's own O.K. Corral.

Duane Dupree is now a hero. And my father is all over TV, saying all the right things, nodding in all the right places. He is smart, brave, concerned. Just like when Nellie Banner-Ross died in our upstairs bathtub. Just like when my mom disappeared. Always fucking pretending.

I found out about the shooting while my father and I were sitting down alone to Thanksgiving supper. I was across from the empty place still laid out for Anne Hart. The phone rang and I thought it was her calling to tell him she'd changed her mind, felt better after all. But when he looked at the incoming number for a long time, I knew it wasn't her. He stared like he wasn't sure what he was seeing . . . like he didn't believe *what* he was seeing. He let it ring and ring.

The TV in the living room was turned down, muted, so everything was silent between us except his cellphone. Anyone looking into our house from the outside would have seen the appearance of normal—a Thanksgiving meal, football on TV, and a father and a son sitting at the table beneath warm lights. But that's all it was—appearance. *Pretending.* Emptiness without depth. A postcard sent from someone else's normal life, and nothing more.

He slowly cut the meat he'd hunted; chewed, took a sip of warm water, as his cell continued to ring.

I asked him if he was going to answer it—*because it might be important*—and he stared back with eyes like a snowstorm, flat clouds blanking the horizon. He put his silverware down, arranged it near his plate while never taking his eyes off me, and finally picked up that goddamn phone. He knew who it was from the caller ID, but even he couldn't hide his expression when he was forced to say Duane Dupree's name out loud, acknowledging the other man's voice on the line.

While he talked to Dupree, I could hear Dupree shouting over the line and saying Chris's name, again and again, and I knew then my father had learned about our meeting at the stadium, maybe even our few texts, and that because of them—because of me—Chris was dead.

I also knew by the way he stared at his phone so long before answering, unbelieving, that Duane Dupree should have been dead as well.

Amé won't talk to me now and I don't blame her. I'm broken, I failed her. I understand, I really do, but it doesn't hurt any less.

I took her out to the Murfee Lights a few times and we tried to find those phantom orbs. I didn't take it seriously; for me it was another chance to be near her. But

sometimes I think she really did believe in them—
standing in the bed of my truck, staring out over the flat
when I so much wanted to hold her hand, both of us
searching the dark. Maybe we were always searching for
different things.

My father is back and forth to El Paso, seeing to Chris,
dealing with the media, dealing with the federal agents
and Texas Rangers who've swept into Murfee and back
out again. He's dealing with everyone and everything else
at the moment but me. But eventually he will. He'll have
to handle his business. Me.

School is almost out for Christmas break, and he'll be
back in Murfee full time. We'll be trapped together here,
we both know it. For all of the hundreds of ways I've let
him down, I finally let him down the only way he can't
overlook. I betrayed him. Worse than that, *I fucking
failed*.

I once wrote: *It might be that if I don't do something,
then no one will.* Maybe no one else was ever supposed to.
So I waited after school yesterday until Ms. Hart left the
building. She walked slow, as if carrying a heavy burden,
but her arms were empty. She was wrapped in a long coat
and it beat against her legs like the wings of a huge bird.
I thought it might carry her away, lift her above the gray
clouds and back to warmth and sunlight—to a better
place far from here.

She looked like my mom, lost in thought, her hair
pulled back. So much so that I stood there for long minutes, lost. I might have to finally accept that's what my
mom did—just flew away to warm sunlight, to a better
place far from here.

I caught up to her near the bench that Amé and I often used, and this time she didn't try to run away from

me. I talked, frantic. I sounded crazy. But I had to pour it all out; otherwise I would have only broken down and cried. I told her everything.

She sat in Amé's place and heard me out, holding back tears of her own. She didn't even stop me when I told her I thought I was going to need her car.

5

DUANE

Truth be told, it was Jamison Dupree who saved Cherry and then made Duane into a hero. Duane might *still* be running if his dead daddy hadn't yelled at him to get his ass back there; that if he didn't stop running *right fucking then*, he was likely running forever. Reminding him that all those bullets filling the dark for Cherry were meant just the same for him, too. Duane wouldn't find any safety by running off into those hills alone, and even if he outran them that night or the next or a dozen more, eventually they'd catch him after all.

Hell, if he didn't *do something*, he was giving the Judge what he wanted anyway, even without a bullet in Duane's skull. Better they both be dead, but *everybody* loved a hero. And if Duane somehow fucking survived the night, *heroes weren't expendable.*

By the time he'd turned around, the plane was already inching across the ground, returning to the sky.

Through the oil light he'd seen those beaners, all shadows and hollows where their eyes should be, trying to grab their fallen, so he threw enough rounds downrange to make them reconsider it. They tumbled back into their plane, sparks dancing on its skin, and he may have even hit one or two as prop wash spun the pie plates skyward, trailing wet fire.

He'd gotten back to the cover of his truck when he saw Cherry crawling on the ground, alive.

It had been a god-awful mess, though, getting Cherry into the truck, begging him not to die and trying to hold his blood in him while driving. At one point Cherry had grabbed his hand tight, like a woman almost, their fingers all twined together, as Cherry's eyes went all glassy and bright. Duane thought he was dead then—even pulled over and put his ear to his chest—put his face up to his lips to catch only the faintest movement of breath on his skin, fading fast. He whispered, "Don't you die on me! Don't you *dare* die on me!" and got so frustrated he punched Cherry in the chest and felt the other man's heart jump when he struck it. Then Cherry had spit up a load of black blood and was breathing again, hard, like a man not quite ready to die.

Duane had gotten back on the road and made a call to the Judge, letting him know they were headed back to Murfee. Also, he wanted to hear the Judge's voice when he realized Duane was still alive.

*   *   *

Being a hero was hard work. Not that he didn't like the attention: the claps on the back and the smiles from people who used to look through him; all the folks lining up to hear his story, and the free burgers at the Hamilton and free drinks at Earlys, if he ever was to become a drinking man.

He could sense, though, every now and then, that a few wondered how he'd escaped without a scratch—how Cherry was the one who'd done all the killing that got them off the Far Six alive. He always had to remind them then, with a sad smile, that the *forensics*—his ten-cent word—weren't all done yet, and it still might be they'd pull one or two of *his* slugs out of those dead beaners

He'd goddamned fired enough of 'em. Those moments then passed with a laugh, his laugh, the biggest of all. The hardest part was that he couldn't get over to Nathan to get some *foco* because now everyone everywhere knew his face. When people slapped him on the back, it made his skin catch fire; when they smiled at him, he was afraid he would burst into flame. Drinking his Dr Peppers was like drinking crushed glass.

He could pinch some from Eddie Corazon, but it was hard to get out to Mancha's as well, because everyone was watching him. He didn't much trust Eddie, either, thought it best to keep his distance after making him come out to the Cut to get him . . . down by the water, after that mess with the agents. So he was back to staring out his windows into the dark, gnawing at himself, knowing that dark was anything but empty. There were still eyes out there everywhere. They never went away; cameras and ghosts and cellphones and wolves and microphones.

He texted his little Mex girl, thinking he might make

her get him some, but like always she ignored him, and he wasn't free enough to track her ass down. So he dug out some makeup and patted it on his skin to hide the yellow color and the hollows beneath his eyes and the places he was picking at on his arms, and people started saying he'd gone Hollywood and was just staying ready for the cameras. He wanted to kill those people, every goddamn one of 'em.

He was dying one piece, one day, at a time, and still hadn't crossed paths with the Judge, who'd been spending most of his time in El Paso, standing in front of cameras while Duane ran the show in Murfee. Circling each other like two dogs Duane had once seen fighting in the street near Rufus. Hackles up, haunches flecked with dust, soon to be blood.

Those dogs had gone at each other growling and barking while Duane sat in his truck, smoking and humming along to Slim Richey and the Jitterbug Vipers. In his mind he'd bet on the bigger, mangier one, a shepherd mix, but the little one—nothing but black and brown spots and broken teeth—got low and at the belly of the other, tore at it but good, until all sorts of important stuff came balling out in a pink and red mess.

The bigger dog tried to drag itself away, but the little one worried at its guts, pulling them farther out. It hadn't fared much better, though, its skull punctured by the shepherd and an eye loose in a socket.

Duane got out of his truck and walked over and put a bullet in both, still locked in mortal struggle. He snapped their picture like that, using his cell camera, the first one he ever remembered taking, and looked at it again and again for weeks after. He once sent it to the Mex girl.

He'd left the carcasses where they lay until the turkey vultures came and took them away.

Duane had bought a few days by not running away at the Far Six, but little else. He still had all his ghosts waiting for him. He still smelled the ash of the burning girl, forever caught in his hair, in his skin.

He still had the Judge to deal with.

Heroes weren't expendable, true. But they could be hunted, forever haunted. In the end, you could never outrun all the things you'd done. From his side of the grave, his daddy had somehow forgotten to tell him that.

6

ANNE

She was cursed. *A bad penny*, her dad would say. She
didn't want to think that way, but how else could she
explain the horror of Lucas Neill and watching and feeling her husband die in her arms? What other explanation
was there for Chris Cherry, nearly killed in the desert?
They were saying all around town his heart may have
stopped one or two times before he decided to stay alive.
She saw the bloody pictures in the newspaper, that awful
handprint against the glass, and it made her remember
Marc's own bloody hands on her . . . his fingers touching
her face, and later, standing in front of a mirror, not
wanting to wash those stains away.

She knew it was as futile as reading tea leaves, searching for a pattern in a spiderweb or falling snow—counting
butterfly wings a thousand miles away. Part of her knew

there was nothing to link those tragic events of her life, but she was having trouble sleeping all the same, plagued by a carnival of bad dreams, unable to ignore the only connection that did exist. Two men she'd known, a thousand miles apart, a lifetime away. One she had loved with everything in her, the other she could have easily grown to care about, after fearing nothing might ever blossom inside her again.

But instead, just so much blood. And nothing between them but her.

Two days before Marc died, they made love.

He came in late from work; he was on one of those odd swing shifts, and she was long asleep when he slipped into bed next to her. The window was open, wet Texas air moving through the blinds and wandering around the room— invisible hands turning the blades of the box fan she'd left off—and the heat of his body woke her.

He got into bed, naked, something he rarely did, slipping his arms around her. She could feel him pressing against her, urgent, and she responded. He used his fingers to get her ready, and she rolled into him, opened herself to him, and he held her down, their fingers laced together, his face between her breasts. He threw the sheets off and they both lay exposed, the light outside magically turning them into weird shapes on the walls and ceilings—performers in their own spotlight. She tasted beer on his tongue, her own tongue, knew he'd sat in his cruiser with Lieutenant Cafee or Bobby Dale and had a couple before coming home to their bed, and she didn't care. He was so hot she felt her own sweat sizzle against his skin, and even though her hands were pinned, she felt the heave and roll of his shoulder muscles deep in her own legs. She strained off the mattress to reach him, to meet him, and when he came, he'd called her name and threw out a few other words a bit too loud.

He rolled away from her and laughed, tried to get off the bed and brush his teeth, but she wouldn't let go of his hands, tasting herself on his fingers before she let him leave.

Those were the same fingers that left bloody track marks on her face, forty-eight hours later.

She couldn't reach out to Chris. She didn't feel comfortable driving to El Paso to see him or even trying to call him.

Christmas break started in a few days. Caleb had told her the sheriff was due back in Murfee tomorrow or the day after, and was going to stay awhile this time. As a courtesy, Texas Rangers were still on duty 24/7 at the hospital, guarding Chris until he was well enough to come home.

Caleb thought he had a very small window of opportunity to do what he wanted to do, what he felt he had to do, for Chris's sake. He didn't explain it all, and there were very serious parts of it he was leaving out, but he'd said enough that she knew he needed her help.

In his own way, Lucas had asked for her help, too . . . cried out for it, and she'd pushed him away until the very end. As badly as she'd handled it, it had been the right thing to do, although everyone paid a terrible price for it. Was it worse to do the right thing badly or the wrong thing right from the start?

Marc and Chris Cherry. Lucas Neill and now Caleb Ross. She prayed for Caleb's sake that she wasn't their bad penny after all.

7

CHRIS

The stranger held the pictures up again, repeated Mexican names he didn't know, and when Chris asked again, he simply said, "These are the men you killed, Chris, that night out on the Far Six."

Chris didn't recognize the man but knew the voice, the very first ghost from the other end of the line. He was older than Chris had imagined, in dark pants and a button-down shirt in a color Chris couldn't quite put a name to. His cuffs were rolled up to reveal tanned arms and an expensive watch, a silver and black bracelet on one wrist. If he had a badge and gun, Chris couldn't see it. He looked like a lawyer.

Chris felt naked in the hospital bed, even with the covers up. The blinds were cracked but it was dark outside, getting darker, light wavering in the distance. Still, the room was too bright by half, all the machines around him a little too loud, blinking Christmas colors. He'd been awake for a few minutes that felt like hours, and he was already exhausted. He wanted Mel here.

"I don't remember a whole lot," Chris said, his own voice, older and worn-out, surprising him.

"No, I imagine you probably don't. You've been through a helluva lot. I'm not going to take up too much of your time, but we've never had the chance to talk face-to-face. We spoke on the phone, but maybe you don't remember that, either. You also called me the night all this happened, and I'm sorry I didn't get back to you fast enough. I'm not sure it would have changed anything, but still . . ."

"It's good to finally meet you, Chris. My name is Joe Garrison. I'm with the DEA. We've had our eyes on Murfee for a while." He shifted photos around, showed Chris a picture of the burned-out Tahoe.

"Darin and Morgan were two of my agents, looking into the disappearance of Rodolfo Reynosa. Of course, you and I both know where he was." He raised a yellow envelope with a Texas DPS stamp on it. "This is the complete forensic file on the remains you discovered at Indian Bluffs. The file you called me about."

Garrison reached down, picked something off his pants. "Rudy came to us to be an informant. He worked for Nemesio—major, major bad guys right across the border. He also claimed to work with bad cops. He was scared shitless, and in way, way over his head. He strung us along, saying a lot without saying anything important, if you know what I mean, but more than enough to keep our attention. He wanted assurances, money. He wanted promises. He hinted that he got recruited into Nemesio by an uncle, *family*, but was worried about a younger sister, still living in Murfee . . ."

"America," Chris said.

"Yes, I think that's her name." Garrison nodded. "Anyway, our boy Rudy was playing all ends *and* the middle, and most of us figured he got himself killed because of it. He fell off of the earth before we had the chance to bring him in. That's why Darin and Morgan were down there, looking for him . . . unofficially. Darin was big on working solo. He was probably that kid who colored outside the lines, who never read the directions for anything. But he had a nose for the job, and he had a feeling about Reynosa. By then you'd already found him."

"Who killed him?"

"Ten-million-dollar question. Nemesio? Someone else?" Garrison reshuffled his pictures. "My bet is on someone else. There have been rumors for a while that Murfee is bad . . . sold out to the narcos, helping get dope through down there, protecting loads. With all the problems in Juárez a few years ago, the Big Bend has become a lot more attractive. Nemesio has owned it for a while, and they are evil motherfuckers. It's all religious, mystical bullshit with them. They're dangerous, crazy, and lately they've been leaned on hard by another cartel, a newer one, the Serrano brothers, who've moved into smuggling routes and areas Nemesio have long considered sacred. Fucking cartoon characters, the whole lot of them . . . but cartoons with machetes and guns and too much time on their hands. They're very, very creative in that way. But the three men you killed weren't Nemesio, although I think we were meant to believe they were, so if we came looking, we'd look the wrong way. They were Serranos, looking to touch off another drug war down there with our help, like the one we experienced up here. They didn't land that plane to drop off dope or pick up money. They weren't couriers or smugglers, Chris, they were known *sicarios*, assassins." Garrison held up a picture, the face on it a blank slate, the eyes empty and vacant and uncomfortable to look at for long. "Our intel on this one is that he's killed twenty people. Twenty." He put the picture down. "You put two bullets in that fucker, by the way, and I want to personally thank you for that. One right between the eyes. Goddamn amazing shot."

Eyes he couldn't look at. Chris stared out past Garrison to the window, to a distance full of lights.

"And he . . . they . . . were here to kill me?"

Garrison leaned back. "Now, what do you think?" He followed Chris's gaze to the window. "Do you know how many people were murdered over there just a few years ago? Over three thousand. That's nine people *a day*. Another two thousand plus, a year after that. Killers killing killers, true, waging their own nasty little war, but that's still a lot of dead people. And too many of them *were* innocent, just bystanders . . . mothers or wives. Not to mention all the other bad men using the cover of that bloodshed to have a fucking field day. That's Ciudad Juárez you're looking at, all those lights. For a while, short of a real war zone, one of the most dangerous places on earth.

"But during that time, do you know how many people from this side of the border, U.S. citizens, the narcos murdered?" Garrison held up a solitary finger. "One. A guy they snatched out of El Paso . . . cut his hands off and left them duct-taped to his chest, because they thought he'd ripped off a drug load. He was found in the Valle de Juárez, a message to anyone else who might try the same thing. Allegedly that murder cost about a quarter of a million dollars, because it's not cheap to kill someone here. Not cheap at all. But over there? No more expensive than a bullet." Garrison seemed lost in the lights he was staring at. "How about the number of U.S. law enforcement? That would be *zero*, Chris. Even for the narcos, the smart ones, it's too expensive to kill guys like us, and that's saying a lot, given what they paid for that piece of shit we found in the Valle. They've learned the hard way it's bad for business, not worth it. Right here in El Paso, a couple hundred yards separate Texas and Mexico, yet even with all the violence and mayhem the last few years, they've remained worlds apart. But down in Murfee? In the last couple of months, we've had two federal agents attacked, leaving one dead, and two sheriff's deputies fired upon. It's open fucking season down there. I want you to tell me why."

"I'm not sure what you think I do or don't know," Chris said. "I've barely been in the department a year, and you're not even convinced I'm not one of these bad cops you keep talking about, are you?"

Garrison nodded. "I'm *mostly* convinced, but try harder. Maybe you were and aren't now. Maybe you're just another Rudy Ray, trying to come in from the cold, or were never involved at all. They asked and you said no. If you're not mixed up in it, if you don't know shit, why does everyone want you dead?"

Chris sat silent, and Garrison checked his watch.

"Okay, Chris, I'll trade. Here's what I think. Your department is crooked, through and through. One or more of your buddies there killed Reynosa, either because Rudy knew they were double-dealing Nemesio, or switching sides to the Serranos, or because they pieced together Rudy was a fed snitch. It doesn't really fucking matter. But they also tried to take out Darin and Morgan, and now you."

"My department? Everyone? Me?"

Garrison stared at him. "Like I said, convince me otherwise. Darin and Morgan had their suspicions about Duane Dupree and one or two others, but they wanted to believe you might be righteous. They hoped you were. I do, too. Depending on how things had played out, they might have approached you, like I did, a few weeks ago."

"Dupree saved my life. Doctors said if he hadn't brought me in when he did, I would have died out there."

Garrison shrugged. "Change of heart? Guilty conscience? Dupree doesn't strike me as the head of the snake, never did, and Darin didn't think so, either. Dupree's nothing but a short order cook. I've been in this business a long time. The how and the why aren't even important anymore. It's just the *who*." Garrison put away all of his pictures but one, leaving the heavy packet on the bed. Garrison flipped the last photo in his hand over, held it up so Chris could see it. It was an official picture, a pretty young woman in a dark business suit, trying to smile serious.

It was different from the one he'd seen in the paper, but still he recognized her, there was no way not to. It reminded him of the picture on her license.

"She doesn't look anything like this anymore, and never will, even if she lives. She's here, Chris, down the hall, in the burn unit, if you want to visit her. You don't want to talk to me? Deal with me? Fine. You can explain it all to her.

"Here's the thing. Maybe you're protecting someone, or you think you're being a hero. It doesn't matter. My people were hurt, one of them is dead. I don't forget that. I can't. I'm not going to, ever. And I'm not going away, ever. That's not how this works. You can't outlast me or outwait me. I'm patient, and I've got time. How much time do you think you have?" He pointed at the DPS report. "You can't even die and take your secrets to the grave, Chris. I won't allow it. When all this is done, with or without your help, I'll bulldoze that little town of yours, and everyone and everything in it." He stood up, stretched. "Of course, I might not have to do a fucking thing. Remember Nemesio, those professional madmen? They're still out there. They aren't smart . . . they don't follow the rules of business. Whoever dealt with them, crossed them, has no idea what they are dealing with. No idea at all."

Garrison gathered up his packet, although Chris could still feel the weight of the pictures and reports on his bed. "I had to wait to talk to you until most of your department returned to Murfee. I have people watching *your* people. Why is that? You know what I said about the head of the snake? It's like this sign I once saw outside a little jail near Arco, Texas. It said 'Beware of snakes,' in both English and Spanish. Grass all around the place was tall, uncut, like a fucking swamp, dangerous as hell. And right now? Murfee makes that place look like a fucking paradise.

"I've been looking forward to meeting you, Chris. I really have. But not like this. Never like this."

Chris raised his hand, the one that had been shattered by a bullet. The one he used to throw with. The last wound he had received, lying on his back, reaching skyward, waiting to die. A part of him wanted to get his thoughts in order, make sure Mel was safe. The world was still just so much smoke, so much broken glass; so many pieces that had to be put together. And everything inside him was broken too, a thousand pieces of himself to put back together as well. Still, he raised that damaged hand, holding Garrison back. He was so goddamn tired, but he knew where to begin. One piece at a time.

"It started with zip ties. You know, FlexiCuffs? It's all there in the DPS crime lab report. That's what I saw out at Indian Bluffs. That's what got my attention. Another second or two, and I would have walked away, and no one would ever have checked again."

He walked Garrison through the car stop out on 67, and the video. He talked about that day with Dupree at Mancha's and the back of Dupree's truck, and although he didn't specifically say Caleb's name, he did say that Rudy's sister might have information that could directly link Rudy and Dupree. He described how Eddie Corazon talked about picking up Dupree, smelling like gas. Garrison asked him how high it all went, and Chris said he didn't know, wasn't sure, but was afraid it went as high as it could go. He said the sheriff's name out loud, once, and left it at that.

He said he would do whatever Garrison needed him to do.

Later, after Garrison left, he realized the agent had left the DPS report envelope behind, empty except for one thing—her picture.

He got one of the nurses to wheel him down the hall to her. He wasn't supposed be up and about, but she understood without him really having to explain, and so did the big Texas Ranger sitting outside his door, flipping through a magazine.

He could see her only through thick glass, in her own magic bubble, floating, suspended, in the middle of the burn unit in a medically induced coma. It was still unknown if she would ever come out of it on her own. Or if she'd want to, knowing what had happened. Maybe she did know. Remembered it, dreamed it, reliving it . . . over and over again. She looked so goddamn small, held in the hands of the huge machines keeping her alive. Chris sat for a half hour watching Morgan Emerson lost in her own twilight.

8

AMERICA

She didn't know what to expect, so she tried not to expect anything at all.

She had her mama's fat friend, Pilar, drive her to Mancha's even though she could have walked—gave her fifty dollars of Rodolfo's money for her to wait in the car and keep her mouth shut—only to discover he was already there, leaning against the wall outside the bodega, drinking a horchata. She walked past him, just to be sure. She went inside and bought a pack of gum and cigarettes and counted her steps in the tiny aisles, and came back out to find him in the exact same position, watching her. She knew it was him because of the red boots. The voice on the phone had told her all about the boots . . . *rojo*.

*   *   *

He was young, close to her age, wearing a silly movie T-shirt, thin and frayed, with a thinner jacket, like a *fútbol* zip-up, tied at his waist even though it was chilly enough to raise bumps on her skin. He had tight jeans she always associated with Ojinaga, and those nice boots peeking out from underneath them. The boots were easily worth fifty times his clothes and the money she'd given Pilar. His hair was dark and pushed back high on his head, a thick black wave, and he was razor thin, like he barely ate. He had a small backpack sitting on the ground, right at the bright red toe of one of his boots, and wore a small braided rope—a bracelet—far too large for the wrist it circled.

He smiled at her, said *hola*, and tossed his empty cup into the trash can, hitching up the backpack, which she thought seemed awfully light.

Whatever she'd expected, it wasn't this.

She gave Pilar another fifty, bought her a *TV Notas* magazine and a Coke, and told her to sit in the car and wait some more. Pilar kept staring around her shoulder, asking who the boy was, since she didn't recognize him, but Amé told her that it was okay, all okay. *Todo está bien*.

They sat together on one of the benches lining the lot, where she knew her papa came and drank and sometimes fell asleep with his shirt unbuttoned and empty bottles sprawled around him in the gravel. The same lot where she'd met Deputy Cherry, what felt like years and years before. She pulled out the phone Rodolfo had given her and put it on the table. He pulled out his own, too, and side by side, they were nearly the same. He whisked them both away with one sure move of his hand, reminding her of a cat, slipped them into his backpack, and sat back to look at her. He turned his head this way and that, and said she looked like Mayrín Villanueva, a Mexican actress, and asked if Amé knew who she was. She said she wasn't sure, but guessed it was a compliment.

He laughed, said *sí*, very much so. She asked him about the ranch, but he didn't want to talk about that, even when she pushed. She wanted to know if it was just like Rodolfo described. She asked about the peacocks, and when he finally broke down and said *sí*, it was all true—they were like blue and green metal—she let herself believe that her *magia* that night had worked. Deputy Cherry hadn't died out in the desert then, and she was glad for that. But he was far away, might never return, and none of that mattered anymore anyway. It was too late. Her *magia*—Rodolfo's phone—had summoned this thin, dark-eyed boy. He was sharp, like a knife. Even standing still he was in motion. He watched her closely, but then again, he watched everything.

He told her he had come to deliver *un mensaje*, one that could only be delivered *a mano*. He held out his hands to her then as if they weren't empty, as if there was something there only she might be able to see. They were slimmer, more delicate than her own.

She asked if he had a place to stay and he shook his head, but said it would be *no problemo*, he'd take care of it. But she glanced at Pilar, watching them both through her windshield, and had an idea. It would take the last of Rodolfo's money, but that didn't matter anymore, either. There was so much she needed to know, everything— how he'd gotten to Murfee, how long would he stay? Why were the men from the ranch willing to help her? What did he really plan to do, and most important of all, when could she return across the river with him? Some things she guessed he couldn't answer; others he might not want to. So instead she asked him his name. He was surprised, suddenly shy, as if it might never have occurred to him that she would want to know that. He scuffed his expensive boots in the gravel, like a kid pretending to be an adult and suddenly caught at it, but smiled anyway when he finally answered.

"*Máximo. Me llamo Máximo.*"

9

THE JUDGE

He drove through a storm. It was all cold wind around Van Horn—the air static like wool and metal shavings, a sky colored dust and bone. It was impossible to see where the highway ended and heaven began—as if a huge eraser had dragged across the edge of the world. But he'd never believed in God or heaven, not like his father and Hollis, or his grandfather, who'd said prayers while whipping him as a boy. God's words were on his lips when the flames had flicked up the side of his canopy bed. Praying hadn't done him any damn good.

He did, however, believe in judgment. In his office was an original gold scale in a mahogany and glass case. It was a heavy thing, serious—scratched from use and still slick from the sweat of other men's hands. There was a brief gold rush in Texas in 1853, in the hills around Austin, but nothing much had come of it. There was also the old folklore about gold that centered on Murfee itself—the Lost Nigger Gold Mine. In 1887, the four Reagan brothers picked up an illiterate Seminole, William Kelly, as a ranch hand. Kelly was known as "Nigger Bill"—what you called any mixed-blood in the Big Bend in those days. Kelly, only fourteen at the time, claimed to have discovered a gold mine, showing off a lump of ore as proof, and although no one believed him, Kelly abandoned his work and went on to San Antonio, still talking up his stake. He got an assayer to verify it—seventy-five thousand dollars to the ton—and then came back to the Big Bend.

Some said he returned to the Reagans' ranch, where the brothers killed him and dumped his body in the Rio Grande, having finally come around about the boy's claim. Others said he fled over the border on a stolen Reagan horse, never to be seen again. Either way, the Reagan brothers spent the rest of their lives poking around for that damn mine—the last of them searching the dirt as late as 1930. In a copy of the *Victoria Advocate* from 1935, the Judge had read an interview with Lee Reagan, who dismissed the stories of Nigger Bill's death, claiming he last saw him riding off on a stolen pony, and downplayed his family's efforts to find the mine. But other treasure hunters also set out looking for it, and although there were whispers through the years that the mine had been rediscovered, something bad always befell the whisperer before they could pass on their secrets.

He had a first edition of J. Frank Dobie's *Coronado's Children*, taken from his grandfather's library before it burned, which recounted all about the mine and other stories of gold. It was possible Kelly's gold wasn't actually gold ore. Another writer, Haldeen Braddy, thought it was just a worked piece left by the Spanish. Or it had been dropped by a group of Mexican *banditos* fleeing the *rurales*—the Mexican Guardia Rural—abandoning their prize because it was slowing them down. He'd named his hunting lands El Dorado as a secret nod to those old stories, because one edge of his property encompassed the Reagan brothers' original 1887 ranch. He'd never seen treasure, though—nothing sparkling in the wallows, not even the gleam of fool's gold flecking a granite rock face, but it was a helluva story anyway. You can't find what isn't there, and never was.

In his days traveling back and forth, Murfee had come to look different to him now, as if he had been away for decades rather than days: the shape of it unfamiliar, the shadows longer, its people unknown to him. Duane Dupree and Chris Cherry hailed as heroes, and strangers walking the streets. Questions would get harder.

William Kelly lost his mine—his life—when stronger men, more violent and determined and ruthless men, took it from him. It was blood and judgment. It was the old way of the West he knew and understood and accepted. It was Murfee now.

There was a cell message waiting for him when he cleared Valentine, after he got through the dead spot in coverage after Van Horn. There were spots like that all over the Big Bend, all the way up to Sierra Escalera and his own El Dorado. Dead areas like graves. But he recognized the number, and of all the people he'd expected to hear from, she was the last. They hadn't spoken since Thanksgiving morning, nearly a month ago, but he hadn't forgotten her, far from it.

It was Anne Hart.

10

MELISSA

Chris was as thin as she'd ever remembered.

He joked about it when she helped him to the bathroom, how he was on one helluva weight-loss plan. *It wasn't for everyone, but it damn well worked.* As tall as he was, he weighed nearly nothing leaning against her, and that scared her more than anything. If he lost a few more pounds, he might disappear altogether. He saw the look on her face and told her it was okay. He was going to be okay. She searched his eyes and wanted to believe him. He asked her to open one of the windows, but they were sealed shut. Instead she pulled the shades back and the blinds up and let the late-afternoon sunshine fill the room. It glowed on his bed, turning everything white, revealing just how pale he was.

He drifted in the sunlight, held up his own hands,

even the damaged one, and looked at them, turning them back and forth, as if amazed by them. He fell asleep in mid-sentence, right at the point when he said he had something important he wanted to tell her.

It was dusk when he came to, startled awake, as if he'd been dreaming about things that had scared him. Moving and flinching, dodging imaginary bullets. He reached out a hand to steady himself and she grabbed it, squeezed it, and he squeezed back. He'd called out a name too, just before he woke up, but she couldn't tell who it was.

He sipped some water, asked her how everyone had been treating her, how the hotel was. She told him everyone was nice, the hotel not so much. She asked how everyone had been treating *him*, how he liked the hospital. And he laughed; she'd made her point. She told him the sheriff had returned to Murfee with the rest of the department; they were still trying to find the other men who had done this to Chris. He hadn't killed them all, and a few might not have escaped on the plane. They might still be out there hiding in the desert, waiting for another chance.

Chris said it didn't matter, they could look all they wanted. They were all gone now, all phantoms to begin with. In the end, they had never really existed anyway. Then he told her about Joe Garrison's visit.

"That man thinks you had something to do with those agents being attacked?"

Chris shook his head. "No, but he thinks I might know why they were."

She didn't want to ask, didn't feel the need to. He'd tell her if he wanted to. And he did. Everything.

Then it was her turn.

She'd already told him about the video, but wanted to tell it all again. Just like him, everything, all of it. She'd learned sometimes you have to say something twice for it to matter. She told him how she'd been following him around, searching through his things, but he didn't ask her what she was looking for or why she'd mentioned it to Duane Dupree at all. He didn't need to. *He knew her.* The only one who ever had, ever would.

"They hurt you because of what I said, right?"

Chris shook his head, slow. "It doesn't matter, babe. It has nothing to do with you. I did this. There are a lot of things I could have done different."

She looked out the window, not wanting to see his face when he answered, not wanting him to hide what she would see there. "Is this going to keep happening, Chris?"

"I don't know. I really don't. I mean, Duane could have left me out there and we wouldn't even be talking right now. Not sure why he didn't. It doesn't make sense. Do you know they tell me my bum knee giving out is what saved me? I fucking fell down so I didn't get shot in the back of the head as I ran. And then Duane got me out of there, kept me alive."

She made a face. "Fuck Duane Dupree. Seems to me he owes you, too. What about this Garrison, what's he going to do?"

A welcome smile at her old anger, then a shrug. "He thinks our department is corrupt. He'll keep digging. His people were hurt, one's dead. He doesn't have a choice." Chris reached out, took her hand. His was cold. "I saw her, that woman, again. That woman I met on 67. Her real name is Morgan Emerson. She told me it was Sara. She's in a room a few doors down."

Mel knew that, had heard it from the other Murfee deputies. She walked by the room every day, but never looked in. "You didn't hurt her, Chris, that's not on you. You didn't do anything wrong."

Chris looked at her, looked close. "No, babe, but I didn't do a helluva lot right, either."

He slept again, and she brushed his hair out of his eyes. Talking to her had exhausted him, exhausted her, too. He'd been carrying all this around with him, these sharp, silent burdens, and they almost cost him his life. She'd been telling herself she hated Murfee because she didn't understand it, but the truth was she understood it far too well. There was a side of it no different from the city across the river, from the motels she and her daddy had bounced around—dangerous and desperate. Places where most people didn't matter all that goddamn much, and where someone like Duane Dupree could do anything he pleased, hiding in the dark and neon. She was not going to allow him or anyone else to hurt Chris again.

Chris sighed, rolled away from her. She adjusted his sheets and his skin was hot, burning. He'd been so cold earlier. He flinched from her touch, clawed out with his wounded, pale hand, and she knew he was once more dodging dream bullets.

11
MÁXIMO

Pilar's apartment was small, and she talked far too much. She had two little dogs he hated, who got hair all over everything, and she reminded him of his *abuela*. She talked about her *hijo* in San Elizario who never visited her anymore, and watched Máximo with her small eyes—always wanting to know what he liked on TV or what he wanted to eat. She burned the tortillas and her rice was no good, but if he asked, she always drove down to the market and got him cold Tecates.

More than once he caught her staring at him as he tried to sleep on her couch, as large and pale as the moon and blocking the kitchen light behind her, breathing heavily. He knew he was going to have to fuck her. The money America had given her would not keep her quiet, not for long. Her *hijo* was far away and she was lonely and her little apartment felt empty, even with both of them in it. She worked with America's mama at the dry cleaners, and she would talk if he didn't do something about it, something for her.

So he had her buy him beer—he wouldn't drive on his own, careful because he'd never really driven a car and didn't have a license—and sat on her bed and drank as many as his stomach could take and told his jokes and she laughed too loud and too long. He even sang "Cielito Lindo" to her.

He thought the beers would make it easier, but it didn't. Her eyes were *pesos* and she talked so fast, so nervous, he thought tiny birds would fly from her mouth. Finally he unzipped and grabbed her fat hand and put it down the front of his jeans, heard her gasp as she fumbled with him while he finished off a Tecate and tried to watch *fútbol* on the TV over her shoulder.

She may have even started crying as he pushed inside her. She said a name that wasn't his—her *hijo*, that rotten boy, in San Elizario. But he was thinking about America all the time.

All America wanted to know about was the *rancho*.

He told her other things he thought she might want to hear—some true, some lies. She wanted him to take her there, but she didn't know what she asked. They wanted him to bring her there, too. But it was no place for her . . . no good would come of it. If he took her there, he would never see her again.

He'd beaten men to death with wooden planks, helped shoot crossers in an abandoned house down by the water. He'd stacked heads in a bloody pyramid and pointed a rifle at two dozen *niños* and *niñas* no older than him and walked them ten miles to the border, one carrying two bundles of *heroína* taped to her legs. He'd tossed a grenade from a ten-speed bike into the open door of a disco.

He'd seen worse things at the *rancho*.

Instead, he asked her about Hollywood, where they made movies, and Houston and New York and Miami— cities he'd heard of. She'd never been to those places, but she said she had pictures of them all, taped to her walls. Then she showed him a picture that the *ayudante del sheriff* had sent to her phone, this gringo she knew as Dupree, who the others at the *rancho* had named Perrito. He read the words with the picture and deleted it for her.

Staring hard into his eyes, she finally demanded to know if he'd come for her at all, or just for Perrito, and this other gringo she called El Juez. Did she matter? Did her *hermano*, Rodolfo? He asked her what *she* wanted, and after she told him—after she told him all the things Perrito had done to her and all the bad things he'd promised—he said with a smile, *Te prometo que nunca te hará daño de nuevo*, and they never talked anymore about the things he'd come to do.

They borrowed Pilar's car and America drove, as she showed him her town and the places he'd asked to see. On the road near Mancha's they sped by three Mexican boys and a Mexican girl, running in the tall dead grass. The *niña* was smallest of all, with a dirty baseball hat shoved down on her head, but she was running so fast, faster than her *hermanos*, laughing at them and leaving them behind. He laughed too; pointed her out to America, who watched and smiled. After they passed her, the *niña* was still running beneath the biggest sky he'd ever seen, trying to race their car.

On their way out to the place where her own *hermano* was found, they went past the *ayudante*'s little house, but America didn't say his name. She didn't have to. She just pointed it out, tucked past a pecan grove, and kept going. Later, when she finally parked, they leaned against the car, against the wind. He put an arm around her, careful, because she was shivering.

She didn't know exactly where Rodolfo had been found, couldn't point it out, but looked out over the fence line as if she could still see him there; then past that, to the scrub and caliche and the mountains in the distance—everything purple and gold and red. A couple of big black birds sat on the wire fence itself, bouncing in the breeze, staring at them with small eyes. Máximo waved his arms at them, made cawing noises to drive them away, but this was their place.

She asked him if he'd ever met Rodolfo, and he wanted to lie and say *sí, claro*, but told her the truth instead. He hadn't known him, may have met him once in passing, but couldn't be sure. Either way, it didn't matter. He didn't need to know him.

They stood and counted the birds together for a while, letting the sun go down around them. She could have gotten back in the car, where it was warmer, but seemed content enough to let him keep his arm around her, as if for the moment, there was just enough warmth and safety there.

12
CALEB

My mom disappeared without her truck, her phone, or her wallet. Anything that might have been used to find her, trace her, was left behind. Every connection to her life in Murfee was discarded, including me. Some people asked—not many, not enough—how a woman could leave a note and simply vanish from a place as small and rural as Murfee. Did she hitchhike? Did an old friend come get her? Did she make her way to the bus station in Midland and buy a ticket with cash, heading nowhere, to lose herself from all of us?

It's unthinkable that my mom chose to abandon my father and me. I've heard her called a coward or worse. But if that's what she did—run away—there's another way to look at it. That it took unbelievable strength and courage—the sort of courage that makes the unthinkable bearable. The only choice.

Dear Mom,

I have started this a hundred times, and I never finish it. There is so much I want to say, but you'll never hear these words, never read them.

They're like messages in a thousand bottles that will float forever lost, like you.

There was a time where every single night I dreamed of finally finding you, of catching a glimpse of your face in a huge window, or seeing someone on a street corner I know without a doubt is you. In those dreams, we look right at each other, and for a moment—an eye blink—I think I see you smile, but when I run to catch you, calling your name over and over again, you are already gone— just another faded reflection in glass, another stranger's face in the crowd.

After a few months my dreams changed.

Then when I see that hazy reflection or the face in the crowd, I don't quite recognize it. I think it is someone I once knew, but I'm not so sure anymore. I don't run to catch you. I stand in place, trying to recall who you might have been and why it once mattered so much that I remember you.

Now I don't dream about you at all.

Please know I haven't given up.

I just don't know where to look anymore.

13

ANNE

Sheriff Ross picked her up from the house an hour or so after she'd left school, just like she'd asked. She'd stayed late that last day before Christmas break, getting her final work done, so it was dark by the time he pulled up. Most of the students had long ago headed over to the Hamilton for burgers and were going to a bonfire after that. She told him she thought Caleb was one of them. She had him for the last period of the day, and overheard him talking with Carl Tippen and Dale Holt about it.

The sheriff knew all about the bonfire. It was a high school tradition. The kids had been doing it for years on the last day of school before winter break. A lot of the kids drank there and it was never a problem, but he always kept a deputy nearby, just in case. This year it would have been Chris Cherry, but now it was Miller or Dupree.

They'd planned it for Tippen's place, but he asked them to keep it a little closer to home this time around. He wasn't sure where, but Duane would tell him.

It was still early, though, and as they drove north out of Murfee, they both saw Caleb's little Ford Ranger parked with all the other cars in the lot at the Hamilton.

They didn't go to the same place in Artesia, but another place, much farther away, that she'd picked outside Terlingua. She told him that Lori McKutcheon had told her all about it, and she wanted to try it herself. But it was Caleb who'd given it to her. He'd calculated the mileage, worked out the timing. The sheriff said it really was a good Mexican place, authentic, although the menu wasn't that extensive, and it was a helluva drive.

Over cold margaritas he told her about all of his media interviews, his time in El Paso, and his visits with Chris. He said Chris had been shot in the left shoulder, the right hand, and most serious, a bullet to the chest, but eventually he'd be all right. He said Chris was as strong as a horse. It would take more than a little lead to bring him down.

"I'm surprised you called, Anne, pleasantly surprised."

"I am too, I guess. There's so much going on right now, I know, and it'll only get busier. But I wanted to apologize for Thanksgiving. I owed you this second invitation."

"Well, given how it turned out, it was probably for the best. You really must not think much of our little town right now."

"Do you mean Chris and Duane? That can happen anywhere. As horrible as it is, it seems to happen everywhere."

The sheriff turned his glass up to the light, content to watch the last of the ice slide to nothing. "True, but it has been rare here. This has been a safe place for a long time because a lot of blood was spilled in Murfee's early history to make it that way. There was a time when all of this was bandits and Indians and Mexican rustlers. Wearing a badge in these territories was deadly work. Many men sacrificed. Their families did. I don't want to see it like that again."

"I'm sure they'll catch whoever who did this."

Sheriff Ross ordered her the fresh margarita she'd asked for. "I'm sure we will."

He was distracted throughout dinner; still charming, witty. And she did her best as well. Talking, laughing, making sure to order more drinks for the both of them. She checked her watch twice when she went to the bathroom, but otherwise ignored it and her phone. That was the hard part, not looking at her phone. But all in all, she thought she did a pretty damn good job. Thespian troupe good.

She even pretended not to notice how when they walked across the parking lot toward his truck, he kept one step behind her, one hand at her elbow, his eyes searching the shadows. Once on the road he glanced at his mirrors and drove back a slightly different way from how they'd come.

He'd had a lot to drink, refusing to turn down the ones she'd ordered, and she could see each one in the red cast to his eyes, the slight sway in his step when they'd walked out to the truck. Driving, he was still observant, careful. Sitting near him in the cab was like holding a hand over a naked blade. He told her how he hoped she might decide to stay in Murfee, said it a second time about halfway back to town. He made a point of letting her know he would really enjoy seeing her again.

Later they sat in his truck in front of her house while

she thanked him, not for the dinners but for everything else he'd done for her—getting her to Murfee, making her feel welcome. She wasn't a hundred percent sure she could or should stay, but was warming up to the idea. She leaned forward, forced herself to hug him, smelling alcohol, and let him kiss her on the cheek good night. He lingered there, a bloodless gesture, without warmth.

She guessed his eyes were open, staring into the dark, the whole time.

He got out and opened the door for her, his hands brushing her shoulder, her breasts, and it took all she had not to recoil. He waited as she walked toward her door, watching both her and the night. She braced then for him to call out, not believing he wouldn't. He'd been so careful all night, always on guard. After all, there was no way he could miss it, but she finally shut the door on him still standing silent by his truck. She turned on a light, too afraid to stay in the dark, and stood by the front door, listening for his truck to leave.

He lingered out there forever, waiting for her to come back out and invite him in, before his truck roared to life. He drove away, leaving her shaking and holding herself up against the hallway wall. She wanted to throw up dinner, get in the shower and scrub him and this entire night off. Then she wanted to get in her car and drive as far away as possible and never look back. But she couldn't do that, not now, and she was thankful that he'd missed it, too. That he never got around to asking her why her little driveway was empty. *Where on earth might her car be?*

14
CHRIS

Chris was surprised when Caleb came in.

He looked as tired as Chris felt, grayish circles under his eyes, carrying a plastic bag in his hand. Caleb took it all in, the stark white of the room, the humming chrome machines, and the TV turned down low, fixed to a corner between the ceiling and the wall. It was showing an old black-and-white movie, one Chris didn't recognize and couldn't imagine that Caleb did, either. They watched it together for a while anyway, before Caleb asked if it was okay if he sat down.

Chris told him of course, no problem, and then asked what had been on his mind the moment Caleb entered the room. *Did the sheriff know that he was in El Paso, visiting Chris?*

Caleb smiled, his eyes far older than they had any right to be, shook his head, and sat down.

"I guess it's late for visitors, they didn't want me to disturb you. I had to use my father's name, tell them who I was, and then it was no problem. They may call and check, who knows? Can you believe that? Even now his name is like a goddamn key." Caleb looked at him, studying him. "You're going to be okay, right?"

"It's your name too, Caleb." But Chris knew Caleb didn't want to hear that, so he held up his hand. "Probably not throwing any footballs for a while—actually, like forever—but I'll be fine."

Caleb eyed him more. "You don't look fine."

"That makes two of us." Chris punched the remote off, sat himself up a little straighter in bed and tried not to wince. "You shouldn't be here, Caleb, shouldn't have come. I appreciate it, but there was no need."

"I know. It's not just about you, though. I wanted to thank you for believing me, and Amé, too."

"Well, nothing's come of it yet. But it will when I get out of here."

Caleb shrugged. "It doesn't matter, though, does it? Not really. We can be right, all of us, and it won't mean a damn thing." The words didn't sound like him; they sounded borrowed and probably were—Amé Reynosa outside Mancha's, abandoning her cigarette, letting it fall to the ground. *Do you think it matters, really?*

Chris hardened. "Rodolfo Reynosa was murdered at Indian Bluffs, just like you said. I can prove that. I can prove who did it, and I have people who will help. People who believe me . . . believe *us*. Don't tell me what happened to me won't matter."

Caleb shuffled his bag from one hand to the other. "We'll all be gone by then."

Chris thought it was a weird thing to say. "Look, there are others who know about this now. What you did took courage, and you should be proud of that. This is far from over."

Caleb laughed, brittle. "No, that wasn't courage, it was fear. I've been afraid forever. And this was over the minute I got you involved. It was over the minute my mom disappeared and I didn't do a damn thing about it."

"Jesus, Caleb, what else do you think you could have done? What are you trying to say?"

"I've already said it all." Caleb raised the bag. "Here." He put it at the end of the bed, like Garrison before, and stood to leave.

"Did you drive here by yourself? Is America with you?" Chris asked.

"No, I came alone."

"The sheriff will find out you're here." It wasn't so much a question. "He'll be looking for you."

"I don't think so. I had a little help. Right now, I'm at Tippen's bonfire. Goodbye, Deputy Cherry. Get better and get the hell out of Murfee."

"Wait." Chris struggled, trying to sit up, stand. "What sort of help?"

Caleb stood at the door for a second. "Someone was nice enough to let me borrow her car."

Chris sat for a while, staring at the space where Caleb had been and also at the pile of books on his bedside table that Mel had left him. Trying to avoid the bag Caleb had left behind. She'd dug through the boxes he'd put away, and brought ten or fifteen of his old books, a random collection, anything she could grab, figuring he would want them while trapped in the hospital. Even *Something Wicked This Way Comes.* She said she didn't know if these were ones he liked, didn't know anything about them, but brought them for him anyway. He told her he loved them all.

He struggled to reach down and pick up the bag Caleb had left. He could have called the nurse to do it, but didn't. Whatever was in the bag was for him alone. It felt like a book, too. And it was—a small, thick notebook, like a real diary, loosely wrapped in even more plastic, smeared with what appeared to be dirt, as if it had been buried. Chris's hands were dusty by the time he got it exposed. He turned it over, looking for something to identify it, a name or title, but there was nothing.

When he opened it, his fingers passing over the stiff pages, money fell out.

Dozens of hundred-dollar bills, trapped between the pages, now free, fluttering over the white sheets around him. He went to the first page, nervous. A very real part of him wanted to wrap the book up again and have Mel take it, burn it, rebury it. Part of him wanted to do anything but read it.

His heart hurt at the neat writing, the words.

"My father has killed three men . . ."

15
MELISSA

She woke to the sound of a phone ringing, couldn't figure out if it was the hotel phone or her cell, fumbling for both. The shades were drawn but it was still dark outside, twice as dark, and she had no idea exactly what hour it was. By the time she got her cell in hand the ringing had stopped—*missed call*—but she recognized it. It was the hospital. She sat in bed and held on to the phone, used it to keep her hand from shaking. She didn't want to call back, didn't want to have to face what that call might mean. Chris had been pale, weak, but he had been okay. He'd been cold, then hot. *He had told her he was going to be okay.* Fuck him all to hell if he'd lied. God help Murfee if he was dead.

She was halfway to tears when her phone rang again, and she counted to five before she answered. She held it as far away as she could; she'd still hear the voice, barely, but it wouldn't be so close. Still not far enough away that the words, however bad they might be, wouldn't touch her. It was Chris, calling out her name, so she had to bite her free hand to keep from crying, relieved.

She listened, trying to sort out what he was saying. He wanted out of the hospital. The doctors would fight him, even he knew he wasn't well enough to be up and around, but he didn't think they could actually stop him if he demanded it. Plus she would be there with him, supporting him, helping him. He added something strange too, almost as much for himself as for her—that they needed to be gone and on the road before anyone in Murfee figured out he'd left.

She wanted to know what the hell he thought he was doing, what was going on. Where did he need to be other than a hospital? Which, as near as she could figure, was the only place on earth a man who'd been shot three times should be. He said he knew, understood. But she needed to hear him out. Really hear him and trust him. He'd explain it in the car. It was about Caleb Ross, who wasn't returning his calls now, and the sheriff.

The morning was too late, and none of it would matter anyway if they didn't get on the road. They were going home.

16

DUANE

He was at the bonfire, the flames rising and falling. Faces leered out of them; a few he recognized, but most he didn't. One even looked like his own, staring back, mute, without a goddamn thing to say.

She texted him, wanted to meet out at the Comanche. Said she had what he needed . . . what he'd been wanting all along. Then she sent *him* a picture. Naked skin, the curve of a shoulder, hair a beautiful mess, dark eyes beckoning—staring right through him. She'd never answered his messages before, never even acknowledged him at all, and here she was, sending him a picture that made his hands shake—not that they didn't do that on their own now.

She had what he needed. What he wanted. She couldn't even imagine what that was anymore.

She was up to something, something *bad*, but he didn't care. Someone else was up to something, too. He noticed it when Dale Holt pulled up in Caleb Ross's truck, without Caleb. Duane sat around for another hour at the far edge of the fire light, not once seeing Caleb with the other kids. Curious, agitated, gnawing his lips, he walked up to Holt and finally asked him about it, leaving the other boys around him to scatter into the dark. Holt was nervous, looked so much like his dead older brother that Duane had to look twice to make sure it *wasn't* him. Holt smelled like weed, beer; stammering over every word, even *Hello, sir.* Duane wanted to grab him by the throat and scream into his face, eat out his goddamn eyes, because he had to admit he was barely in control of himself anymore, but forced a smile anyway that was probably twice as terrifying, and eased the scared boy along by telling him he knew that Holt and Ross weren't really friends—hell, everyone knew Caleb Ross didn't have friends.

So why the fuck was he out and about in Caleb's truck? And by God, he'd get an answer one way or another. Holt did come clean eventually, nearly pissing himself, admitting Caleb had paid him a few hundred dollars to drive the truck around a bit and keep his mouth shut about it—then leave it parked a few streets over from the Hi n Lo.

Duane mapped it in his head, saw a street lined with poplars, and knew exactly where it was and what it meant. He didn't even have to ask Holt where Caleb might have gone. He thanked the boy, told Holt that was all just fine and dandy—and that he'd better keep his hole shut and start running, fast, unless he wanted Duane to cut out his fucking tongue with a fucking knife. Not before reminding him not to get too close to the bonfire, so he wouldn't get burned.

After that he drove over to Mancha's, found Eddie Corazon, pointed his gun right into Eddie's face and shoved him into his truck in front of an audience yelling, *Hey, you can't do that, he ain't done nothin'*, all in thick accents. He took him to the beaner's trailer, where he pistol-whipped him until Eddie gave up his stash. He kept it hidden in tinfoil in his freezer. Duane didn't care anymore, felt so sick he couldn't stand, so he took it all.

And then for one long moment he was back . . . *walking among his daddy's fields, a boy but all done up in his deputy's uniform, carrying his grandaddy's Smith & Wesson and shooting his cows all over again. Except now they had human faces, all of Murfee kneeling in the grass, staring at him, calling his name. Even his favorite, Big Boss, wearing the face of the Judge . . .*

He may have left Eddie Corazon dead too, didn't stick around to check. There sure was a lot of blood on the floor.

17

CALEB

He'd gotten a pretty decent head start to El Paso by skipping out of the last period of school, so even with driving all the way up there in Anne Hart's car, he was on his way back to Murfee before the bonfire was really going. More or less about the same time Anne and his father were halfway to Terlingua.

His phone had lit up most of the drive back, though—calls and messages from Chris that he ignored, let go. He wanted more than anything to see Amé, make sure she understood the note he'd given her at school, and before heading up to the house he stopped at her place, but she wasn't around; his own texts and calls to her were still unanswered. He knew she wouldn't have gone to the bonfire, but couldn't guess where she might be.

When he asked her mother where she was, using all

the Spanish that he remembered, she said nothing and pushed him away from the door, back into the darkness and away from her light, and shut it in his face.

He drove around Murfee a little more, up Main Street, toward Archer-Ross. He drove out to the Hi n Lo, counted people coming and going for a bit. Saw John Snowden, the dentist, walk out with a small bag and get in his car, where his wife was waiting. In the brief moment they were illuminated by the car's dome light, he bent forward, kissing her as if he'd been gone a long time, to a place far away. Caleb left them like that, circled his hometown once, twice, and then he was done.

He dropped off Anne's car like they'd agreed—a couple of streets over from her house but close enough for her to walk to it—and turned for home. He walked fast, past so many darkened houses. By the time he got to his street at the edge of town, he was running, trying not to cry.

When he got inside he took the Ruger out of the gun locker, loading it with the stolen shells he'd recovered two days earlier from his hiding place down by the creek. He wiped and cleaned it till it shined, checked his work twice, and slipped it beneath his bed to wait.

18

AMERICA

She sat in Pilar's car near the edge of the Comanche lot, where she'd sat with Dupree before. She had the engine off and the radio on, listening to a Mexican station from over the border. There was no music, just words; a *fútbol* game somewhere over there, but for her, still so much closer than the school bonfire. She'd never gone to it, didn't even know where it was.

Máximo had kept begging her to be patient, *tener paciencia*. He was in no rush and she couldn't figure out why. Maybe he was in no hurry to get back over the river, but over *here*, she needed it done now. He just wanted to look at her and hold her hand and tell her it already was.

She'd sent Dupree a picture of her own for once, one she'd snapped in her bedroom, but he hadn't answered her. Not yet. She had never taken a picture of herself like that, and wondered what Caleb would have thought of it, or Máximo. Máximo had wanted Dupree way out here, away from Murfee and everyone, but she didn't tell him about the picture she'd made to draw him out of town. Draw him *to* her. She'd stared at it a long time before sending it, afraid to let it go, wondering if it even looked like her, because the girl in the photo was so different. Someone she didn't recognize, because she never looked at herself anymore, avoiding even the mirror in her bathroom, since Duane Dupree. Wondering if this was how Caleb and Máximo saw her, wondering if she was pretty. Before deciding that *sí*, the girl in the picture was, very much so.

She was about to give up when he finally called, said he would come. But his voice sounded strange, lost, like each word burned or there were other voices speaking for him. He giggled, whispered things so that she knew he was high, *drogado*, as high as she'd ever heard him. She wasn't sure if that made him more or less dangerous, but at least he was coming. She texted Máximo, let him know Dupree was on his way. She wished she could be more like Máximo, who acted like he had all the time in the world. Like he wanted *more* time. And maybe he did. He never talked about what waited for him back across the river, what waited for them both.

Caleb had given her a note at school before disappearing during his last period. Once she had it in her hand, felt it, she'd realized it wasn't a paper note at all, so she went into the bathroom, stood in the stall with the door shut, to look at it alone. She'd unfolded it and it was the picture he'd taken down from her wall, when he'd last been in her bedroom. That magazine cutout of a city skyline along a beach, once glossy but now faded. The picture with the numbers she'd written down on the back, including Dupree's, over a year ago. So many times before she'd looked at that picture and wondered if the colors were real—the blue of the sky and the blue of the ocean. A blue so bright and the pale white of those tall buildings the same white of the coldest desert moon, taller than any she had ever seen with her own eyes. She'd played a game with herself, picking out a window in one of those buildings as her own, the highest point, imagining herself living there, staring out that window, looking back at herself, waving goodbye. Caleb had written a few words right across *her* window, as if he'd known which one it was all along.

Dupree's truck pulled in, slow, pinning her beneath his headlights. He sat like that for a long time, the rumble of his engine carrying low across the gravel lot. But he didn't pull forward or shut off the truck, just smoked his cigarettes. He was watching, waiting, wary—as if he knew there was trouble, as if he could smell it. She tried to will him over to her, make him cross that distance, and when that didn't work she got so frustrated she almost got out of Pilar's car and walked right over, even though she didn't want to be that close to his truck. It was an open hole, ready to swallow her up. If she got too close, he'd make her disappear for good. If she didn't know any better, she thought she caught Dupree's eyes glowing red in the truck's cab, but it was only the flare of his matches, the tip of his cigarette burning bright with each breath. Minutes passed. There was the flicker and flash of the luminous screen of his phone as he took a call or a picture, maybe both. A *puta* phone call.

Ten paciencia.

Ten paciencia.

Máximo had wanted her to stay in Pilar's car, do exactly what he'd told her, exactly *how* he had told her to do it. He was worried about the *ayudante* springing his own trap, but with Dupree alone, only feet away, smoking without a care in the world, it was so hard. She held her breath, but didn't know if she could hold it much longer. Her window was down and through gritted teeth she could smell cigarette smoke, Dupree's skin. The same smell that had been trapped in her clothes and her room for what felt like forever. What happened next wouldn't make it go away, not at first, but it was a start. A start she could live with, that she would have to.

Ten paciencia.

She took her eyes off of Dupree, taken for a moment by the stars. Wondering if they were the same ones she had watched from her bedroom window the night she'd dreamed of Rodolfo, after Caleb had come to her. Maybe they'd been following her all along, right up to this moment, watching down on her, without judgment. She knew she loved the stars here, the way they hung above the mountains, shined across the desert, glittered high over the town. She hoped they'd be the same everywhere, that they would always follow her, no matter where she went, but wasn't sure, a part of her understanding that it was possible to see *real* stars only in a place like this, far from big city lights. That's when she truly understood the stars weren't just scattered points, but were so many and so close they could light the sky with a fierce radiance, bright enough to read by. At times close enough to reach up and grab, so bright they hurt. So hot any one of them would burn to touch. She had been Rodolfo's *estrella*. All he'd asked of her was to *glow* for him—to wait for him, to guide him. But he never found his way back to her, because she had become lost, too. She'd been all alone, needing a light of her own to show her the way.

When she was gone, she'd miss the stars here. She was

still looking up, searching for her star, when her phone buzzed, a text from across the parking lot. Not from Máximo . . . finally, *Dupree*. But just another picture . . .

. . . of a man's face up close, eyes bruised and open. Out of focus and gone away, and there was dirt in them . . . in his hair. There was blood too, on his pale lips, spotting his cheeks like tears. Everything else was blackness. It was a picture of a starless night, a shuttered room—of nothing at all; a square of dark like the deepest well or a grave in the desert or a hole to nowhere.

And Duane Dupree had taken a picture of her dead brother deep down in that hole, staring upward at the last thing he ever saw.

Then she was out of the car, running toward him, screaming. But before she got there, Dupree gunned the engine on his truck, pulled it in a wide circle, and with a wave of his hand was gone.

She had thrown her phone and its horrible last picture after him, crying too hard to stop, when Máximo walked up from where he'd been hiding in the dark. All of his patience, all of his worry and caution, and he'd waited too fucking long. Instead he put his arms around her, holding her close, still holding Rodolfo's gun.

19

CALEB

His father got home late, poured himself a glass of whiskey, and sat in the kitchen by himself. Caleb tracked the steady clink of the glass on the wood, a drinking rhythm. From his bedroom window the sky had long gone blue to purple; above that, a deeper darkness and the lonely burn of brighter, distant things. Some of them moved left to right—planes or satellites passing far overhead.

His father finally came up the stairs and his weight moved past Caleb's bedroom, stopping only long enough to peer in, where Caleb lay sideways on his bed, asleep, still wearing his earbuds. But there was no music in them, no sound, and Caleb wasn't asleep. He listened to his own heartbeat and the sound of his father standing at his door, watching him; holding his breath, because of his damaged ear from the night on the mountain. Finally, faintly, catching the echoes of his father walking down to his own room. Caleb said his mother's name three times and reached down under his bed for the Ruger.

In his mother's mirror, his father moved, shapeless. Caleb thought he might take a shower, but instead he just pulled off his boots, lying down on the bed, unsteady. He was drinking downstairs for a while; too long, too much, and he'd probably had a few during his dinner with Anne. His father's reflection reclined and came to rest, motionless, hands across his chest. Caleb waited and tried not to breathe, tried not to cry anymore, as his father turned into one shadow among many, threatening to disappear altogether.

Caleb was paralyzed, knowing he was waiting too damn long. He hadn't planned on shooting a sleeping man, but he would. Then he was in motion from where he crouched in the hallway. The gun heavy, so goddamn heavy, he thought it would pull him through the floor. He'd never held anything with such weight, such importance—all the years between them and all the years that would never be—and he struggled as he burst into his father's bedroom, the muzzle leading him more than he wanted.

He glanced up quick enough to see the bed was now empty, nothing reflected in the mirror. His father had disappeared, faded away right in front of him as he tried not to shoot himself in the leg. The gun's impossible weight threatened to bend him in half, leaving him kneeling on the floor, as if he were praying. His finger slipped on the trigger when he fired blind, shooting out his own reflection and anything that hid within it.

He never heard his father, never saw him, when he was struck hard and sharp across the mouth, tasting blood.

20

THE JUDGE

The room was full of sudden rage, the one bullet shattering the old mirror. It rang like a church bell. And then the boy lay sprawled on the floor covered in broken glass, the rifle a handspan away. The Judge marveled at the gun, as if he couldn't imagine such a thing, while he fought for his balance and shook the muzzle blast free from his eyes.

He'd gotten up to take a piss and was coming out of the bathroom when Caleb stumbled into his room, yelling. But he saw the rifle first and hit Caleb as hard as he could across the mouth, surprising him. Still, the boy was not half as surprised as he was. He wasn't angry or particularly scared, either. He'd had too much to drink, and it had nearly cost him, but getting up to piss it all away had probably saved his life.

He thought about just kicking the gun clear, but instead bent over, picked it up, checking to make sure it was still loaded. It was. He leaned against the dresser, steadied himself, and then pointed the Ruger at the crown of his son's head.

"Damn, boy, goddamn." He had to say it loud, since they were both still half deaf from the gun's blast. But Caleb looked up, heard him clear enough, his eyes dark. He had a cut on his cheek from the mirror glass and blood crawling down his face, mixing with what was already running from his mouth.

"I know what you did," Caleb breathed.

"Is that the truth now?" He raised the gun to make his point, took a step back, opening distance between them. "What exactly would that be?"

"You're not going to kill me, not here. Not like this." Caleb pulled himself up, and he could see now just how tall the boy had grown; still thin, but tall, nearly his own height. He couldn't remember when Caleb had gotten big, maybe because his son was always hunched over, disappearing into his clothes, or maybe because he hadn't been paying enough attention. Or he saw only what Caleb had showed him.

"Don't test my patience, boy. You'd be surprised what I am capable of."

"No, no, I wouldn't. I'm not surprised at a goddamn thing." Caleb touched his mouth, leaving blood on his fingers. He wiped them on the bedcover. "There's not a thing about you that surprises me anymore. Once I really understood that, I wasn't scared of you anymore, either. It made picking up that gun a lot easier. I had to do it, no choice. *You* are my business to handle, always have been. It was in my blood all along." He held up a stained hand. "I am my father's son."

"What the hell are you talking about?"

"You killed my mother, you fucking monster, and Rudy Reynosa. Tried to kill Chris Cherry, and God only knows what else you've done. No one in this town knows what you're capable of, but I do. I've known all along. I believe it all."

"Your whore of a mother ran off." The Judge ignored the rest of it.

"Don't you talk about her like that, don't you dare say that. You don't get to do that anymore."

He lowered the gun, his old Ruger that he hadn't shot in years. He couldn't imagine why Caleb had chosen that one, when there were a dozen others that would have done the job better. And he was tired, as tired as he'd ever been. "You were going to kill me over her? She left us . . . left us both."

"She wouldn't have done that. She never would have left me with you."

"Are you so sure? Do you really believe that? I don't think so. You didn't know your mother half as well as you want to pretend." Doubt flickered in Caleb's eyes. "Ah, but you suspect, don't you? You've suspected all along. I can see that you do. What sort of mother leaves her son behind? *But what sort of son were you, that she was willing to do it?*"

Caleb pushed his hands against the side of his head. "Is there anything that comes out of your mouth that isn't a fucking lie? Do you even know what the truth is anymore?"

"You just haven't been listening, Caleb. I've been telling you the truth your whole goddamn life. Hard words . . . *hard truth.*"

Caleb laughed, crazy. "So this was all somehow for my benefit, your way of making me a man? Jesus Christ."

He nodded at the boy, took the Ruger, put it up on the dresser—still within his reach but out of Caleb's—and raised his hands. "Man enough. You tried to handle business just now, and I'm proud of you for that."

Caleb kept his eyes on the gun, breathing hard. "Do you fucking hear yourself? You're crazy . . . fucking crazy."

"I'm your father," the Judge said, smiling. "As much as neither of us might want it, you are my blood. You see that now, you said it yourself. I love you the only way I know how. I know you, and you know me.

"Like father, like son." They stood that way for what seemed like forever, watching each other, listening to each other breathe.

He knew Caleb could still make a move for the Ruger. It was even money as to whether he would try. He had Evelyn's eyes, the way she'd always stared at him—that same intensity, all the same questions. Full of mysteries, deep as the ocean. There were no answers there, ever.

Caleb broke the silence. "I know what's up in the attic. I found what you've been hiding there. All that damn money . . . I guess that was the price of your family, this whole town."

Now, *that* did surprise him. He didn't have anything to say but didn't have the chance to anyway, because right then someone started hammering on the front door. It echoed throughout the otherwise still, silent house. The aftermath of the gunshot.

"Expecting visitors?" He glanced at the windows, the stairway walls, waiting for the smear of reflected blue-and-red lights. It wouldn't be his own deputies coming for him, but he wondered if Caleb or Chris Cherry had already talked to the feds or the Texas Rangers. But Caleb looked twice as surprised. He glanced down the hall, as if he might see a ghost walking toward him.

The Judge reached out and hefted the gun, pointed it at his son, making him lead the way.

"Clean your face and get the goddamn door, Caleb. Let's see who we have for company."

21
ANNE

She wasn't sure what she'd see, still in mid-knock, when Caleb opened the door. He was pale in the porch light, unmoored, translucent, and there was red at his mouth and a cut on his cheek, another smaller one on his forehead, both weeping blood. If it had been warmer, there would have been bugs fluttering against the light, battering against them with soft wings as they stood there, urging them on. But it was too cold for that, so it was just the two of them, their breath in streamers, the only thing moving in the chill.

"Oh my god," she said, almost reaching up to touch his face.

"Why are you here?" Caleb said, hoarse.

"Please get your things, Caleb, you're leaving, now. Chris sent me. You haven't been answering his texts or calls, or mine . . ." She trailed off as Sheriff Ross appeared behind his son.

"Anne, do you want to explain why you're telling my son to leave with you?" The sheriff put a heavy hand on Caleb's shoulder, his fingers pressing down. He tried to stare her down, make her go away.

She held her ground. "Chris Cherry wants you to come down to your office. He's waiting for you there."

Chris had called, begging for her help. It was more than he had any right to ask, he knew that, but he had no one else. He explained most of what had happened with Caleb in El Paso—what he'd read in Caleb's journal and the money he'd found there.

He'd already left the hospital with his girlfriend Melissa, driving back to Murfee, but was afraid he would be too late—kept saying it, over and over again, *too late, too late*—and she could tell that he wasn't doing all that well himself. He laughed that he was bleeding on everything, making a goddamn mess, just to make her smile over the phone, but told her none of that mattered. He'd whispered every word, each one an immense weight. Too hard, like Marc, the night he'd died.

He needed to get Caleb away from the sheriff, but Caleb wasn't answering his goddamn phone and there was no one else he could trust, no one in all of Murfee. She was the one who had to make sure Caleb was okay, stop him before he did something stupid, something fatal. Chris knew she'd helped him earlier tonight by lending him her car and now she needed to help him again. If she could do that, Chris promised to take care of the rest. She asked him what would make either of them—Caleb or the sheriff— listen to her? Then he told her what she had to say.

"Chris wants you to come tell him face-to-face why you tried to kill him and Duane Dupree."

The sheriff blinked. "That's what he said? Those exact words, to you, about me?"

"Yes."

"And you believe him?"

"Does it matter? Caleb is coming with me now, and you can go deal with whatever you need to."

"You're going to talk to me like this, on my own porch, my house? Anne, I thought you were smarter than this. This is ridiculous. Chris is . . . well, Chris is still suffering a lot of trauma."

Anne's heart hammered. Caleb looked at her, pleading silently with her to go away, but everything had come down to this moment. There was nowhere else for her to go, not alone. Not without Caleb. "Chris said if you don't come right now, he's going to the federal authorities. He hasn't yet, but he will."

"With what? About what?"

"I don't know, don't care. But he said you would." She repeated it just like he told her. "He said you needed to remember your talk at El Dorado. How you said secrets lead to trouble and to good people getting hurt."

She thought the sheriff might reach out and strike her, grab her hair and pull her into the house and swallow her up along with Caleb. In the dim light, for one horrible moment, he looked so old—ancient, mortal, collapsing right before her eyes.

"And if I say no to all of this?"

She looked at him, then to Caleb. They were all standing too close in the small circle of the porch light.

"Please don't," she answered, adding her own words, not Chris's: "Either way, you're not going to hurt anyone anymore, so I don't think you have a better choice."

*   *   *

The sheriff drove away while she waited in the front hallway for Caleb to grab a few things. She looked around for
signs of disturbance, something to show there had been
a struggle, but from there, everything was in place. Only
the smell of smoke in the air.

Still, if half of what Chris had revealed about Caleb's
journal was true, there'd been constant struggle in this
house—a battle of wills between a father and a son. Chris
was convinced it was coming to a head tonight, and
maybe it had. She had no idea what she interrupted when
she came to the door. The only hint was Caleb's pale face,
the cuts and the blood. When she asked him about that,
he had nothing to say. They didn't talk anymore, even
when they came out of the house and both saw a truck
sitting in the shadows up the street, idling. At first she
was afraid it was the sheriff, returned and waiting for
them, but that wasn't it. Caleb saw it, recognized it, and
didn't say anything at all. He left the front door open,
though—wide open—as if expecting someone.

22

CHRIS

He sat at the sheriff's desk, surrounded by all his relics of people and places that no longer existed. Of a time that no longer existed.

He had a gun on the desk in front of him, next to a few of the dollar bills that had fallen out of Caleb's notebook. The rest were tucked safe inside the envelope with Morgan Emerson's picture, waiting for Garrison back in El Paso.

He didn't have the key for the office, but Miss Maisie kept spares and a master in her cube downstairs. Mel had helped him break into her file cabinet to get it. He'd unlocked the office, leaving the door wide open behind him, waiting for the sheriff to walk through it.

Chris prayed he didn't bleed out before that happened.

*   *   *

Sheriff Ross was wearing his duster and his black Serratelli, as if he'd stepped right out of one of his old pictures on the wall. He laughed when he saw Chris sitting at his desk, a sound without light or heat, and pointed a gloved finger at Chris, as if to confirm he was there. *Marking him.* And Chris caught a faint smell of whiskey.

He leaned against the doorjamb and crossed his arms, ignoring the money and the gun on the desk. "Well, I guess you decided you're ready for that chair after all." Adding, "You don't look well, Chris. Not at all. You shouldn't be out of the hospital." He glanced down. "You're bleeding all over my goddamn desk."

"This is over tonight, Sheriff."

The sheriff examined the wooden doorframe. "What exactly would that be?"

"Everything. I know about those agents being here in Murfee. I know *why* they were here. I know about Rudy Reynosa and I've read a journal that Caleb's kept for years." He pointed at the money with his bandaged hand. "I know about the money . . . all of it."

The sheriff nodded. "I see . . . a journal." He pushed away from the frame, took a step into the room, his boots loud on the wood. "Do you think anyone is going to care, much less believe, what Caleb wrote? He's a boy." Another step. "And we already know that no one gives a damn about Rudy Ray and never did." Another. "And if you know anything about those agents, well, then you know a helluva lot more than me. So where does that leave us?"

Two more steps, moving just like Duane Dupree had at Mancha's. Then a final one that left him looming over the desk, huge. "With some money you say you've found? You're going to make something out of that? You haven't thought this through, Chris. Not long enough, not hard enough."

Chris picked up the big gun with his unbandaged left hand and aimed it unsteadily at the sheriff, roughly at his heart. He recognized it the second Chris touched it, and the way it gleamed in the light. The Model 1847 Colt Whitneyville-Walker, once owned by Texas Ranger Sam Wilson; for a while the most powerful handgun in the world. The one that had made Sam Colt himself say it'd take a Texan to shoot it. Chris's service weapon had been taken by the state lab for his part in the Far Six shootout, so he'd pulled this one from the sheriff's collection.

"I've thought it through plenty, all the way on the drive back from the hospital you fucking put me in."

23

MELISSA

S he sat out in the car, watching shadows move through the bottle-green glass of the windows upstairs—Chris and the sheriff. She'd thought this entire idea was crazy, told Chris as much, but when he was unable to reach Caleb Ross, he'd become convinced it was the only way. They fought with the hospital to release him, before the on-call staff finally threw their hands up in defeat.

On the long drive back she'd offered to go to the sheriff's house, begged him, but he told her the teacher would do that. She listened when he made the call near Presidio, where they had cell service; heard the familiar way he talked to her, but also heard everything that *wasn't* there. Afterward, when he leaned his head against the window and grabbed her hand—held it tight as he could—that had been enough. It would have to be. Instead, he'd needed Mel's help to get him upstairs to the sheriff's office. He leaned on her the whole way up, unable to stand, and she knew he wouldn't be able to get out from behind that desk without help. He was trapped in there alone, but wouldn't let her stay.

He kissed her when she had propped him up—no better expression for it—like a store mannequin, plastic and bloodless. He told her which gun to get out of which case and how to check if it was loaded. He had her wipe off her fingerprints, like any of that would matter if he had to use it. Then he'd smiled from somewhere behind bloodshot eyes and told her to get the hell out of there.

When she came back to the car there was blood on the seat from his wounds. The car was filled with copper, *with Chris*, but she kept the windows rolled up anyway, even if that meant staying trapped with that awful smell of him bleeding. *Dying*. Then she'd searched around in her purse for that folded napkin Duane Dupree had given her, and dialed the number.

Now she kept watch on the window, guessing at shadows . . . phantoms. Guessing at what they said, what might happen next—one of them near dying and the other already dead, because no matter what, the sheriff wasn't escaping tonight. She'd talked to Dupree . . . and also because, if it came to it, there was a second gun, another she'd taken from the sheriff's collection, sitting heavy in her lap, cool to her touch. Chris never saw her slipping it away.

24

CHRIS

You're done here, done with Caleb. Use tonight to get whatever you want, and then get the hell out of town."

"That's it? You're riding me out of Murfee? Out of my town? *My home?*" The sheriff didn't take his eyes off the Colt 1847. They were gunmetal gray, flat and unreflective and unresponsive. But his voice thundered. "Son, I made this town. *I am this town.*"

Chris nodded toward the pictures on the wall. "It was here before both of us, it'll survive long after we're both gone. You can wait here with me until the feds show up, or you can start walking. I'm giving you a chance you never gave me, for your son's sake. So he doesn't have to live with your fucking shame. Do you really want to stay here, answer all the questions? Read about yourself in the paper? Have to look the people of this town in the eye? That's the deal. There is no other."

"Or what?"

"Or . . ." Chris shrugged. "Or I guess I'll have to shoot you right where you fucking stand."

The sheriff shook his head, like he was shaking away other voices. "You won't shoot me, Chris, it's not in you. *It's not you.*"

Chris tried to hold the heavy gun higher, knew it was shaking because it was in his weak hand. All of him was weak. "Tell that to the three men I left dead out at the Far Six."

The sheriff paused. "Shooting a man in the dark where you can't see his face is one thing. Putting a bullet right here"—the sheriff pointed first at his chest, then his head—"or *here*, like this, where you can see his face and feel his breath and see the blood? That's a whole different kind of thing."

"Maybe, I guess you'd know. But know this too, you kill me now and everything is out for everyone to see. It's done, all done. Just walk away, keep walking."

The sheriff spoke low. "Do you really think you have enough friends to help you, to save you . . . to see this through? Melissa, Caleb? That goddamn whoring school-teacher? That's not much of a posse, Chris."

Chris used everything he had left to hold the gun firm. He zeroed in on a point between the sheriff's eyes, right behind them. "Don't make me, but I will. I promise." The gun didn't waver. "You can't kill us all, Sheriff. Not everyone. And I only have to fucking kill you."

The sheriff nodded slow, once, twice, and backed toward the door. A hand hovered near his Colt.

"So now we draw, see who's faster?"

"My gun's already out, Sheriff. Seems like I've already won."

Chris cocked the hammer.

The sheriff raised both hands. "Okay, *Deputy* Cherry. Okay."

Chris pointed the gun barrel at the money. "Some of what's happened I can understand. I can almost wrap my head around." He shook his head. "But we both know you didn't want me dead over Rudy Ray, least of all that. That never even mattered. Or even because of what I knew about those feds. In the end, it was because of *Anne*, right? That was it all along. Between you and me, it always was.

"You wanted her."

The sheriff didn't answer, just raised his chin, defiant. It was the one thing Chris had never told Garrison—the one thing that made the most sense, and still somehow didn't make any sense at all.

"And why did you kill Evelyn? For God's sake, why did you kill your wife?" But he was asking emptiness, because by then the sheriff was gone.

25

THE JUDGE

He saw her sitting in the car, waiting for him. He could have put his hands on her then, hurt her, put the muzzle of his gun against her head, and told her to beg him to stop. He could have circled it around her eye, up and down her cheek, across her mouth, like a god-damn kiss.

Chris would have heard the shot from the office but wouldn't have been able to do a damn thing about it, no more able to stop it than catching smoke. He would have been left stumbling and falling down the stairs, into the street, looking for her, afraid of what he'd find but knowing what it would be all the same, leaving his blood behind with every step. Always carrying the burden of what had been done to her. It wasn't that the Judge *couldn't* do such a thing—that even in his situation, as bad as it was, he wouldn't contemplate making the time and then finding some small pleasure in it.

But what stopped him was the way Melissa Bristow stared back without blinking. Working out his thoughts, not afraid of them, as something rose in her eyes like the moon over the Chisos. Not fear or worry. *Just anger.* She raised another of his own goddamn guns, held it high. Shooting through the windshield might hurt her as much as him, might send the bullet wide or leave her blind. That was a chance she was willing to take. Up in his office he wasn't sure Chris could pull the trigger, but he had no doubt this goddamn woman would. No matter the damage, no matter the cost. No doubt at all.

He drove away, down Main, past the Hamilton with the broken N, like a fist had been put through it, and the Dollar General and Modelle Greer's and Bartel's Gas. Past the Sonic drive-in and the Radio Shack and the sign for Donnie Ray Royal, Attorney at Law, and the small U.S. post office. He sat for a bit beneath the sodium yellow lights of the Hi n Lo and then took the long curve of Appian Way past Big Bend Central and Archer-Ross Stadium. He turned circles in the stadium's lot, round and round, as the stars above wheeled in the opposite direction.

He cruised out to Beantown, to Mancha's, which was strangely quiet and dark, and all the small homes nearby, clustered together and painted in garish colors. He made them brighter, driving up and down the dusty alleys with his lights flashing—a blue-and-red electrical storm that brought no one to their windows. No one even looked out, no one cared. He might have been all alone in the world.

He took 67 and drove out toward the Lights as fast as the truck would go—all the windows down and the inside of the car like a captured tornado. The truck rattled and shook, and when he got to the little pavilion for the Lights he drove right on through the gravel out onto the caliche itself, bouncing over rocks and ruts, crushing ocotillo and anything else that wouldn't get out of his path. The only lights were his own high beams, and had there been other wraiths waiting for him, he would have chased those as far as they could take him. Instead, he turned his head lamps off and screamed at the top of his old lungs and plowed through the darkness trying to find the end of the world, to drive off it, but there was no end. The Big Bend, the Far Empty, just went on forever and ever and ever.

Dirt and rocks sprayed against his windshield like gunfire and he fought the wheel and himself and when the ground did not finally raise up to swallow him whole and drop him down a black throat, he knew he was done. He ground the truck to a halt and listened to the engine tick, as all the echoes he'd thrown slowly worked their way back to him over the desert. Even his own, still screaming.

Then he turned around and drove for home.

26

DUANE

He realized, as he searched for a Dr Pepper in the kitchen and then wandered through the rooms, that he'd never actually been in the Judge's house. Through the years, he'd been summoned up to the porch, stood in the driveway. He'd been out back in the yard and may have made it as far as the garage, but never, ever inside its walls. The Judge liked his privacy and his safety. He often talked about a home being a *sanctuary*, and had a three-thousand-dollar alarm system to prove it. So it had been all the more strange when Duane walked up and found the door already standing open for him, waiting. *Don't mind if I do!* He thought he saw his daddy there, holding it ajar for him, and thanked him for his help.

He wandered a bit, eventually went upstairs and

searched Caleb's room and found kid stuff. Then he went into the Judge's room and tossed a few things around. He sidestepped the shattered mirror and found the Ruger rifle behind the door; thought the grip still felt warm where it had recently been held, checked to make sure it was loaded. He carried it with him as he moved along.

It had been while he was out at the Comanche, watching his little Mex girl and waiting for her to work up the nerve to finally try and kill him, that Melissa's call had come through. She'd been angry, near screaming—told him everything he already knew about the Judge, how Duane was supposed to have died right along with Chris at the Far Six. She told him Caleb had come to see Chris, and now Chris, who was still hurt—more than bad—was coming back to town to end it, once and for all. Murfee wasn't big enough for all of them anymore. The world wasn't big enough.

Then she'd offered Duane anything—everything—if he promised to make sure the Judge never hurt anyone else ever again. *You kill that son of a bitch, Duane Dupree, you kill him . . .*

There was a woman lying in the bathtub, and he had to admit, it startled the hell out of him. He walked into the Judge's dark bathroom and she was there, reclining in the big old dry tub, her pale skin holding its own light, like moonbeams on glass. Her eyes were closed and her dark hair was a tumble that was her only pillow. Her long, thin hands were at her side, one of them lying across a belly that he knew would be as soft and warm to the touch as anything. He followed the gentle path of her body down to her legs, to the darkness between them, and felt himself get hard in a way he hadn't in weeks.

He recognized her even though he'd never seen her quite this way. It was Nellie Banner, who'd been dead for

more years than he could quite remember. She was another ghost and her eyes were open and they were wolf's
eyes just like his, glowing and hot and angry, and her lips
moved as she whispered, *Come closer, oh, please come closer.*
She had so many things to tell him, and he was welcome
to look at her while she did so. *You kill that son of a bitch,
Duane Dupree, you kill him . . .*

She wasn't reflected in the bathroom mirror, but for
that matter, he wasn't, either. He was a ghost, already
gone, a dead man. He knew none of it was real, just the
foco turning the last of his sanity to dust, but he didn't
care. So he went and knelt next to Nellie, smelled water
that wasn't there and put his ear close to her dead mouth,
and listened to all of her secrets.

He'd taken so much *foco* he thought his heart would
explode. He could feel each individual beat, each one
labored, popping a bloody sweat right off his skin. He'd
already thought about taking his old buck knife, his daddy's Model 110, and cutting his skin off. He didn't need
the skin now—it was too tight and too hot and it squeezed
him something terrible—so earlier he *had* cut himself a
little before heading out to the Comanche, just to test the
thought: a slice across his arms, across his belly, and even
with a fair amount of his very real blood, he'd known it
was the right thing to do. It wasn't the blood or the pain
that finally stopped him. In fact he didn't really feel any
of the hurt, and the knife edge proved no different from
picking at his skin with his own nails. Later, if he survived
any of this, he was going to start in earnest at his face and
work down, shedding it all. Revealing once and for all the
wolf underneath. He'd stopped only because he had a few
other things to attend to first—things that definitely
needed human hands.

He was curled in the Judge's bed, naked and bloody,

when the door opened downstairs, the one he'd closed and locked behind him. He was grinning when he popped up and went to the hall, the Ruger out in front of him, his shotgun slung over his back. He'd left the lights off, just like he found them, but it didn't matter because it seemed to him that everything glowed green, clean and clear and visible. He came to the top of the stairs and saw the crown of the Judge's head passing below him, moving toward the kitchen. The fridge opened, and light bloomed bright. He had to blink back tears, it was so hard to see through. When his vision cleared, he came down the stairs slow, cautious, and backed into the family room, gun pointed at the open arch where he knew the Judge would appear.

The Judge nearly walked into the open mouth of his gun. In the gloom his eyes went wide, caught their own startled light. He had a Lone Star in his hand, and he let it slip from his fingers. It hit the ground between them, rolled in a tight circle, bleeding beer in its wake. His hand moved toward the gun at his hip, his Colt XSE—a gun that had been given to him as a present by the Sheriffs Association of Texas—but Duane shook the Ruger at him to let him know he was serious. Dead serious.

"Just slip the hand back, Judge. Sorry you had to waste a cold one. Guess I got the drop on you."

The Judge gaped at him, unbelieving. "Dupree, get some fucking clothes on and get that fucking gun out of my face. You hear me? Or I will whip the dog shit out of you." The Judge looked closer. "Fuck, are you bleeding?" His voice had a tightness that Duane had never heard. If he didn't know better, it sounded like goddamn fear.

The Judge finally raised a hand, just one, not his gun hand, though. "Look, don't make this worse, right? I saw

Cherry just now. He's out for both of us. That's our problem."

"Naw, he's really out for just you, Judge, *just you*. You can't slip out of that noose. Now comes the *reckoning*."

"Goddammit, Duane, you're not the first person to point a gun at me today, but by God, you will be the last."

Duane laughed. "You might take that as a hint, Judge."

The Judge spoke slowly, carefully. "If you don't stop now, you're not walking out of here. I can't allow it. You know that."

"Oh, I know it. Don't care. Not really atall." Duane loosened his shoulders, relaxed and breathed and took better aim at the Judge's face. As jittery and wired as he'd been for months, he was suddenly calm, cool, like he'd been standing still for hours in the cold desert night. And then Chava was standing in the hallway behind the Judge, his gold tooth grinning in the dark—a skull. Chava waved at him, urging him on, empty eye sockets and face curtained with blood. Duane waved back. Next to Chava was Rudy Ray, screaming silently.

"You eat your own, Judge, that's what you do. You eat your own." Chava was gone now, replaced by the girl he'd set on fire. She glowed and smoldered in the dark, ash drifting from the hand she pointed at him. She smeared the air, like a dirty fingerprint on glass. "Everything I ever did was on your word. 'Cause of you."

"Now *that* is horseshit, Duane."

"I see their faces and they have holes where their eyes should be. All the things you did, and it's *me* they're comin' for . . . I'm haunted, Judge, so haunted. And they've been waiting for this for a long time." The air between them was charged, moving on its own, as if they had an audience. "I even talked to Nellie upstairs in the tub. Goddamn, she was a beautiful woman. They're here right now. They're holding breath they don't even have and they're waiting to clap their dead hands after I blow your head off."

"It's okay, son. I understand. I really do."

Duane sighted down the rifle at the Judge's empty, open mouth. "There's no way you can."

"No, Duane, no, goddammit." The Judge pointed at him. "You're sick, dying . . . a goddamn dead man."

Duane saw all the rest of the dead staring at him, and spit blood at the Judge's boot.

"We all are."

The Judge went for the Colt.

The room lit up with muzzle flashes, everything so loud. Duane fired round after round, standing stock-still, bracing himself with his legs, leaning into the rifle's kick. It was smooth as oil, greased like lightning, the finest gun he'd ever shot. Someone had taken real good care of it, for just this moment. A window blew out and stuffing from the couch floated in the air. He thought he might be hit, but couldn't quite feel it and couldn't have cared less. It was possible the Judge's head came off in a powerful spray, so hard and fast that it hit the ceiling. There was a lot of blood, he knew that—so much blood, like Eddie Corazon's—and all of it everywhere and on everything. A real goddamn reckoning right here in the living room.

He knew it was all over when he heard the ghosts clapping.

27

MÁXIMO

It was cold outside, and he hugged his arms against his body to keep warm.

She'd dropped him at Pilar's, still crying, and wouldn't talk. But he'd gone out right after she left, begging Pilar to show him how to start and stop her little car, giving her a kiss with lots of tongue for her efforts and leaving her smiling. He'd paid close attention when America first brought him out here, and it wasn't hard to find again. Everything here was straight lines, one direction. The roads had been his alone, and although he had trouble bringing the car to a nice stop, he did well enough to leave it crooked in the dark against a fence line, off the road. The only crooked thing in forever, all the fences like chewed toothpicks, thin and broken, marching off into the distance. He walked the rest of the way, cutting across pasture and broken land and pecan groves, guided by moonlight to the little house out here all alone. He curled up at the corner of the porch, and waited. *Ten paciencia.* He was still there when truck headlights came down the gravel drive.

He smelled blood, a smell he knew all too well. The man reeked of it as he stumbled free of the truck, tried to walk toward his front door, and Máximo knew in a way he couldn't say that not all the blood on the man was his own, but enough of it was. Enough that if Máximo melted back into the darkness, this man might fall down and die on his own. But he might not. And all Máximo had to do was remember America screaming and throwing her phone after him, her tears and the darkness of her eyes, to push him forward. He remembered what his *abuela* once said, while he sat with a face like a rock after his papa had gone away—

Llora, niño, porque los que no tienen lágrimas tienen un dolor que no se acaba nunca.

Cry, for those without tears have a grief that never ends.

He hadn't cried, not then, not later. He'd since learned there were so many other ways to deal with grief. He rose out of the darkness by the porch, came straight at the man, who rocked on his feet and spotted him, neither surprised nor afraid nor anything at all.

The man might have said, "Daddy?"

He didn't even bother with Rodolfo's old gun. Máximo brought a knife to the man's throat. It was bloody work, so much blood, to take the man's head. And the knife wasn't a good one, just something he'd taken from Pilar's *cocina*. Not that he needed the head—not that America would want to see it or that he could take it back

across the river to show what he had done. He did it so
that *after*, when he went to her and said something funny
and made her laugh and wrapped his tired arms around
her, she would feel them still quivering from all his effort,
and she would *know* that it was done. He knew, in the
same way he knew that all the blood was not the man's
own, that the other gringo he'd come for—the real *jefe*—
was already dead as well. The killing was done.

He set the head aside and pissed on the body, and then
kicked in a window of the house and searched around.
He was supposed to look for the *dinero*, but there was
very little, not enough, and those across the river did not
want it anyway—it was tainted, *venenoso*. They would not
dirty their hands with it—planning to burn it as a
sacrifice—because it was never about the money for them,
until it was. Just ask Chava. No, the *ayudante*'s ruined
body was the *mensaje*, all because they'd felt disrespected,
cheated, and because of whatever visions floated in that
oily mixture of blood and water swirling in their big
bowls. Whatever their reasons, they were not his reasons
now. He did this thing for her.

He kept looking until he found enough matches and
oil and dirty clothes, piling them throughout the living
room and out onto the porch, dumping an armload of
newspaper over the body. He sat the head on top of that
and filled its mouth with the small amount of money he'd
found, and lit that on fire. Flames moved inside the skull,
behind the eyes, glowing, as Máximo set the rest of the
house on fire.

When he jumped off the porch, he thought he spied a
creature slinking off into the darkness with him, something that had been watching him all along—a *lobo*. The
only ones he'd ever seen before were caged at the
rancho—dirty, desperate things, and he had always

wanted to see one free, running wild. He would tell America about it, and they could guess together at what it might mean.

He didn't look back, not once, didn't think any more about the man or the house or the blood or the fire. He kept walking until the burning house was well behind him; then he broke into a run, pretending that he was a *lobo*, wild and free, forever. The flames at his back rose higher and higher and higher until they washed away the whole sky.

✴ GHOSTS ✴

1

ANNE

They saw each other every once in a while in passing, as they had before, but different. They couldn't really talk, not then, but he smiled at her and she smiled back, if they thought no one was looking. It had finally started to warm up, the wan earth gaining color, coming back to life.

Like so many things.

It was a week before school was due to let out when they ran into each other outside the Hi n Lo. Chris looked so different, thinner but healthier, even with the cane he needed to walk. But she looked different too, letting her hair go back to its normal shade, wearing her contacts again. She was afraid he might just say a quick hello and keep going, but he didn't. He asked her to stay awhile, and she did.

They talked about all that happened *after*—all the noise that had surrounded Murfee, as if the Fall Carnival had returned and spilled out over the wide streets. There had been so much shock and sadness at Sheriff Ross's death at the hands of Duane Dupree, and then Dupree's own fiery demise. Everyone knew the story, or as in any small town, *thought they did*—a popular sheriff betrayed by his chief deputy, his best friend, who'd been corrupted and paid for it all with his life. They both agreed it made a good story—a damn good one. And when all the investigations and media inquiries failed to turn up anything different, and then after those had all gone away too, the story was all anyone had left.

Sheriff Ross was buried a hero, a true lawman of the West. Over two thousand people showed up at his funeral.

She asked how he liked being sheriff now, and he said it wasn't permanent, not yet. He'd cleaned out the department, fired nearly everyone except Miss Maisie, and although the town council had handed him the badge, there was still an open election set for later in the spring. So far no one had come forward to oppose him, but he'd have to wait and see. He guessed everyone liked a hero.

Truth be told, he wasn't sure Murfee was ready for a sheriff with a bad leg and a damaged shooting hand and a weak heart, but she laughed and said that was exactly the sort of sheriff they needed, now more than ever.

She said that Caleb had been doing all right, all things considered. He'd missed a ton of school the past semester, but was going to enroll in a prep school in Virginia for the summer to finish up his credits and try to get started on college the following spring, maybe at Brafferton, or even Mary Washington, the same brick-and-ivy place where she'd done her undergraduate work. Her father had not so subtly mentioned it to Caleb a couple of times, having taken a real interest in the boy's well-being.

Caleb talked about writing. He thought that's what he wanted to do. Be a writer. He'd turned eighteen two weeks after his father was buried, so he really was free to do anything he wanted. For now, Caleb was going to stay with her and her family in Virginia until he sorted it out.

Everyone thought it best he get out of Texas for a while, maybe forever.

"What about you, what are you going to do?" Chris asked, squinting at the sunlight, at her.

"I don't know. I'll go back with him, of course, get him settled. My parents are thrilled about that. After that, we'll see."

"No chance of staying here? The school could use you."

She laughed. "I've heard that line before. No, no chance." She measured his thin face, the way he leaned against his cane. The gun at his hip, now on the left side in reach of his good hand, helped pull him back to center, kept him balanced. He looked more like a cowboy than ever, even more than that first night they met, beneath carnival lights. "What about you? Are you ready for all of this? Is this what you want?" She waved at Murfee, at everything around them.

"I don't know, either, to be honest. But for now it's what I have to do. After that, we'll see." He twisted his cane in his hand, the one he kept gloved. "What about Amé Reynosa?"

Anne shook her head. "I was going to ask you the same thing."

He joined her. "Nothing, gone." He looked down the

road. "I met her, talked to her just before everything went bad at the Far Six. She told me to be careful. Guess I should have listened." He smiled. "She seemed tough, tougher than all of us. A real survivor. I've talked to her father and mother a few times, and all they'll say is she went back to Mexico, to stay with family there."

"Do you believe that?" she asked.

"Do you?"

She let it go, not willing to ask if he thought Amé had anything to do with what happened to Duane Dupree. Not wanting to know. "I've asked Caleb once or twice about the money, the money he found hidden in his mother's things in his attic. He still won't say what happened to it."

"It doesn't matter, I guess. I'm not looking for it. Garrison isn't, either. It might as well not exist, if it ever did."

Anne let a car pass them and then drive on before she got to the question she'd had all along. "Do you think the sheriff really killed Evelyn?"

Chris frowned. "I still don't know." He poked at the gravel, digging with his cane, like he might uncover an answer there. "So many things I still don't know. Don't understand . . . and guess I probably never will."

And they left it at that.

He walked her to her car, tried to be a gentleman and hold the door for her, but it was too much. She reached in for the present she'd made for him—had been driving around with it for weeks like he'd once driven around with a book for her. She got them off eBay, had them framed: a pair of vintage carnival tickets, sepia-colored; a Wild West show, from long ago.

She took his hand, held it gently, didn't care who was

looking. He squeezed back with all that he had and that almost brought her to tears. In that moment, in their fingers, passed all the choices and chances and roads they would never have and could never take. It was done.

"Take care of yourself, Sheriff Cherry. *Please.*"

"And you do the same. Do the same."

She shut the door—too fast, far too fast, so he couldn't see her cry. Still, goddammit, it seemed to take forever.

2

AMERICA AND MÁXIMO

He wouldn't take her back with him to Mexico. Told her it was not for her. It wasn't safe, never would be. She told him it wasn't safe for him anymore either, so they'd go to Houston instead, like Rodolfo had always promised. He asked how they could do that when they had nothing.

She'd gone out to the place Caleb had told her about, that he'd reminded her of with the few words he'd printed on her magazine cutout, the last time she saw him. Out beneath a desert willow at Coates Creek she found the place where he had buried his notebooks, his poems and stories. She found a stack of them, glanced through them once, but as much as he may have wanted her to have them, she left them behind.

She did take the suitcase he'd left for her. Heavy . . .

filled with what seemed to her to be all the money in the world. They paid Pilar for her car, drove it to Midland and sold it in a bar, buying a Charger from a used-car lot with cash, a lot like the one Rodolfo had owned. Different color, nicer, but close enough. They slept during the day and drove at night, by the light of oil-rig fires across the flats.

She told Máximo how Rodolfo had called her his *estrella*, and he told her that was perfect, *perfecto*, and he put his arm around her as she drove and he told her all his stories and jokes. He even sang her songs, making them up on the spot.

They stayed outside Houston for a few days in a nice, not great motel. But parts of the city reminded her too much of Murfee, and parts of it reminded Máximo too much of Ojinaga, and they both laughed at that. He wondered where she wanted to go next, and she said she had an idea. She showed him the magazine picture of the skyline and the beach. He stared at Caleb's words, but didn't say anything about them.

She stood outside in the parking lot, searching for stars. In the city, you couldn't find them at all. In Murfee, they'd been everywhere, every night. You couldn't escape them if you'd wanted to. She missed them.

She'd left Máximo asleep in their room, to stand out here and breathe for a moment alone and find them. He'd drunk too many beers and had passed out whispering to people who weren't there, people who haunted him. They hadn't talked about his showing up to her smelling of oil and smoke, his face smudged with ash, embers dying in his hair; blood on his hands. How he'd been smiling. Now, standing in the dark, she held tight her picture of the beach, the one Caleb had left for her and she'd showed Máximo. She ran her finger over Caleb's handwriting there, tracing it. It was hard to know if that picture was really hers anymore, or his; just another city where she wouldn't be able to see the stars.

On the road she'd dreamed over and over again of that little girl she'd seen with Máximo, the one running in the dead grass, leaving her brothers far behind. Running so far, so fast, but never getting anywhere safe. Not alone. *Our town*—that's what Deputy Cherry had said before he'd almost died to make that real for her. The dreams of the running girl had replaced all the ones of Rodolfo. She'd been his *estrella*, always would be, but she thought he'd understand.

Still, she couldn't go back now, not yet. After all, she still wanted to see the beach, the ocean, at least once. She owed herself that, at least. But after that, who could say? She'd follow the stars, see where they led her, and that made her smile, bouncing the car keys in her hand.

And she glowed.

Y ella resplandeció . . .

When he awoke, she was gone.

He ran to the motel window, naked, and the car was gone, too. On the little table next to the bed was a newspaper, and inside it was a thick stack of money. Not all of it, but plenty. And on top of that was the gun. Silver and pearl—etched with the Virgen de Guadalupe and Pancho Villa and Jesús Malverde.

All of its *calaveras* grinning goodbye at him.

3

MORGAN

A nd she opened her eyes . . .

4
CALEB

I'm starting this new journal on the plane, high above Texas. Murfee is somewhere below me. Before too long, it will all be behind me. But can I ever truly leave it behind? That place? All that happened to me? I don't know. I think it will always be a part of me, forever. Maybe it's supposed to be. It's in my blood.

Anne has said I'll love Virginia. She talks about the *green*, all the green, like it's an actual place or a living thing, and in a way, I guess it is. I do look forward to seeing that—trees and green grass and water. She won't admit it, but she's even more excited than I am.

In the airport I thought I saw Amé—a brief reflection in glass, her face turned away, laughing. I walked toward her, got ready to call her name, but when she turned toward me, I realized it wasn't her at all.

Just someone who looked a lot like her.

This is the thing I understand . . . that I've come to accept. I will forever be searching for Amé's face—my mother's face—in every place, in every crowd. I'll always wonder . . . I'll always picture them out there, in some distant somewhere, a place as real as Anne's *green*.

They're *my* Murfee Lights, and I'll forever wait for them—ghosts. I'll just never know if they're only haunting me. Or I them.

END

SHERIFF CHERRY

He drove out to Indian Bluffs, parked as near as he could remember to the same place he'd parked before . . . when he first walked out to the body of Rudy Reynosa.

There were flowers now, blooming after last night's rain, and they ran into the distance, every color in the world, and more he couldn't name. They ran all the way to the mountains and beyond. The sky was pearl, bright, like it had been shined hard with a cloth. It dazzled and hurt his eyes, and it took his breath away. He'd grown up here, always thought it was so goddamn small.

Now he realized it was infinite.

He'd been more or less truthful when he told Anne he didn't know whether Sheriff Ross had killed his wife. He had ideas, ones that crept into his mind late at night, whenever he thought about that wild place the sheriff called El Dorado. You could get lost there—no one would ever find you. But he also knew now you didn't even have to go that far.

Behind him was the shotgun Mel had bought as a present, a Browning A5 Ultimate. Still affectionately called the Humpback, it was the modern version of the world's first semiautomatic shotgun—a shotgun once carried by Clyde Barrow. She had the barrel cut down so it'd be lighter for him, easier to wield; it had a beautiful walnut stock and the receiver was etched in black and gold leaf. On one side was a desert sun coming up over mountains that looked vaguely like the Chisos. On the other, intricate scrollwork surrounded three words that would mean nothing to anyone other than him and Mel:

Let 'Er Rip.

He had no idea where she got it or what it cost, but she made him promise to always carry it, and he would. It was still so new he could smell the oiled wood and metal. He was going to practice with it, and knew he'd soon get to the point where even with his wounded hand he'd be able to pull the trigger with ease.

A great bird circled high above, vanished before he had a chance to find it in the sky again. He let it go, didn't wonder where it had gone. Instead, he started up his truck and headed out for the road. Just as before, cell service was still bad out here, and he needed to get back close to Murfee so he could call Mel and tell her that he was finally on his way home.

ONE YEAR LATER

She'd called the department, but had agreed only to meet way out here, not quite ready to come into town. The remains of the house were still visible, loose piles of burned, weathered lumber; a wooden skeleton left to bleach in the scrub, most of it already taken back by javelina bush, althorn, and white guara. The guara's flowers were still in bloom, pale, like white stars in the grass, growing thick through the broken planks. The pecan grove south of the house had gone completely wild, a tangle so thick it was difficult to see where one tree began and another ended, the upper branches patrolled by crows fighting over the split hulls of nuts.

Once, on a hunch, he'd come out to look for shell casings out near those trees, but a rare rain—the sky dark as a bruise, scarred by lightning—had turned him away. He hadn't been back since.

She'd changed her hair, cut it short, but she was still pretty. More than that, she was beautiful; taller, her dark skin tanned something deeper, tropical. He'd last seen her in a sweatshirt and glasses, pulling on a cigarette. The sweatshirt was long gone, replaced by a T-shirt revealing slim arms, but the glasses remained, still hiding her eyes. There was no cigarette in her hand, and he guessed she hadn't smoked in a while, maybe not since she'd left. Her truck, a late-model Tacoma, almost new, was parked by a large ocotillo, obscuring the plate. He couldn't see if it had luggage or other bags. Anything. He had no idea where it had come from, where she had been.

She was staring at what was left of the house when he walked up, lost in thought.

"No one likes to come out here. They say it's haunted," he said.

She shook her head. "No, I think maybe it was before, but not now. Not anymore." She turned, smiling. "*Sheriff* Cherry," and then she surprised him by hugging him. She stood back, taking in his official uniform—jeans and a button-down shirt, a black Stetson Brimstone. His badge and his gun.

"America, it's been a while." He wanted to say so much, hardly knew where to begin. "It's good to see you. Good to know you're okay. I always wondered . . . Well, I always wondered what happened, where you went."

She laughed. It was a clear sound, real. "I went to the ocean, that's all."

He laughed with her. "And how was it?"

"Blue and big." She gestured at the sky. "And still not as blue and big as all of this."

They stood silent together, watching clouds roll away along the horizon. "Are you back for good?" he asked.

She looked at the ruins of the house, at Duane Dupree's old place. *"No sé."* She hesitated. "But I missed the stars here, too. It sounds silly, but I did. I thought they'd be the same everywhere, but they're not. Or maybe I just wanted them to be."

He nodded. "No, I get it, I do."

"And things are okay now?" she asked.

He shrugged. "Things are better. There's still work to do. I'm trying." He picked at a guara, tossed it into the wind. "This town has a goddamn mind of its own . . . set in its ways. Old attitudes, older prejudices. I think this whole damn place is frozen in time. Some folks just can't accept the world outside of here is different now. It's changed . . . *we've changed.*" He grabbed at a second flower, tossed that away, too. "Well, no matter what, Murfee is going to change as well. It has to."

She stayed silent, following the flowers he'd thrown. One barely missed the ocotillo near her truck, escaped skyward, and was lost.

"The last time we spoke, I said I needed your help. I still do, you know."

She shook her head. "I don't understand."

He slipped the badge off his belt, the gold star. He pressed it into her hand. "You said you missed the stars. How about this one? I need a Spanish speaker, someone who grew up here and lived all this and understands it." He laughed. "God knows the department could use a woman."

She shook her ahead again. "I . . . I don't know. This place isn't ready for that. *Ahora no.*"

"No, probably not. But that's okay. We have to start somewhere. It's *change.* It's good. It's necessary."

She turned the badge over and over, a star shining in her hand. "A badge?" She smiled, stole a glance at his holster. "A gun, too?"

"Everything," he said.

She considered the badge, his words, like she was weighing both. "I've been gone awhile. It seems so long ago . . ."

"But you're here now, Amé. You're home."

It was turning dusk, the sky already burning red deep in its heart, catching the mountains on fire. All of the Big Bend, the whole world, it seemed, suddenly ablaze. It was beautiful, a helluva show, the type of sunset you could get only in the West. Night would soon follow, and with it the stars, flickering alive one by one by one, just to set the sky alight all over again.

Amé bounced the star in her palm one last time and then put it in her pocket.

"*Muy bien*, Sheriff Cherry. *Muy bien*. What now?"

He smiled, put a hand on her shoulder. "Okay, *Deputy*, let's see if you're any good with a gun . . ."

ACKNOWLEDGMENTS

Writing a book can be a solitary endeavor, but publishing one is definitely not.

I have to start by thanking my amazing agent, Carlie Webber, who first saw some potential, and then Nita Taublib and my wonderful (and very patient) editor, Sara Minnich, as well as everyone else at G. P. Putnam's Sons, who pushed me to realize it and made it all come true. Of course I could never have gotten this far without my family: my sister, Torri Martin, and my parents, Dan and Vickie Scott (who wondered why it took so long); my girls, Madeleine, Lily, and Lucy (who cheered me on); and my best friends, Brian, Tom, and "Doctor" Todd (who heard it all for years).

Also, special thanks go out to fellow writers, including Brian Panowich and Kate Brauning, who were gracious

ACKNOWLEDGMENTS

enough to answer my many how-to questions, and Sheila in Portland and Brian (again) in Tucson, who took the time to read my "other" first novel, even if it wasn't this one.

As always, nothing is possible without Delcia . . .

. . . And this book was fueled in large part by the music of Whiskey Myers and a lot of cold bottles of Rahr & Sons Texas Red lager.

Murfee, Texas, and Big Bend County don't exist, but they are stitched together from real places: Brewster and Presidio counties and Big Bend Ranch State Park and Big Bend National Park. I took some necessary creative and geographical liberties, but I hope I did justice to this wild and beautiful part of the country. This story doesn't exist otherwise. As always, all true errors are mine.

Finally, I've carried a badge and gun for twenty years, and have been privileged to work alongside hundreds of dedicated, honest, and self-sacrificing agents and officers from all over the world, most recently in the DEA's outstanding El Paso Division. There's no career, *no calling*, quite like it, and other than writing, it's the only thing I've ever wanted to do.

To all those out there chasing outlaws each and every day, stay safe.

—JTS

TURN THE PAGE FOR AN EXCERPT

When a local Rio Grande guide is brutally murdered, the ongoing
investigation is swept aside by a secretive federal agent, and
novice sheriff Chris Cherry realizes just how tenuous his hold on his new
badge is. As other threats rise right along, nothing can prepare Chris
for the cost of crossing dangerous men such as a high-ranking
member of the Aryan Brotherhood of Texas and the patriarch of a
murderous clan that's descended on Chris's hometown of Murfee—or
a part-time pastor and full-time white supremacist hell-bent on founding
his violent Church of Purity in the very heart of the Big Bend.

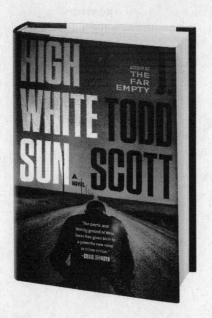

1

It was damn hard to follow a blood trail at eighty miles per hour.

Not that Sheriff Chris Cherry needed to see actual *blood*; he knew it was there all the same. Thick drops of it all down U.S. 90, bleeding off the rear fender of the Nissan Maxima that was trying hard to disappear in his windshield and throwing up dust as it swerved across lanes and the shoulder.

All that blood from one of his deputies, Tommy Milford. Chris still didn't know whether he was alive or dead.

Another of his deputies, Dale Holt, was ten miles back with him. He'd been riding shotgun with Tommy when it all happened, and although he was barely one year older than the injured boy, when Chris had left them both behind, Dale had been holding Tommy's hand like a father might a son, telling him over and over again to *hang in there, brother, hang in there* while they waited for the ambulance, because no one had been sure if it was a good idea to move Tommy or not. Honestly, it hadn't looked good either way. But Dale, even before calling it in—even before kneeling down next to his damaged friend and grabbing his shaking hand and shielding his body with his own—had gotten off a handful of rounds at the fleeing Nissan, and after this was all done they'd be out here looking for them in the desert, shining bright among the ocotillo and the cat's-claw and the creosote; prying them out of the car's metal body. At least one had definitely punched through the rear windshield, spider-webbing the safety glass and X'ing the spot where a passenger's head might be.

Chris tried hard to focus on *that*, rather than his deputy's blood drying on the asphalt.

He prayed that Tommy was hanging on to Dale's hand right now, squeezing back just as hard with each heartbeat, letting Dale and everyone else know he was still alive.

Hanging on tight.

Please don't die. God not today.

Not today. Not Tommy's first damn day on the job.

Deputy Amé Reynosa blasted past Chris, shooting up the shoulder, close enough they almost traded paint. He'd already barked at her once on the radio to stay behind him but she wasn't listening and clearly wasn't going to. They were both pushing ninety now, heading toward a hundred, chewing up the distance on the Maxima, whose back end suddenly fishtailed, brake lights flickering on and off. The driver must have seen the red and blue strobes on Chief Deputy Ben Harper's truck up ahead, bright and clear and ominous even in broad daylight, leaving him surprised and *really* scared and unsure of what to do; maybe even bleeding out, if Dale's bullet had bent the curve and clipped the driver while passing through the car's interior. Harp had been out at Artesia most of the day but had been rolling back to Murfee when Dale fired his first shot, which put him right in the path of the fleeing car, so Chris had radioed for him to lay up at mile marker 67 and toss out the spike strip.

Chris glanced over at the small green signs blurring past his window.

MARKER 65

The strips were an expensive Stinger Spike System. He'd been reluctant to buy them at first, reading that some officers and deputies had been killed trying to deploy the damn things—struck by the very cars they were trying to stop—and Harp hadn't helped the cause by admitting that the Dallas PD had recently banned them.

But out here there was so much empty space, so much straight-line *nothing*, that you could chase someone all the way to El Paso or right down to fucking Mexico if you didn't have a way to slow them down.

So Harp had pushed and pushed for them, and in the end, Chris had agreed. *Caved.* That had become the defining nature of their relationship.

In fact, Chris had ordered *two* sets for each patrol truck, enough to cross both lanes. They'd proved easy enough to set up when his deputies had practiced it out in the department parking lot, but so far they'd never been used—not in *real life*, not like this.

MARKER 66

Almost there.

Chris backed off the gas and hoped those damn spikes worked . . . and hoped to hell that Harp was out of the way.

The Nissan's tires grabbed the pavement *hard*—spitting rocks and boiling smoke—as the driver locked them up, with both car and driver holding on for life as the Nissan started to slide sideways. It tipped ever so slightly *up*, catching air as the whole car shuddered, looking for one horrible second like it might roll and tumble down Highway 90 in a mess of buckled metal and broken glass, before straightening out and hitting the strips square at sixty miles an hour. The hollow spike tips punctured all four radials clean, and Chris swore he saw a dance of bright sparks beneath the Nissan—a July Fourth light show—as it plowed over the strips and kept going even as its tires died beneath it.

Chris drove off the shoulder into the scrub, giving the strips a wide berth and catching air himself, as Harp's truck roared to life and paralleled him from where it had been parked on the opposite shoulder. Harp *had* gotten clear from the truck, never even bothering to use it for cover in case the Nissan's driver lost complete control and plowed into it. Instead, he'd been crouched low with his Colt AR-15 aimed straight and steady into the other car's oncoming windshield. As it slid past, he'd calmly stood up and tracked it with his sights, before running back to his own truck.

Now, he and Chris were slow-rolling up to the Nissan, which had finally come to rest in the middle of the road, nose canted at an angle, the driver's door visible to both of them but still closed. The car sat wreathed in smoke,

all of its tinted windows dirty. The car itself looked exhausted, worn out; sporting an ugly metallic scar down
the left flank—another one of Dale's bullets.

And Tommy's blood, which had been so bright and
visible to Chris only moments before, was now lost to the
dust.

Chris got out with his Browning A5 and positioned
himself behind his engine block, while Harp opposite of
him did the same. Amé rolled to a hard stop behind them
both, and with his attention full on the Nissan, Chris felt
rather than saw her join him at his shoulder.

She was breathing hard, her Colt 1911 resting over
the hood.

"Son of a bitch," she said. *"Pendejo."*

"Exactly," Chris agreed. He stole one glance at her;
hair in her eyes and those dark eyes narrowed and angry,
trying hard to see beyond the Nissan's windows. And for
the first time since he'd made her a Big Bend County
deputy, he was regretting it. Not that she wasn't capable—
she'd more than proven her worth and was tougher than
he could ever have hoped—but because of moments like
this one, right now.

He didn't want to send her in harm's way and he knew
that he was going to have to.

In two years as sheriff, none of his deputies had gotten
hurt on his watch. It was like a run of cool, calm weather,
or a desert rain. It couldn't last forever and maybe it
wasn't supposed to.

But he was going to make damn sure it wasn't two in
one day.

"Sheriff, time *is* wasting." Harp's voice carried over the
road.

His chief deputy was pushing, his idea of subtle. Harp always complained that Chris was too slow, too measured; *too goddamn deliberate* . . . just like their long debate over ordering the Stinger system. Even though he won more than he lost, the older man still liked to needle Chris: *It's all about action versus reaction, Sheriff . . . you can't finish what you don't start.* These were Harp's idea of *lessons*, freely and frequently given, and Amé Reynosa had already taken way too many of them to heart.

It didn't take much for Chris to imagine what his two deputies would think about his first impulse here and now: to keep them all safe behind their trucks and just wait the fucking guy in the Nissan out.

All afternoon if they had to; hoping against hope that he got tired and gave up.

Now *that* was goddamn deliberate.

But there was another of Harp's sharp lessons: *Chris, hope is not a strategy . . .*

Sheriff, time is wasting.

Fuck me.

Chris took a long breath, turning to Amé. "Okay, I'm going to call him out. If we're lucky, there's only the one and maybe he's already hurt. I'm going to walk him backward between us and when I stop him and tell him to get on his knees, you're going to go up, put him facedown, and cuff him. I'll stay covered on the car in case someone else is in there. I've got the best angle on it, so Harp is going to stay covered on *you*. If our bad guy so much as flinches, reaches for anything, even breathes too hard, Harp will take the shot. Got that?"

Amé nodded, already grabbing for cuffs and making ready to move down to the rear of the truck, near to where she'd have to expose herself. It wouldn't be much and it wouldn't be long, but it would be enough.

Chris put a hand on her shoulder. "You're angry, we all are. It's not personal. Just do it by the numbers. Wait till he's on his knees." Chris let her go. "You good?" he asked.

She smiled, grim. *"Bueno."*

Chris waved toward Harp to get his attention, raising his voice. "I'll call the guy back. Amé is contact, you're cover." Harp never took his eyes off the Nissan, didn't respond, but hitched up a thumb . . . *okay.*

In a perfect world, Chris would've put hands on the guy himself, but he didn't have faith in his bad knee. It had never fully recovered after he'd reinjured it at the Far Six. *You've never fully recovered.* He pushed that cold thought away. But fortunately Harp had spent almost three decades on the Midland PD, many of those years as part of their SWAT team. Even though he and Amé had spent a lot of free hours together at the makeshift range near Chapel Mesa, and Harp claimed she'd developed a hell of a shooter's eye, Chris still felt comfortable with Harp taking a tight shot more than anyone, far more than even himself. The chief deputy was the only person who had killed more men than Chris. That left Amé as the best choice, the only choice, to approach the driver if he ever showed himself.

Chris took another deep breath, steadied himself. He squinted past the shortened barrel of his A5 to the Nissan. Still there, still waiting.

Waiting for *him* to do something. Just like his two deputies.

"Driver, roll down the windows and throw out the keys. Then extend your left hand through the window and open the door." His voice surprised him, too loud.

Nothing happened and the Nissan kept idling.

"Driver, roll down the windows and throw out the keys." *Or what, exactly?* Chris didn't want to send Harp and Amé up to the car to forcibly pull the driver out, there was too much open ground to cover and it was too naked, too exposed. And they sure weren't going to start pumping lead into it from here. Even if he made that threat, would the driver believe it? Could *he* even make it sound believable? Maybe he'd get his wish after all and they'd just sit here the rest of the day like Old West gunfighters in a duel, forever trapped at high noon; neither of them ever drawing.

Fuck me.

Sweat collected in his eyes. None of his options were good, all of them just different kinds of bad. His shirt stuck to him like a second skin; that high, white sun hammering hard. It had been infernal hot for days, with no end in sight. The scrub all around them was burned brown, skeletal; brittle and quick to turn to dust. Except for the yucca standing tall and crowned with its ivory flowers and marching into the distance toward the mountains, the rest of the world out here looked and felt lifeless. Like a hot breath would be all it'd take to set it aflame.

The air above the car rolled back and forth in waves, reflecting the engine heat back skyward, where it got lost.

Impatient, Amé started inching forward, moving beyond the safety of his truck's tailgate; too far away from him to pull her back. Just like he feared, she'd been listening to Harp too damn much.

"*Driver. . . .*" He started again, angrier, but before he could call out anything else, the driver's-side window slid down.

Chris braced, found a point in the darkened interior

and kept his A5 on it, realizing the engine had also stopped.

The car was now silent, still.

Long moments passed, everyone holding their breath.

Then keys tumbled out of the open window, jingling loudly, and landed on the asphalt.

Followed finally by a slim arm, grabbing the door handle as he'd instructed and opening the door.

A man got out.

No, that wasn't quite right; he was younger than that, early twenties, maybe, a Hispanic male in black jeans and a white T-shirt. His hair was slicked back and he still had sunglasses on—metallic, small frame, designer.

There was no sign of blood.

Chris put the A5 on him. "Driver, turn around once, and then lock your hands together behind your head and walk backwards . . . slow . . . until I order you to stop."

The kid—and that's how Chris saw him, even though Chris wasn't a whole lot older than him—did as he was told. The watch on his wrist was big and looked expensive. It caught all of that impossible, fiery sunlight, and winked it back at Chris and his deputies as he put his hands behind his head. They might have been shaking, too, just a slight tremble matching the kid's heartbeat. He started walking backward, trying to catch a glance over his shoulder.

"Look straight ahead and keep walking. Slow." Now that the door was open Chris could see all the way through the cabin. There was no one else in the front passenger seat, but that didn't mean there wasn't someone curled up in the back. He still needed to clear the car while Harp and Amé dealt with the kid.

He heard it then, tinny music echoing over the desert. Some popular rap song he might have dialed past once or twice on the radio. It was the same few bars, over and over again—*a ring tone*—a cell phone somewhere inside the car. Is that what the kid had been doing while fleeing, making a call? *Waiting* for a goddamn call back, while Tommy Milford bled out on the asphalt behind him?

By the time the driver backed within the arrow formed by the two trucks, the cell had stopped.

"Driver, take five more steps. Count them with me and then get on your knees. Keep those hands behind your head."

One.

Two.

If the kid was counting along, Chris couldn't hear him.

Three.

Four

Five.

The kid's knees had barely flexed when Amé was already in motion, clear of the truck, handcuffs carried like a church cross in her right hand, moving toward him.

Goddammit.

Impatient.

Chris shifted aim and tried to zero in on the black mouth of the car, the open door, scanning for movement. But he couldn't help keeping one eye on Amé as she went to put her free hand on the back of the kid's head, her hand over both of his, ready to push him facedown. And just like that, inches away, the kid turned to stare at her, quick as a snake. His chin was up, like he was looking her up and down and giving her a once-over. Even hidden behind his expensive glasses, Chris had the idea there was something important passing through the kid's eyes . . . *recognition* . . . and then he said something to her, lips clearly moving, but whatever it was it was low and fast so that only she could hear.

She didn't respond, just pushed him down hard and straddled him as she cranked his hands behind his back to get him cuffed. *They look so young* . . . his deputy and her prisoner. It was easy to imagine them as kids roughhousing in the yard, a brother and sister with their matching dark hair. Without too much effort she pulled the kid to standing and started to drag him back behind their trucks, while Harp moved toward the abandoned car, his AR-15 sweeping left to right; smooth, steady, like the hands of a clock. Now that Amé was clear with their prisoner, Harp could work up the passenger side and Chris could move in on the open driver's door, so they could finish clearing the car and then figure out what the hell was going on.

But then the kid said something *else* to Amé. Louder this time, in Spanish, just before he flicked his tongue out—quick, again, like that goddamn snake.

The kid was still talking, fast.

Chris held up, now forgetting Harp and the car. As hot as it already was, the temperature seemed to boil up another few degrees, releasing sparks and turning the air around them all to embers.

"Amé . . . *no* . . ."

It was hard to read her face: anger, surprise, something else. Or nothing at all. She nodded, like she was considering whatever it was the kid had said or maybe Chris's warning, and then she hit the handcuffed son of a bitch anyway in the face as hard as she could.